Praise for Daryl Wood Gerber's first Fairy Garden mystery

A Sprinkling of Murder

"Enchanting series launch from Agatha Award winner Gerber. . . . Cozy fans will wish upon a star for more."
—*Publishers Weekly*

"Likable characters . . . and an entertaining but not-too-intrusive fairy connection make this a winner. . . . Fans of Laura Childs' work will enjoy Gerber's new series."
—*Booklist*

"Full of fun, whimsy, and a baffling whodunit. . . . After finishing the book fans might want to try their hand at making their own fairy garden, or test the delectable recipes in the back of the book." —*Mystery Scene*

"A charming murder mystery. . . . The addition of real fairies adds a delightful twist. . . . Courtney is an engaging heroine backed by a fun, diverse cast." —*Criminal Element*

"*A Sprinkling of Murder* is an enchanting mystery that asks you to believe. Believe, not only in fairies, but in yourself and the intrinsic goodness of people." —*Cozy Up with Kathy*

Kensington books by Daryl Wood Gerber

The Fairy Garden Mystery series

A Sprinkling of Murder

A Glimmer of a Clue

A Glimmer
of a Clue

Daryl Wood Gerber

KENSINGTON
PUBLISHING CORP.

www.kensingtonbooks.com

Thank you, Sparky, my darling dog. You make life joyous.

Acknowledgments

Creativity is a habit, and the best creativity is the result of good work habits.
—Twyla Tharp

Creativity is not easy, no matter what anyone tells you. I don't sit down and write beautiful prose every time I'm at my computer. Sometimes writing is like pulling teeth. Painful. But I do it because I'm a glutton for punishment and because I want to write the best stories I can. For you.

I have been truly blessed to have the support and input of so many friends, family, and associates as I pursue this wild, chaotic, creative journey.

So let me start by saying thank you to my family and friends for all your encouragement. Thank you to my talented author pals, Krista Davis and Hannah Dennison, for your words of wisdom. Thank you to my Plothatcher pals: Janet (Ginger Bolton), Kaye George, Marilyn Levinson (Allison Brook), Peg Cochran, Janet Koch (Laura Alden), and Krista Davis. It's hard to keep all your aliases straight, but you are a wonderful pool of talent and a terrific wealth of ideas, jokes, stories, and fun! I adore you. Thanks to my Delicious Mystery author pals, Roberta Isleib, Krista Davis, and Amanda Flower. I treasure your creative enthusiasm via social media. Thank you to my Facebook fan-based group, Delicious Mysteries, as well as my review crew. I love how willing you are to read advance copies, post reviews, and help me as well as numerous other authors promote whenever possible. We need fans like you.

Thanks to those who have helped make the Fairy Garden Mystery series come to life: my publisher at Kensington, Steve Zacharius; my editor, Wendy McCurdy; my publicist, Larissa Ackerman; my production editor, Carly Sommerstein; and the rest of the Kensington team; my agent, John Talbot; and my cover artist, Elsa Kerls. Thank you to my biggest supporter, Kimberley Greene. Thank you to Madeira James at Xuni for maintaining constant quality on my website. Thank you to my virtual assistants, Marie McNary and Christina Higgins, for your novel ideas. Honestly, without all of you, I don't know what I would do.

Thank you to Chief Paul Tomasi of the Carmel Police Department for answering all my questions. Any mistakes as to police department procedure are my own.

Last but not least, thank you, librarians, teachers, and readers, for sharing the delicious world of a fairy garden designer in Carmel-by-the-Sea with your friends. Dream big, my friends, and savor the mystery.

CAST OF CHARACTERS
(listed alphabetically by first name)

Humans

Brady Cash, owner of Hideaway Café
Courtney Kelly, owner of Open Your Imagination
Didi Dubois, owner of Sport Zone
Dylan Summers, detective, Carmel Police Department
Elton Lamar, car dealership owner
Eudora Cash, romance author and Brady's mother
Glinda Gill, owner of Glitz Jewelers
Hattie Hopewell, Happy Diggers garden club chair
Hedda Hopewell, loan officer
Holly Hopewell, cottage landlord and neighbor
Jeremy Batcheller, owner of Batcheller Galleries
Joss Timberlake, assistant at Open Your Imagination
Kenny Chu, trainer at Sport Zone
Kipling "Kip" Kelly, Courtney's father, landscaper
Lana Lamar, art critic
Meaghan Brownie, half owner of Flair Gallery
Lissa Reade, aka Miss Reade, librarian
Pauline, perky front desk attendant and assistant manager at
    Sport Zone
Redcliff Reddick, police officer
Renee Rodriguez, owner of Seize the Clay
Tish Waterman, owner of A Peaceful Solution Spa
Ulani Kamaka, reporter for *The Carmel Pine Cone*
Victoria Judge, defense attorney
Wanda Brownie, art representative, Meaghan's mother

Yvanna Acebo, employee at Sweet Treats, weekend baker at
    Open Your Imagination
Ziggy Foxx, half owner of Flair Gallery

Fairies and Pets

Fiona, a righteous fairy
Merryweather Rose of Song, a guardian fairy
Zephyr, a nurturer fairy
Pixie, Courtney's Ragdoll cat

Chapter 1

*Come, fairies, take me out of this dull world, for I would ride with
you upon the wind and dance upon the mountains like a flame!*
—William Butler Yeats

"That woman is going to be the death of me, Courtney."
Didi Dubois bustled from Open Your Imagination's main
showroom onto the slate patio.

I was standing at the far end, beside the rectangular table in
the learning-the-craft corner, creating a fairy garden using a
three-foot tall, wide-mouthed blue glazed pot. I loved spend-
ing time on the patio, an outdoor garden space with a skylight
in its pyramid-shaped roof. Good vibes radiated everywhere.

"I swear her tongue is a dagger and her fingernails are
talons," Didi carried on.

With long strides, she made a beeline past the wrought-
iron tables and ornate fountain carved with fairies and gnomes
to the verdigris bakers' racks. Recently, I'd doubled the stock
of fairy figurines and fairy equipment and accessories we carried at Open Your Imagination. Customers had been thrilled.

"If she morphed into the tigress that she is," Didi said,

"she would eat me for breakfast, lunch, and dinner." Didi could be quite dramatic. When not working out or playing pickleball, like she obviously had today, judging by her outfit of spandex shorts and tank top, she dressed as dramatically as she came across, in colorful dresses and lacy shawls. "I need to make something that will calm my nerves," she said loudly.

A few of the customers who were communing near the vines and ficus trees that adorned the patio were glancing in Didi's direction. She was oblivious.

"Any fairies about?" she asked.

The scuttlebutt in Carmel-by-the-Sea was that a number of fairies resided at my fairy garden and tea shop. In fact, there was only one—Fiona, a fairy-in-training. I'd come to meet her a little over a year ago when I'd quit my job as a land-scaper for my father's company and dared to open my own business. I'd lost my ability to see fairies after my mother died twenty years ago. Fiona said it was the leap of faith to start something new that had opened my heart to the unimaginable again.

Fiona should have been a full-fledged fairy by now, with three full sets of adult wings, but she'd messed up in fairy school, so the queen fairy had subjected her to probation. Fiona was working her way to earning her wings. As part of the probation, Fiona was not allowed to socialize with other fairies, although she could attend one-on-one classes with a mentor the queen fairy had assigned to her. Because Fiona was classified as a righteous fairy, which meant she needed to bring resolution to embattled souls, she could earn her way back into the queen fairy's good graces by helping a human. Only last year did I learn that there were classifications of fairies in addition to varieties of fairy *types*. Classifications included in-tuitive, guardian, nurturer, and righteous. Types were what most people understood about fairies; there were air fairies, water fairies, and woodland fairies.

"Help, Courtney," Didi wailed. "I need to rid my mind of these negative thoughts."

"Sure thing. Pick a pot first," I suggested.

The size of the planter determined the number of plants and figurines a fairy garden maker would need.

Didi wandered among the many selections the shop offered and stopped beside a hanging pot dressed with moss. "I like this one."

"Terrific. That's one of my favorites," I said. "Next, pick some plants. I like the Pink Splash hypoestes and baby tears, but if you're going to hang that in hot sun, you might want to consider succulents."

"What's that you're planting?" she asked, circling my work in progress.

"This is a bonsai. To be specific, a dwarf jade." It was one of the easiest to grow and recommended for beginners.

"I heard you're making a pot for the Beauty of Art Spectacular," Didi said.

"Yep. This is it."

The Spectacular, an annual fundraiser to raise money for community outreach programs in the arts, took place the first Saturday in September—two days from now. Wanda Brownie, the event chairwoman and mother of my best friend, had commissioned the garden that I was making. Because she desperately wanted to meet a fairy, I'd encouraged her to help me. I'd reminded her that working on a garden might open her spiritual portals, but she'd pooh-poohed me. Her loss.

"It's quite pretty," Didi said.

"Thank you." For the theme, I'd decided to create an antique-style cityscape. As a focal point, I'd planted the twelve-inch bonsai at the rear of the pot and was currently creating a walkway to it using glass mirror chips. How they sparkled. "It's taking a bit—"

Didi was no longer listening. She had moved away and

was swaying in a bell-like motion, her beaded salt-and-pepper cornrows swinging as she gathered items: a dancing fairy, a reading fairy, and a miniature pig in a pink tutu. She appeared to be humming. That pleased me. I wanted those who came into my shop to find a sense of peace and well-being. Making a fairy garden was an imaginative adventure.

She returned to me. "Okay, now what?"

"You're not very focused," I joked. To date, Didi had made four gardens. Not once had she needed me to hold her hand.

"Tell me about it."

"So who has you wrapped around the axle?" Once a week, Didi and I played pickleball in a league. She was eons better than I was, but then she had been playing ten years longer than I had and worked out constantly at Sport Zone, the athletic club she'd inherited and managed since her husband passed away.

"Who do you think?"

"Lana Lamar."

"Bingo." Didi rolled her eyes. "That woman thinks she is God's gift to mankind. Honestly, she has no sense of anyone else. She's a total narcissist. If only she were happily married like you, maybe she'd settle down."

"Actually, I'm not married."

"You're not? Where did I get that notion?"

"I almost was. Years ago." The day after our co-ed bridal shower, my fiancé announced he never wanted to get married. Ever. And, yet, he did get married, just not to me. He and his wife had three kids, last I heard.

"I'm sorry. My bad. I should have remembered that."

"No worries."

"Well, Lana is married, but not happily. She'll mess it up like every other relationship she's had."

Lana Lamar was a forty-something antique and art critic

who wrote a column for a number of syndicated newspapers. She'd been married once before, prior to marrying Elton. Lana believed she was beautiful beyond words. She wasn't. Nor was she objective and fair-minded, as she liked to claim. In truth, she was hypercritical of everything. Nothing cut the mustard. How did I know her so well? Whenever she wasn't working, she was at the athletic club using the StairMaster, which happened to be my machine of choice. Side by side, we would step for an hour. Lana was more than happy to talk about herself. The last time I'd run into her, she'd recited her latest review to me: *Without a doubt, Betsy Brahn's work adds up to a big ego trip. The last time I saw a painting as deluded as Miss Brahn's witless work, I was ten. Seriously, Miss Brahn, have you no one who will say this to you? Stop. Now. Quit painting. Spare us all. Find another career.* The harshness of her words had nearly knocked me off my machine. True to form, Lana had found my stumble amusing.

"What did Lana do this time?" I asked, offering a darling set of miniature fairy signs to Didi. One read: *Fairies love to read*.

"Ooh, I adore this." She set it in her basket.

"Lana," I pressed.

"She bought a third home. In Lake Tahoe."

"Okay." I wasn't following why that upset Didi. The more Lana traveled to her other homes, the less we would all see of her. Good riddance.

"Uh-uh, not okay. She thinks that because she won't be here as often, she deserves an exemption when it comes to the pickleball championship."

For fourteen years, Lana had been the reigning champion. Years ago, she'd trained for the Olympics as a long-distance runner, but a bout of mononucleosis had benched her. Ever since, she had striven harder. At tennis. At racquetball. At weight lifting.

"What kind of exemption?" I asked.

"Sport Zone has rules and regulations about how many rounds one has to play in order to compete in any competitive sport."

"Yes." I might have been a newbie, but I understood the rules. Even though I never wanted to compete, if I were to do so, I would have to wait an entire year before I'd qualify, and in any given season I would need to compete a minimum of six times to maintain my competitive status.

"Well, she doesn't want to comply with the rules. She believes she should be able to compete no matter what. No minimums. No qualifications. End of story. 'Once a champion, always a champion.'" Didi said, mimicking Lana's strident voice. "No strings attached."

"Give me a break."

"I know, right? The name Lana means 'child.' That about sums it up." Didi picked up a ten-inch-tall Schleich Griffin knight. He was clad in white-and-blue robes and holding an ice bolt and awesome spear. "I love this guy."

"He's pretty incredible but too big in scale for what you're planning."

"I could just buy him and put him on my bookshelf, couldn't I? Next to my voodoo doll."

"Let me guess. The voodoo doll is for Lana?"

She let rip with a rollicking laugh. "I made it on my trip to New Orleans. We went to a graveyard. . . ."

As Didi reminisced, Fiona flew to me. "*Psst*. Courtney." She hovered nearby, her green wings working hard, blue hair shimmering, her silver tutu and silver shoes sparkling in the sunlight that filtered through the overhead skylight. She whispered, "Didi is really negative. She needs something to lighten her up."

Didi stopped talking and tilted her head. She was looking in Fiona's direction, but I was certain she couldn't see her.

Negativity made it difficult for anyone without innate ability to perceive other beings.

"So what are you going to do about Lana?" I asked Didi.

"Block her at every turn, which means she'll lash out."

"She wouldn't hit you—"

"There's no telling what she might do. I've seen her attack other women. It's not pretty. Don't worry. I'm prepared. I've got my weapons."

"The voodoo doll?"

"And other tools of the trade."

That sounded ominous.

"The pen is mightier than the sword." Didi raised a finger in the air to make her point.

"Oh, I see. A poem." In addition to running the athletic club, Didi did live readings of her poetry at Harrison Memorial Library. "Will you read it aloud?"

"Perhaps I might." Didi cackled. "Plus, I have a few more tricks up my sleeve." She kissed my cheek and hustled into the main showroom to buy her purchases. "Thanks for the help."

I wasn't sure I'd given her much. On the other hand, sometimes a receptive ear was all anyone needed to erase negativity.

Fiona plopped onto my shoulder and fluffed her first set of adult wings, which she'd acquired after helping me solve a crime. She was quite proud of them. They were striated with filaments of blue and green. "Didi needs a potion or a spell to lighten her spirit."

"Can you do that?"

"My mentor is teaching me how."

"I mean, are you allowed to?"

"I'm allowed to practice." She mumbled a phrase that sounded like, *"By dee prood mahaw."*

I'd heard her utter words in her native language before, but I could never determine what she was saying. Back in college, I'd read *The Canterbury Tales* in Middle English, which our professor said sounded like Erse and Gaelic. Fiona's language reminded me of that class. I'd figured out a few terms she used, like *ta* meaning "thanks," *littlies* meaning "babies," and *furries*, meaning all small creatures like dogs and cats, but the rest sounded like gobbledygook. I did know that *by dee* meant "may God."

"Courtney!" Meaghan Brownie, my best friend since college, beckoned me from inside the French doors leading to the main showroom. "I'm so glad you're here." Her curly brown tresses bounced the more she waved. She, like Didi, loved wearing bohemian-style clothing. Her white crocheted dress draped her lithe form nicely.

I joined her. "What's up?"

"My mother needs two fairy gardens, not one."

"Two?"

Meaghan and I had met in our sophomore year in college. When she visited me one summer in Carmel, she fell in love with the place, gave up her pursuit of becoming a professor, and decided to move here and devote herself to art and beauty. After Meaghan graduated, her mother, Wanda, moved to Carmel, too, and was now one of the premier artists' representatives.

"Can you make another fairy garden in time?" Meaghan asked as she toyed with the sleeve of her dress.

"Sure I can. No problem. Does your mother have a theme in mind?" I asked. "She wanted the first to be relevant to antiques, so I decided time should be the theme."

"*Time.* She'll love that. And how apropos for her."

In addition to managing the Beauty of Art Spectacular and representing artists, Wanda brokered antique deals, played a mean game of pickleball, and offered assistance at Sport Zone to help Didi Dubois. She had also taken on the position of president of the women's association at the club. Meaghan worried that her mother's chakras were out of whack because she never slowed down. Wanda didn't give a hoot about chakras. After she'd kicked her abusive husband out of her life—Meaghan had been five at the time—Wanda had been determined to live life to the fullest.

"Let me see what you've done so far," Meaghan said.

"It's about time gone by."

"Dinosaurs?"

"No, silly, dragons." I led her to the project. "I found a miniature castle called the Dragon's Keep."

"It's so big."

"Not every fairy garden has to be made with teensy fairies," I said. "This one is oversized. I started with this ornate purple warrior dragon with a tooled letter opener as his sword." I lifted him from the setting. "Hold him."

"*Oof.* He's heavy. And ominous."

I replaced the dragon and said, "To combat him, I've added Eyela." She was a radiant Schleich fairy dressed in a turquoise gown and sitting atop a white unicorn.

"Awesome. I love the sign."

I'd set the stone-carved sign *Warning: Dragon training site this way* prominently in the front of the design and had created a primordial ooze behind and around the castle using a glue gun, a plastic bag, and lots of pebbles. In addition, I'd added a fiddlehead fairy—not the prettiest of fairies, closer in likeness to a gnome with huge pointed ears and hooked nose—at the top of the keep. Who would mess with him?

"As a contrast to the first garden, why don't you make the second theme beauty?" Meaghan said.

"Beauty it is. Pick out the fairies I'll need."

"Me? Shouldn't Mom have a say?"

"She gave me carte blanche."

Over the past few years, Wanda had become like a second mother to me.

"This will be fun," my pal said as she browsed the figurines.

Meaghan was the reason I'd risked investing in Open
Your Imagination. She'd known how unfulfilled I was when
I'd worked as a landscaper.

"Select a few accessories, too," I added, "like some twinkling lights and a lantern or two."

"Is she here?" Meaghan peered past me into the patio.
Though she'd chanced upon Fiona a while back—she had felt
her presence and seen a glimmering—she had yet to have a
face-to-face with her. Up until then, Meaghan hadn't believed in fairies. The near encounter had changed her mind.
Now she wished Fiona would land on her shoulder and reveal
every last wing of herself.

"She's by the fountain." I wiggled my fingers. "Playing
with Pixie."

My creamy white Ragdoll cat was on her hind legs batting
the air, the flame markings over her eyes squinting with focus.

Meaghan squinted like the cat and shook her head. No
luck.

"I'll be right back," I said. "I've got to check on Joss. She
looks swamped."

From the patio, I could see everything that went on in the
main showroom. The French doors and beveled casement
windows of the L-shaped space provided a full view. My assistant, Joss Timberlake, who was in charge of all financial deal-
ings for the store as well as making sure we had enough
change on a daily basis for cash transactions and guaranteeing
that monies were deposited in the bank account, was a whiz
when it came to dealing with customers. At least four of our
regulars were waiting in line at the register and yet none appeared to be put out.

I moved into the shop and felt the lovely breeze floating
through the open portion of the Dutch door. Carmel-by-the-

Sea was blessed with Mediterranean-style temperatures. The Cape Cod feel of the Cypress and Ivy Courtyard, of which we were a part, had set the standard for the interior décor: white display tables and white shelving, with a stylish splash of blue and slate gray for color.

"Hey, Joss, need help?" I said, towering over her the way Meaghan towered over me.

"I'm good to go." She finished wrapping a set of fairy-themed wind chimes in silver tissue paper and then packed up a teapot and a pair of matching cups and saucers in Bubble Wrap.

From the outset, we'd stocked the shop with an assortment of tea sets, garden knickknacks, wind chimes, and bells—fairies, Fiona informed me, loved anything that made an angelic sound. We also carried miniature plants, pots, tool sets, and aprons.

After Joss packed the items into a tote bag and thanked the customer for her patronage, I said, "We've dressed alike again."

Joss was twenty years older than me, but we had similar taste in clothes. I didn't think either of us needed to dress *up* for work. We were gardeners. Today, we were each wearing a T-shirt with overalls. Hers was green; mine was red. I loved how powerful I felt whenever I wore the color. "You look elfin," I said.

Joss swept her pixie-style bangs to the right and rubbed her pointy ear. "What can I say? I'm partial to green. I'm surprised you're not, Miss Kelly, seeing as you're the one with Irish blood."

"My skin tone doesn't go with green."

"Good morning!" a lean man in a serge suit—our book rep—called as he entered rolling a dolly filled with boxes. A month ago, Joss had suggested that we start selling books about fairies, both children's literature as well as adult literature. We displayed them on a swivel stand by the Dutch door. I'd fallen in love with *The O'Brien Book of Irish Fairy Tales and Legends* and *Jamie O'Rourke and the Big Potato,* a beautifully illustrated Tomie dePaola folktale.

"I'll handle him," Joss said, and hitched her chin. "I think those ladies could use some of your expert advice. Why don't you cozy up to them?"

Across the shop, by the antique white oak hutch that held a host of cups and saucers, stood a gaggle of ladies. As I drew near, I realized they were admiring a teacup fairy garden I'd set out last night. Although fairy gardens came in all sizes, from large pots to Radio Flyer wagons to four-, six-, and eight-inch pots that were perfect for a tight corner, teacup fairy gardens were the ideal fit for someone who didn't have much space or a green thumb. I had adorned the pink-themed cup they were admiring with a moss base, silk plants, and a crouching pink-and-purple fairy inspecting a snail.

"This is so cute, Courtney," one of the women said. "Promise me that you'll have a class so we can make one of our own."

"I offer classes already. Pick up a schedule sheet at the register and check out the dates I've set for workshops for the remainder of the year. Don't miss the holiday one. We'll be making—"

Crash! Outside the shop, pottery hit the ground. Followed by raucous shouting.

Chapter 2

I threw open the Dutch door and dashed through. I peered up the courtyard toward Dolores Street. A crowd was gathering by Flair Gallery at the far end of the courtyard.

People squawked: "Oh, no!" "Goodness." "Can you believe it?"

A woman shouted, "How dare you!"

Another woman screamed at the top of her lungs, "Let me go!"

Joss yelled from the shop, "Courtney, what's going on?"

"I'm not sure. Tell Meaghan to come quick." She was half owner of Flair. Ziggy Foxx was her partner.

Fiona joined me. "What happened?"

"Beats me."

Fiona trailed me as I jogged up the steps that made Cypress and Ivy Courtyard multilevel. In addition to Wizard of Paws, the pet-grooming salon across the way from our store, there were five other businesses in the Cape Cod–style courtyard, including Flair Gallery, the Sweet Treats bakery, the Glitz jewelry store, a high-end clothing shop, and a collectibles store. Carmel-by-the-Sea was known for its charming courtyards and secret passageways.

I neared the oft-photographed fountain that featured a floating bronze sphere atop a twisted bronze base and peered through the throng.

Lana Lamar, in body-clinging butter-yellow spandex pants and crop top that revealed her amazing abs, was holding Wanda Brownie by the ponytail.

Wanda and her daughter, Meaghan, resembled each other right down to their towering height and curly brown tresses. Now, however, bent backward at the knees, her body parallel to the ground, with one hand grasping Lana's wrist for dear life while trying to save what was left of her hair and dignity, Wanda reminded me of a limbo dancer in extreme pain. A glazed pot lay in pieces by her feet.

If I were to guess, I'd bet this conversation had started inside Flair Gallery and had moved outside with the toss of the pot. Lana had to have thrown it. No way Wanda would damage a piece of art, especially given the price. Artwork displayed at Flair ran upward of two thousand dollars a pop. Why had Lana destroyed it? Who would pay for the damage? Flair Gallery had insurance, but the deductibles were steep. Maybe Lana's husband, Elton, would make reparations. He was one of the primary buyers of art at Flair Gallery, the more avant-garde the better.

"You can't do that," Lana said, clearly in the middle of an argument with Wanda.

"Yes, I can," Wanda managed to say through gritted teeth.

Do what? I wondered.

"You can't take it away," Lana persisted. Her cheeks were flushed, her neutrally colored lips drawn tight.

"Didi can, and as president of the women's association, I'll make sure she does," Wanda said. "You cheat."

"I do not cheat." Why did Lana always sound like she was shrieking? I imagined her as a child demanding this and that of her parents, winning arguments because they couldn't stand the whining. "I have never cheated. It is beneath me to cheat."

"Cheater, cheater, cheater," Wanda said, not ceding an inch.

Truthfully, it was beneath her to act so petty. What had instigated this madness?

Lana sputtered, "You . . . you . . . liar."

Fiona flicked me with a wing. "Do something."

I scanned the group. There wasn't a policeman anywhere. No security guard, either. All the shop owners and passersby stood in a frozen tableau. I spotted a hose with a spray nozzle that the courtyard's weekly gardener used to water plants and bolted to it. I switched it on. Water didn't gush out; I needed to depress the nozzle's trigger to release the flow.

I tore to Lana and aimed the nozzle at her. "Let Wanda go."

"Or what, Courtney, you'll drench me?" Lana's mouth pulled back in a vicious sneer.

"If I have to."

Meaghan burst onto the scene. "Stop hurting my mother."

"She started it," Lana tried as an excuse.

Writhing under Lana's firm grip, Wanda snarled, "I did not *start* it," the emphasis on *start*.

"Yes, you did. You said you'd tell Didi to rescind my membership at Sport Zone because I'm a cheater."

"Lana, you demented fool," Wanda said in a disparaging tone, "this all *started* because you had the gall to denigrate one of my artists whose work is on display in my daughter's gallery."

"I will denigrate whomever I choose."

"You are a hack." Wanda smirked.

"What? You are such a—"

"You couldn't write an honest critique if it killed you."

"The piece of art was garbage with no redeeming values. A gimmick. A fiasco."

"Art is in the eye of the beholder."

"As is a review. I get paid for my opinion. Do you, Wanda? No, you do not." Lana raised her narrow chin without releasing her prey. "I know of what I speak."

"Hogwash. I'm a respected art connoisseur, and you're just a know-nothing who makes a living trashing people who actually create art. Have you ever considered rewriting your reviews? You use the same trite sayings and despicable words week in and week out. 'Banal style,' 'Boring inspiration,' 'Blatant self-aggrandizement.'" Wanda *tsk*ed. "You wouldn't know a good piece of art if it stabbed you in the heart."

The crowd gasped.

Lana snarled.

"Lana, let her go," I ordered.

"Not until Wanda promises that she won't tell Didi to rescind my membership at Sport Zone. I am not a cheater."

Where was Didi? I didn't see her in the crowd. Was she at Sport Zone sticking pins in her Lana voodoo doll? Had the voodoo jabbing mystically goaded Lana into lashing out?

Wanda said, "Sport Zone members have to obey rules and be ethical and kindhearted, none of which you care to do or to be, Lana Lamar."

"Where does it say that exactly?" Lana demanded. "Where?"

"Actually, it says it in the bylaws," I stated. I'd read them front to cover. My father was a stickler for agreements. He never took on a client without presenting that client with a contract and then reading the contract aloud with the client so all the terms were distinctly understood. I'd gotten my creativity from my mother; my business sense came from Dad. "Let's discuss this civilly, Lana," I suggested. "Over a cup of tea. On me." We served tea at Open Your Imagination on weekends, but we could muster up a cup or two to initiate a détente. "Say yes." I raised the nozzle.

"Go ahead, Courtney. Spray away. Make my day."

Fiona whispered, "I don't have a good feeling about this."

Neither did I, but what choice did I have? Someone had to maintain the peace. If my father were here, he would take the reins.

Pressing my lips together, I pulled the trigger. Water blasted Lana. She howled at the top of her lungs and released Wanda, who fell to the pavement.

Luckily, Wanda was able to break the fall with her hands and not land on her face. Meaghan rushed to her and asked if she was okay. Wanda scrambled to her feet and brushed off her blue knit top and skinny jeans.

Meaghan glared at Lana. "You . . . you . . . bully."

But Lana wasn't listening to my pal. She turned to me, claws bared. "How dare you, Courtney Kelly. You have overstepped, fairy girl."

Fairy girl? Not taking it as the insult she had intended, I smiled. "You did the overstepping when you decided to make a public scene. Sport Zone has a board of directors. Take this up with them."

"Didi Dubois runs it. Everyone on the board hates me."

For good reason, I wanted to add, but bit my tongue.

"Lana." A black-haired woman in a brown cloak stepped from the crowd. I recognized her although I'd never met her. She was the woman who lived near me in a yellow storybook cottage. I'd often seen her silhouette through the sheer drapes dancing around the living room. From a gym bag, she pulled a white towel. "Here. Take it."

Lana gaped.

"I'm on my way to work out." The woman had a dulcet voice, like a symphonic radio announcer. "It hasn't been used."

After a moment, Lana grudgingly accepted the woman's generosity.

A ghostly gray cat with a white muzzle bolted to the peacemaker, weaved around her ankles, and then dashed through the crowd and disappeared beyond the fountain. Someone behind me yelped.

"Jamie says hello, by the way," the woman added. The knees of her leggings were dusted with dirt. Where had she been before joining the onlookers? And who the heck was Jamie?

Lana's face turned ashen at the mention of Jamie.

"He hopes you're enjoying your nightly runs," the woman whispered.

"Stop. Don't say another word." Lana glanced right and left as if scoping out the area for an escape route.

Before she could run, however, Didi Dubois broke through the crowd and strode to Lana, blocking her exit. She was carrying a pink bag from Sweet Treats. Was the bag holding a cream pie? One could hope.

"Lana, dagnabbit!" What Didi lacked in height she made up for in attitude. "What is wrong with you, creating all this chaos?" Didi handed the pink bag to a woman in the crowd and shot a finger at Lana's chest. "Have you no shame? No dignity? What were you thinking, taking on Wanda in front of all these people?"

Lana's eyes grew steely. "I didn't start it. She took me—"

"Do not rationalize. No, no, no." Didi sliced the air with her hand. "You are in the wrong. Admit it. It's why so many people don't want to play with you anymore."

"You aren't calling me a cheater, too, are you?" Lana demanded.

Didi cut a look at her friend. "Oh, Wanda, you didn't."

"It just came out," Wanda rasped.

"Well, are you, Didi? Calling me a cheater?" Lana's hands balled into fists. Was she going to pop Didi in the nose?

I raised the nozzle.

"Wait, Courtney. Let me handle this," Fiona whispered in my ear.

She flew to Lana and circled her head while sprinkling her with a sparkly green dust. How she could come up with fairy dust on the spot baffled me. I was pretty sure it had something to do with her adult wings. Her mentor, she told me, was leading her one lesson at a time to her adulthood.

Lana blinked. She took a step backward, her features softening.

At the same time, Wanda, looking exhausted, accepted the arm Didi offered her.

"Honestly?" Lana abandoned whatever had mellowed her. "You're a united force? Fine. Whatever. Just lay off my membership, Didi. I pay my dues—*full* dues—even though I could claim out-of-town residency."

That's a stretch, I mused. Her primary residence was in Carmel.

"I have no violations and no infractions at the club," Lana continued. "My record is clean. No one other than you and your cronies are against me."

Seconds ago, she'd said everyone on the board hated her. Maybe she actually had some allies among the members.

Didi said, "Everyone at Sport Zone has to obey the code of conduct. Everyone has to follow the rules. Everyone has to be nice."

Lana pursed her lips. "Where does it say I have to be nice?"

"C'mon, Lana." Didi huffed.

A nasty smile pulled at the corners of Lana's mouth. "I'll do my best."

"Not good enough," Didi said. "Your membership is revoked."

"You can't do that."

Suddenly alert, Wanda glowered at Lana and folded her arms. "Oh, yes she can."

Lana's eyes grew dark. "Over your dead body."

Chapter 3

The fairy poet takes a sheet of moonbeam, silver white;
his ink is dew from daisies sweet, his pen a point of light.
—Joyce Kilmer

I invited Wanda, Didi, and Meaghan to have a cup of tea, but all of them turned me down. Meaghan, after reassuring herself that her mother was no longer in danger, needed to address the broken pottery, and Didi and Wanda, to work out their frustration, said they were going to Sport Zone to play a rousing game of pickleball. In truth, that sounded like a fib. I would bet they planned to call an impromptu board meeting to get the wheels in motion regarding Lana. She would be livid, but I couldn't change the tide.

Returning to the shop, I was surprised to see that it was packed with customers. Nothing like a little animosity between rivals to make people hang around the courtyard shops hoping to pick up a piece of gossip. Some of the lingerers were interested in whether my fairy had something to do with Lana's change of attitude. I decided to keep mum. Fairies wanted newbies to become believers naturally, not out of a desire to see magic. Instead, I directed customers to the wind chimes and bells and sign-up sheets for upcoming do-it-your-self fairy garden classes, advising them that if they wanted to experience fairies, they had to open their hearts to the reality. A few of them giggled. One woman murmured that I was loony. I knew I wasn't; many in Carmel could see fairies.

By the end of day, chatter about Lana and Wanda's set-to abated.

After work, to decompress and review the day's events, I went with Meaghan, Joss, Pixie, and Fiona to Hideaway Café, located across the street in the Village Shops. Carmel was a unique town; many businesses were pet-friendly. Animals accompanied humans often.

Like the other buildings in the Village Shops, the café boasted a striking dark red wood-and-stone façade, but the café had added bowers of flowers and beautiful English gardens to both their front and rear patios.

A waitress showed us to a white iron table on the rear patio. The strains of jazz guitar music filtered through a speaker system.

Pixie nestled in my lap. Fiona flew into the trees. I knew she wouldn't dare search for other fairies—she had a number of hurdles to overcome before the queen fairy would allow that—but she loved communing with nature.

"Aren't the lights pretty?" Joss asked.

Strands of twinkling lights, similar to the ones on our patio, arced across the expanse. Whereas our roof was permanent with a skylight, Hideaway Café's was draped with tent-like material.

Brady Cash, the owner of the café, strolled toward us, a grin on his face. He and I had gone to high school together; I'd been a freshman and he a senior. I hadn't seen him in years until we'd reconnected in late April.

He greeted us warmly and handed us menus. "How's your dad?" he asked me.

"Doing well. Yours?"

"Serving the greater community of Monterey with gusto." His father owned the Cash Cow, a diner where my dad hung out.

"I saw your mother has a new novel out." Brady's mother was the well-known novelist Eudora Cash. I'd read all her books without realizing they were written by the woman I'd grown up calling Dory.

"She does. *The Pirate's Affair.*"

"Sounds spicy," I said. "I'll have to buy it." In addition to reading mysteries, I loved historical romance novels.

"She's doing a book signing next weekend."

"Here? In town?"

"At Pilgrim's Way."

The shop had been open for over fifty years and was the only remaining bookstore in Carmel. The owners were proud to provide a wide variety of new titles, from best sellers to classics. In addition, Pilgrim's Way boasted the most adorable Secret Garden with fountains and collections of plants and locally made gifts.

"I'll have to go," I said.

"She would love to see you." Brady eyed Meaghan. "And how are you tonight?"

"Fine. You're looking as handsome as ever," she said, staring at him appreciatively.

Brady was muscular and tan, everything Meaghan's boyfriend, a temperamental artist who preferred staying indoors, was not. In addition to Brady's good looks, I was partial to the deep dimple in his right cheek, the hank of hair that fell on his forehead, and the casual way he dressed for work—Pendleton shirt open at the collar and jeans.

Joss spoke up. "I saw that your ex-wife's husband landed a new film."

Brady's ex had left him for a popular actor in Los Angeles. "What a joke," he replied. "He's going to play the president of the United States. Like, get real. Are you kidding me?"

"All he has to do is memorize the lines," Meaghan said.

"And act," I joshed.

"Act. Ha! That would be refreshing." Brady laughed. "I relish the fact that my ex will have to go to premieres and smile as if she thinks he pulled it off. What can I get you?" As the owner of the café, he didn't have to wait on us, but he enjoyed it.

We each ordered a glass of Chardonnay and the café's specialty appetizer, mushroom cheese puffs.

When he left, Meaghan said, "How's it going between you two? Are you dating yet?"

"No, we're not dating. We're hanging out. We're friends."

"As in, the two of you are at the same place you were back in high school? Totally platonic?"

Joss chuckled. "She's taking it slow, which is the right way to go."

"Slower than a snail." Meaghan propped her elbow on the table and braced her chin on her hand. "Boring."

Joss wagged her finger. "Slow is good when you've been burned."

"Heaven help me. She's taking romance tips from you now?" Meaghan teased.

"Better than from you," Joss replied. "Aren't you the one with the boyfriend who doesn't lift a finger or give you a compliment?"

Meaghan frowned. "Okay, touché."

Despite the tone of their banter, they really liked each other.

"But c'mon," Meaghan said, "shooting hoops and taking photography walks? That's it? Courtney needs more from a relationship. She realizes that, doesn't she?"

"Yoo-hoo." I waved a hand. "I can hear you."

Fiona plopped onto my shoulder and giggled.

I flicked her away.

"He's so handsome," Meaghan continued. "Not to mention he reads, he cooks, and he looks good in jeans. Worth the time and effort, if you ask me."

Truth be known, I did like Brady. A lot. But he hadn't pushed to broaden our relationship over the past few months, so I was comfortable with what we had. I treasured the friendship. I didn't have any other male friends. Getting a man's perspective—from someone other than one's father—could be enlightening. I didn't want to overreach and scare him away.

Changing the subject, I said, "By the way, Hideaway is providing the food for the Beauty of Art Spectacular."

Meaghan whooped. "At least if things go south between my mother and Lana, we know we'll eat well."

"Speaking of your mom," I said. "Is she all right? Have you heard from her since she left with Didi?"

"I have, and get this. Lana has already hired a lawyer who wrote the board a letter demanding they cease and desist in regard to limiting her competition requirements. Lana is claiming that they are discriminating against her."

"No way." Joss gaped.

"*Way.*" Meaghan leaned forward on her elbows. "If they don't grant her everything she wants regarding competition, she'll file a lawsuit. Apparently, her husband has a lawyer for everything."

Joss scoffed. "Elton Lamar is a joke."

"Why do you say that?" I asked.

"Lana only stays with him because he's wealthy."

Elton owned a number of car dealerships. I'd bought my Mini Cooper from him.

"He's not bad on the eyes," I said. "I've seen women fawning over him."

"That's just it." Joss snapped her fingers. "He could have anyone. Why settle for Lana, who doesn't love him? If you ask me . . . not that you did, but if you did . . . he'd do well to divorce her and move on. She will drain him of every last cent."

I whistled softly. "I had no idea you felt so strongly about Lana, Joss. What else aren't you telling me?"

"Telling *us*," Meaghan said.

Joss shifted in her chair. "You know that Lana was married before, right?"

I nodded.

"Well, her first husband was the only man I ever loved."

I felt gobsmacked. "Really?"

Joss's chin quivered. "Don't get me wrong. He never had eyes for me. We were buddies. Pals. Fellow geeks. We could talk bottom line all day. When he became a fabulous investor and rich beyond words, Lana set her sights on him. How could he resist? He fell for her and fell hard. So I left Carmel and moved to Silicon Valley. Out of sight, out of mind. But I kept track of him. A few years later, when Lana took him to the cleaners in the divorce, he never recovered. Overwhelmed by grief, he overdosed."

"Here we go, ladies." Brady returned with our appetizers and our wine and a glass of water for himself and pulled up a chair. "Are you discussing this afternoon's free-for-all? I've got a few minutes. Clue me in."

Quickly, Joss took a sip of wine. I would discover no more of her story.

Meaghan said, "Okay, Brady, here's the scoop. Lana Lamar might sue Sport Zone. For discrimination."

"Does she have a legal leg to stand on?" Brady asked.

"Mom doesn't think so." Meaghan downed a mushroom cheese puff and purred her appreciation. "This is scrumptious. I want the recipe."

Brady grinned. "You always want the recipe. Have you cooked any of the ones I've given you so far?"

"I can dream." Meaghan wasn't much of a cook, but she loved food as much as I did.

I took one of the appetizers and almost swooned. Flaky pastry with a creamy warm center. "Gruyère?" I asked.

"Good palate." Brady eyed me. "Is it true you hosed Lana?"

I nodded. "When I was a landscaper, the best thing to do when a feral creature encroached on a property was to soak it. They usually turned tail and ran."

"But Lana isn't running," Brady said.

"Nope." I took a sip of wine, savoring the vanilla and peach flavors. "She's fighting mad."

Brady turned to Meaghan. "What do you think your mother's going to do?"

"Didi runs the show. She wants Lana out. Mom will go along with whatever Didi says. They're crafting a response right now."

Joss hoisted her wineglass. "Let the fur fly."

I said, "By the way, does anyone know the name of the lady in the cloak? The one who offered Lana a towel to dry off? She lives near me, but we've never met."

Meaghan said, "Tamara Geoffries. Therapist to the rich and famous."

I raised an eyebrow. "Really? A neighbor said she was a high-end, by-invitation-only antiques dealer." Many sellers operated that way because foot traffic might not happen. Who wanted to sit around for hours without meeting a single customer?

"'High-end' is the key word," Meaghan said, coquettishly coiling a lock of hair around a finger. "Who do you think gets an invitation? The wealthy. And who need therapists?"

Joss said, "The wealthy."

Lots of affluent and famous people owned second homes or vacationed in Carmel-by-the-Sea. Being a therapist might explain Tamara's dulcet voice. She probably hypnotized some of her clients.

Meaghan said, "Tamara doesn't hang out a shingle because famous people don't want it known that they seek help. While selling them an antique piece, she helps them work through their problems."

"Years ago, she traveled to meet clients," Brady said, "but now they come here."

I peered at him. "You know her?"

"A lady has to eat. This is her go-to place." He hooked a thumb. "In fact, she's right over there. She's the one who suggested that the group doing the Beauty of Art Spectacular hire me." He brushed my shoulder with his hand. "I've got to go. The hostess is signaling me."

I swiveled in my chair. Tamara Geoffries, who was once again clad in a cloak, the cowl hanging down her back, sat at a table in the far corner. She had a gorgeous profile and beautiful olive-toned skin. I pegged her at somewhere in her forties.

"Why do you want to know about her?" Meaghan asked.

I replayed her conversation with Lana and the mention of someone named Jamie.

"Don't know him," Meaghan said. "Or her, if it's a *her*."

"*Him*. She said, 'He hopes you're enjoying your nightly runs.'"

While stroking the ears of the Angora that was sitting in her lap, Tamara's mouth moved. She wasn't speaking into a cell phone and her menu was closed, so I presumed she was talking to the cat. Above Tamara's head, I noticed a shimmering, and then I spied Merryweather Rose of Song, Fiona's mentor, as she flew into view. She had iridescent gossamer hair like Fiona, but that was where the similarities ended. Unlike Fiona, her cheeks were plump, her loose-fitting dress was a regal crimson, her wings sported matching polka dots, and she was much older.

Fiona shot off my shoulder and soared toward Merryweather. The two conferred.

Seconds later, Fiona returned to me, a pained expression on her face. "Uh-oh."

Meaghan didn't notice my fairy, but Joss did and gave her a wink. I nodded for Fiona to continue.

"Merryweather is quite concerned about the woman in the cloak. She said she's mumbling and saying it was her fault."

I cupped a hand around my mouth and whispered, "What was her fault?"

"That's just it." Fiona opened her palms. "Merryweather can't figure it out."

Merryweather, a guardian fairy, wasn't assigned to any particular human; however, she spent most her time at the library. According to Fiona, she was one of the wisest fairies ever to have lived.

I studied Tamara Geoffries again and noticed a tear slipping down her cheek. What was wrong? What was her fault? A moment later, Tamara rose from her chair with her cat in tow and left the restaurant.

I loved going home to Dream-by-the-Sea, the cottage that I rented from my neighbor Holly Hopewell. Many of the homes in Carmel had clever names instead of addresses. Holly owned five houses in Carmel and by her own right was a talented artist. We knew each other because she had taught my mother how to paint. When Holly discovered I was branching out on my own, she took me under her wing and offered me the cottage on Carmelo Street at a discount. She'd said the cottage was run-down. Blessed with a keen eye for possibility, I'd seen beneath the jungle of plants and realized the cottage was a jewel. Over the past year and a half, I'd made it mine. The front yard was a proper English garden now, with geraniums, lavender, catmint, and larkspur growing in harmony. The flagstone walkway was free of moss and grit. The front door, with its fresh coat of periwinkle-blue paint, made me smile. And the cottage was a mere two blocks from the ocean. I loved long walks on the beach.

On my way inside, I batted the new hummingbird wind chimes hanging on the scroll of the lamp by the door and said to myself, "Time to get cracking, Courtney. You have one more fairy garden to put together and not a lot of time."

I set Pixie on the floor. She scampered ahead of me into the kitchen. Fiona trailed us. Meaghan had put the items she'd selected for the beauty-themed garden in a tote bag. I couldn't wait to see what she'd chosen.

Semi-full from the mushroom puffs at Hideaway Café, I decided to forgo dinner and I settled for a couple of slices of cheese and a glass of sparkling water so I could get right to work. However, once I entered the kitchen, which was one of my favorite rooms in the cottage, I changed my mind. The aroma of herbs planted in each of the white mugs on the tiered glass shelves by the window made me crave something more gourmet.

I moved to the white hutch, fetched a Royal Doulton Pacific Splash pattern plate, and sprinkled the plate with chopped oregano. I doused the herbs with olive oil, cut two fresh slices of sourdough bread for dipping, and unwrapped a portion of Boursin cheese. For Fiona, I set out sliced grapes. Pixie always thought a can of tuna was an epicurean delight.

We dined at the kitchen table. As I spread the Boursin lavishly on the bread and nibbled slowly, my thoughts ran the gamut from Tamara Geoffries to Lana Lamar to Brady Cash and back again to Tamara. What had she been crying about? What was her fault?

Knowing that I couldn't solve all the world's problems, and particularly Tamara's, I polished off my meal, washed my dishes, and headed to the backyard with Meaghan's tote bag in hand.

I'd almost landscaped the backyard to my liking, with wisteria, impatiens, and herbs growing naturally beneath the towering cypress trees. I'd created a number of fairy gardens, which I'd set in the corners and along the fence, but I wanted to add one more: a five-pot, blue-themed cascade held together by a garden stake. I'd seen something like it online and thought it was quirky and artistic. I also had my heart set on purchasing a copper fountain featuring a fairy pouring water into a shell. Its cost was steep; I'd started saving.

"This way," I said to Fiona, who'd asked to accompany me. Pixie had chosen to snooze on her pillow in the living room.

I crossed the yard to the six-by-eight polycarbonate greenhouse I'd installed and slipped inside. I inhaled the aroma of the herbs and wood shelving and murmured, "Heaven."

All the tools I needed were in the greenhouse: a rake for loosening soil, a trowel, a variety of spades, and an assortment of good shears. In addition, I'd stocked the place with fairy figurines, pots, miniature plants, and fairy garden environment pieces like slides, swings, trees, and boulders. Each item was in its place, a requirement drilled into me by my father, who was fierce about organization. It was one of the reasons he was in demand as a landscaper.

"Let's choose a pot," I said.

One of the most important things before creating a fairy garden was selecting the proper container. I opted for a narrow, blue-glazed pot that would go nicely with the one I'd used for the time-themed fairy garden. I packed it with soil that I made myself—a mixture of peat, moss, bark, perlite, and not too much sand or else the soil would become too porous. When I'd completed that task, I realized the design would be so heavy I'd need a dolly to wheel it to the event site, so I quickly sent myself a voice message as a reminder.

"Let's see what Meaghan chose." I opened the tote bag and smiled.

She'd selected three hand-painted fairies with exotic eyes, white swans, white birds, white marble statues, and frosty white lamps, all in 1:12 scale. As in buying things for doll-houses, a fairy gardener needed to anticipate the scale of the project she hoped to create. One of the most common scales was 1:12. It was the simplest to calculate. For every twelve inches of normal size, the gardener would use one inch for miniature size. For example, a round table might measure three feet. A miniature version, in 1:12 scale, would measure three inches.

"Aha," I said to Fiona. "I'm going to need to build a mountain." Meaghan had also included a premade waterfall, as well as green beads to represent the water in the pond that the waterfall would create.

To fashion the mountain, I turned a six-inch clay pot up-side down on the soil, hot-glued moss to it, and positioned the waterfall against it. When I was sure it would stay in place, I gath-ered a set of natural rocks to surround the pond and stepping-stones to lead up to the waterfall. Rather than plant live plants, I opted to use fake plants so this particular display wouldn't need watering. I'd stocked up on loads of beautiful pine trees and shrubs, like the kinds used when creating miniature rail-roads.

Fiona settled at the top of the waterfall and crossed her legs. "Why do you think that woman was crying?"

"Tamara Geoffries? I'm not sure." People wept. It didn't always mean the situation was dire.

"What if it had something to do with that Lana person?" Fiona asked. "Did you see how shocked Lana was when Tamara offered to help her?"

"Definitely." Lana rarely was taken aback.

I affixed miniature pine trees and bushes at the top of the waterfall, perfect for the overall scope of the setting, and then finished the pond by surrounding it with the natural rock, filling it with the green beads, and setting the swans on top of the beads.

Fiona preened her wings. "On the other hand, it could be something else. Something personal."

"Well, we can't worry about it," I said, even though talking about Tamara had re-ignited my concern. "I'm sure she has friends who will help her with whatever her problem may be."

"She doesn't."

"Doesn't what?"

"Have friends. Merryweather told me."

My heart snagged. No friends? How was that possible? Tamara was a therapist to the rich and famous and a respected antiques dealer. She must have lots of friends. Plus, there were other antiques dealers in town. She had to be friends with one or two of them, didn't she? I stroked the silver locket with my mother's portrait inside. An image of a fairy not dissimilar to Fiona was etched into the lid and the word *believe* engraved on the underside. As I rubbed, I considered what my nana or mother would have done. Would they have gone to Tamara's house and knocked on her door? Would they have asked if she'd needed help?

No. I couldn't. If I did, Tamara might think I was poking my nose where it didn't belong.

"Merryweather must be wrong," I said. "I'm sure Tamara has someone in her life who can help."

Fiona clucked her tongue.

I ignored her and continued putting the finishing touches on the garden. I inserted the decorative statues and lamps at the base of the waterfall and then found locations for the three fairies, each turned toward the other. I preferred that my fairies looked like they were carrying on a conversation; it helped the scene come to life.

Fiona fluttered near and inspected my work. "Are they gossiping?"

It sounded like such a funny word coming from her lips. "Why would you ask that?"

"Because that's all I can think about after seeing Lana and Wanda going at it. Tongues were wagging." Fiona orbited the blue pot, inspecting this way and that. Suddenly, she pulled to a stop, midair, and gazed soberly at me. "Nothing good comes from gossip. Nothing."

Chapter 4

Life itself is the most wonderful fairy tale.
—Hans Christian Andersen

Friday at the shop sped by. A couple of tour groups wandered in during the morning, each group hoping for an impromptu class. I obliged. Over the course of the afternoon, I heard a little gossip about Wanda's set-to with Lana, but to my surprise the spat hadn't made the local news.

Saturday started out in much the same way as Friday. In the early morning, I delivered the fairy gardens to the site where the Beauty of Art Spectacular was to be held. By mid-morning, a couple of large groups had come and gone.

Around noon, however, I was surprised to see Lana Lamar stroll into my shop. She pushed through the door and did a spin to close it, which made the flute of her multicolored skirt billow up. When it settled over her long legs, she did another spin to move forward. I'd seen her do similar moves on the pickleball court. She was nothing if not elegantly athletic. She tugged the hem of her short-cropped yellow sweater over the waistline of her skirt and swept toward me with intention, arm extended.

"Courtney, so good to see you." She clasped my hands.

Anyone watching might think we were best friends. After watering her down yesterday, I'd expected to receive a punch to my nose at our next meeting.

"Love, love, love your place." Lana released me and strode to a selection of wind chimes. She ran her hand along the rods. A symphony of sound resonated. "I must buy one." She lifted a sea glass and driftwood set, one of the artiest chimes I'd discovered, and held it high. "Look how the sun shines through the glass. Exquisite." She offered me a radiant smile and looped a hand around my elbow. "Take me on a tour. I hear the patio is a delight."

Joss was gaping at me. Mentally, I was gaping, too. What had come over Lana? Better yet, what did she want?

"Sure." I gestured for her to follow me.

Setting the chimes on the counter, Lana said to Joss, "Wrap these up for me. I'm sure I'll be back with more."

As we moved through the patio door, I glanced over my shoulder at Joss, who threw me a cockeyed look. Was she thinking about the man she'd lost to Lana? Or was she trying, like I was, to figure out what Lana was up to?

Fiona sailed to Lana and soared around her head. "What's her plan?" she asked, echoing my concern.

Lana didn't react. She couldn't hear Fiona. However, she was peering toward the ficus trees, not the fairy figurines, suggesting she had learned that Open Your Imagination might have a resident fairy. "Courtney, I've heard so much about this place from Didi, but I haven't had a chance to stop in until now. It's magical." She tilted her head right and left. Was she trying to get a better angle so she could spy a fairy?

"Love the fountain," she said.

I steered her toward the verdigris bakers' racks. "These are the figurines we use to make gardens. And these are the pots we sell." Brandishing an arm like a TV model, I said, "And this—"

Lana spun me around to face her. "Wanda and I have made up. I feel the need to tell you because, well, you were furious with me."

"I wasn't furious with you. I was upset for both of you."

"Wanda and I were"—Lana licked her lips—"imprudent. Grown women, fighting like that in full view of the public." She tsked. "It was wrong. Dead wrong."

I couldn't help myself from agreeing. "Look, I know you have control of your emotions when you're on the court."

"I do."

"So I couldn't understand what could have made you . . ." I searched for a word.

"Snap?" Lana moved with me to a table and she slumped into a chair. She pulled my hand so I would sit, as well. When I did, she leaned forward and whispered, "I don't know what came over me. I've been under a lot of pressure. I need to make some life decisions sooner rather than later, so I've been preoccupied. When Wanda called me a cheater and threatened . . ." She fanned the air. "Threatened is a harsh word. When she said she'd tell Didi to rescind my membership, I . . ." Lana pressed a hand to her chest. "It hurt. Like a dagger to my heart. I know you understand. You do, don't you?"

What could I say? My father, who raised me after my mother passed away, had taught me that publicly airing a feud was not the best way to resolve hurt feelings. He advised that the best way of handling a conflict was to do so privately, one on one.

Lana squeezed my hand and popped to her feet. "Good chat. Thanks for listening. I knew I could count on you."

"For what?"

"For being on my side when the time comes."

"Your side? When *what* time comes?"

"Why, the hearing with the board at Sport Zone." Lana grinned.

"I'm not on the board."

"You're not? But I heard—"

"From whom?"

"Wanda said—" Lana's grin turned into a snarl. "Oh, I get it—"

Fiona whizzed into the air, laughing hysterically. "Meaghan's mother has no shame," she said, but of course only I could hear her.

With great effort, Lana suppressed whatever aggravation she was feeling and smiled beatifically at me. "Well, your place is lovely. I'm glad I stopped in. Good luck with . . ." She twirled a hand toward the ficus trees.

"The fairies," Fiona chirped.

"We all need a little make-believe in our lives, don't we?" Lana blew an air kiss and whisked out of the shop with the same energy as when she'd entered.

She didn't purchase the wind chimes. I didn't care.

Midafternoon on Saturdays, we served high tea on the patio. Once a month, we offered a book club tea. Yvanna Acebo, our weekend baker who held a steady job at Sweet Treats, had outdone herself for today's tea. She'd made a variety of tarts, cookies, and muffins. My favorite was the lemon bar—lemon curd on a shortbread cookie. It was melt-in-your-mouth good. Usually Meaghan served as the harpist at our teas, but because she was helping her mother prepare for the Beauty of Art Spectacular, I'd hired a lute player. The young woman entertained for nearly an hour and a half, wowing our customers and providing a wonderful atmosphere to browse and shop and enjoy delectable food.

Around five p.m., I left Open Your Imagination in Joss's capable hands so I had ample time to go home and get ready.

At seven p.m., after donning my earrings and grabbing my evening purse, I kissed Pixie good night and walked, with Fiona riding on my shoulder, from my cottage to the event.

There were plenty of venues and gorgeous hotels in Carmel-by-the-Sea that hosted events like the Beauty of Art Spectacular, but scoring the Meeting Hall had been a coup for Wanda and her team. The sprawling center, run by a non-profit organization and done in Mission Revival style architecture, was an amazing place. A state-of-the-art facility with a main foyer as well as a rear foyer, the Meeting Hall offered banquet sites, conference rooms, and six exterior bungalows. The pièce de résistance was the botanical garden. During the course of the evening, there would be ongoing tours. My fa ther had designed the garden using only indigenous plants. It was one of his premier accomplishments.

When Fiona and I met Meaghan by the entrance gate, I asked about her absent boyfriend. She said he'd opted not to attend. He was suffering an acute migraine. After giving our names to the guard, we followed a stream of people along the cobblestone walkway to the grassy expanse behind the main building. Fiona made a crack about Meaghan not needing this guy in her life. I told her to mind her own business. She didn't know him. She didn't understand the complexities of why humans fell in love and stayed in love.

Irritated by my response, Fiona flew off in a huff. I didn't worry. She would find ways to entertain herself and not get into trouble. Fairies loved art and particularly enjoyed fund-raisers because the *give, give, give* vibes were incredible.

"Wow," I said as Meaghan and I walked through the arch of roses leading to the venue.

Although the guest list was elite and not everyone in town had been invited, there were nearly three hundred in attendance. The men had donned traditional black tuxedos, but color, not neutrals, was the recurring theme for women's attire. I'd dressed in an ocean-blue sheath and sling-back silver heels. Meaghan had donned a chic burgundy flapper-style dress. Both of us had brought matching shawls.

"Your mother and her team of volunteers have outdone themselves," I murmured.

"She'll be thrilled to hear that. She said art galleries and antique stores from all over the central coast have donated works to display and auction, and a variety of garden shops have contributed gorgeous potted plants. Speaking of which . . ." Meaghan pointed.

Wanda had placed my two fairy gardens by the entrance to the rear foyer, which for tonight's event would serve as the bidding room.

"Mom hopes the *Donated by Open Your Imagination* sign above your fairy gardens will prod attendees to *open* their wallets."

"Crossing my fingers." I peeked in on our way past. "Nice digs."

Two wood-framed leather sofas, in keeping with the Mission Revival style, stood against the walls on either side of a guard desk. Talavera tile mirrors hung over each sofa. Added for the event were cloth-covered tables with bidding sheets, pencils, and photographs of each donated item. Bidding would open at seven p.m. At eight forty-five, the bidding would close. An hour before the end of the event, Wanda would announce who had "won" what. The guard desk was unattended. It didn't need to be manned. Only the hallway to the restrooms was accessible during the event. The second-floor ballrooms and such were closed to the public.

"Ready to see who's who?" Meaghan said.

"Sure."

We strolled on, taking in a few of the donated items. Auction number plaques stood beside or hung on each antique, artwork, or potted plant set around the semicircular grassy area and by the bungalows that flanked the expanse. An ornate armoire intrigued me. So did a Degas-like painting of a cypress on the beach.

Seated on the event stage situated in front of the entrance to the botanical garden was a string quartet. They were playing Mozart's "Spring."

"Love the music," I said.

"Mom said there will be a jazz band later. There she is." Meaghan gestured. "With Didi. See her? By the bar."

Both women had worn teal, but that was where the similarity ended. Wanda was dressed in a smart pantsuit, her hair in a loose chignon. Didi's billowing teal chiffon gown was a tad over-the-top but fun. She handed Wanda a glass of champagne and toasted her.

"Didi is her second-in-command tonight," Meaghan said.

"The logistics of this had to have been quite a challenge."

Beyond them, near the bungalows on the left, stood the buffet and six food stations. A variety of small café-style tables and chairs were clustered nearby, all occupied. I didn't see Brady, but he was probably overseeing his people in the kitchen.

I said, "Your mom has to be exhausted after putting this thing together."

"She's a warhorse. She'll survive."

We sauntered toward Wanda and Didi, but before we could reach them, Lana Lamar and her husband, Elton, approached them. Lana was wearing an ultra-tight lemon-yellow sheath and stacked heels. Elton, who typically had a penchant for colorful clothing, was clad in basic black tuxedo and black tie. A few weeks ago, while stair stepping at Sport Zone, I'd overheard Lana giving him an earful about his flamboyant workout outfit. Maybe that was why he'd toned down his attire tonight, although he hadn't toned down his mop of bleached-blond hair. He swept a thatch of it off his handsome face and scanned the crowd.

Wanda thrust her hand at Lana, but Lana didn't take it. She said something that made her mouth curl up in a snarl. Didi recoiled and stared daggers at Lana.

Elton's mouth moved as he ran a finger under the collar of his tuxedo shirt.

Lana shot him a wounding glance.

"Uh-oh," I murmured. "Your mother might not survive tonight if the vibes resulting from that exchange mean anything."

I scanned the area for a hose but didn't see one anywhere in sight. Good thing. I wasn't sure my trigger-happy finger would be able to resist blasting Lana if she overstepped.

Meaghan said, "Lana is going through with the discrimination suit. I'm sure that's what they're discussing."

"Oh, no. Really? You'd think a lawyer would talk her out of it. It's petty."

"No one can talk Lana out of anything."

After my encounter with her yesterday, I wasn't surprised to hear that. She had been determined, even then, to have the upper hand. Why? At what cost? I couldn't imagine why anyone would care about competing for a title at a small sport facility, but Lana did. She lived and breathed *winning*. Was a lawsuit the *life decision* she'd been concerned about?

As we drew nearer, I heard Didi say, "We're through discussing it, Lana. Elton, you look handsome tonight. I like the way you're wearing your hair. And those glasses are nice. Are they new?"

"Yes." His wire-rimmed glasses made him look professorial.

"How's the auto business?" Didi asked.

"Selling cars like hotcakes."

"Don't lie, darling." Lana picked something off her husband's jacket. "If you'll recall, I sat in on a meeting last week and your people weren't happy with you."

"Not true, darling," Elton countered. "You misread the cues. They weren't happy with *you*." He said to Didi, "I told my lovely wife that she could attend a sales meeting, but she was not to chime in. Did she listen? No, she—"

"Darling, hush." Lana put a finger to her husband's lips. "Don't let toads pop out of those beautiful lips. You can't take them back." She kissed his cheek and slipped her hand around his elbow.

"Stop!" Elton wrested free and threw both hands in the air. "You don't—" He pressed his lips together, breathing angrily through his nose, and stormed away.

Lana swapped a bleak look with Didi and Wanda, and then rushed after him.

Chapter 5

Each fairy breath of summer, as it blows with loveliness,
inspires the blushing rose.
—Anonymous

Meaghan hurried to her mother. I trailed her.

"Golly, Mom, Lana can't help herself, can she?"

"It appears not."

Didi frowned. "What Lana needs is an intensive class on how to win friends and influence people."

Maybe Tamara Geoffries offers that kind of therapy, I mused.

"Lana, Lana, Lana," Wanda chanted. "She loves to ridicule anybody and everybody. You'd think Elton would have a spine, what with all of his success in business, but his wife invariably gets the upper hand."

"He does," Didi said. "Whenever he's working out at Sport Zone, he's strong. Fierce."

Wanda bobbed her head. "Until Lana shows up; then he's namby-pamby."

Didi said, "*Shh.* Kenny is coming this way."

Kenny Chu, a trainer at Sport Zone, strode toward us. Tamara Geoffries, looking delicate in a wispy pink frock, clung to his arm as she hopped forward, trying to right a shoe that had come off. Were they a couple? Prior to living in Carmel, Kenny had worked as a stunt man in Los Angeles. In one movie, he'd stood in for Jet Li, the famous martial arts expert.

"Ladies," Kenny said, "you all know Tamara Geoffries, I assume."

"I don't." I raised a hand. "I'm Courtney Kelly."

"Hi." Tamara broke free of Kenny and sidled away from him.

Aha. They were not on a date. He'd apparently been a gentleman and lent her an arm while she'd struggled with her shoe.

"Courtney, you own Open Your Imagination, don't you?" Tamara had the kind of voice I could listen to all day—symphonic radio announcer calm. "I've been meaning to stop in. Although I'm not much of a gardener, I've always wanted to try." She swept her long hair over her shoulder and toyed with one of her dangling diamond earrings. "Does a fairy really live there?"

"You'll have to come see for yourself." I offered a friendly smile, dying to ask her who Jamie was—the name she'd uttered that had rattled Lana on Thursday—but I knew it would be inappropriate at a social function.

"Maybe I will."

"I saw the armoire you donated," I said. "It's exquisite."

Tamara lowered her chin demurely. "Vintage nineteenth-century French country walnut."

"I'd love to see what else you have in your shop." In addition to adding a fountain in the rear yard, I wanted to purchase a few specialty pieces for the cottage. A girl could dream. "Do you think I might score an invitation?"

"Maybe." She was nothing if not cryptic. "Oh, I see a few friends of mine across the way. Thanks again, Kenny, for offering your arm. Bye." She strode toward a gathering of women.

For the next hour, Meaghan and I said hello to everyone we knew and introduced ourselves to those we didn't know but should. *Big-bucks people*, as Wanda dubbed them, the kind who could help both Meaghan's and my businesses grow. Then we toured the grounds to view more of the artwork, antiques, and plants up for auction. When I spotted an antique Amish wagon that would make a great container for a fairy garden, I knew I had to have it, so I went to the bidding room and entered my offer. Four people had bid before me.

"I hope I get this." I couldn't go higher. I was at my limit.

"I hope you do, too. Bidding will close soon."

When Meaghan and I finally succumbed to our craving for food, we joined her mother in the line at the buffet. I scanned the crowd for Fiona but didn't see her anywhere, although I did notice light and movement in the trees. Perhaps she had found Merryweather and they were having tea. The queen fairy would approve of that social nicety.

"Kip!" Wanda waved. "Over here. Doesn't your father look handsome?" she said to me.

"Very."

My father was tan and rugged, like a man who worked the land all day should be. Before turning to landscaping, he'd been a cop. A freak accident while chasing a thief had ruined his knee and ended his career. In spite of the chronic pain, he'd maintained his muscular physique.

"Nice tuxedo, Dad," I said. He must have rented it; I didn't think he owned one.

"Pretty dress." He pecked me on the cheek. "Goes well with your see-no-sun skin."

"I spend time in the sun, Dad." Sun block and sun hats helped me protect my pale Irish skin.

He kissed Meaghan's and her mother's cheeks. "What a gala, Wanda. You've nailed it."

"I couldn't have done it without Didi Dubois." Wanda's

eyelids fluttered; she stifled a yawn. "By the way, thank you, Kip, for providing such lovely plantings."

"You did, Dad?" I raised an eyebrow. "Where are they?"

"All over. Here and there." He brandished a hand.

"I thought only local garden shops had donated."

"Wanda asked. How could I refuse?"

He smiled impishly at her and alarm bells rang out in my head. Were they flirting? My father hadn't dated much since my mother's death twenty years ago. Although he'd hidden it better than I had, he'd been heartbroken. Stoic ran in his veins, Nana had said. Oh, sure, he'd gone out to dinner or to a movie with a woman or two, but he hadn't gotten serious with anyone.

Meaghan must have noticed the flirting, because she elbowed me.

Wanda bit back a second yawn. "Sorry."

"Why don't you go to the lounge?" my father suggested. "Just beyond the rear foyer in the main building. There's a sofa in the anteroom. You can lie down. Put your feet up."

"Good idea. A power nap. Just what I need." Wanda blew us all a kiss and wended through the crowd.

At the same time, Brady came into view. Dressed in a tuxedo, he looked as handsome as all get-out. Desire stirred within me. I tamped it down. *Friends.* We were *friends.*

"Having a good time, sir?" Brady shook my father's hand firmly.

"Indeed. It's a wonderful affair." My father patted him on the back. "The food is terrific. I'm particularly fond of the stir-fry station. I must have eaten a dozen dumplings."

Wanda said, "The teriyaki kebabs are to die for."

"Save room for dessert," Brady said. "Don't miss the chocolate fountain."

Meaghan moaned in a good way. "I saw it and gained five pounds just looking at it. Mini cream puffs and peanut brittle dipped in chocolate? Inspired."

Brady thanked her. "Where's your guy?"

"Home sick."

"Sorry to hear that." He turned to me, a twinkle in his eyes. "Are you on your own, Courtney?"

"Seems I am. Nobody asked me to the prom."

He chuckled. "If I'd known, I would have blown off this gig and asked you myself. Heck, I'd have even bought you a corsage." He was teasing, but the banter felt fun. Relaxed.

Friends.

"Catch you later." He hooked his thumb over his shoulder. "I need to make the rounds."

"Me too," my father said. "There are a few clients I've got to see."

Both men headed off, leaving Meaghan and me to our own devices. We filled up our plates with appetizers, each fetched a glass of sauvignon blanc from the bar, and found a table.

As we sat, the jazz band Wanda had promised kicked into high gear. The band's rendition of "It Don't Mean a Thing" was rousing. People in the audience hooted their approval.

"Look at those two," Meaghan said between bites. "Don't they ever stop talking pickleball?"

"Which two?"

She pointed at Kenny and Didi, who were moving toward us, each pantomiming a ground stroke.

As they neared, we could hear every word of their conversation.

"The serve should be executed near the center line so that the server can effectively cover both sides of the court when the serve is returned," Kenny said. In addition to being the premier trainer at Sport Zone, he taught pickleball.

"Of course, Kenny, except everyone knows that's the strategy, so where's the finesse?"

"Kenny! There you are." Lana cut through the crowd and sidled to Kenny, brushing his arm with hers.

Kenny turned three shades of pink and inched away.

"Didi," Lana said, "I couldn't help overhearing."

Did she have supersonic hearing or had she been eavesdropping?

"You're forgetting that most players have a weaker backhand than forehand." Lana mimed slicing the air with a paddle. The muscles of her perfectly formed arms rippled with the effort. "You have to force your opponent to use the weaker side."

Didi said through gritted teeth, "What I was going to say before you rudely interrupted me is the dink is the finesse. Especially the cross-court dink, which you seem to have trouble returning."

Lana flinched. "I do not."

"It is your Achilles' heel."

"Ha!" Lana's scornful laugh could have cut ice. "I've beaten you in every match, so it's not much of an Achilles' heel."

Didi winked. "But now that everyone knows it—yes, I've told everyone who will face you in competition—you'll be toast."

Lana let out an angry little shriek and rushed Didi.

Didi dodged her. Lana tripped but righted herself by catching the back of an elderly woman's chair. The woman startled. Lana apologized and whirled around. Didi spread her arms and crooked her fingers, daring Lana to take her on. What had gotten into Didi? Had she had too much to drink? I'd never seen her acting so frisky. Maybe there were pixies about. They loved to create mischief.

Fiona soared to me and hovered in front of my face. "What's going on?"

Merryweather trailed her.

"Isn't it obvious?" I said. "The onset of another squabble." In high school, these kinds of public quarrels were to be expected, but between two grown women? At a major event? Ridiculous.

"Ladies." Kenny held out both arms. "To your corners."

He looked ready to brace the women by their foreheads if necessary, which made me flash on a scene in an old Three Stooges movie, Moe holding off Curly and Larry. After my mother died, my father and I had watched a lot of comedies. We'd needed a respite from the sorrow. If this set-to between Lana and Didi weren't such a tense scenario, it would be comical.

"You've got to stop them, Courtney," Fiona said. "It's bad. I can feel it in here." She thumped her chest.

"Do you see a hose?" I asked. "No, you do not. I'm not the savior to the world. They have to fix this themselves."

Fiona huffed and flew to Merryweather. They huddled. Fiona glanced over her shoulder at me. Her face was pinched with worry. Did she really sense something awful was about to happen? My insides snagged.

"Kenny," I prompted.

"Ladies," Kenny said, his voice edgy, "I will not warn you again. Back. Off."

Didi huffed and obeyed. Drawing in a deep breath, she held up her hands, palms forward. "Truce."

Lana grumbled. I was pretty sure she said *truce*, as well.

Kenny breathed easier. "Lana, I've told you over and over again that you need to see a therapist. I've got the perfect—"

"Do not tell me what I need, Kenny. Ever." Lana's eyes glinted with loathing. "I tell you what *you* need. Do you understand? So back the heck off or else."

Her warning sent a shiver through me.

At a distance, I glimpsed Tamara Geoffries nibbling a teriyaki kebab. A smile tugged at the corners of her mouth. When she caught me staring at her, she turned heel and disappeared into the crowd.

Elton Lamar, carrying a bottle of beer by its neck, passed

Tamara without giving her a second glance. Even from a distance, I could see his eyes glinting with malice. He strode purposefully across the grass to his wife, clutched her by the elbow, and said something in her ear.

Although public displays of affection or disaffection made me uncomfortable and usually caused me to turn aside—toward the end of my relationship with my fiancé, Christopher, he had been prone to the latter—I remained riveted. I caught a snippet of what Elton said: ". . . a fool of me."

Lana glowered at him. "Grow up, Elton," she said under her breath, but her clipped words were completely audible. "Honestly, at times you're like a petulant child. Nobody made a fool of you at that sales meeting except yourself." She wrenched free and marched away.

How adult. *Not.*

Elton's face turned as red as rhubarb. His jaw started grinding from side to side. Was he wishing he had a snappy comeback? After a long moment, he crossed to Kenny. "Man, go after her, will you? Calm her down. She'll listen to you."

"Uh-uh." Kenny threw up both hands. "Ain't my problem."

I couldn't blame the guy, not after the way Lana had belittled him.

"But . . ." Elton sputtered. "C'mon—"

"No way, man. Your wife. Your deal." Kenny strode to the nearby no-host bar and purchased a bottle of beer, then he swung around, propped his elbow on the bar, and raised a toast to Elton.

The fairies broke from their huddle and flew in the direction Lana had gone.

I said to Meaghan, "Whew. Who knew tonight would be so lively?"

"Do you think any of the patrons are wondering whether the tête-à-tête was staged for their benefit?" she asked. "Some are staring in this direction."

"If they believed that, they would have offered a round of applause."

"Good point."

I shook my head. "Sadly, this will probably be fodder for the gossip mills tomorrow."

"Mom will rally. At least this time, she wasn't the center attraction." Meaghan draped her shawl over her shoulders.

I did, too. The weather had turned cool. "I'm ready for dessert," I said. "How about you?"

"You're reading my mind."

A half hour later, after we'd had our fill of peanut brittle dipped in chocolate and chocolate-drenched cream puffs, Meaghan said, "My mother's been gone a long time. Come with me. I'm going to the lounge to check on her."

As if sensing I was on the move, Fiona returned. I hung back from Meaghan and held out a finger. Fiona alit on it.

"Where have you been?" I asked.

"Merryweather gave me a task. We set off after Lana Lamar. She led; I followed. But midflight, Merryweather changed her mind. She decided we couldn't help Lana—anger has to run its course sometimes, she said—so she made a new plan, and we flew from plant to artwork to antique to douse each with a special money potion. Just watch. All the guests will bid high."

"Money potion? That's a new one."

"It's so cool. Merryweather taught me how to make it. We used all sorts of green plants. We can't use the potion for personal gain, of course."

I smiled. "You are natural do-gooders. Wanda will be so thankful. She—"

"Courtney!" Meaghan raced from the main building waving her arm frantically. Her face was ashen. "Come quick."

Chapter 6

The dances ended, all the fairy train for pinks and daisies
searched the flow'ry plain.
—Alexander Pope

Fiona and I followed Meaghan into the foyer.

"Oh, no!" I cried, stopping abruptly. I put my hand on my friend's arm to hold her back. "Wait."

Lana Lamar lay on the parquet floor, eyes open, the contents of her purse scattered, cell phone face down. Wanda was kneeling beside Lana, her hand wrapped around something jutting from Lana's chest. Was it the dragon's sword—the letter opener? Yes, I could make it out now. The tooled hilt jutted from between Wanda's hands. Bidding papers were scattered on the floor. Wadded brown paper towels lay beneath the tables. The time-themed fairy garden had been shattered; shards of the garden's pot lay on the floor beside Lana. Wanda's eyes were dull and unfocused, as if she was in a trance. No one else was in the vicinity.

Wanda glanced in our direction, but I wasn't sure she saw either her daughter or me. She muttered, "What have I done?"

"Heavens!" a woman exclaimed.

I released Meaghan and peered over my shoulder. Tamara Geoffries, who had donned a full-length coat, scarf, and gloves, was standing in the doorway, her hand covering her mouth.

Through widened fingers, Tamara said, "Did Wanda kill Lana?"

No way. She couldn't have. Wanda was a sweet, gentle soul.

"Stay back!" I commanded as emotions caught in my throat. "Meaghan, help your mother to her feet."

Without saying a word, Meaghan rushed to her mother and pried her hand off the letter opener. As she ushered her mother away, I knelt beside Lana, clasped her right wrist, and felt for a pulse. I couldn't find one. I tried her other wrist. Nothing. A sob escaped my lips. I had never liked Lana. She was a bully and an egotist who had never had a kind word for anyone, but that didn't mean I'd wished her dead. She must have had some good traits. Some dear friends. A sister or a mother who adored her? A competitor who admired her? Someone.

"She's gone." I rose to a stand. "Wanda, what—"

"Don't wake her." Meaghan put a finger to her lips. "She's asleep. She . . . she sleepwalks."

"Sleepwalks?" My mouth fell open.

Tamara said, "It's a form of parasomnia."

"I know what it is," I said, not meaning to sound so snappish. "What I meant was how could she be sleepwalking now?" It was barely nine thirty in the evening.

"Remember? She came in here to take a nap," Meaghan explained. "She must have fallen into a deep sleep. She sleepwalks when she's in full REM mode."

Tamara said, "Your mother killed Lana."

"No," Meaghan said. "She did not do this. She couldn't have."

Tamara aimed a finger. "Wanda said, 'What have I done?'"

"That wasn't an admission!" Meaghan hissed. "She's confused."

Tamara pursed her lips. "A sleepwalker can do all sorts of things, including kill someone."

"Stop. Please. She didn't—" Meaghan bit back a sob. "Let's talk about this later. Right now, I need to wake her. Slowly."

"Right now, we need to alert the police," Tamara said.

I glared at the woman, anger fomenting inside me. Why was she here? In the vicinity? The bidding had ended over forty-five minutes ago. Tallying the winners wasn't supposed to occur for a while. She should have been with the other guests. Maybe she'd needed to use the restroom, except there were plenty of other facilities beyond the stage where the band was playing as well as in the bungalows. I flashed on her give-and-take with Lana during Lana's set-to with Wanda. And earlier this evening, I'd noticed Tamara jubilantly watching Lana argue with her husband. Did Tamara have a reason to want Lana dead?

"The police," Tamara repeated.

"Yes, of course." I pulled my cell phone from my clutch.

"I'll stand guard outside and make sure no one else comes in." Tamara hooked a thumb in that direction.

"Thank you." I stabbed in 911 and quickly explained the situation.

As I ended the call, Fiona flew to Lana and cruised over her face.

"What are you doing?" I asked her.

"Examining the body."

If the moment weren't so serious, I might have laughed. "You're not a coroner."

"I'm looking for clues."

In addition to learning fairy magic, Fiona had also been reading the complete collection of Sherlock Holmes stories. She had a particular fondness for *A Study in Scarlet*, the first Holmes story.

"We need hard evidence," she said, as if she were Sherlock Holmes in the *fairy* flesh.

There was hard evidence, I thought. Wanda had been gripping the murder weapon.

Merryweather flew into the foyer and screeched to a halt, metaphorically speaking. Like Fiona, she hovered over Lana. "Oh, my," she and Fiona intoned like a Greek chorus.

"Merryweather," I said. "Track down Didi Dubois. She'll need to take charge when the police arrive."

"She won't be able to hear me." Merryweather had a burbling, cheerful voice, even when tense. "She's not a believer."

"Right." I wasn't thinking clearly. My mind was churning.

"I'll fetch Miss Reade," Merryweather said. "She's close by."

"Good idea."

Miss Reade was a librarian at Harrison Memorial Library. Merryweather assisted at the library by giving inspiration to its patrons. I didn't even know Miss Reade's first name, I suppose because I regarded her as an authority figure like my teachers in my school days, and I would never have called any of them by their first names.

Merryweather vanished and returned in a flash. With her came the librarian, a spry woman in her early seventies who appeared much younger than her years, thanks to her sense of style and chic haircut and inquisitive personality.

"Oh, my," Miss Reade said. "This afternoon, Merryweather told me she had a bad feeling about tonight. I'd dismissed it. Poor Lana. How she adored reading about sports."

"She patronized the library?" I asked.

Miss Reade bobbed her head. "Indeed. It might surprise you to learn that, in addition to lapping up everything about sports, she devoted one Saturday a month reading aloud to a girls-in-need club."

Sadness coursed through me. How little I had known about Lana.

Miss Reade took in the mess in the foyer. "Did Wanda do this?"

Meaghan had moved her mother to the far side of the room and was coaxing her to sit on one of the wood-framed leather sofas, the one to the left of the guard desk.

"No," I said. "I mean, I don't think so. She couldn't have. She's a sleepwalker. She doesn't have a clue what happened. But . . ."

Tears glistened in Meaghan's eyes. I mouthed that I was *sorry*. She mouthed, *Me too*.

"A few killers have gotten off with the defense of sleep-walking," Miss Reade said.

Tamara Geoffries had also said a sleepwalker could kill. Was she nearby? Again, I questioned why she'd been lurking about.

"Wanda couldn't have done this," Fiona said. "She's too nice."

I recalled the set-to between Wanda and Lana on Thursday and wondered how *nice* a person had to be to *not* commit murder. If pressed against the wall, wouldn't anyone? Hadn't we all fantasized about killing someone? I had. Not in grue-some detail, but even so . . .

Had Lana goaded Wanda into an argument? Had she irked someone else? Had that other person—the murderer—set up Wanda to be the fall guy?

I cleared my throat and revised that thought—fall *woman*.

"Fiona," I said, "go to Meaghan. She won't see you, but you can comfort her." Then I turned to Miss Reade. "Could you please find Didi Dubois? She's Wanda's second-in-command tonight. I've called nine-one-one."

As if on cue, a siren pierced the air. The Carmel police station wasn't far from the Meeting Hall.

Miss Reade hustled out of the foyer and returned in a few moments with Didi, who was clutching her teal shawl tightly at her neck. Her hairline looked moist. What had she been doing to work up such a sweat? Miss Reade must have explained what had happened, because Didi's skin was ash gray.

When Didi caught sight of Lana lying on the floor, she moaned. "How? Who?"

A few other guests trailed her in. Some wheezed. Others began to whisper.

"Coming through," a man bellowed from outside.

Two emergency medical technicians hustled into the foyer, the male built like a Mack Truck, the female as athletic looking as Lana.

"She's dead," I said to them.

"Let us be the judge, ma'am," the Mack Truck said. He and his partner conferred.

"Move, everyone. Out of the way!" another man yelled from outside. "This is a crime scene. Back away, but don't leave. We'll be getting your statements soon."

Detective Dylan Summers strode into the foyer. Clad in what I liked to think of as his work clothes, khaki trousers and white shirt with the sleeves rolled up, he looked rested. I attributed that to his romance with his former partner Renee Rodriguez—*former* because she'd quit the force. After dealing with a murder, she'd decided she couldn't take it any longer. Renee had recently opened a pottery school and store. As it turned out, she was quite deft at throwing pots. I'd purchased a few for Open Your Imagination.

Summers's new partner, Officer Redcliff Reddick, a lanky redhead in his early thirties—a good twenty years younger than Summers and taller by six inches, no easy feat since Summers stood over six feet tall—accompanied him. Both donned latex gloves. I'd met Reddick before. He had worked the previous murder.

Tamara slipped in behind them and stayed close to the wall. Tears pressed the corners of her eyes.

Summers caught sight of me. "Well, well, Miss Kelly, as I live and breathe."

The Mack Truck peered over his shoulder at Summers. "She's dead, Dylan."

"I didn't do it," I joked, halfheartedly. Summers and I had met a few months ago when the owner of the pet-grooming business across the way from Open Your Imagination was found dead on the shop's patio. For a nanosecond, I'd been a suspect in the murder.

"Is that Lana Lamar?" Summers asked.

"Yes. How do you—"

"I'm a member at Sport Zone."

I'd never seen him there, but that didn't mean a thing. I didn't follow a schedule or routine. I went whenever I could and on rainy days. On clear days, I preferred long walks or runs on the beach, shooting hoops, or taking a bicycle ride along the coast.

"Lana has quite the reputation," Summers said, his tone dry.

"That's an understatement," Didi quipped.

"Detective Summers, this is—" I balked. "You probably know Didi Dubois."

"Indeed. Mrs. Dubois."

"Lana's husband, Elton, is at the party," Didi said. "I'll find him." She turned to leave.

"Didi, don't go!" I yelled.

Chapter 7

Fairies have to be one thing or another, because being so small, they unfortunately have room for one feeling only at a time.
—J. M. Barrie, *Peter Pan*

"You're in charge now, Didi," I said.

"Why me?" she asked.

"Because you're Wanda's assistant at this soiree, and seeing as she can't manage, you"—I swallowed hard—"have to take over. With the police." I motioned to Wanda. Was she awake yet? What were the risks of waking her?

"What's going on with her?" Didi squinted.

"She was sleepwalking." Tamara stepped from the wall.

"Sleepwalking?" Summers asked.

"When we arrived," Tamara went on, "Wanda was kneeling beside Lana, her hands on the knife."

"The letter opener," I said with venom, angry that Tamara was implicating Wanda.

Didi pulled her shawl tighter, as if steeling herself for worse news.

"Letter opener?" Summers studied the body.

I nodded. "It's a decoration from the fairy garden." The *broken* fairy garden, I thought. Had there been a fight? I noticed dirt on Lana's hands but not on Wanda's. Had Wanda cleaned her hands with the paper towels? "It's actually the dragon's sword."

Tamara said, "I heard Wanda say, 'What have I done?'"

Stop now, I willed Tamara.

But she didn't. "Wanda hated the way Lana had critiqued her clients," Tamara continued. "I know because a few of her clients have shown artwork in my gallery."

"I thought you only sold antiques," I said.

"And a few pieces of art."

"The reviews were harsh?" Summers asked Tamara.

"One in particular was scathing. For Betsy Brahn. Wanda's client."

I groaned. I couldn't help it. Had the review Lana recited to me at Sport Zone incited Wanda to murder? Wouldn't Miss Brahn have lashed out instead?

"Betsy's in Europe right now," Tamara added, as if reading my mind.

Summers met my gaze. "Miss Kelly, did Mrs. Brownie kill Mrs. Lamar?"

"What? No." I glowered at Tamara, feeling like I'd been sucker-punched. And why was she wearing a coat? A shawl like mine would have been enough. It wasn't that cold.

"Miss Kelly?" Summers said. "Were you first on the scene?"

Through gritted teeth, I said, "Yes. Actually, no. Meaghan was first. She yelled at me to come quick. Wanda . . . Mrs. Brownie . . . was here. Kneeling beside Lana. And, yes, her hand was on the weapon, but she was in a daze." Was that how sleepwalking could be described? "She didn't have a clue what she was doing. Perhaps she found Lana stabbed and thought if she pulled out the letter opener—"

"Did anybody else touch it?" Didi asked.

"Good question." Summers regarded me again while removing a small leather notebook from his pocket. He took off the rubber band that held it together and slid the pen from its loop. Slowly, deliberately. At times, he could be so old-school. And aloof. And a real pain.

"No," I said in response to Didi. "I mean, yes. I touched it. When I made the fairy garden." My cheeks flamed hot. With guilt? Not a chance. I did not kill Lana, but my gut told me Wanda hadn't, either. To cover my frustration, I turned to Miss Reade, who was keeping quiet. "Would you mind finding Elton Lamar?" I described him and what he was wearing.

"On it." Miss Reade scuttled away with Merryweather soaring after her.

Reddick said, "Sir, this looks like a crime of passion."

"Are you supposed to offer opinions while determining what happened?" Didi asked, sounding as miffed as I felt.

Summers scowled. "Let's not discuss anything but the facts, Red."

"Yes, sir." Reddick pressed his lips together. Despite how cool Summers could be, he was a good and fair cop. Reddick would learn a lot from him.

"I'm going to talk to Mrs. Brownie now," Summers said.

"There's probably blood on her hands," I stated, "because she touched the weapon, but sir, I really do think she was trying to help Lana, not hurt her."

"As I told Officer Reddick, let's not make assumptions, Miss Kelly."

"Can't you call me Courtney?" I rasped. He knew me by now.

"No, ma'am." Summers offered a compassionate smile. "Please stick around. First people on the scene—"

"Notice things. Got it."

"What about me?" Tamara introduced herself. "Should I stick around?"

"Please wait outside, Miss Geoffries," Summers said.

Tamara retied her scarf and shambled out.

Didi sidled up to me. "This is horrible. Awful. What a loss. I know it sounds trivial, but . . . even though Lana was a lousy sport, she actually was a really good pickleball player."

I found it interesting that people often felt the need to say something nice about a victim, likability notwithstanding.

"Elton will be heartbroken," Didi went on. "Luckily, they didn't have kids. Lana didn't want them. She thought pregnancy would ruin her shape. You know what a stickler she was for having less than two percent body fat. She was a consummate athlete. She—" Didi's voice caught. She pressed her lips together and covered them with her fingertips.

"Didi, you look like you've just run a marathon," I said. "What's up?"

She rolled her eyes. "I got an alert that an alarm went off at Sport Zone. Worried about a break-in, I zipped over. It was nothing, but then . . ." She sliced the air with her hand. "Honestly? I was so ticked off at Lana after our to-do earlier that I switched into workout gear and hit balls with the pickleball tutor." The tutor was an auto-return machine. "Owner's privilege to be able to use the club even when it's closed. I—" She braced her cheek with a hand. "Oh, my, my, my. If I'd been here instead of there, maybe—"

I touched her arm. "No. Don't blame yourself. None of us could have seen this coming." Well, one person could, I supposed. The murderer.

I gazed across the room. Summers had moved to Meaghan and her mother and stood towering over them. Wanda gazed up at him. She appeared more alert. And frightened. Her eyes were blinking rapidly, her skin pale. Summers's mouth was moving. Wanda glanced at Lana's body and shook her head vehemently.

Summers squatted in front of them and squinted at Wanda. He put a hand on hers. Was he judging her condition? Testing her pulse to determine whether she was faking the sleep-walking?

Didi said, "What if Wanda isn't the killer and the real killer is roaming the party?"

Fiona whizzed into my line of sight. "Something's afoot."

I raised an eyebrow. "Don't go all Sherlock Holmes on me."

"Me?" Didi pressed a hand to her chest. "I would never."

"No, I . . ." *Oops.* "Sorry. I'm on edge." I squeezed her shoulder to reassure her.

"I mean it," Fiona went on. "The whole thing looks staged to me."

Why did she think that? I eyed the crime scene. If Lana and Wanda had gotten into a fight, they could have knocked over the bidding tables as well as the fairy garden. The pottery could have shattered. Wanda, in her trance, might have picked up a shard to defend herself, but Lana advanced on her. Taunting her. Threatening to overpower her. Even in her dazed state, Wanda would have realized a shard wouldn't stop Lana. In a flash, she saw the dragon lying on its side. Maybe the letter opener had fallen loose. She picked it up and—

"That gavel," Fiona said. "What is it doing there?"

The gavel, the one Wanda was to use when announcing the winning bids, was lying beneath one of the tables.

Did Wanda strike Lana with the gavel, thus rendering her incapable of fighting back, after which she stabbed her with the letter opener? No. I had to stop thinking Wanda had anything to do with Lana's death. She had gone to the ladies' room to take a nap. She was in the wrong place at the wrong time.

I tried to imagine another scenario: Wanda woke up because of a noise. She must have heard the killer and Lana going at it. The killer had used the gavel and tossed it aside. By the time Wanda arrived on the scene, Lana was on the floor dead; the killer had fled. Wanda went to help Lana, but she fell into a state of confusion by the time we arrived.

I scanned the room again. How long had Lana been dead? Had she come to this room to make a bid? Or had the killer lured her here after the bidding had closed? Had framing Wanda been part of the killer's plan?

"Why didn't anybody hear the fight?" Fiona asked.

I craned an ear. "Because the band had started up."

In fact, it was still playing. The jazzy rendition of "Ruby Blue" wasn't earsplitting, but it was loud enough to cover a quarrel. If Wanda was asleep, she wouldn't have heard anything. Except she must have, which was why she'd roused.

Four officers charged into the foyer—two uniforms and two technicians. Reddick gave the uniforms the task of securing the perimeter. The technicians started to collect evidence.

Before the officers could move outside with yellow crime scene tape, a man yelled, "Where is she?" Elton Lamar pressed through the crowd. "Lana? Darling?" He stopped cold and pressed a fist to his mouth. "Omigod." I noticed that a bandage covered one knuckle. Had that been there before?

Didi released me and hurried to Elton. She looped her arm around his back and said, "I'm so sorry for your loss."

Summers abandoned the Brownies and strode to Elton. "I'm Detective Summers, sir, and you are . . ."

"Elton Lamar. Lana's husband." His bow tie was loose. His fingers looked damp, as if he'd recently washed them.

"Sir, I'm afraid your wife has met an untimely death."

"I can see th-that." Elton's voice caught. He shrugged off Didi and finger-combed his hair. "What happened? Who did this?"

"We're not sure yet," Didi said.

Summers threw Didi a look, which she missed. He repeated with more authority, "We're not sure yet, Mr. Lamar." He proceeded to ask Elton the basics: his age and profession and how long he'd been married to Lana.

"Fifteen years, going on sixteen." Elton's voice snagged. "Our anniversary . . . it's next week. We were planning to travel to Seattle. She's always wanted to see the Space Needle. Then we were going to one of the islands off British Columbia. We had been planning the trip for—" He moaned. "I'm going to be sick."

Didi said to Summers, "I can take him to the restroom, Detective."

Summers nodded.

As Didi and Elton walked past the guard station down the hall, Kenny Chu stumbled through the doorway. "What's going on? I heard—" He gawked at Lana's body. "Lana! Oh, man, no." His words slurred together. "Is she dead?" He made a gagging sound. "Was she stabbed?"

Summers barked, "Reddick, get that perimeter established! No more guests come in without my say-so."

"Sir." Reddick rushed out.

Summers asked Kenny his name. Chu came out sounding like *Shoe*. How much had he had to drink?

"How did you know Mrs. Lamar?" Summers inquired.

Kenny's voice cracked with emotion. "I was her pickleball trainer. Her friend. Her . . ." He blanched.

Her *what*? I'd seen them earlier. He'd made eyes at her. She'd brushed his arm, accidentally on purpose? Had he and Lana been an item? Had they been having an affair?

My imagination went wild. What if he'd met Lana in the foyer and asked her to leave Elton for him? What if she'd turned him down? Kenny had removed his tuxedo jacket since I'd seen him. Where was it? Had he thrown it away because there was blood on it? The cuffs of his shirt were wet. Had he gotten blood on them and washed it out? A bit of dirt was on the hem of his pants. Could it be soil from the broken fairy garden pot?

Stop, Courtney. Not everyone is a killer. Kenny might have taken a tour of the botanical garden.

Summers eyed Kenny's shirt sleeves. "Where's your jacket, Mr. Chu?"

Kenny grimaced. "I'm a slob. I spilled soy sauce on myself. It really stains. I dumped it in my car."

Summers regarded Kenny's freshly buffed black loafers. "Did you also spill soy sauce on your shoes?"

"Yeah." Kenny drew in a deep breath and let it out. "Why?" He seemed oblivious to Summers's line of questioning, but clearly, Summers was wondering what I was— whether blood splatter had gotten onto Kenny's jacket.

"Where have you been over the course of the last hour, Mr. Chu?" Summers asked.

Kenny scratched his cheek with a finger. "That would be, what, since eight thirty? I left the party for a bit. I needed to think, so I . . ." He worked his tongue inside his cheek. *"So I went to the library."*

"With anyone?"

"No," Kenny said, and swallowed hard. "I realized I'd had a lot to drink, and I wanted to walk it off."

He didn't walk it off enough, I mused.

"Is the library open this late at night?" Summers asked.

"No. It was closed. But I could at least see the bookshelves through the windows. Maybe it sounds strange, but looking at books always calms me."

"Can anyone corroborate that you were there?"

Kenny's eyes widened as he sobered. "Whoa, man, I

mean, sir. Detective. You don't think I had anything to do with this, do you? I wouldn't. Lana and I, we were . . ." He rubbed the back of his neck.

"You and Mrs. Lamar were what?"

"Friends. Good friends. I was her coach, too. We didn't have any issues."

Summers regarded him for a long moment. "I'm going to need a statement from you, Mr. Chu." He signaled one of the officers who had secured the perimeter. "Take this gentleman and get his particulars."

"Do I need a lawyer?" Kenny asked, his voice bristling with tension.

Summers inclined his head. "I don't know. Do you?"

Chapter 8

May you touch dragonflies and stars,
dance with fairies and talk to the moon.
—Anonymous

The way Summers had lit into Kenny made me feel better. Maybe Wanda, despite the incriminatory evidence, wasn't his only suspect.

I recalled the way Lana had demeaned Kenny publicly earlier. I could imagine that he might have texted her and asked her to meet him at the bidding room so he could read her the riot act. Had she shown up with attitude and lashed out? I imagined Kenny picking up the gavel and threatening her with it and Lana growing livid and rushing at him, claws drawn. They struggled. The fairy garden tumbled. Papers flew. Ultimately, Kenny prevailed and stabbed her with the letter opener.

The timing seemed particularly important. The murderer would have needed to have killed Lana and escaped before Wanda had walked out of the restroom in a trance. I flashed on the paper towels among the rubble. Had Wanda entered with them in hand, or had Kenny brought them with him? If that was the case, why? In order to wipe off blood that might splatter onto his clothes or clean the weapon. Did that imply premeditation? Why leave the paper towels?

"Detective, my mother needs some air," Meaghan said. "May we step outside?"

Summers nodded. "Don't go far."

"May I join them, Detective?" I asked. I needed to get the lowdown.

"Sure."

Before I left, I said to him, "Lana's cell phone." I pointed to it. "Is there a text message on it? Maybe the killer summoned her here."

Summers picked it up. "It's password protected."

"Her fingertip might . . . you know . . ." A bitter taste flooded my mouth.

He followed my suggestion and placed Lana's finger on the Open button. It worked. He scrolled through her text messages. "No recent ones. The last was at six p.m. from her husband."

"I suppose a message could have been erased?"

Summers frowned. "I'll consider it."

Sensing he didn't want more of my input, I slipped outside.

Meaghan and her mother were sitting on a cement bench near the bidding room entrance.

I perched on the opposite side of Wanda and slung an arm around her. "How are you doing?"

"Not well. I didn't . . ." She let the sentence hang.

"I know you didn't."

A huge crowd had gathered beyond the yellow crime scene tape. Each person was goggling in the direction of the bidding room. The band had stopped playing. The officers Reddick had put in charge of the perimeter were doing their best to keep people quiet and respectful. I noticed Brady among the crowd. He beckoned me.

I said to Meaghan and Wanda, "I'll be right back," and strode along the walkway to him. Staying within the perimeter, I said, "Hey, Brady."

"Hey, yourself. Is it true? Lana Lamar is dead? Murdered?"

"Mm-hm."

"What a shock."

"I'll say."

Quickly, he recapped what he'd heard so far, about the crime scene, and Wanda, and the sleepwalking.

I wasn't sure from whom he would have gleaned all of that. I didn't ask. Maybe Miss Reade had revealed what she'd seen while on the hunt for Elton. Or Tamara Geoffries had spilled everything. Where had she gone? I scanned the crowd and spied her standing near Kenny Chu. Earlier, he'd helped her while she'd struggled into her shoe, causing me to wonder whether there had been something between them. Would she cover for him if there was?

"Everyone has an opinion," Brady added.

"Like . . ."

"Tish Waterman said she heard a cat yowl at nine o'clock exactly."

A while back, Tish Waterman, who owned A Peaceful Solution day spa, had had it in for me. Believing my fanciful shop was wicked, she'd campaigned to force Open Your Imagination to close its doors. Thanks to a nurturer fairy who Tish had denied existed until Fiona interceded—actually, Tish had erased the fairy from her memory because life had thrown her a curveball—we had resolved our differences.

Brady added, "She thinks nine p.m. might be the time of death."

Out of nowhere, a ghostly gray cat with a white muzzle darted by our feet. Was it the same one I'd seen on Thursday in the courtyard when Tamara had shown up? Where had it come from? It scampered toward the estate abutting the Meeting Hall property. I noticed a large crypt on the other side of the wire fence, nearly ten feet tall and ten feet wide, and a shiver ran down my spine. Was the property a cemetery? I'd never paid attention.

Shaking off the notion, I said to Brady, "What else have you learned?"

"Hattie Hopewell saw Kenny Chu arguing with Lana tonight."

Hattie was a flamboyant redhead in her sixties. She regularly made fairy gardens and was the chairperson for the Happy Diggers garden club.

"Did she hear what they were arguing about?" Maybe Kenny had followed Lana after all, as Elton had urged him to do.

"Not specifically, but Hattie said there was a lot of finger-pointing."

Maybe Kenny hadn't needed to text Lana; he'd merely moved their argument into the bidding room. He made his final point by stabbing her in the heart.

"Thanks," I said. "I'll let the detective know."

"Wait." Brady placed a hand on my shoulder. His touch felt reassuring. Wonderful, in fact. "How are you holding up? This can't be easy. You. Murder. Is it dredging up memories?"

A chill ran down my neck. I was the one who'd found the groomer in our shop a few months ago. "It's not something I'll ever get used to, but I'm fine. I'm not a suspect." Honestly, I hadn't been thinking about me at all. Wanda had been my sole focus. "But Wanda Brownie is, and she's like my second mother. I've never seen her so fragile, Brady. And Meaghan?" I shook my head. "I ache for them."

Brady squeezed my shoulder and released me. "Hang in there."

"Keep listening to the scuttlebutt. I want a report."

"I'm all ears." He waggled them comically, bringing a smile to my face.

I returned to Meaghan. She and her mother were still sitting on the bench outside the rear foyer, but Wanda was leaning forward, elbows on her knees, her head resting in her hands. I whispered, "Meaghan—"

Wanda sat up abruptly. "I didn't do this, Courtney. I did not kill Lana."

"Do you remember what happened?" I asked.

"Mom and I have gone over it a couple of times," Meaghan said. "She went to the ladies' room. She took a nap, woke up, and found herself . . . there." She jutted a hand toward the foyer.

"Wanda," I said, "walk me through it. Maybe I'll hear something new."

Wanda sat up, eyes clear. "I went to the ladies' room. There's a small settee inside, as your father indicated there would be. I laid down. If only I'd napped sitting up—I don't go into a heavy sleep that way—but the champagne and wine had made me sleepy, and I was tired to begin with. This event has been the death of—" She gasped. "I didn't mean . . . bad choice of words. Poor Lana." She took a moment to regroup. "At least we won't have to read any more of her horrid critiques, and my clients won't be the recipients of her feral harangues."

"Mom. Stop. Talking." Meaghan clipped off each word. "Did you hear yourself? What you said sounded like . . ."

"Motive," I whispered.

Meaghan nodded. "I'm hiring a lawyer. Right now."

"I don't need one," Wanda snapped, and smoothed the

lap of her pantsuit. "I'm sure Detective Summers will realize I'm telling the truth."

"Mom, the evidence—"

"Hush." Wanda put a finger to her daughter's lips. "Whoever did this had a reason. I have none. No motive whatsoever."

Other than the one she'd just uttered and Tamara had confirmed, I thought. Was disliking someone's reviews enough reason to kill the person? Would the police think that Wanda had taken revenge on an enemy? Did Kenny Chu or Tamara Geoffries have a better motive to want Lana dead? And what about Lana's husband? Lana had humiliated Elton in front of all those people. How many men would sit idly by and take the abuse?

I caught sight of Tamara slinking toward the foyer doorway. She waved her hand at someone inside. "Detective!" she called. Was she hoping to repeat what she'd uttered earlier, ready to throw Wanda to the wolves at whatever the cost?

"I'll be right back," I said to Meaghan, and made a beeline for Tamara. I tapped her on the shoulder.

She whipped around. Her eyes widened. "Oh, it's you."

"Sorry if I frightened you. Not many other guests hanging around."

"I think we're all on edge," she said, her voice faint.

"Did you think of something else? Is that why you want to get the detective's attention?"

"I . . . yes." Tamara licked her lips.

Summers moved into the doorway, the light from the foyer casting a glow around his rugged silhouette. "What do you want, Miss Geoffries?"

"*Mrs*. Geoffries," Tamara stated, while fiddling with a wedding ring on her left hand.

I'd never seen a man at her house. She danced alone each night. Was she a widow?

"I saw Wanda and Lana arguing on the street yesterday," Tamara stated.

My stomach clenched. No question about it; she was intent on throwing Wanda to the wolves.

Fiona whizzed to me. "What's wrong?"

I wanted to ask where she'd been, but I didn't want to miss whatever Tamara said next. I held a single finger near my cheek, hoping Fiona would get the hint that I needed a minute. She did. She settled on my shoulder.

"What were they arguing about?" Summers asked Tamara.

"About Lana's membership at Sport Zone," she said. "I know this is old news after the free-for-all between them at Cypress and Ivy Courtyard on Thursday—"

"What free-for-all?" Summers raised an eyebrow.

"Why, Lana attacked Wanda," Tamara replied. "In public. Didn't you hear? She even broke an artist's creation, a glazed pot, at Wanda's daughter's gallery. It was quite the to-do. Wanda was upset with Lana for panning one of her daughter's artists."

I silently cursed. This did not look good for Wanda.

"Courtney used a hose on Lana when she wouldn't back off," Tamara added.

Summers studied me. With respect or veiled humor I wasn't sure.

"But the other thing I wanted to tell you, sir," Tamara continued, "is that I saw Wanda yesterday and she'd appeared dazed. Is it possible she was sleepwalking when she was arguing with Lana? I only say this because my mother was a sleepwalker, may she rest in peace. So I'm not sure Wanda would even remember quarreling with Lana. And, just for the record, I don't think she killed Lana tonight."

Talk about a case of whiplash. Now Tamara was standing up for Wanda? Why? Was she hoping that by acting like a Good Samaritan she could make herself look innocent, as well?

Summers said, "Thank you, ma'am. I appreciate your candor. If you would provide Officer Reddick with your statement, then you'll be excused." He retreated inside.

I watched Tamara converse with Reddick. He, like Summers, jotted the conversation in a notebook, and then Tamara ducked under the yellow tape and melded into the crowd.

"Where have you been?" I whispered to Fiona, who flew off my shoulder and floated in front of my face.

"Merryweather and I were flying among the bystanders, listening."

"Is that allowed?" I asked.

She folded her arms and raised her chin. "It's not socializing."

"Okay, don't get huffy." I held out my hand and she settled onto it, crossing her legs. "What did you learn?"

"Not many are sorry that Lana Lamar is dead."

I winced.

"To a person, everyone thought she was a formidable athlete, but many dismissed her art critiques as tripe. They questioned how someone with her talent could be so vicious. Only one woman said Lana was a good person because she read to children at the library."

"Did anyone confess?"

Fiona shook her head. "A woman said there were quite a few artists' representatives, in addition to Wanda, who weren't happy with Lana's reviews."

"Did you get the feeling Lana fought with everyone?"

"Apparently so." Fiona fluffed her wings. "By the way, did you notice the dirt on the hem of that woman's coat?"

"Which woman?"

"Tamara Geoffries. What if she's the killer and the dirt came from the broken fairy garden?"

I'd wondered the same thing when I'd spied the dirt on the cuffs of Kenny's trousers. "Interesting idea, except Tamara didn't enter the crime scene, and she arrived at the same time we did."

Fiona scratched her ear. "Did she?"

Over the course of the next hour, while the Monterey County coroner inspected Lana's body and CPD officers collected evidence and took photographs, Summers and Reddick moved to the café-style tables on the grassy expanse by the event stage and interviewed guests. I couldn't sit in on the interviews, but I noticed that Summers paid particular attention to those who had known Lana best. Only a few of the staff from Sport Zone, other than Didi and Kenny, were in attendance. At one point, I spotted Summers talking to Tish Waterman. She tapped her watch as if she was supplying specifics. He also corralled two of the Hopewell sisters, Hattie and Holly. I hadn't seen Hedda in attendance. Hattie, who was the easiest to spot with her red hair, did most of the talking. My landlord, Holly, added a word or two.

Then Summers re-interviewed Meaghan with Wanda and, after that, Wanda alone.

At eleven p.m., he asked for me.

"Tell me again what happened, Miss Kelly." His voice lacked energy.

I bit back a yawn and took him through each phase. My arrival at the party. The various guests. The food. How the music had switched from Mozart to jazz. How Wanda had grown tired and my father suggested she take a rest in the ladies' lounge located in the hallway beyond the foyer.

"Go on."

I replayed the dispute between Lana and Didi over pickleball and the altercation I'd witnessed between Lana and her husband that had made Lana run off. "Supposedly, she'd made a fool of him at his work, but I'm not sure how or why."

"Noted."

"Directly after, Elton Lamar suggested Kenny Chu go to Lana and calm her down. I got the impression that he thought Kenny had a way with Lana, but Kenny wanted nothing to do with it. He went to the bar. I think he downed quite a few beers."

Summers's gaze narrowed. "Why wouldn't Elton deal with his wife himself?"

"I got the feeling he was afraid of what he might say. Maybe Kenny had talked her down before, like after bad games of pickleball. Lana hated to lose."

Summers poised his pen over his notebook. "Tell me more about the set-to between Mrs. Brownie and Mrs. Lamar on Thursday in the courtyard."

I groaned, hoping he'd forgotten about that. "It was nothing."

"Nothing? You hosed her." He suppressed a smile.

Somberly, I summarized the event and included Tamara Geoffries's puzzling reference to Jamie.

Summers cocked his head. "'Jamie says hello.' Those were Mrs. Geoffries's actual words?"

I nodded. "Why?"

He didn't reply, but he jotted the sentence in his notebook, making me again wonder about Jamie. Who was he? Why would Tamara make a point of uttering his name while Lana was in the throes of an argument? And why on earth had Tamara tried to implicate Wanda at first and vouched for her later on?

"Okay, we're done, Miss Kelly." Summers turned to Reddick. "Have you got what you need for now, Red?"

"Yes, sir."

"Bring me Mrs. Dubois."

Reddick headed out of the building. When he returned, he had Didi in tow. Her lipstick was eaten off. Strands of hair frizzed out from her beaded cornrows. Usually bubbling with energy, she appeared drained.

"Detective," she said, her voice thin and gaze wary. "More questions?"

"No, ma'am. We're done with the guests. Go ahead and announce that the party is over."

"We didn't finish the bidding."

"You can attend to that in the morning with an officer present."

"Of course. Thank you." Didi pulled her shawl tighter. "What a fiasco." She scanned the area. "May I say a word to Wanda Brownie first?"

"Of course."

Wanda was slumped in a chair beside a table. Meaghan stood next to her mother, one hand on her shoulder.

Didi went to her. I followed.

"Wanda, I'm so sorry—" Didi didn't finish the sentiment. "I know we'll get this sorted out. You did not do this. Certainly not with malice aforethought."

"Or at all," I inserted.

"Correct. *Or . . . at . . . all,*" Didi sputtered. "Wanda, I'll touch base with you tomorrow. Sleep well." She bussed Wanda on the cheek and then, like a woman on a mission, strode to the event stage. The band was long gone. She tapped on the microphone. It was live and crackled. "Everyone, gather around please."

The crowd listened attentively as Didi introduced herself. She apologized for Wanda being under the weather and then asked all to bow their heads in a moment of prayer for Lana, after which she declared that the bidding announcements would be sent in a mass email within a few days and the art, plantings, and antiques would be distributed forthwith.

"As you can imagine, the bidding room is—" Didi's

voice broke. "It will take some sorting out and . . ." Her shoulders slumped. She scanned the crowd, looking for someone to save her.

Kenny sprinted to her side and threw a supportive arm around her.

"Bless you," Didi said to him, and added into the microphone, "Thank you all. Good night."

As people meandered toward the exit, I noticed Summers conferring with the coroner as well as a technician who had collected evidence. Summers's face was grim.

Moments later, he broke from the impromptu conference and strode quickly to Wanda and Meaghan. I caught the first words he said, and I shuddered.

"Wanda Brownie, you have the right to remain silent . . ."

Chapter 9

The iron tongue of midnight hath told twelve.
Lovers to bed; 'tis almost fairy time.
—William Shakespeare, *A Midsummer Night's Dream*

As I trudged home, Meaghan's pitiful plea as I left the event cycled through my mind: *Courtney, do something. Help us.*

To soothe my uneasy mind, I decided baking would be my best plan of action. My mother had been a stress baker. Cakes, pies, biscuits. My favorite was her double-chocolate cookies. So easy. So scrumptious. There was nothing like chocolate to comfort my soul.

I gathered the ingredients and set everything on the counter, wet ingredients to the left and dry to the right, as my mother had taught me. Next, I prepared the baking sheets, lining them with parchment paper, and I turned on the oven so it would preheat.

For the half hour while stirring, mixing, and molding the dough into requisite walnut-sized balls, I found myself breathing easier. As I performed each step, Fiona flurried around me, her nose twitching with joy. She loved the aromas when I baked. Pixie had hopped onto a chair at the kitchen table to get a better view. She knew she wasn't allowed on the counter when the mixer came out.

The recipe suggested refrigerating the dough, but I didn't want to wait. I was salivating. So I bypassed the step and baked the cookies. A firmer dough would make a firmer cookie, but the flavor would be the same.

An hour later, I moseyed to the front porch with a plate of cookies and a glass of milk and sat in the weather-resistant mission slat rocking chair.

At two a.m., I could have kicked myself. Chocolate? Before going to bed? Was I nuts? I lay under the quilt in my bedroom, staring at the ceiling, my mind whirring about Wanda and Meaghan and how to help them out of the mess. At two thirty, I sat up, turned on the lamp on the stand beside my bed, and read. A chapter of a mystery. A chapter of a romance. A chapter on indigenous plants of the Carmel Valley. The latter made me yawn, but I didn't doze. Pixie tried to calm me by nestling in the crook of my arm and Fiona sang lullabies. I finally drifted off, but I tossed and turned and awoke out of sorts.

Wanda arrested. Impossible.

Determined to refresh my mind, I ran along the beach while drinking in the crisp air and the roar of the surf. Seagulls cawed overhead. A couple of early-bird surfers were out and testing the modest waves. Thirty minutes later, I returned home feeling somewhat better. Pixie dined on tuna and Fiona on bits of apple. I drank two cups of chamomile tea to calm my nerves and nibbled an omelet made with Herbs de Provence. The latter settled the gnawing in my stomach.

After a brisk shower and dressing in a pink blouse and pink capris to enhance my mood, I flipped through the contacts on my computer. Sunday wasn't the best day to reach out to a lawyer, but Victoria Judge, who had represented me last spring, told me I could call her anytime, anywhere. I had liked the way she'd conducted herself. She'd reminded me of my mother, confident and cool under pressure. Who better to represent Wanda?

When Miss Judge answered, I filled her in on what had happened. She'd heard about the murder on the morning news. She requested that I tell her everything, leaving nothing out. I started by describing the weapon and mentioned the time of death. I suggested that the window of opportunity had to be narrow, after bidding closed and before Meaghan and I had arrived on the scene, so between eight forty-five and nine thirty. Miss Judge questioned me about Wanda's health and such. I mentioned the issue of sleepwalking. She murmured her concern. I was pretty sure she'd mumbled, "Not good." A half hour later, when Miss Judge asked all she'd wanted, for the time being, she urged me not to worry. She was on the case.

Edgy and nervous—okay, downright disheartened—I nabbed Pixie and Fiona, and we traveled the short distance to Lincoln Street and 8th Avenue serenaded by church bells.

"Morning," Joss said as I entered Open Your Imagination. She often beat me to work. How lucky I was that on her fiftieth birthday she'd decided to leave her Silicon Valley accounting job and seek a simpler life. She was fanning herself. Joss often needed to cool down. Hot flashes came at all times of the day for her. "Hope you have a lot of energy because—" She pressed her lips together and skirted the counter. "Lordy, what's wrong? You look like you've been run over by a truck."

And here I thought I'd done a pretty good job of sprucing myself up. So much for pink making me look perky. "You haven't heard the news?" I asked.

"Heard what?" Joss didn't read newspapers. She kept up with the latest headlines by *tweet*.

"Lana Lamar was murdered last night."

"Heavens. Who did it?" Joss rasped. "Why?"

"I don't know who or why, but the police arrested Wanda Brownie."

"No way. Wanda is salt of the earth. She wouldn't hurt a flea. She even gathers spiders in their webs and takes them outdoors to find new homes."

"Unfortunately, that endorsement won't satisfy the authorities." I told her how Meaghan and I had found Wanda in a daze, kneeling beside Lana, her hand on the weapon, and how after consulting with the coroner and a technician, Detective Summers had lowered the boom.

"Sleepwalking. Wow, I've heard about people doing all sorts of things while in a trance, looking as if they were awake, but I've never run into anyone who has done so."

I went on to describe the crime scene.

Fiona flitted to Joss's shoulder. "I think it was staged. Courtney doesn't agree."

"I didn't say that."

"Why would it be staged?" Joss asked.

"To make Wanda look guilty," Fiona said. "Maybe the killer was waiting for her to wake up."

"That sounds like iffy timing, don't you think, boss?" Joss poured me a cup of coffee and pressed it into my hands. "Here, a little caffeine will do you good." She leaned one elbow on the counter and addressed Fiona. "Go on. Tell me your theory." Fiona was the only fairy Joss could see. Neither of us was sure why. Her heart was open. She'd traveled to Ireland and kissed the Blarney Stone. She loved to make fairy gardens and planted lots of flowers and herbs to attract fairies to her home. Perhaps it had something to do with the fact that she was so concerned about her elderly mother that she didn't have room for anything fanciful. "If you have a theory," Joss added.

"I do," Fiona said. "I think the killer created a mess to cover a clue."

Joss nodded. "A killer often does that." An avid mystery reader, Joss was the one who had hooked Fiona on Sherlock Holmes. "What else?"

"There were paper towels on the floor."

"To wipe off the blade?" Joss asked.

Fiona shook her head. "No. They weren't bloody. I checked."

I gawped at her. "When did you check?"

"When the technicians had set them aside and had moved on to another task."

I nodded, impressed.

"Wanda was probably using them to dry her hands when she entered the foyer," I said. "She dropped them when she spotted Lana."

"'The Adventure of the Speckled Band.'" Joss hoisted a finger, citing one of Sherlock Holmes's famous cases. "It's all in the clues."

In "The Speckled Band," Sherlock Holmes waited until the very end of the short story to summarize the combination of clues that painted a picture of premeditated murder.

"Staging a crime scene suggests premeditation," Joss added.

"I agree!" Fiona exclaimed.

As the two of them theorized using Sherlock Holmes's cases as comparatives, I headed to the patio to straighten up and set out items for today's private lesson. While I did my mindless chores, I imagined the crime scene: the shattered pot; the letter opener freed from its dragon; the gavel lying beneath the table; the bidding sheets scattered everywhere.

"Hello, we're here!" Hattie Hopewell traipsed into the shop with her sister Holly.

"Where's Hedda?" I went inside to greet them. I'd agreed to give a private fairy garden lesson to all three sisters. Hattie was a veteran. Holly had become passionate after pruning her first bonsai tree. Hedda had yet to make one.

"She's running late." Hattie flapped a hand. "She had to finish up a loan."

"On a Sunday?" I asked.

"She is devoted," Holly said.

The three sisters couldn't have been more different. Holly, a sprightly sixty-something, enjoyed painting and donning arty clothing, liked today's Picasso-style T-shirt over holey jeans, while Hattie liked to garden, dress in outdoorsy clothes, and dye her hair various shades of red. Hedda, the youngest by twelve years, was all about dollars and cents and maintained a tailored look, although she did like to wear flashy eyewear. She had set up the loan for me to open my business. Occasionally, we met for coffee.

Hattie clapped her hands. "Let's get cracking. Do we pick out our own teacups?"

I'd agreed to focus our lesson on mini fairy gardens. Hattie had fallen in love with the one I'd displayed at the front of the shop and thought it was a perfect start for someone like Hedda.

"Yes."

At the far end of the patio where we displayed the pots we sold, I'd created a learning-the-craft corner. A cabinet held most of the teaching supplies. A rectangular table and benches served as the workstation.

"I've set out a selection of wide-mouthed cups as well as a sample teacup fairy garden on the instruction table." I'd used a creamy white teacup and adorned it with a miniature dancing fairy figurine in a white tutu as well as white silk daisies and the sign *Fairies Dance Here*. "If we plant in too narrow a cup," I went on, "it can topple."

Hattie chose the Wedgwood Butterfly Bloom Posy pattern teacup and saucer for herself and a Lenox Butterfly Meadow pattern teacup and saucer for Hedda.

"You should let her choose her own," I said.

"Trust me. This is the one she'll select. It's simple and elegant."

"Here we go." Holly set a country-style Villeroy & Boch Basket Garden pattern teacup on the table and slid onto the bench. "What a night last night at the Spectacular, right?" She reached across the table and petted my hand. "How are you doing, dear? You didn't sleep well. I could tell. You kept turning on and off your bedroom light."

"I'm sorry if I disturbed you."

"Nonsense!" Holly said. "I rarely sleep, especially when one of my Poms is suffering." She owned an adorable pair of Pomeranians.

"Which one is sick?"

"Neither. Did I say suffering? I meant insufferable. The youngest wants to play nonstop."

I bit back a smile. The dog played because Holly toyed with her *nonstop*.

"She's six, but she thinks she's a puppy." Holly smiled indulgently.

"Where are they today?" I asked.

"At the groomers. Let's hope that tires my pretty girl out." In addition to grooming, Wizard of Paws, the shop across the courtyard from ours, offered doggie daycare services. "I didn't want them with me, disturbing my concentration. But back to you, you poor thing. Stumbling across another dead body."

"You mean poor Lana," I mumbled.

"Yes, of course." Holly shook her head. "I can't believe Wanda is guilty."

"I don't think she is."

"But they—you—found her there. Holding the weapon."

Hattie twisted her teacup to inspect all sides. "I saw Elton Lamar this morning. He appeared quite buttoned down. Suit. Tie. Stoic face. Men hold things inside, don't they? He was walking alongside Glinda Gill's boyfriend."

My ears perked up. Glinda's boyfriend was a prominent attorney. Was Elton seeking legal advice because he had something to worry about?

Hattie added, "I assume they were discussing Lana's will."

Maybe I was jumping the gun. I recalled Meaghan saying Elton had an attorney for everything. Glinda's boyfriend took on a variety of legal cases including estate planning, real estate issues, and the occasional defense matter. I supposed he and Elton could have been discussing Lana's will. Had she written one? Not everyone did so. Did she have sizeable savings? How much did an art critic make?

Hattie said, "I don't know why Elton would care about Lana's money. He's wealthy in his own right."

"Not necessarily." Holly shot a finger into the air. "A rumor is circulating that his business is struggling."

"Hoo-boy." Hattie whistled. "I heard Lana received a tidy sum from her previous husband. If that's true and Elton is struggling, and if he was named in Lana's will, that gives him motive."

Chapter 10

I love fairies. If you don't believe in them, your loss.
—Anonymous

Even though Hedda hadn't shown up yet, I started her sisters on their projects. As I showed them how to cut green Styrofoam to create a wedge in the bottom of the teacup, I thought more about Lana and the *tidy sum* she'd received from her first husband. If he hadn't died, I would have considered him a suspect in her death.

"Do you know what Elton's alibi was last night?" Hattie asked.

"He was at the party," Holly said.

"Yes, but"—Hattie leaned forward—"I heard he left and went for a walk around Devendorf Park."

Devendorf Park, located at Ocean Avenue and Junipero, was Carmel's central gathering place—home to plein air painting, Veterans and Memorial Day remembrances, and the annual tree lighting.

"Says who?" Holly demanded.

"Says Elton." Hattie shot her sister an exasperated look. "After he visited with his attorney, he moseyed into Percolate."

Percolate was a local café that I often frequented.

"He goes there every day, I heard." Hattie hummed as she fitted the Styrofoam into her cup. "People can be such creatures of habit."

"Did you follow him there?" Holly asked. "Were you snooping?"

"Of course not," Hattie sniped, clearly not appreciating her sister's inference. "I go there, too. You know I can't make a cup of coffee to save my life and I burn toast."

Holly tittered and assured me that her sister was a lousy cook.

"Elton was chatting with the barista," Hattie went on. "Upon closer inspection, despite his natty attire, I realized he seemed frazzled, like he hadn't slept. He confided to the young woman that he'd taken a walk during the Spectacular because he was upset after Lana and he had quarreled." She regarded her sister. "I didn't witness the quarrel. Did you, Holly?"

"No."

"I did," I said. "They didn't go at it tooth and nail, but it was intense."

As the two sisters debated the difficulty of marriage— Holly was a widow with one adult son; Hattie was a divorcée with no children—I pondered alibis. Had every suspect left the party at one time or another? The party had been lively, the music loud, and the chaos around the auction itself intense. A quiet walk, I supposed, could have cooled heated emotions.

"Courtney," Holly said, "we're ready for the next step."

"One piece of Styrofoam won't do it," I said, refocusing on their projects. "You have to cram little pieces around the wedge you've inserted. Hot glue is the trick that holds it all together." I handed each of them a preheated glue gun. "Have you ever used one of these? Be careful because the glue is really hot! Just drizzle a little over the abutting edges of the Styrofoam."

"Speaking of hot," Hattie said, expertly dispensing the right amount of glue, "Didi Dubois was a hothead this morning at Sport Zone. Whewie."

I had forgotten about Didi. She had left the party to handle an alarm, only to return to find the police questioning Wanda, thus leaving Didi in charge of the party and the auction. Of course she'd be stressed. Had she straightened out who had "won" which auction item yet? Was anyone helping her with the task? I hadn't received an email. I pondered whether mine had been the final bid on the antique Amish wagon and instantly felt sickened that I cared.

"Since when did you join Sport Zone?" Holly asked her sister.

"Since I started dating that adorable gentleman who owns Carmel Collectibles." Carmel Collectibles was one of the shops at the far end of Cypress and Ivy Courtyard. I loved visiting it near Christmastime. The owner, Cliff, adored the holidays. He enjoyed dressing up as Santa and doling out candy canes. "I decided my figure needed a little toning."

"Toning." Holly snorted. "At our age? *Pfft.*" She fluffed her gray-streaked curly brown hair. "And you're doing it for him? Why, for heaven's sake? He's no slim chicken."

"I want to look my best." Without rising, Hattie twisted to show off her curves.

"I can see a difference," I said, judiciously.

"Thank you, dear."

"Why was Didi so irate?" Holly asked, disinterested in her sister's preening.

"She kept invoking the name of her dead husband while

saying Sport Zone was a money pit," Hattie said. "The air conditioning had blown the fuse box. The sink in the mini kitchen where they make all the protein drinks was clogged. And the security system was on the fritz.

"I swear she was near to tears," Hattie went on. "Money. It's all about the mighty dollar." She rubbed two fingers together, the universal sign for *money*. "I'm glad I have a property manager who takes care of those things on my behalf." Like her sister, Hattie owned a number of homes in Carmel-by-the-Sea. Their grandparents had been original settlers in the area, way back in 1906 after the San Francisco earthquake drove artists, authors, and actors southward. The cultural migration was one of the reasons why there were so many art galleries in town.

Fiona flew to the table. "Joss and I are done theorizing. May I join you?"

I nodded.

Fiona skated along the rim of Hattie's cup and leaped to Holly's.

Though neither Hedda nor Holly could see Fiona, Hattie sensed her but often gazed in the wrong direction. I believed Holly would see her soon. I'd noticed fairies in Holly's garden playing pranks trying to get her attention, the exact kind of imps with whom Fiona was forbidden to associate.

"Okay, let's set the moss on top of the Styrofoam," I said.

"Hello-o!" Hedda ran in. "Sorry I'm late." She shrugged out of her linen jacket and laid it neatly on the bench beside her. "Do I select a teacup?" She noticed the cup Hattie had chosen for her. "Oh, I see someone has done so already. Perfect, Hattie. Thank you. It's lovely."

Hattie winked at me.

I doubted Hedda would ever put up a stink. She didn't like to ruffle feathers.

"Courtney, I heard the news about Lana Lamar." Hedda

slipped onto the bench and smoothed the wrinkles from her linen skirt. "How horrible to have another murder in our fair city, and how horrible for you to have found her."

"Meaghan and me."

"And me," Fiona chimed.

"Shocking," Hedda said. "My customer told me all about it. Wanda in a trance. The mess in the bidding room."

"You didn't attend the party last night, did you?" I said.

"Oh, no." Hedda adjusted her bright red Tory Burch glasses. "I was invited, but I never go out on Saturdays."

"You should." Holly inserted silk flowers through the moss into the Styrofoam below.

"Poppycock," Hedda responded.

Holly cut a sad look at her sister.

Fiona settled onto Hedda's shoulder and caressed her hair.

Hedda squirmed under her sister's gaze and swept her hair over her shoulders upsetting Fiona's balance. I questioned the significance of the sisters' testy exchange but didn't ask. Whatever it was had a sad memory attached, explaining why Fiona had tried to comfort Hedda.

"These are so cute, Courtney," Hedda said. "Help me get started. I see I have to fashion a wedge of Styrofoam." She began sawing off the edges of a square piece.

"Hot glue next."

Fiona spiraled into the air. She did not appreciate the hot-glue gun.

Wielding the gun, I showed Hedda how to stick the pieces together and tuck them into the cup. Though Hattie was the most creative of the three, I knew Hedda would be the best at following instructions. A loan officer rarely missed a step.

When Hedda had caught up with her sisters, I said, "Now let's pick a fairy figurine for each of your designs."

The sisters moved to the verdigris shelves of figurines and cooed.

"So cute," Hedda said, choosing a teensy pink fairy kneeling beside a flock of ducks.

"I adore this one." Hattie picked up an exotic fairy dressed in yellow with golden hair.

"This one is perfect for mine!" Holly exclaimed, choosing a fairy dog with a bone in its mouth.

When they returned to the table and took their seats, I said, "Now set the figurine on the garden. It's important to center it because—"

"Wait!" Hattie cried. "Take a look. The one I picked reminds me of Lana, don't you think? Look at the haughty expression." She turned the exotic yellow fairy toward her sisters.

"She does," Fiona said, inspecting more closely. "Right down to the color of her eyes."

"Oh, my," Hattie said in a somber tone. "Let's toast Lana." She set the fairy on her teacup garden, placed the teacup on its saucer, and lifted the set into the air. "To Lana. May she rest in peace."

Each of us raised a teacup and recited the blessing.

Fiona settled on my shoulder and added, for my ears only, "May we solve the murder quickly so Carmel can heal."

Amen.

After lunch, eager to talk to Meaghan and find out if she had consulted Victoria Judge, I left the shop and headed up the steps of the courtyard to Flair Gallery. Fiona accompanied me. I entered and scanned the store for Meaghan. She wasn't anywhere. Ziggy Foxx, Meaghan's partner in the enterprise, an eccentric gay man in his forties with ice-white hair always gelled to within an inch of its life, was discussing a huge oil painting of the California coastline with a customer. I caught his attention and mouthed, *Meaghan?* Ziggy shook his head: *No clue.*

For Meaghan not to be selling art on a Sunday, things had to be dire. My stomach sank.

As I traipsed toward our shop, Hattie's new beau, Cliff, a cherry-cheeked sixty-something with a sizeable belly, standing outside Carmel Collectibles drinking in sunshine, waved to me. I responded in kind.

Due to the distraction, I nearly ran into Tish Waterman and her identical Shih Tzus as they were exiting Sweet Treats.

"Watch out!" Fiona cried.

I pulled up short. "Sorry, Tish."

"No worries." Tish was whip thin with carbon-black hair and a scar down her abraded cheek. After a night of self-pity, she'd suffered a terrible fall and had grazed her cheek on an exterior wall. She often said the scar was a reminder of the life she'd led before. She yanked on the dogs' dual leash. "Hush, babies." They weren't upset; they were clamoring for my affection.

I bent to pet them and received appreciative licks. In Carmel, people went everywhere with their four-legged friends. Though the Shih Tzus used to be snippy like Tish, once she transformed they seemed to have, as well.

I rose to standing. "What did you buy?"

Tish was carrying a pink paper bag with the Sweet Treats logo on it. "My daughter's favorite. Sugar cookies."

My eyes widened. "Is she . . . Have you . . ."

"No, not yet." Tish's eyes grew misty. Twenty years ago her seventeen-year-old daughter had joined a cult, and she hadn't been seen since. I didn't know the name of the cult or what it professed to believe. "However, I received a postcard. The first ever."

"That's wonderful."

"It was postmarked Aspen, Colorado. No specific location, but it's something." She fished it from her purse and read: "'Hi, Mom. I'm fine. Hope you are, too.—Twyla.'"

She showed it to me. "It looks like her handwriting. See the big loop on the Y? That's just the way I write mine. I taught her to write in cursive."

How I hoped Tish was right and she wasn't being tricked by someone hoping to fleece her.

Tish held up the pink bag. "Zephyr said to set these on a plate and let the aroma call Twyla home." Zephyr was a nurturer fairy who had manifested herself to Tish moments after Tish took the horrible fall. At the time, Tish believed she was seeing things and had blocked the memory from her mind, until recently when Zephyr—thanks to Fiona's urging, an act approved by her mentor—had reached out again to Tish and had finally persuaded Tish to acknowledge her existence. In an effort to ingratiate herself with Tish so Tish wouldn't ban her again from her memory, Zephyr had vowed to track down Tish's daughter. Sadly, Zephyr hadn't been able to locate the girl—now a grown woman—yet.

"Will such an enticement work?" Tish eyed the pink bag. "One can dream."

"We should help Zephyr find her," Fiona said to me.

I eyed my sweet fairy. Though she had been given the permission to reach out once to Zephyr, I would bet she wasn't allowed to do so again without the queen fairy's blessing.

I shook my head.

Fiona stamped the air with her foot.

Tish didn't acknowledge Fiona. Like Joss, she could only see one fairy—hers. "The detective I've hired doesn't seem to be able to do anything further," Tish said. "He tracked down the person at the post office who'd canceled the postcard in Colorado, but that's as far as he's gotten." She moved away from me, paused, and did a U-turn. "Isn't it horrible about last night? I didn't like Lana. I don't think anyone did, honestly. She could be imperious and condescending and, well, downright irascible. She never had a facial that she enjoyed. And she didn't tip. But she didn't deserve to be murdered at such a lovely event."

Or at any time, I mused.

"What is this world coming to?" Tish asked.

I was stumped for an answer. "Tish, Brady told me you heard a cat yowl at nine o'clock."

"I did. A gray cat with a white muzzle."

That same cat again.

"Do you think that could be significant?" Tish asked.

"I'm not sure." I recalled the window of opportunity for murder that I'd given the attorney, Miss Judge. Nine would have been near the middle. Had the cat heard or seen Lana fighting with her killer? "I'll let you know if I find out."

As Fiona and I neared Open Your Imagination, I paused. "Can you communicate with a cat?" I asked her.

She smirked. "What do you think?"

Chapter 11

We the Fairies, blithe and antic, of dimensions not gigantic,
though the moonshine mostly keep us,
oft in orchards frisk and peep us.
—Thomas Randolph

The moment I entered the shop, I called Meaghan's cell phone. She didn't answer. I left a message. When she didn't respond, not even with a text message, I stewed. How I wished I could do something to help her.

Late Sunday afternoon, Glinda Gill, owner of Glitz, the jewelry store situated in the middle of the Cypress and Ivy Courtyard, popped into the shop. She was holding hands with an adorable preteen who was the spitting image of Glinda—bobbed blond hair, full lips, and alert eyes. Glinda wasn't married and didn't have children.

"Is this your niece?" I asked.

"Sure is. Georgie, say hello."

The girl nodded. Both were dressed for a game of tennis in gold-and-white body-hugging tennis dresses.

"You're the phenom," I said to Georgie. Tennis cognoscenti had dubbed her the ice princess of the court. At the tender age of twelve, she had nerves of steel and never let her opponents see her sweat.

"I don't know about being a phenom," Georgie said softly, batting her eyelashes in the same way Glinda would, coyly but keenly aware.

"You're really, really good," I went on.

"I practice."

Fiona flapped into view. "Practice makes perfect."

Georgie glanced in her direction but didn't make a sound.

"Georgie is determined to make a fairy garden," Glinda said, "but her mother told her she might not have saved enough of her allowance yet."

I bit back a grin, loving that. The girl was on the path to glory and fame and possibly earning megabucks from sponsors, but her parents had her on an allowance.

"I have thirty dollars," Georgie said. "Will that cover it?"

"That will easily pay for your first garden," I said.

"Why don't you show her how to build an eight-inch fairy garden?" Glinda suggested.

As I led them to the shelves on the patio that were filled with fairy figurines, Fiona flew beside me.

"Glinda is quite something," she said.

I nodded. Glinda was full of pizazz. She breezed into a place and took over the room.

"Ooh, this one," Georgie said, instantly falling in love with a blue-and-green girl fairy figurine. The girl was reading a book. "I love to read, too." She added that taking quiet time for herself helped her stay focused in sports.

After selecting the figurine, she chose the rest of her items modestly, to stay within her budget. A few succulents. A cat to keep the fairy company. I provided a pot gratis, guided her to the workstation in the learning-the-craft corner, and gave her a few instructions.

As Georgie was installing the plants, Glinda pulled me to one side. "I heard about last night."

"Heard? You weren't there?" I raised an eyebrow. "I could've sworn I saw you."

"Must have been some other pretty blonde," Glinda joked. "I had a personal thing to attend to." She said the word *personal* so softly that I didn't feel it was proper of me to pry. "How horrible for you," she went on. "And for sweet Wanda."

"And for Lana."

"Well, that's a given." Glinda peeked over her shoulder and returned her attention to me. "Between you, me, and the lamppost, Lana was getting ready to leave her husband."

"Are you sure?"

"Certain. She was in last week to buy a pair of glitzy earrings, and while she was browsing, she told me she wasn't sure Elton loved her anymore. He was acting all"—Glinda twiddled her fingers by her head—"weird."

"That doesn't mean she planned to leave him."

"Well, no, of course not, but women like us"—Glinda wagged a finger between us—"sense things." She claimed her ancestors were pirates who had terrorized the California coast. She said it was the fey spirit of her pirate blood that helped her see alternate realities, although she had yet to mention whether or not she had the ability to see a fairy.

Fiona fluttered near my ear. "Ask about her boyfriend. The attorney Hattie saw walking with Elton. If Lana had been planning to divorce Elton, and if she did have a lot of money that he might inherit, if she died, then maybe he killed her before she could pull the plug."

Sometimes it jarred me that my sweet fairy could think in such dastardly, human terms, until I reminded myself that she was a righteous fairy that read Sherlock Holmes stories.

"Glinda," I said, "stop me if I'm overstepping, but I heard

Elton Lamar was seen with your boyfriend. He handles estates and wills and such, right?"

"He does, but I'm not privy to any of his business. If he revealed something confidential to me, that would be unethical." She cocked a hip. "So if you're asking me if I know what they discussed, I don't."

Rats. Shot down before I got out of the gate.

"Glinda, you should inform the police about what Lana said in your shop."

She rolled her eyes. "Are you kidding? They won't listen to what I say. I sell jewelry for heaven's sake. They think I'm frivolous."

"Don't let their bias—or your belief in their bias—hold you back. You have information to impart."

She screwed up her mouth and thought about it for a moment. "Okay, you're right. I'll do my citizenly duty."

"That's the spirit."

"Courtney, are you okay?" Glinda asked.

I wasn't. I was ticked off that I couldn't find someone else to blame for the murder. However, I said, "I'm fine," and set a hand on Georgie's shoulder. "You're doing great, young lady."

She blushed at the compliment. "I love this kitten with its belly in the air. My cat does the same thing."

Fiona zoomed to Pixie and rallied her to play. When she coaxed Pixie to roll onto her back, feet in the air, she whistled.

"Look, Georgie," I said. "Pixie is pretending to be like your cat."

Georgie laughed.

"Aw." Glinda looped an arm around her niece's shoulders.

I felt a pang of jealousy seeing them bonding. I didn't have a sibling. I would never have nieces and nephews. On the other hand, Meaghan was as close to a sister for me as anyone could ever be, so if she ever decided to have children. . . . *If.*

At the end of the day, by the time the last customer exited, I was spent. I poured myself a cup of Peppermint Rush tea to revive my energy, slumped into a chair at the chalked chestnut desk in the office—Pixie settled onto her pillow—and brought up our website on the tabletop computer. I hadn't blogged in a few days. I needed to write something to drive traffic to the site. Plus, I needed to post photographs on a variety of social media sites. I let out a deep sigh, overwhelmed by the public relationship side of business.

Joss poked her head in. "Aha. I see you're brainstorming."

"Brain-deading is more like it," I said. "What's up?"

"I'd like to update our website tomorrow, if you don't mind. I'll add photos of some of your new creations, in particular the dragon one you designed—"

"Having a picture of a murder scene fairy garden won't endear us to our fans."

"Oh, heavens." She swallowed hard. "That was insensitive of me. We should *not* post that one. What was I thinking?"

"It's all right. We all stumble when tragedy strikes. Why don't you add photos of the Mary Poppins garden?"

There were no specific Mary Poppins fairy figurines for sale, but I had loved the movie so much—it had been one of my mother's all-time favorites—that a month ago I'd decided to make one. I'd used a huge square pot, created a London rooftop out of plaster of Paris, and added a number of chimneys to re-create the skyline. Then I'd painted six dancing fairies a sooty black and I'd hot-glued an umbrella to each. For the finishing touch, I'd added a Mary Poppins garden stake, with Mary and her umbrella rising into the air. It was whimsical and one of my most unusual creations. *Whatever the mind can imagine,* my father had told me when landscaping. I'd carried that premise forward in my fairy gardens. My mother and nana would have been so proud.

Fiona flew into the room. "May I help with the website?"

"Do you know how?" I asked.

"Joss will teach me. I can press keys on a computer."

She wasn't a speed demon typist—no sixty words a minute for her; more of a hunt and peck with her toes—but I loved how determined she was to grow and learn.

"Sure. Have at it."

Before heading home, I telephoned Meaghan again. She answered, sounding weary.

"You don't call; you don't write," I said, teasingly, doing my best to lighten the mood.

She heaved a sigh. "Sorry. They—" Her voice cracked. "They won't release Mom on bail without a hearing. There's just too much against her. Caught in the act. Her hand on the weapon. Miss Judge contacted me. She's going to try to free Mom tomorrow, but for now, my mother has to spend the night in jail. It's—" She sniffed. "Courtney, I'm worried about her. What if she has another sleepwalking incident? Who will help her?"

"I'm sure the guards are decent and attentive."

Meaghan tamped down a sob. "I've got to go." Abruptly, she ended the call.

On my way home, I stopped by a deli and picked up a bottle of wine and some Gouda cheese and crackers. I wanted a snack for dinner, not a meal. My appetite was nil knowing I couldn't help Meaghan. Fiona flew beside me, chattering nonstop about something she was learning from Merry-weather. Pixie seemed intrigued; I tuned her out.

As I was passing Tamara Geoffries's storybook house, I paused, captivated yet again by the vision of her silhouette dancing around what I presumed to be the living room. The sheer drapes prevented a full view. Who was this woman?

How I wished I knew more about her and her relationship to Lana.

Fiona darted in front of me. "Go to the door," she urged, as if reading my thoughts.

"No. That would be intruding."

"She's alone."

"How can you be sure?"

"Only the dark blue Toyota is in the driveway." Fiona tugged a lock of my hair. "Go."

"Cut it out."

"Merryweather said the way we learn is to ask questions."

Emboldened, I strode along the path admiring the lemon balm, sea thrift, mint, and thyme growing on either side of it and the wisteria spilling through the trellises. Normally, wisteria only bloomed once a year. Tamara or her gardener had to be deadheading it, which forced it to flower.

I reached the door and heard music playing inside— Johnny Mathis singing "Misty." I shivered as I recalled the psychological thriller *Play Misty for Me*, which had been set in Carmel and told the story of a disc jockey whose female fan had repeatedly requested he play the jazz standard "Misty." I'd watched it on Netflix. The final scene had been harrowing.

Suddenly, a cat popped onto the porch. Not just any cat. It was the ghostly gray with the white muzzle. Did it belong to Tamara? Pixie's nose twitched. She was curious to get a closer look. I set her on the doormat. Before she could check out the cat, it scampered away.

"Fiona, did you see the cat?"

"Yes."

"So I wasn't dreaming? It was real?"

"Yep. Very real. Not a spirit."

"Can you, um, talk to it if it returns?"

"I'll do my best." She saluted me.

Drawing in a bit of Carmel fresh-air courage, I pressed

Tamara's doorbell. It didn't ring. I knocked. The music stopped; the sheer curtains parted slightly. An inch of Tamara's face emerged between the break. I waved.

Seconds later, she opened the door. She was wearing a slinky black dress and black heels, her long hair woven into a braid. "What do you want?" she asked, her tone icy. It sounded nothing like the warm, dulcet timbre she typically used.

I cringed, hating that I'd infringed on her private time. If I could have slinked away without conversing, I would have. "I'm sorry. I was in the neighborhood. Actually, I live nearby. On Carmelo." I pointed. "Dream-by-the-Sea. The cottage with the blue door." I was blathering.

"I've seen it. Your garden is nice."

"Thanks. I saw your silhouette and wondered, if you were alone, whether you'd like to share a glass of wine." I held up the grocery bag. "I also have cheese and crackers."

"Thank you, no." She started to close the door.

Quickly, Fiona circled Tamara's head and sprinkled her with a shimmering gold dust.

"Ask her again," Fiona whispered.

I said, "Are you sure? It's a really nice sauvignon blanc."

Tamara wrapped her arms around herself and peered past me. "Are you by yourself?"

I gestured to my cat, who had tucked herself behind my ankles. "It's just me and Pixie."

Fiona kicked my ear. I bit back a laugh. I didn't think that adding, *As well as my fairy*, would win an invitation.

"Pixie?" A smile tugged at Tamara's lips. "What a sweet name."

The Angora I'd seen with her at Hideaway Café peeked from behind her ankles and meowed at Pixie, who took that as an invitation and padded inside.

"Wine sounds lovely." Tamara beckoned me to follow her.

Bless fairy magic, I mused.

Tamara guided me toward the kitchen at the rear of the house. On our way, I sneaked a look into the living room. It was an antiques dealer's delight, boasting a floral Victorian sofa and a pair of couture wingback chairs. Tiffany standing lamps provided the only light. A bookshelf held a variety of silver-framed photographs, but I couldn't make out any of the faces from this distance. A mahogany Victrola record player stood against the far wall, its lid open. I didn't see a coffee table or carpet, which I presumed made it easier to dance.

Fiona said, "I'll be right back," and disappeared down a hallway.

"Did you just get off work?" Tamara asked over her shoulder.

"Yes. I walk to and from the shop."

"I do the same. No sense in driving. Carmel is so lovely, day or night."

"I agree."

The kitchen was painted white and the tiles were white, as well, but that was where the modernity ended. A mahogany hutch was filled with blue-themed teacups and matching teapots. A well-used chess and backgammon table with scrolled legs stood in the dining nook.

"Sit." Tamara gestured to the Napoleon-backed hardwood chairs. She pulled two Baccarat wineglasses from a cabinet and opened the wine. As she poured, she said, "I'm still shaking from last night."

"Me too."

"I've never seen a murdered . . ." She let the sentence hang.

"The image will fade," I assured her. "Not quickly, but it will." I wasn't an expert, but after a few months I was no longer dreaming of the body I'd found on the patio of my shop. Thank goodness.

Tamara hummed her agreement.

"Your house is lovely," I said.

"It's quaint. Just the right size."

"Are those Victorian Flow Blue?" I gestured to the hutch.

"You sure know your china. Yes, they're nineteenth century, made by Thomas Morris. I carry a lot of tea sets in my shop."

Fiona zipped into the room, out of breath. "She's married. To Jamie. There are photos of them at their wedding in her bedroom. The frames are etched with *Tamara and Jamie*. Ask about him."

I sputtered. My fairy had had the audacity to scope out Tamara's bedroom? Oh, my! We'd have to have a chat about privacy. "So, um, are you married, Tamara? You're wearing a wedding ring. I've never met your—"

"No." Tamara whirled around. Her cheeks tinged pink. "My"—she drew in a deep breath—"husband died." She placed a wineglass on the table in front of me and turned away.

"I apologize. I had no idea." Well, that was embarrassing. I shot Fiona a scathing look.

"You might as well know"—Tamara arranged the cheese and crackers on a crystal plate—"Jamie . . . my husband was killed in a car accident three years ago."

Jamie says hello, Tamara had said to Lana. Why? Had her husband spoken from the great beyond? Had he known Lana?

"The accident . . ." Tamara's shoulders looked as taut as wire. "It happened at night. It was very dark."

"I'm sorry for your loss," I murmured. "I can tell you loved him very much."

"He was the love of my life."

I took a sip of wine. "Did he like to dance as much as you do?"

Tamara peeked over her shoulder. "You can see me dancing?"

"Your silhouette."

"I knew I should change the drapes." Tamara set the plate of cheese and floral cocktail napkins on the table and took a seat. "As a matter of fact, Jamie was a ballroom dance instructor. That's how we met. I wanted to learn to waltz before my sister's wedding. The moment I met him, I fell hard." She laughed softly. "I had two left feet, but he had the patience of Job." She nibbled on a piece of cheese and took a sip of wine. "This was nice of you."

I didn't admit I'd planned to have it as a solo dinner. Why spoil the mood? "How long were you married?"

"Sixteen years until—" She pressed her lips together.

Fiona *tsk*ed. "There's something more she's not saying."

I sensed it, as well.

Fiona snapped her fingers. "Remember how Merryweather was worried about Tamara because she was mumbling that something was her fault? Maybe she killed her husband."

I lifted a finger to silence Fiona and returned my focus to Tamara. Gently, I said, "I get the feeling the accident wasn't Jamie's fault."

"No. He . . . She . . ." Tamara swept her braid over her shoulder. Through tight teeth, she said, "Lana Lamar was running in the fog along a narrow stretch of road that night. You know how the fog can roll in."

I did. We often got heavy pea-soup fog when the warm wind coming off the Pacific Ocean hit the cold water in the bay.

"Lana shouldn't have been out. It was wrong of her to be running." Tamara's voice held an edge. "At the last second, I saw her and screamed. Jamie swerved to avoid hitting Lana. The car careened off the road. Into a tree." Tamara's breath caught in her chest. After a long, tense moment, she exhaled and continued. "Jamie died instantly. I . . ." A single tear trickled down her cheek. She wiped it with her index finger. "I didn't."

Fiona let out a moan and flitted to Tamara. She kissed her cheek. Tamara touched the spot briefly.

"You have to forgive yourself," I said.

"I do. I have."

Even so, Tamara had every reason to hate Lana. Was it possible she'd killed her? When she'd joined me near the crime scene, I'd noticed she was wearing a coat. And gloves. It hadn't been that cold. Had she donned them to cover blood splatter?

"You're wondering why I was in the vicinity of the crime scene, aren't you?" Tamara asked, leveling me with her gaze. "You'd like to know my alibi."

Gee, she was perceptive. I supposed she would have to be in order to have been successful as not only an astute antiques dealer but also a therapist to the rich and famous.

"Yes," I murmured.

Since she wasn't rising from the table and dashing over to fetch a knife from the wood block, ready to do me in, I breathed a little easier.

"The property next to the meeting hall is owned by an older woman who was my client," Tamara went on. "I say *was* because she went blind. She loves the antiques she owns because she can feel them and knows what they looked like, once upon a time, but she doesn't want to purchase anything new; hence, *was*. Even so, I like to visit and chat with her."

The alibi came out so easily that I thought of a tidbit Meaghan had said the other day about Brady's ex-wife's actor husband. All he had to do was memorize the lines. Had Tamara rehearsed her story?

"Does your client—former client—live on the property with the crypt?" I asked.

Tamara nodded. "When one of her cats dies, she inters them there."

"One of?"

"She owns eight right now. She's had as many as twelve at any one time. The crypt is a cat spirit paradise." Tamara fanned the air. "Anyway, I went to visit her during the event because I was bored out of my mind by all the talk about art by people who don't understand art in the least."

Could a blind woman be able to confirm Tamara's account? Of course she could. She would know Tamara's voice.

"But she wasn't home," Tamara went on. "So I spent time with her cats."

Whoa. There went that option. The police wouldn't accept a cat's meow as an alibi. I thought of the ghostly gray cat that I'd seen three distinct times, all while Tamara was nearby. "Does the old woman own a gray one?" I asked.

"She does. He was born the night Jamie died."

I shivered at the same time Fiona whispered, "Ooh."

For another half hour, Tamara and I chatted about Carmel and customers we had in common. When we hit a lull, I begged off and headed home. I couldn't prove or disprove her alibi—that would be up to the police—but I liked her and I wanted to believe she was innocent.

As I ambled up the path to my cottage, the shadow of a person loomed on my porch. The light by the front door cast a halo around the figure making it impossible to determine size, sex, or features.

Fiona whispered, "Stop."

I did. "Dad?" I rasped. My father had been known to surprise me on occasion. I'd often teased him, saying he was trying to spy fairies when I wasn't around. He was a true-blue nonbeliever. "Is it you?"

The person didn't answer. My skin prickled.

"Speak!" I shouted, ready to turn tail. "Or I'm calling the police." I waggled my cell phone.

"It's me," a female said. "Ulani." She rose to her feet and moved to where I could make out her face. Ulani Kamaka, a reporter for *The Carmel Pine Cone* whom I'd met a few months back.

"What do you want?" I asked, drawing nearer.

"May we go inside?" Lustrous black hair framed Ulani's pretty face. Her floral silk dress showed off her nice shape. I should have known she was my visitor. I'd seen a two-toned Mini Cooper like mine parked on the street. When she'd first approached me last April, she'd claimed she was writing an article about my shop and the possibility of fairies. In truth, she'd wanted the scoop about the murder of Mick Watkins, the pet-grooming shop owner. I rebuffed her. In the end, she gave up writing the scoop and actually followed through with a delightful piece about Open Your Imagination, so we'd buried the hatchet.

Fiona, who hadn't trusted Ulani from the get-go, flew to the reporter, circled her head once, and returned to me. "Humph," she muttered.

"What's up, Miss Kamaka?" I set Pixie on the ground and strolled to the porch.

"Ulani, please. And I'd rather speak in your house if that's okay."

For a public figure, she could be quite jumpy. Early on, I'd learned that she didn't like photographs of herself posted anywhere. She didn't have any kind of social media presence, which was rare for a reporter. When I'd asked her why, she'd said her parents didn't know where she was and she wanted to keep it that way; they didn't share the same surname. Back then I'd speculated on whether she was in danger, but recently I'd seen a movie that I'd missed in the theaters, *Crazy Rich Asians*, which made me wonder whether Ulani was simply a wealthy young woman trying to forge her own path without interference by overbearing parents. Whatever her story was didn't involve me.

"Follow me." I opened the door and stepped inside. Fiona sailed past and hovered in the air, arms crossed, foot tapping. A few months ago, she had perfected the impatient fairy look. It usually made me laugh. Not tonight. "Tea?" I switched on the lights and led Ulani to the kitchen.

"Yes, thank you."

As I brought a kettle of water to boil, I fetched some sugar cookies from the freezer—my nana's recipe, made special by the half pecan that decorated the center of each cookie. I always had some on hand. I placed four on a Royal Doulton plate and set the plate on the table.

"What brings you to my humble abode?" I asked.

"You know."

"No, I don't." I could play coy.

"Last night." Ulani pulled a pen and notepad from her purse and used the blunt end of the pen to scratch beneath her chin.

"If you get the scoop," I said, "people will want to take your photograph."

She snorted. "As if. All I want is to put together an article. A well-written investigative piece. Just to prove to my editor that I can."

The kettle whistled. I poured two cups of Earl Grey and set them and a bowl of sugar on the table. "Milk?"

"No, thanks." She set her notepad and pen aside and prepared her tea with one teaspoon of sugar. "So . . ." She arched an eyebrow. Her almond-shaped eyes glistened with hope.

Fiona said, "Have her do you a favor in return. Have her help with Tish's situation."

What a great idea. I winked at my fairy and then said to Ulani, "Okay, but I'd like a little tit for tat."

"What exactly?" Ulani tilted her head.

"A friend of mine is looking for her long-lost daughter. A detective she hired is having no luck. Maybe you, a talented reporter who can loosen lips, might have a better chance of getting information."

"Talented." She smiled. "Go on. I'm all ears."

Chapter 12

⚜

*Come away, O human child! To the waters and the wild
with a faery, hand in hand, for the world's more full of weeping
than you can understand.*
—William Butler Yeats, "The Stolen Child"

I slept better than I had in a few days. In the morning, I rose
with a spring in my step. I loved working, but I truly enjoyed
my single day off each week. On Mondays, I often puttered in
the garden or took a long walk on the beach. Sometimes, I
reveled in a mini vacation: a bike ride along the coast, a photography trek into a forest, or a visit to the Monterey Bay
Aquarium. A few weeks ago, I'd joined a walking food and
wine tour with five people I didn't know. Delightful. As we
wandered from restaurant to watering hole to food shops, our
tour guide told us all sorts of things about Carmel that I didn't
know. And I knew a lot. While growing up, and on into college, I'd made it a point to study the history of the area.

But on this particular Monday I couldn't laze about. At
nine a.m., Meaghan and Victoria Judge were convening with
Wanda at the County Jail in Salinas. Afterward, they were
meeting me so they could clue me in.

I took a run, showered, dressed in white shirt and jeans and my favorite sandals, grabbed Pixie, and hightailed it to Hideaway Café. Fiona had gone off somewhere, probably a magic class with her mentor.

By the time I arrived, Meaghan and Miss Judge were already seated at a table on the rear patio, Meaghan in a tight-fitting blazer, Miss Judge in elegant Armani with her hair swept into a soft chignon. Both had been served tea. A plate of cinnamon swirl scones sat between them.

"Good morning, Meaghan." I nodded to the attorney. "Miss Judge."

"Please, call me Victoria. We have too much history between us to be so formal."

"Victoria." I sat with Pixie in my lap and ordered tea. I was too wound up to eat anything. "So? Fill me in."

"Mom's okay. Frazzled." Meaghan shrugged off her jacket and fluffed the sleeves of her silk blouse. "A polyester jumpsuit isn't the best style for her." She tried to laugh at her joke, but the *heh-heh* sounded stilted. "We talked for quite a while. She wants me to bring her a book about fairies."

"I've got just the one. *Fiona's Luck,* a witty story about a girl who must outsmart clever leprechauns." I clasped my friend's hand. "Maybe she'll find inspiration in the girl's pluck."

"Sounds perfect." Meaghan forced a smile.

"We'll have a bail hearing in a day or so," Victoria Judge said.

"Not right away?" I asked.

"The wheels of bureaucracy move slowly."

Meaghan grunted. "At a turtle's pace."

"The court has asked for a tox screen and urine test." Victoria took a sip of tea.

"Why?" I eyed Meaghan. "Your mother wasn't drunk."

"It's protocol in a sleepwalking case," Victoria said.

Meaghan said, "It's possible someone might have induced Mom's episode."

"Induced," I repeated. "That's a possibility I hadn't considered. That would indicate premeditation on the part of the killer."

Meaghan nodded. "Mom ate and drank with a variety of friends and clients. You saw her."

Victoria said, "Who might have known about Wanda's ailment?"

"Anybody," Meaghan said. "Mom didn't hide the fact."

"Which broadens our list of suspects." Victoria took a sip of tea.

"That's what Mom, Victoria, and I talked about at the jail," Meaghan said. "The party. Mom's friends. Her clients."

"No leads?" I asked.

"Mom can't imagine anyone would have deliberately drugged her." Meaghan sighed. "And then, eager to change the subject, Mom wanted to talk about Didi. She's worried about her. Ever since Didi's husband, Davis . . ." She waggled a hand.

When Davis, a former professional weight lifter, had passed away, Didi had been thrust into the role of businesswoman, a position for which she had been ill prepared, not to mention his death had thrown her for a loop. Healthy one day; dead the next. Well, not completely healthy. Davis had suffered hypertrophic cardiomyopathy the year before, but even so, his heart attack had been shocking.

"Mom isn't sure Didi can manage all by herself," Meaghan continued. "It's one of the reasons why Mom accepted the position of president of the women's association, so she could be available if Didi needed her."

"She's a good friend," I said, "and she has a right to worry. Didi told Hattie Hopewell that Sport Zone is a money pit. What else did you discuss about the murder?"

Meaghan glanced at Victoria Judge and back at me. "Mom started going on about how much she hated Lana for demeaning artists and her scathing reviews. Of course, Miss Judge—Victoria—put a quick stop to that. She urged Mom to hush and motioned to the surveillance cameras in the jail. She said someone might be listening in on our conversation."

Victoria was reviewing text messages on her iPhone and didn't respond.

Meaghan took a sip of tea and set her cup down. "Of course, Mom blanched, which made me wonder whether she'd been talking to her cellmate. So I asked her if she had. She swore she hadn't."

Brady sidled to the table. "Everything all right, ladies?"

"As right as it can be," I said. "Meaghan just visited her mother in jail."

Brady's face turned appropriately solemn. "Please give her my best. We know she didn't—"

"No, we don't," Victoria said, crisply. "We don't know anything, Brady Cash. That's why we will do discovery and get to the bottom of this."

"Yes, ma'am," he replied, sufficiently chastised. A smile tugged at the corners of his mouth. Apparently, Victoria Judge and he had history. She must have been the attorney for him in his divorce. How many times had she needed to rein him in so he wouldn't give away the store?

Brady signaled our waitress to refresh the hot water in our teapot and moved to another table. He caught my eye and hitched his chin in Meaghan's direction, the concern in his gaze palpable. I mouthed, *She's okay.*

"By the way, Courtney," Victoria said, "your father visited."

"Does he need legal advice?" Dad, not Brady, had introduced me to Victoria Judge.

"He didn't visit me. He came to the jail to visit Wanda. While we were there."

I eyed Meaghan.

She smiled meekly. "He brought flowers. Mom couldn't receive them, but the gesture was nice."

The alarm bells that had pealed in my head at the Spectacular rang out again. Were my father and Wanda dating? If they were, I'd be happy for him. Wanda was a wonderful woman. But what if she was convicted of murder?

No, no, no. I could not think in those terms. She was innocent. We just had to figure out who killed Lana. I thought again of what Fiona had said, that she believed the crime scene had been staged. Had the killer induced Wanda's episode? Could the killer have planned down to the minute when Wanda might waken? Had he or she counted on Wanda stumbling upon Lana lying on the floor and rushing to help at the very moment Meaghan and I would come upon the scene and hear Wanda say, *What have I done?*

A notion struck me. I tapped the table. "Surveillance cameras."

Meaghan shuddered. "They creeped me out, I've got to say."

"No, not the ones at the jail. At the Meeting Hall. There must be some. What if they caught the real killer in the act?"

Victoria said, "I'm sure the police will have—"

"Let's go to the precinct right now and find out." Meaghan bounded to her feet.

"I can't," Victoria said. "I have a meeting with another client."

"It's my day off," I said. "I'll go with you."

As Victoria paid the bill, Meaghan grabbed her jacket, and she, Pixie, and I hustled to Carmel Police Department.

The precinct, which was located on Junipero at 4th Avenue, was a modest cream-colored building. From the foyer, I addressed the reception clerk through the bulletproof window via one of the inset voice boxes and asked for Detective Summers. He was in, but he only had a few minutes to chat, she told us. He had a meeting with the chief. Seconds later, Summers appeared.

Standing in the foyer, with wanted criminal flyers as his backdrop, Summers regarded me and only me. He folded his arms. "What could be so important that you needed to grace this fine establishment with your presence, Miss Kelly?"

"Are there any surveillance cameras at the Meeting Hall?" I asked.

"There are, and we've viewed the footage from last night, but"—his face turned grim—"there are only cameras in front of the building and in the business office. There are none capturing activity at the rear of the property."

"Why not?"

"Because the powers that be didn't think it necessary. There's nothing to steal back there except exotic plants. In order to keep costs low, the nonprofit didn't install them. The twenty-four-hour security guards at the front gate monitor all comings and goings."

Prior to the party, we'd all had to pass through the gate and have our names checked against the guest list.

"Do you think the killer knew there weren't any cameras?" I asked.

"The killer, as in Mrs. Brownie?" Summers asked.

"Not my mother!" Meaghan cried. "She didn't do this. The real killer."

I placed a hand on her arm. "The killer might have known that he . . . or she . . . could do the deed without being seen."

"Possibly," Summers admitted, "but that doesn't lead us to any suspects other than Mrs. Brownie."

"At this time," Meaghan asserted.

Summers nodded. "At this time."

★ ★ ★

As I was leaving Meaghan's house—I'd walked her home and settled her in; she hadn't wanted company—my cell phone rang. It was Brady.

"What's up?" I asked.

"I'm taking the night off. How do you feel about a picnic and some sunset photography?"

"Absolutely." I didn't want to be home alone and rehashing everything I'd learned today, especially since I didn't have a clue how to help Wanda. Maybe an evening out would recharge my beleaguered brain. "I'll bring the wine. What do you fancy?"

"Anything red."

At home, I switched into cutoffs and a Carmel-by-the-Sea T-shirt. Fiona hadn't returned yet, but I forced myself not to worry. She wouldn't jeopardize her standing with the queen fairy. She knew the parameters. To be honest, I wished she could use a cell phone and touch base with me.

Minutes after I'd jammed my tote bag with a sweater, my Nikon Coolpix, a bottle of Scheid Vineyards pinot noir, a wine opener, and two acrylic glasses, Brady showed up at the front door dressed in khaki T-shirt, camouflage shorts, and sandals.

"Are we feeding the troops?" I gave his hefty backpack a friendly pat.

"I've loaded enough to feed an army."

"Smells divine. Chicken?"

"Fried."

With Pixie in tow, we headed to the beach. The roar of the surf grew louder as we drew near. When we arrived, the wind was at a standstill and the scattering of sunlight by the atmosphere was creating an orange-and-yellow masterpiece in the sky.

"Perfection," I murmured.

"Sure is. Especially the lack of activity."

Mondays were ideal for a picnic. Unlike on weekends when the beach was crammed with folks and their pets, now there were merely twenty people, and only a few with dogs.

After laying out a blanket and anchoring it with Brady's backpack, we slung our cameras around our necks and snapped off a round of photographs. Then Brady uncorked and poured the wine, and we kicked off our shoes and took a walk bare-foot, wineglasses in hand.

"Nice pinot," he said.

Scheid pinot noir was one of my favorite wines. I relished the flavors of raspberry, spice, and the subtle hint of oak.

Brady said, "I gathered from how uptight Meaghan was earlier that the visit with her mother at the jail didn't go well?"

I filled him on what had happened, as well as the meeting with Detective Summers. "It doesn't look good."

"For now," he said.

"For now." I liked his optimism.

Up ahead, I noticed a woman pulling the hood of a cloak over her head. Seeing her made me think of Tamara Geof-fries. "Hey, Brady." I whirled on my heel, kicking up a swirl of sand. "You know that woman who frequents your café, Tamara Geoffries, the one with the Angora?"

"Sure. What about her?"

"She was at the event Saturday night."

He bobbed his head. "I saw you talking to her."

"Something felt off."

"Off?" He guffawed. "Were your Spidey senses working overtime?"

I'd never read a Marvel comic book or seen any of the movies, but I knew what Spidey senses were. Spiderman could detect imminent danger.

Brady twirled a hand. "Go on. Tamara. Felt *off*. Why?"

"She showed up right when we found Wanda hovering over Lana."

"Um, I hate to point out the obvious, but so did you."

"Because we were looking for Wanda. What was Tamara's excuse? My fai—" I balked.

"What about your fairy?" Brady hadn't seen one, but he'd told me he wanted to. Unlike my father, Brady was open-minded and knew how spiritually active Carmel-by-the-Sea was.

"My fairy encouraged me to stop at Tamara's house and ask her a few questions. She lives in that yellow storybook cottage near me."

"I know the house. Love the bougainvillea." He lifted his camera and took a picture of a dog frolicking in the surf. Salty foam lapped the dog's ankles. "Did you stop?"

"Yes." I gave him a quick recap, ending with Tamara's motive for wanting Lana dead.

"My father and Jamie were friends," Brady said. "Dad was broken up when he died. He felt Lana was in the wrong, but Lana never admitted responsibility. People run all the time in the fog, she'd said. Drivers had to be more careful. The police didn't cite her. It was ruled an accident, not even involuntary manslaughter. Lana didn't send flowers."

"Maybe she'd thought if she had, the gesture would have made her look culpable."

"Or she was as hard-hearted as everyone believed." He grunted. "I have to admit I'd never thought about Tamara wanting retaliation."

"Did Tamara sue Lana?"

"A civil suit? Nope. As far as I know, insurance paid all the bills and Tamara collected on the life insurance policy, which is how she was able to remain in her house." Brady started walking again. "Even so, between you and me, I don't think she killed Lana."

"Her alibi is weak." I told him how she claimed she'd left the party and gone to visit the blind neighbor, who turned out not to be home. "She said she was playing with the woman's cats."

"I'll admit that sounds pretty feeble. Did you tell the police?"

I hadn't, but now, after rehashing with Brady, I would.

Brady said, "Hungry?"

"Starved."

"Race you back to the picnic."

"You're on." Holding my camera steady with one hand so it wouldn't pummel my chest and extending my wineglass with the other so the wine wouldn't slosh all over me, I tore ahead.

As we neared the blanket, Pixie, the scamp, jumped right in front of us. I dodged left; Brady went right. We crashed into each other, our wineglasses went flying, and then we tumbled to the sand. Like a gentleman, he tried to break my fall and protect my camera all at the same time.

Laughing hysterically, we lay there for a full minute, his arm cradling my neck, his face close to mine.

Without budging, Brady broke the silence. "'Well, here's another nice mess you've gotten me into, Ollie.'" His eyes sparkled with impishness.

"You can quote Laurel and Hardy?" I asked.

"Absolutely. I can also recite the 'Who's on First?' script verbatim."

"Me too."

Brady brushed bits of sand off my cheek and studied my face. Did he want to kiss me? Did he think I wanted to kiss him? What if we did and the kiss was horrible?

I nudged him with my shoulder and said, "Let me up, you goof, and pour me some more wine. Next time, watch where you're going."

He chuckled. "Tell that to the cat."

Chapter 13

*A fairy-lock did greet me as I woke. What imp hath played
with mine hair?*
—Daryl Wood Gerber

The dinner Brady brought was yummy: fried chicken, car-
away-laced coleslaw, and honey butter with biscuits that he'd
kept warm. Throughout the meal, we didn't talk about
Tamara or Wanda or the murder. Instead, we chatted about
apertures and lenses and our memory card strategies. Nerd
stuff. Around nine, he escorted me home and gave me a
friendly hug.

As I climbed into bed, I didn't think about our near kiss.
Okay, I did. And, if I was truthful, I wanted to kiss him.
Would a kiss ruin our friendship? I spanked the comforter.
Honestly, Courtney, are you back in high school?

Pixie butted me with her head.

I drew her close. "It's okay, kitty. Just arguing with myself."

Around eleven as I was placing the mystery I'd been reading on the nightstand, Fiona flounced in.

"Where have you been all day?" I asked, sounding like a worrywart mother of a teenager.

"Out."

"With Merryweather?"

"No." She did a twirl. "With Zephyr."

I gasped. "That's not allowed."

"Yes, it is."

I narrowed my gaze. "Says who?"

She gave me a peeved look, one I knew I made. Fairies could mimic all of our human expressions. "Merryweather okayed it. I'm on a quest for all the right reasons, to bring resolution to an embattled soul."

"Your mentor has the authority?"

Fiona bobbed her head. "Directly from the queen fairy herself."

"Why was Zephyr involved?"

"Being a nurturer fairy, she can ease hearts and minds."

Her answer sounded credible. "What was the quest?"

"Tailing that reporter."

"Ulani Kamaka? Why?"

"To ensure she makes good on her promise to you and stays on track. Tish really wants to find her daughter. Zephyr wants to help Tish, and I want to help Zephyr. And do you know what?" Gleefully, Fiona threw her arms wide. "Ulani is trying. She made a lot of calls. I mean, a ton. Whee!" She did a loop-de-loop and hovered midair. "She might have a bit of detective in her after all."

Tuesday morning arrived with a bang. Literally. My alarm wasn't set to go off for another thirty minutes when I heard the noise. I dashed to my window and peered out. Catty-corner across the street, at the Congregational church, a Ford truck was trying to parallel park. It must have hit the green sedan behind it.

"I'm up," I grumbled, although I wasn't unhappy to have been torn from a nightmare about dueling letter openers.

Given the extra half hour, I decided to allow myself a luxurious shower. As water cascaded over my head and shoulders, I thought of Wanda. In jail. No amenities. Bread and water for meals.

Okay, that was probably an overreach. Even so, the notion made me feel as if I'd been doused with a bucket of ice water. I switched off the shower and got moving. I had to get Wanda out of jail. Fast. Thanks to my nightmare, I was pretty sure I knew how I could accomplish that.

I slipped into a peach pin-tuck dress and comfy espadrilles—the temperature was supposed to be close to eighty degrees later in the day—and I hurried to Open Your Imagination, ready to fight for my friend's innocence.

"Morning," I said to Joss as I breezed through the Dutch door.

"Hey, sunshine." Joss was unpacking a shipment of Royal Doulton Kirkwood teacups and saucers. The floral pattern on her shirt almost matched the china's yellow-green-and-purple pattern. "Aren't you a sight?"

My short hair had to look a mess after my speedy walk. Fiona, who had flown ultrafast to keep up, was out of breath. Pixie seemed rattled by the bumpy ride in my arms. I set her on the floor, pushed her rump, said, "Go have fun," then finger-combed my hair.

Fiona and Pixie romped onto the patio and immediately started playing Fiona's favorite game: Try to Catch Me. She was such a tease. Pixie leaped after her.

"You look smug," Joss said. "What's up?"

Pouring myself a mug of freshly brewed Kona coffee, I said, "I've divined a way to help Wanda."

"Do tell."

"The letter opener." Too hyper to drink the coffee, I set

the cup aside and started helping Joss unpack the teacups, taking care not to let the Styrofoam peanuts fall to the floor. One nibble by any animal that traipsed in could hurt it. "The letter opener not only had Wanda's fingerprints on it; it had mine, too. Remember how I removed it when I placed the dragon into the garden?"

Joss grunted. "You can't tell the police that. Do you want to get yourself arrested?"

"Of course not, but having two sets of prints on a murder weapon will confuse the techies. Won't that create reasonable doubt?"

Joss's forehead crinkled. "This idea needs more tweaking. You'd better chat with an attorney before you hurry to Wanda's defense."

I frowned. "You're probably right." Often, my father said I rushed into things. I had to formulate a concise plan of attack.

"In the meantime"—Joss motioned to the patio—"you have to set up for the pottery-breaking class. It starts at ten. Twelve people have signed up."

"On it."

I strode to the patio and gathered some of the items I would need for the class—one eight-inch clay pot per student as well as hammers, rubber-headed mallets, bracing sticks, and sandpaper. Although breaking a pot to make a fairy garden seemed counterintuitive, a broken pot could make such a distinctive display. If the fairy gardener already had a broken terra-cotta pot, perfect. Terra-cotta didn't last forever. But if she didn't have one on hand and wanted to make one, she had to destroy a perfectly good pot. Sure, a gardener could buy a prefab broken pot on the Internet, but the fun was in the making.

After viewing YouTube how-to videos online, I'd designed a few broken-pot gardens. My favorite was the one in the far corner of the patio. First, I'd shattered the front third of a large twenty-one-inch pot, set that shard aside, and packed the remaining pot with moist soil. Next, I'd broken the front-third shard into three shards, plus a few remnants, and inserted the trio of shards into the soil, creating tiers. Then, using the remnants, I'd fashioned stairs to the tippy top. On the bottom tier, I'd set a white wire gazebo fitted with a table and tea set inside. On the top level, I'd placed a teetering tree house. On the middle, I'd placed two fairy figurines, one swinging and the other dancing. I'd planted the garden with six different kinds of succulents in a variety of colors. *Which way* signs directing the fairies from one tier to the next created the story.

Fiona drifted near. "I was thinking about that gray cat we saw at Tamara's house. Pixie was upset by it."

A shiver ran down my spine. "Is it possible that you were wrong and the cat was a ghost, or the reincarnation of Tamara's husband?" If I believed in fairies, then I had to admit ghosts could be real.

"Of course not." Fiona tapped her neck. "The cat was wearing a collar."

"It was?"

"Mm-hm. The collar was dark gray so it matched the cat's coat."

"You're observant, aren't you? And into everything lately. Solving Tish's problem. Helping Wanda."

"I am, and it's making a difference. Take a peek." Fiona lifted her first set of adult wings. "I'm growing a second pair. See the buds?"

"I do. I'm so proud of you. Now what about the cat?"

"Why was it there? Why has it attached itself to Tamara?"

"I don't have any answers for that, but I'll think about it. In the meantime, scoot." I blew her a kiss and brushed her away. "I've got to get cracking."

"Cracking." Fiona did a somersault. "You're doing a

pottery-breaking demonstration and you've got to get *cracking*? You're *cracking* me up."

"Hysterical." I mock-frowned. "Get out of my way."

"Okay. I'm going to take a nap." She yawned and disappeared into the ficus trees.

"I'm here!" Didi Dubois called as she breezed onto the patio, her *Love Pickleball* T-shirt drenched, her flounce skirt showing off her toned legs. Her face glistened with perspiration.

"Did you just finish a set?" I asked.

"I had to work out my frustration somehow. To get one more level of *buzz*, I ran all the way here. Adrenaline"—she sighed—"is the universe's natural healer. Now where . . ." She clapped a hand over her heart. "You must think I'm horrible, boasting about energy when Lana . . ." Didi tossed her tote and light sweater on a wrought-iron table. "I can't believe she's gone. Everyone in town is heartbroken."

I doubted the killer was shedding a tear.

"And Elton?" Didi shook her head. "The guy is mooning about. He looks lost without her."

"I can imagine."

"Kenny is, as well. He adored Lana."

Had Kenny wanted her for himself? Had he pressed Lana to choose between him and Elton?

"By the way, you won," Didi said.

"Won what?"

"The antique Amish wagon. I'm sending out emails this afternoon." She whistled. "It was quite the process going over all the bidding papers without Wanda." Her eyes misted over. "She's the one who knew the provenance of each piece. Have you visited her in jail? I've been meaning to get there, but work has gotten in the way."

"I have. She's fighting the good fight."

"I'm glad to hear that." Didi scanned the table. "How can I help you set up? As usual, you look superorganized."

"How about fetching a dozen bottles of water for the at-tendees?"

"Sure thing." Didi crossed to the mini refrigerator beyond the fountain and loaded her arms with bottles. She returned and tumbled them onto the instruction table. As she set them upright, she said, "No way Wanda killed Lana."

"She didn't."

"But she was there. You saw her. Holding the knife."

"The letter opener. Yes, she was holding it, but I didn't see her stab Lana. I think she stumbled upon the scene." *The staged scene,* I mused. "She asked about you. She's worried about you and Sport Zone."

"Why?" Didi opened a bottle of water and drank a swig.

"Hattie said . . ." I paused.

Didi clucked her tongue. "What did Hattie tell you?"

"Is Sport Zone a money pit?"

"A money . . ." Didi sputtered. "Dratted Hattie. That woman can't keep a secret to save her life."

"Is it true?"

Suddenly, tears welled in Didi's eyes. "Yes, it's true. The business is sucking up every penny I have in savings. My sweet Davis, may he rest in peace, would be so upset if he knew things weren't going swimmingly. It was his baby. He was such a sports nut. He lived and breathed health, until . . ." Didi polished off the bottle of water. "I haven't done anything wrong, mind you. I've dotted all the i's and crossed all the t's, but if one more thing goes awry, Sport Zone will go under." She gazed at me. "You know how it is. Open Your Imagination needs customers to thrive, and heaven forbid a shipment arrives late. It's the same at the club. A member or two quits. A pickle-ball net tears. A treadmill motor bites the dust. I have repair-and-replacement insurance, of course, but I also have a huge deductible. My accountant says not to fret, but I'm waiting for the other shoe to drop." She dumped the empty bottle in the recyclables trash bin. "But enough about me. Back to Wanda. How does she look? Do they feed her green leafy vegetables?"

I doubted those were on the jail's menu.

"She doesn't have an ounce of fat on her," Didi continued. "She can't go long without a good meal. If only we could find a way to exonerate her."

"I might have a way," I said.

At that moment, Joss strode onto the patio carrying a tray set with a crystal pitcher of lemonade and twelve glasses. "Do. Not. Say. A. Word." She glowered at me as she neared. "Plus, if it doesn't work, you don't want to look like a fool. Now greet your attendees."

I swear, at times I felt like Joss was channeling my grandmother. Nana would've said the same exact thing. The day after my mother died, my grandmother told me: *No time for crying. Get on with life.* I was ten. But Nana had been adamant. So I'd cried in private.

Three newbies strolled onto the patio. I said hello to each. Cliff, the cherry-cheeked owner of Carmel Collectibles, followed them, as did Hattie and six of the Happy Diggers garden club members.

When the twelve students were settled at the table, I dove into my spiel about how much fun it was to make a do-it-yourself project. I pointed out the eight-inch pots, the pieces of wood, and the rubber-headed mallets and iron hammers I'd set in the center of the table.

"There are two methods for breaking a pot," I began, all eyes on me. "One involves turning your pot on its side and hammering from the inside. Two requires standing the pot normally, bracing a piece of wood on the inside of it, directly behind the portion you wish to crack, and hammering from the outside." From the far end of the instruction table, I demonstrated the latter technique. *Wham!* An irregularly shaped piece broke inward. "Voilà."

Many of the students laughed. A few appeared frozen with fear.

"Relax." I set the hammer down. "Don't be scared. There is no right or wrong here. Whatever you get is what you will work with. By the way, some people like to sand the broken edges of the pot. I don't think that's necessary unless children are going to be touching your creations. You decide." I gestured to the sheets of sandpaper. "Once you've gotten the hang of it, you can graduate to a larger pot if you so desire, but let's all try with these first. Later, we'll plant them."

Fearlessly, Cliff shoved the wood inside his clay pot and whacked the pot with a hammer. A shard burst from it. He hooted with glee. Hattie, who was seated next to him, chose a hammer, turned her clay pot on its side, and daintily tapped her pot from the inside. Nothing broke. Batting her eyelashes deliberately, she asked Cliff for help. He—now a pro—was more than happy to oblige. One of the Happy Diggers threw Hattie a knowing look. Hattie didn't give her the satisfaction of a response.

For the next few minutes, I circled the table to supervise.

Didi had selected a rubber-headed mallet instead of a hammer. She brandished it in the air. "Be bold, right, Courtney?" She rose from the table to get what she hoped would be a good angle. With one deft blow, she slammed the mallet into the pot. The whole thing shattered. She squealed. "Oh, no! Clearly, I don't have the knack."

"Don't worry, Didi," I said. "We'll use those pieces for tiers and stairs." I handed her a new pot and said, "Try again. Maybe strike a little softer this time."

As she drew back her arm to whack the pot again, out of the blue an image of the crime scene came to me—Lana knocked to the ground and the dragon fairy garden I'd made for the event smashed to pieces.

It hadn't taken a *knack* to do either. It had taken pure hate.

Chapter 14

There's no star too far and no dream too grand.
So shake the fairy dust and make a wish;
the magic's in your hands.
—Anonymous

An hour later, as the class was disbanding, Fiona flew into the courtyard, her face pinched with concern. "What a mess." Fairies didn't appreciate messes. I should have warned her before she'd gone for her nap.

"It's all good," I lied, my insides snarled because of my thoughts about the murder.

"You get to clean it up," she admonished.

That made me chuckle. "Don't worry. You don't have to get your pretty hands dirty. You can play with Pixie."

After I'd put the patio back to rights, I decided to work out during my lunch break. Like Didi, I felt the need to burn off some steam. Fiona opted out. She and Pixie were having too good a time playing chase beneath the patio tables.

Sport Zone wasn't packed midday on a Tuesday. The pickleball courts were empty. So were the racquetball courts. The gym, which boasted over one hundred machines, was half full. A StairMaster was available. Sweet.

I strode into the ladies' blue-white-and-brown-themed locker room. There was no one standing at the white marble counters blow-drying their hair and no one preening after a sweaty workout. From where I was standing, I couldn't see along the three aisles of walnut lockers, but I didn't detect chatter.

Needless to say, I was surprised when I rounded the middle bank of lockers and caught sight of Kenny Chu fiddling with the keyless push-button lock on the locker two down from mine—Lana's locker, distinctive because of the plentiful three-inch-long gold plates on its door, each plate depicting one of Lana's wins as *Women's Pickleball Champion*.

"What are you doing, Kenny?" I asked.

He whirled around. His compression shorts and fitted sleeveless top showed off his muscular body. His skin glistened with perspiration in a good way, like he'd worked out but not too hard. However, there was no doubt in my mind that his cheeks had turned crimson at being caught in the act.

"What are you doing?" I repeated.

"Looking for Hattie Hopewell." Kenny checked the read-out on his black Apple watch. "Did you see her on your way in? We have a lesson."

"Nope. She was just at my shop. She might be detained." In fact, I knew she would be late because she'd gone for coffee with Cliff after class.

"Thanks for the heads-up."

"Didi should be here soon if you need to get something out of Lana's locker."

"Lana's lock—" Kenny did a double take at the locker and scratched his chin. "Ha. No, no. My mistake. I thought this was Hattie's. She likes me to get her paddle and warm it up."

"Her locker is in the next aisle." I narrowed my gaze. Maybe Kenny had made an honest mistake. Hattie's locker was in the proximate location as Lana's.

"Right you are."

"Um, Kenny, shouldn't one of the female attendants get that paddle instead of you?"

"They were all busy. I figured I'd do it myself. I announced myself before coming in. The locker room was empty."

He had an answer for everything.

When Kenny exited the locker room, I switched into my workout clothes and looped a sweatband around my hair.

As I returned to the gym and made my way onto the Stair-Master to start my workout, I saw Kenny chatting with a young woman at the smoothie bar. She was flirting with him, but he didn't seem in the least interested. He looked over his shoulder. At me? Did he intend to reenter the locker room when he was certain I was engrossed in my workout? What did he hope to find in Lana's locker? Hadn't her husband cleaned it out yet? Possibly not. There was always so much to do after a death: the will as well as the state's business, not to mention arranging the funeral and interment. After my mother died, my father slogged around for a month. He hadn't been prepared.

"Who are you staring at, Courtney?" Miss Reade asked as she stepped onto the StairMaster to my right. The calf-length leggings and loose-fitting racer-back shirt she was wearing made her look even slimmer than usual.

"No one."

She hummed, not believing me. "I think you and that charming Brady Cash make a cute couple."

"Oh, we're not, Miss Reade. We're . . ." I waved a hand. "We're friends."

"*Hmm*," she mumbled again.

I peered past her at Kenny. I kept picturing him at the crime scene, answering Detective Summers's questions, his tuxedo jacket removed, his shirt sleeves soaking wet.

"How often do you come here?" Miss Reade asked as she entered her workout challenge on the machine and began climbing.

"Once or twice a week, if I can fit it into my schedule. You?"

"Almost daily. If we don't use it, we lose it." She tittered. "By the way, please call me Lissa; it's short for *Melissa. Miss Reade* is so formal. I like when the children address me formally, but my friends should not, no matter what age."

"Lissa. It suits you."

"Thank you."

She peered in the direction I was gazing. "Please don't tell me you have your eye on Kenny Chu. He's too old for you, and he's not much of a reader."

"He's not?" That piqued my interest. "He said he likes to go by the library and look at books."

"*Look* at them, maybe, but he rarely opens them. He comes to use the computers on occasion to watch the stock market." Deftly, she tapped the StairMaster's control screen to enhance her workout. "He's quite the pragmatist. He talks with day traders whenever he gets the chance. Why, I see him go into Carmel Bank on a daily basis. Same time every morning. Supposedly, Lana had advised him on his finances, which had made him obsessed with how much money he netted."

"Lana advised him?"

Miss Reade nodded. "She had received a windfall in a divorce settlement from her first husband."

The man Joss had loved.

"Lana had taken it upon herself to become astute when investing and enjoyed sharing her knowledge with friends," Miss Reade added.

"Aren't you a fount of information?"

"I'm a librarian. It's my duty." Miss Reade paled. "I'm sorry. Talking about Lana in that manner must have sounded crass. Her body is barely cold." She lowered her voice. "Merryweather said she's heard people gossiping that they're glad Lana will no longer be the pickleball champion."

Tongues would wag for quite a while, I supposed. Lana had rubbed people the wrong way.

"Fairies are so unique, wouldn't you agree? Their spirits"—Miss Reade kicked up the intensity of her workout—"bless this world with energy. But back to Lana. You always have your finger on the pulse of these things, so tell me—"

"These things?"

"Murder investigations."

"Only that once. Because I was a suspect."

"But you're sharp, and I know you care for Wanda. So what can you tell me about the investigation so far? Who do you think killed Lana?"

I told her what little I knew. She nodded contemplatively.

Before proceeding, I scanned the workout room for Sport Zone's premier trainer, but I didn't see him. Lowering my voice, I said, "Kenny claimed he left the event that night right around the time of death. He said he went to the library."

"The library was closed by then."

"That's what he said. Would there be footage of him hanging around outside?"

"Excellent question. Why don't you accompany me after our workout, and we'll check together?"

Lissa Reade sat at the desk in her office with a laptop computer open. Four security cameras provided images for the split screen, each displaying a library image—two building exteriors and two building interiors. "This will take some time."

She scrolled backward through the tape, a digital stamp at the bottom of the images showing the time and date. When she reached Saturday evening, six p.m., she cycled forward slowly.

First we saw a group of excited children checking out

their books, and then a couple of women were browsing the aisles of books, and then a man—not Kenny—was strolling through the garden.

Next, we watched as two women at the front door juggled stacks of books while pocketing their cell phones.

At six thirty, the scenarios weren't much different. Typical patrons; typical behavior.

At seven, a group of students entered the reading room while laughing and throwing crumpled paper at one another. A librarian shushed them.

At seven thirty, the students had disbanded and only three elderly people occupied the reading room. Two people were waiting to check out books.

At eight a gaunt male librarian announced closing time, and soon after locked the doors.

Miss Reade continued scrolling through ten o'clock. No one lingered outside the library. Ever.

I thanked her for her assistance and left the library. On my way back to the shop, I phoned Detective Summers and left a message. Kenny Chu had never gone to the library. His alibi was a lie.

Chapter 15

There never was a merry world since the fairies left off dancing.
—John Selden, "Parson"

As I ended the call and hitched my gym bag higher on my shoulder, someone yelled my name. My father hailed me from the middle of the street. He had scored the landscaping oversight of Ocean Avenue a year ago and was on the median, pulling weeds from one of the plantings. Plenty of guys who worked for him could have tended the weeds, but my father took great pride in making sure Ocean Avenue was beautiful at all times.

He strode across the crosswalk to me while lifting his straw hat and mopping his face with a checkered cloth. "What are you doing here?"

"I took a lunch break and went to the gym. I'm on my way back to the shop now." I pecked him on his sweaty cheek.

"Isn't the library out of your way?"

"I like taking the long route. Say, a little birdie told me that you and Wanda Brownie are dating."

"A birdie or a fairy?" His mouth quirked up on one side; he was teasing.

"I heard you visited Wanda in jail and brought flowers."

"I did." My father's mouth pulled down in a frown. "She's innocent."

"I'm sure she is, but the police need more than our word for it. They need a viable suspect."

Dad hitched his chin toward the library. "Is that what you were doing? Looking for suspects?"

I shifted feet.

"You can't help yourself, can you? You solve one murder and suddenly, what"—he snapped his fingers—"you're a detective?"

"I'm doing it for Wanda. She's like—"

"Your second mom. I get it." He placed a hand on my shoulder. "She's a good lady."

"She's smart and energetic and kind."

"And wanted for murder."

"You could do worse." I chuckled. "Honestly, we have to find out who really killed Lana."

"We?"

"No, not you."

"You and your fairy?" The bite in his tone was sharp.

"Dad, c'mon. You know what I mean. Me. Meaghan. Our friends." I waved a hand. "We can ask around."

"As can your fairy."

"Da-a-d." I dragged out the word. "Get real."

"You get real."

I grumbled, "Just because you can't see fairies doesn't negate the fact that a whole bunch of other people can."

"You and your mother—"

"Stop, Dad." I shot a finger at him, bile rising in my throat. We'd had the argument too many times to count. My mother had tried to introduce him to fairies throughout their marriage. He'd resisted.

"Swell." He whipped his hat against his thigh. Dust billowed off his jeans. "My daughter opens her own shop, and suddenly she's bristling with impudence."

I stood a little taller.

After a long moment, he said, "Your nana would be proud."

"I'll take that as a compliment." I kissed his cheek again. "Have fun weeding. I'll let you know if I or my fairy discover anything."

"Hold up." My father placed a hand on my arm. "It dawned on me that the killer might have planned for Wanda to take the fall. Maybe the killer learned she'd gone to take a nap and knew she sleepwalked."

"Miss Judge suggested that."

"She did?"

I nodded. "But it makes me wonder whether the killer is a friend of Wanda's."

"Or a client."

The shop was bustling when I returned. A passel of women who walked their dogs every afternoon had ventured in. Pixie was ecstatic. She adored dogs, especially big ones like the Great Dane and chocolate Lab. I spied her through the glass windows in the main showroom. She was on the patio swatting the dogs with her tail as the dogs' owners browsed the racks of figurines.

I checked in with Joss and then strolled to the patio to assist the customers.

As usual, they were bubbling over with enthusiasm.

"This one reminds me of you," a woman said, lifting a fig-urine of a green fairy sitting on a bench reading. She wiggled it in her friend's face. "When are you without a book?"

"Well, this one reminds me of you," the friend countered. She picked up a big-toothed gnome.

"Very funny. Har-har. I do not have big teeth."

Before I could insert myself into their banter, Fiona way-laid me. "You were gone a long time. Were you investigating without me?"

I gestured for her to follow me to the far side of the foun-tain and told her about Kenny Chu acting suspiciously at the gym and my subsequently discovering that the library's sur-veillance proved he had lied. I added that I'd left a message for Detective Summers, and I reiterated my father's theory.

"Would Kenny know if Wanda was a sleepwalker?" Fiona asked.

"She donates a lot of time at Sport Zone and heads up the women's association. I would imagine they've interacted. He's probably guided her through a workout or two, during which she might have talked about her ailment."

"Hmm. A fairy lives in the garden at the café next to Sport Zone. Maybe she would know the scuttlebutt. I could—" Fiona shook her head. "No, you can't, silly fairy. That's non-sense. No, no, no." Glumly, she flew into the ficus trees.

I ached for her, knowing how much she regretted having messed up at fairy school. How long would the queen fairy subject her to no socializing? Having fun with a human and a cat could not be nearly as satisfying as mingling with one's own kind. On the other hand, wouldn't reaching out to an-other fairy for a clue to help Wanda find resolution, similarly to the way she'd assisted Zephyr in regard to Tish's predica-ment, be an approved interaction?

"Fiona!" I called.

She whizzed to me, tears streaking her cheeks. "What?"

I told her my idea. "Maybe Merryweather would approve this for you."

"You're brilliant!" Beaming, Fiona brushed my cheek with a wing and soared away.

At the end of the day, after selling numerous fairy figurines and tea set items, I said to Joss, "I'm beat."

"Does that mean you're not going to come with the courtyard girls for a night on the town?" Occasionally, the women who worked in the shops at Cypress and Ivy liked to go out together. "We're dining on tapas at that place around the corner. I thought you—"

I held up a hand. "I'll pass. I'm really tired. Another time."

She gave me a hug and said to Pixie, who was happily purring in my arms, "Make sure your mama eats dinner."

Pixie mewed her assent.

As I was walking home with Pixie, I heard the pounding of feet behind me. I whirled around. Brady was running toward me in his work clothes, a jacket slung casually over one shoulder.

"I thought that was you." He slowed when he caught up to me.

"You're taking another night off?"

"If I don't let my assistant manager do something, she'll leave. She wants more responsibility. I want her to have it." He scratched Pixie between her ears. "Heading home?"

"Mm-hm. You?"

"Yep."

A half a block farther, Fiona flew up to us. How I wanted to find out if she and Merryweather had learned anything from the fairy at the café near Sport Zone, but I didn't feel free to ask with Brady tagging along.

As if sensing my question, Fiona fluttered directly in front of me and said, "Nope. Didn't learn a thing."

I blinked. Had she read my mind? Did she have ESP?

She performed a pirouette in front of Brady. "Ask him over."

"Want to stop in for a glass of wine?" I blurted, and ogled my fairy. Had she doused me with a potion? I didn't see anything glittery overhead.

"Sure." Brady grinned. "May I sit in your renowned garden?"

"Renowned?"

"You've talked about how much work you've put into it. I can't wait to check it out. I'm not a master gardener, like you."

"My father is the master gardener, not I."

Dad didn't just do landscaping. Given his extensive knowledge, he lectured and volunteered throughout the community to help beautify the surrounding areas. I had yet to sit in on one of his classes and made a mental to note to add one to my calendar.

"Okay, you're an amateur," Brady said. "Even so, I'd like to see your garden as well as the greenhouse. You've boasted about that so much—"

"I don't boast."

His light blue eyes glinted with humor. "Fine. You don't boast. But you do talk about the greenhouse, and everything that's inside it. I want to see with my own eyes."

"Be my guest."

In the course of a few months of renewing our friendship, I hadn't asked Brady to my house and he hadn't invited me to his. This would be a first. What would he think of my décor? My kitchen? Me?

I pushed niggling thoughts aside and walked beside him in silence for a few blocks. When we arrived at Dream-by-the-Sea, I said stupidly, "Here we are."

He had walked me home before. He knew where I lived.

"Give me the full tour," he said.

I opened the gate and suggested he enter first as I described what I'd done to rebuild the front yard from the ground up. "The path is the original. So is the front door."

He nodded his approval. "I like everything about this place already. The vibes are great. I attribute that to your keen eye."

"You're going to make me blush."

We climbed the steps to the porch and he said, "Nice place to chill."

In addition to the rocking chair, I'd added a verdigris plant stand on which I'd arranged pots of herbs and I'd hung a variety of wind chimes. Fairies loved the sound of chimes and bells.

"This way," I said.

Fiona flew into the house ahead of us.

I set Pixie on the floor and led the way to the kitchen. Brady did what I had at Tamara Geoffries's house. He glanced left and right, taking in everything.

"You have some nice antique pieces," he said.

"Left to me by my grandmother."

"The rolltop desk in the living room is terrific."

"That's my home office. I love all the drawers and cubbies." Knowing I would one day inherit it, Nana had secretly stuffed the drawers with cash. The memory of that discovery after her death made me smile. *Every girl needs a little pin money,* she'd said when I'd turned sixteen. I motioned with my hand like a display model. "White or red?"

Brady's mouth crooked up on one side. He laughed. "Ha. You're asking me about wine. I thought you were testing to see if I was color-blind. The kitchen is white. The accents are blue."

"You passed the test."

"I'll take a glass of white wine. Thanks. Chardonnay, if you have it."

I pulled a bottle from my modest wine refrigerator, opened it, and poured two glasses. I threw together a small plate of appetizers I'd made over the weekend—artichoke cheese bites as well as onion tarts. The bites were easy to make: less than ten ingredients, whipped together in a matter of minutes. I'd used Rogue Creamery cheddar and a dash of Tabasco sauce, which really gave the treat a kick. I often ate appetizers for dinner instead of a full meal because I wasn't hungry at night. A quick zap in the microwave for both appetizers reheated them perfectly.

"This way to the backyard." I opened the kitchen door and let the screen door swing shut after Pixie, Fiona, and Brady exited. Sunlight filtered through the cypress trees. Streaks of orange and gray tinged the sky. A refreshing breeze had kicked up.

Fiona swirled around Brady's head and did a few flips in the air.

"Feeling frisky?" I asked her.

Brady pivoted. "Who, me?"

"No, not you." I batted his shoulder. "My fairy."

He searched the area for signs of her. I think he expected to see a flash of light or something shimmering. Fiona did sparkle, but that wasn't how a person could see her.

"Appetizer?" I offered the plate.

Brady took an artichoke-cheddar bite and bit into it. "Savory. I like it."

I set the appetizer plate on the wicker table and slowly walked Brady through the garden. Over the past few months, I'd created paths like radiant beams of the sun leading from the center of the garden to each corner of the yard.

Brady pointed. "Is that sink a fairy garden?"

I nodded. I'd used an old tub-style sink in the east corner.

"And the wheelbarrow?"

"Yep. Anything and everything can become a fairy garden."

The third was a stack of three pots set on top of one another. Ladders provided access for fairies from pot to pot. In the fourth corner, I would set the antique wagon I'd won at the Beauty of Art Spectacular. I wondered when it would be delivered or whether I had to pick it up. I hadn't received the email Didi had promised to send.

"These are indigenous plants," Brady said, crouching to inspect a few.

I batted his shoulder. "You know more about gardening than you're letting on."

"I'm good with herbs. I like the blue-and-white theme." Brady nodded his appreciation. "And you have a great eye for balance. It must be the photographer in you."

"Or years of my father drumming the notion into me. He believes balance in a garden allows the spirit to calm. That doesn't mean he doesn't like a natural, overrun garden, but to him, balance is everything."

Brady walked along one path and stopped short of the polycarbonate greenhouse. He threw his arms wide. "So this is where the magic happens."

"Don't make fun." I opened the door. "After you."

He stepped inside and drew in a deep breath. "It smells great. Like the damp wood in a forest."

"Because of all the seedlings and plants."

"And it's warm."

"Growing things requires steady temperatures."

Brady inspected the metal shelving that held a wide variety of fairy figurines. "I forgot to tell you my mom was impressed with the garden you made for Hideaway."

"I'm glad to hear that."

A couple of months ago, Brady had commissioned me to create one. Using the café's red color scheme, I'd decided that a tasty meal at the café should be the theme. I found the most delightful fairy figurines, each carrying a different food item, like pie or cake. I'd set out a number of tiny white tables and had hot-glued miniature plates of sweets on top. In the center, I'd planted a beautiful bonsai to represent the trees on the rear patio of the café and strung it with battery-operated fairy lights.

"Let's sit in the yard while the sun is setting," I said.

He held the greenhouse door open for me.

After I passed by, he let the door close and then suddenly clasped my arm. "Is that her?"

"Her?"

"Your fairy." He reached into the void.

I heard a giggle. Fiona was toying with him. Had he really seen her?

He pulled his hand back but didn't release me. I could feel the heat radiating off his body. Turning slightly, I gazed into his face. His kind face. His lips parted. My heart did a hip-hop.

"Hey, you two!" my neighbor called. "Over here."

Brady let me go and stepped into the waning sunlight. I followed him, my insides deliciously jittery.

"Nice night, isn't it, Holly?" I asked.

My landlord was standing beyond the fence that separated our properties. In her arms was her black cat, who was playing with the tassels of her colorful scarf top. I couldn't see her Pomeranians, but I could hear them yapping merrily.

"Nice enough," she said. "By the by, I saw Elton Lamar today, and I got to thinking. You remember how Hattie said she saw him with that attorney?"

Quickly, I recapped the Hopewell sisters' conversation for Brady and then motioned for Holly to continue.

"I recalled seeing him a week ago," she said. "With an attractive brunette outside Carmel Bank."

"Fascinating," Brady said in a teasing tone.

Fiona flew to my shoulder and plopped down. "What's her point?"

A while back, Holly had hinted that the police considered

her a bit of a crackpot. I'd never questioned why. Maybe she'd floated a theory that they'd dismissed out of hand. Perhaps she'd meandered while conveying a story, as she was doing now.

"Something seemed off," Holly went on.

"Off, how?" I asked.

"Well, he was a bit of a mess today. To be expected. But last week, he looked put together. Quite dashing, in fact. I don't dress up to go to the bank. Do you?"

I said, "Maybe the woman he'd met was a loan officer and he'd wanted to impress her."

"Ha! She was way too beautiful to be a loan officer."

"Ahem." I cleared my throat. "Your sister Hedda might take offense at the comment."

"Tosh!"

"She's pretty."

"Don't tell her," Holly said. "She'll get a swelled head."

I smiled. "Holly, you're the one who said to Hattie that you'd heard a rumor Elton might be struggling financially. If he were in debt, that might explain why he'd needed to meet with a loan officer."

Holly *tsk*ed. "Rumors-*schumors*. If I didn't know better, I would have thought Elton was involved with the brunette in a romantic way, except . . ."

Her cat squirmed. She set it on the ground and it jumped to the top of the fence so it could peer down at Pixie. The two cats froze and did a stare-down. Fiona sailed to Holly's cat and landed on its head. The cat swished its tail, ending the stare-down.

"Except they didn't match," Holly went on. "Not like Lana and Elton did. The woman had dark eyes and tanned skin and she was tall. Nearly six feet tall."

Do all couples match? I wondered. Brady and I didn't. But, then, we weren't a couple.

"Well, that's all the news I've got." Holly ordered her dogs inside.

Oh, sure, drop a bombshell, and let me mull it over for the rest of the evening.

Brady and I settled into the chairs at the center of the garden and finished our wine. We didn't talk about Elton or Lana or our close encounter outside the greenhouse. Instead, we grew silent and listened to nocturnal birds wakening.

Around eight, Brady headed home. As I closed the front gate and returned to the house, Fiona winged beside me, rattling off questions about what Holly had said. Elton Lamar had met up with another woman. Was Holly wrong about them not being romantic? Did Elton kill his wife because he'd wanted to move on? Should I loop in Detective Summers?

Despite Holly's prompting, I decided that an idle bit of gossip wouldn't float Summers's boat. I needed more.

Chapter 16

How to tell if a fairy is nearby: mysterious giggling.
—Anonymous

I awoke early on Wednesday morning eager to hear from Meaghan. The bail hearing for her mother was to be held at ten. Feeling antsy, I jogged barefoot on the beach. The crisp air and the aroma of sea salt invigorated me. I returned home and showered and then dressed in my cheeriest orange blouse, white capris, and white sandals. I fetched a matching cross-body purse and went into the kitchen, where I forced myself to eat scrambled eggs even though I wasn't hungry. I knew I'd need protein to carry me through the day.

Fiona, who had accompanied me on the jog, nibbled some pomegranate seeds and stretched. "Ready to go? We have a full day ahead. We're reading to children."

"I nearly forgot."

I nabbed Pixie and raced over to Open Your Imagination.

Lissa Reade, dressed in a royal-purple tunic over colorful parrot-themed leggings—a perfect getup for greeting a group of children—was at the shop sharing a cup of tea with Joss when I arrived. Lissa had arranged the preschool visit.

"Look at the book Lissa chose." Joss handed me a copy of *Fairy Mom and Me*, by Sophie Kinsella. "And she arranged for the local bookshop to provide copies for sale."

"Merryweather helped me select it," Lissa said.

"I like her taste." Flipping through the opening pages, I recognized immediately that it was one we should add to our growing assortment. The drawings were quite clever. Of course, Fairy Mom was nothing like Fiona, but the children didn't need to know that. "Do you think the children will sit still for all of this?"

"They won't have to," Lissa said. "It's a collection of stories. Read one. Twenty minutes max. When you're done, ask the children a few questions, and then move on to cookies and fairy garden magic."

Lissa had designated me as the storyteller. Yes, *me*. I wasn't accomplished at reading in front of crowds, but I figured I could face a sea of smiling children's faces and do just fine.

"Courtney! I'm here." Yvanna Acebo swept into the shop at half past nine carrying a variety of freshly baked miniature cookies on a platter: sugar, lemon, cinnamon, and chocolate chip. She was clad in her uniform, pink apron over white dress, and per usual, she wore her long dark hair in a scrunchie, loose strands dangling around her beautiful face. Her caramel-colored eyes twinkled with mischief. "Any fairies about?"

"Two."

She peered overhead, searching. "If only."

"Someday," I told her.

A while back, I'd asked Fiona if she could sprinkle fairy dust on Yvanna to help her see a fairy, but Fiona had made a face. "You know that's not how it works," she'd said. "Yvanna has to dream and believe."

Yvanna didn't have much time to dream. She'd lost her

parents at the age of twelve, and now she had a family of six to feed—two elderly cousins, her grandparents, her younger sister, and herself.

"Set the cookies on that table, Yvanna." I pointed to the wrought-iron one closest to the fountain. I'd put out fairy-themed paper plates and napkins. "Joss, is there lemonade in the refrigerator?"

"Yep. I added my special ingredients."

Those ingredients included a few squeezes of orange juice and lime juice as well as a pinch of salt. Adults would enjoy it; I wasn't sure about the kids.

"Do we have some for the children?" I asked.

"Of course. This isn't my first rodeo." Joss mimed twirling a rope overhead.

I laughed. "Yvanna, could you spare a few more minutes, or do you have to rush back to Sweet Treats?"

"I can stay."

"Great. Would you pour a dozen glasses of adult lemonade plus a dozen of the kids' version and bring them out?" Our modest kitchen beyond the office, which I'd decorated in neutral tones to make it seem larger, had a double oven, a microwave, a refrigerator, four bakers' racks, and enough granite counter space to set out preparations.

"Sure."

As Yvanna disappeared, I surveyed the patio seating. For our monthly book club teas, we usually set an acrylic lectern at the far end of the patio and the moderator—often Lissa Reade—would stand behind it. For our children's event, I decided to make it cozier. I moved chairs into semicircles facing one chair, where I would sit.

Throughout the setup, even though I knew Meaghan wouldn't contact me until at least eleven, I checked my cell phone. If she needed to chat to keep her anxiety in check, I wanted to be there for her. Before going to bed last night, I'd texted her and suggested she put in her earbuds and listen to harp music. *As if,* she'd replied.

At ten o'clock, we opened the Dutch door and a stream of children accompanied by adults entered the shop. The adults warned the children not to touch anything on the tables in the main showroom, but a few couldn't help themselves, especially when they spotted wind chimes. One girl with pigtails batted a set. The resulting *cling-cling-cling* made the children giggle. The sound was infectious and made me think of Wanda, back in July, at Meaghan's birthday party. She'd *not so subtly* asked Meaghan when she was going to have a child. Meaghan had sneered at the notion. I didn't think she was averse to becoming a mother, but her current boyfriend was not good father material, she'd confided.

Thinking of him made me reflect on Elton Lamar again. He had been married before. He had two grown daughters. Maybe the brunette Holly had seen him with was one of his girls. Yes, that made sense. The girls didn't reside in Carmel, but one lived in San Jose, a stone's throw away.

"Let's get started," I said as the children and adults made their way to the patio and found seats.

Fiona had asked Merryweather to join in the fun. The two of them were flying around the patio, glittery rainbows of color following them as they inspected the children. Those who could see them waved *hello.* Merryweather knew many of the children by name, probably because they were regulars at the library. None of the adults appeared to see them.

When I took my seat, Fiona and her mentor flew into the ficus trees and disappeared. I'd overheard Miss Reade—Lissa—remind them that the children needed to concentrate.

For twenty minutes, I read animatedly from *Fairy Mom and Me,* doing my best to capture the different characters' voices. The children sat attentively. Some crept off their chairs and settled onto the floor, sitting cross-legged, their elbows propped on their knees, chins perched on interwoven fingers.

"And now . . ." I said as I closed the book after the first chapter, "who can tell me what the name of the protagonist is?"

"The what?" a freckle-faced girl asked.

"The main character."

"Ella!" All the children shouted.

"And what is her fairy mother's wand?"

"A cell phone."

I stole a glance at mine. Still no message from Meaghan.

"Last question. Do you believe in fairies?"

To a child, they shouted, "Yes!" Even a few adults cried, "Yes!" A chorus of "Thank yous" resounded and the children bounded to their feet, eager to shop for the fairy figurine I'd promised each of them.

While Lissa Reade chatted with the adults, I moved into the office and phoned Meaghan. She answered instantly.

"Any news?" I asked.

"Yes! Mom is out on bail."

"And you didn't think to text me?"

"We just heard. I was—"

"That's wonderful," I said, cutting her off. "Congratulations."

"One thing." Her gleeful voice turned cautious. "She'll have to wear an ankle bracelet."

"What? Why? She's not a flight risk."

"The judge said it's because Mom could be a danger to herself. It's the main reason the court is letting her out on bail." Meaghan sighed. "As I'd presumed, the jail system can't keep a constant eye on her with her affliction."

Sleepwalking. I nodded.

"She'll be able to move within a five-mile radius," Meaghan added. "That seems restrictive, but it should allow her to go from my house to the grocery store and to Sport Zone with no problem."

"She's staying with you? What about your . . ." I hesitated.

"Boyfriend? I've asked him to move out until this is resolved. He said he gets it." Meaghan went silent. I imagined her twirling a ringlet of hair around her finger, a habit she did whenever she was preoccupied. Then she ended the call.

After the children and adults had finalized their purchases and they'd filed out of the shop, only a few regular customers remained to browse, so I took a moment to sit on the patio and listen to the babble of the fountain. Pixie leaped into my lap. I petted her head and kissed her ears. She peered up at me with her gorgeous eyes and purred.

"Yes, my sweet, I'm taking a breather. You can stay."

She meowed. Was she asking about Meaghan, whom she adored? Had she sensed there was trouble in paradise? I assured her that Meaghan was fine and her mother was going to be released from jail.

Needless to say, the niggling concern that I needed to prove Wanda was innocent roiled inside my mind. Was Detective Summers looking at anyone else? Elton Lamar? Tamara Geoffries? Had my message to him about Kenny Chu fallen on deaf ears? Were there other suspects I hadn't considered, like Didi, who hadn't liked Lana and had wanted her barred from competing at pickleball? How lame would that motive be?

Looking at it from a different angle, who hated Wanda so much that he or she would frame Wanda for the murder, a sentence that would send her away for life?

Joss joined me at the table and pulled a second chair close. She kicked off her clogs and propped her feet on the chair's seat. "I'm roasting." She wagged the hem of her T-shirt to create a draft of air. "By the way, I've been meaning to tell you all morning that I walked past the Lamars' house earlier. Lots of people were roaming the street, staring at the property."

Morbid curiosity in a murder victim and the family was to be expected by the public. Even so, the notion turned my stomach.

"There were a lot of wreaths and bouquets propped against the fence," Joss said. "If I didn't know about Lana's bombastic reputation at Sport Zone, I'd have thought, by the display, that everyone had loved her."

"There were a lot of men at the athletic club who enjoyed playing pickleball with her."

"I doubt they're the ones who left bouquets. Also . . ." Joss glanced over her shoulder. No one was standing at the register. She refocused on me. "Elton came out of the house at just that moment and started shooing people away. He looked, in a word, miserable. Dark circles under his eyes. Rumpled shirt. And then, out of nowhere, that reporter Ulani Kamaka appeared," Joss said. "She begged Elton for an exclusive. I hate to say it, but she grates on me."

"It's because she's dogged. She wants a bigger career."

"By bullying people?"

"By being tenacious."

Thinking of Ulani made me wonder whether she'd dredged up any leads on Tish's daughter's whereabouts.

"Elton wanted nothing to do with her," Joss went on. "He called her all sorts of names and ordered her to leave."

Not cool, dude, I thought. At least I had been polite the first time I'd shunned Ulani.

"He was quite erratic," Joss added. "Almost unhinged."

"It's been a rough few days for him. If he really loved his wife, he might be grieving."

Joss snorted. "If."

Chapter 17

Garden fairies come at dawn, bless the flowers,
and then they're gone.
—Anonymous

Joss rose from her chair, righted the one on which she'd propped her feet, and said, "By the way, Renee Rodriguez phoned. She has those pots you ordered."

"Terrific. I'll pick them up."

Renee Rodriguez, the former police officer and better half of Dylan Summers, if I did say so myself, owned Seize the Clay, which was situated in the Village Shops across the street. The pottery shop supplied all the eight-inch hand-thrown pots we carried. Some were glazed; some were natural; all were unique. Renee had been making pottery since she was a girl and had always deemed it a hobby until she realized she wanted to leave law enforcement. She had staffed the place with eager employees, and within a week of opening, business had soared.

Before heading to Seize the Clay, I sent Ulani Kamaka a quick text asking whether she'd learned anything new about

Tish's daughter. She wrote back immediately; she was *working the case*. I hoped Fiona was right and Ulani did possess good detecting skills. I didn't press the reporter about confronting Elton Lamar. I didn't want to divert her focus.

Speaking of focus, where had my sweet fairy gone? I scanned the patio for her but didn't see her. I asked Pixie where Fiona might be. My Ragdoll meowed as if wondering herself, and then hopped onto a chair, curled into a ball, and fell fast asleep.

So much for feline curiosity.

I decided Fiona must have gone out for a fly-around with Merryweather. A fly-around, she'd explained a few weeks ago, cleared her mind. Sometimes she and her mentor rode fairy horses, which could zoom. Occasionally, Fiona went off by herself and flitted from tree to flower, drinking in the beauty of nature. I tried not to worry whenever she disappeared. She was growing more responsible by the day. I was pretty certain the queen fairy would be pleased with her progress.

"See you in a few!" I yelled to Joss as I left the shop and crossed Lincoln Street.

Similar to Cypress and Ivy Courtyard, the Village Shops were tiered and a staircase wound through the center. Unlike our courtyard, there were a lot more units; three of them boasted two stories. An attorney, a dentist, and a hot yoga studio occupied the upper floors.

Seize the Clay, which stood to the left of Hideaway Café, beyond the art gallery, and faced 7th Street, sported a new A-frame sign on the sidewalk. The sign noted all the events the shop provided: pottery classes, kids' camps, baby imprints, hand-building—which turned out to be sculpture—and private parties.

As I entered, I took in the white walls and white shelving as well as the aroma of wet clay and the scent of artwork fresh from the kiln, and I instantly felt the calm Renee promised to all customers who ventured inside. Soon, I'd have to succumb and throw a pot. As creative as I was, making pottery did not come naturally to me. Painting premade pots was a cinch—I did have an eye for color—but when it came to forming clay, I had heavy thumbs, a college instructor had told me, meaning I hadn't been able to maintain a steady balance between my fingers and thumbs so the pottery would develop evenly. To make matters worse, I hadn't been able to center the clay on the wheel, either.

Two of Renee's assistants, both female, were showing customers around the store. The variety of goods was astonishing: plates, platters, cat and dog bowls—huge sellers in Carmel—utensil crocks, Christmas ornaments, and more.

A thin woman in an abstract floral shift dress was checking out the miniature vases. She turned in profile as she picked up an aqua-and-brown one, and I realized it was Tish Waterman. Had I, having wondered about Ulani Kamaka's progress, conjured Tish's presence?

Renee, who was dressed in leggings and a white smock that hid her athletic figure, was at the register chatting with a man in a fedora. She seemed in her element, her gaze warm and intent, her dark hair cascading in loose curls.

Since she was occupied, I strode to Tish. "Taking a few minutes for yourself?" I asked.

She offered a weary smile. "I'm in a bit of a daze."

"Have you received some news?"

"No. I'm afraid the detective is, well . . ." She set the vase down. "There's no other way to put it. The man is an extortionist."

"How so?"

"He said he has another lead, but he wants five thousand dollars to pursue it. I've already paid him ten."

I gulped. Was that what detectives earned to track down a

missing person, or had Tish been snookered? More than ever, I wanted Ulani to make good on her promise.

"Tish," I said, trying to find the right words, "I'm sure there are more moderately priced detectives who might be able to help."

"He came highly recommended."

"By?"

"Of all people, Lana Lamar."

Why on earth would Lana have needed a detective? I set that question aside and brushed Tish's arm. Dare I offer her false hope?

"Hold off paying him," I said. "I've put some feelers out, as have our fairies. Let's allow them to . . ." I refrained from saying *do their magic*. I wasn't sure this time that magic would work. "To investigate. In a week or two, if we haven't resolved anything, you can reach out to the detective again."

"Okay." She sighed. "I've been wondering about the postcard. Do you think it could have been a fake?"

"You said it was her signature. She didn't ask you for anything. She didn't beg you for money." I thought of all the bogus financial schemes I'd received over the years via email. "So let's assume it's real. She's okay. She's alive. And you'll see her soon."

Tish threw her arms around me and squeezed hard. A boa constrictor or even Joss, who gave mighty hugs, couldn't have done a better job. "Thank you, Courtney. Thank you."

Without buying anything, Tish hurried out of the shop.

I ambled toward Renee, who was finishing up with the man in the fedora and handing him change.

"Are you sure?" she asked the man.

"You set aside time for me. I'm the one canceling. I really don't have it in me today to . . . create. But you deserve to be paid." The man pocketed the change and turned. I hadn't recognized him because of the hat. Elton Lamar, looking as beleaguered as Joss had intimated, slogged out of the shop without making eye contact with me.

Renee caught me staring after him. "He's pretty low."

"Losing a spouse to murder can't be easy."

"Losing anyone to murder isn't." Renee closed the register and skirted the counter, drawing near. "Dylan told me you were at the Spectacular. You were the one to find the body."

I nodded.

"Dylan said you're adamant that Wanda Brownie is innocent."

"She has to be. I feel it in my gut."

Renee was kind enough not to chastise me for having gut feelings. I knew the police, like Sherlock Holmes, judged the evidence, not feelings.

I glanced at the exit and questioned whether Elton, a guy who took pottery classes, would smash a fairy garden pot *deliberately*, given that Fiona thought the crime scene had been staged. On the other hand, my fairy could have been wrong and the pot had been destroyed during a set-to between Lana and the killer. On the *other* other hand, Lana hadn't appeared to have been in a fight. Yes, there had been dirt on her hands, but no visible scratches and no torn clothing, other than where the letter opener jutted from her chest. I stood by my theory that the killer had knocked Lana out with the bidding gavel in a surprise attack and, after she was incapacitated, had stabbed her.

"Yoo-hoo, Courtney." Renee waved her hand. "Where did you go?"

"Nowhere. I'm here. Hey, what's that on your finger?"

Renee flourished her hand to show off the floating halo diamond engagement ring. "Nice, huh?"

"I'm glad he found the courage."

Dylan Summers was a widower. His wife had died in a car accident a week after they said *I do*. I'd hoped he'd take the next step with Renee. Despite the fact that he and I butted heads occasionally, I respected him. He was a decent man who deserved a good life partner.

"He's lucky," I added.

"I'm the lucky one." Renee's cheeks tinged pink.

"I heard you have a few pots for me to pick up."

"Let me show you. If you don't like them, you don't have to purchase them."

As Renee retreated through a white curtain into the room where the kiln fired up and classes were held, I scanned the signs she'd posted on the wall behind the register. One with an image of Michelangelo's Sistine Chapel God, made me chuckle: *And the potter said to the clay, "Be ware," and it was.*

When I'd first met Renee, I'd thought she was stiff and aloof, a real hard-liner. Boy, had I misjudged her.

In less than a minute, she returned carrying a sturdy white bag with looped handles. She set it on the oblong table filled with other items ready for pickup and pulled out two pots that were encased in Bubble Wrap. Using a razor, she sliced the tape holding the wrap in place and unfurled it.

For this round of pots, I'd requested that Renee make them whimsical. She could come up with whatever theme she liked. To my surprise, she had painted a flower fairy on each, not exactly like the Cicely Mary Barker fairies, created during the first half of the twentieth century, but flower fairies just the same, each nestled within a woodland setting, the color of their wings matching the flowers they held.

"Adorable. Sold. Man, Renee, you're really talented."

"Thank you. That means a lot. I've been practicing painting them because . . ." She lowered her voice. "Don't tell Dylan, but I'd really like to see a fairy someday. I think painting them on pots for your store might be the inspiration that will open my eyes."

I gaped at her. For real? She actually accepted that there might be a fairy world? "Um, hasn't Dylan seen your work?"

"Some of it. Most of it. But not these." She frowned and glanced toward the exit, as if flummoxed by something.

"What's wrong?"

"I was thinking of Elton. Pottery has been a creative outlet for him. Lana—" Renee rubbed the back of her neck. "Unlike Dylan, who has been extremely supportive of my new career, Lana trashed every endeavor Elton made."

"Was his pottery awful?"

"That's the thing. No. He's quite good. He has a great aptitude for simplicity. His designs are elegant. I think Lana was jealous that he had talent."

"Why would she care? She excelled at pickleball."

Renee said, "I'm not sure Lana wanted anyone in her sphere to succeed at anything."

Chapter 18

Fairy roses, fairy rings, turn out sometimes troublesome things.
—William Makepeace Thackeray, *The Rose and the Ring*

I returned to Open Your Imagination wondering about Elton Lamar. Had Lana's dismissal of him sent him into the arms of another woman? Had her indifference also persuaded him to kill her to put an end to her ceaseless negativity? As I worked through the theory, I set the new pots I'd purchased with our other assortment on the patio.

Immediately a customer took one. "Isn't this lovely!" she gushed. She trotted off to show a friend.

"I like the pots, too." Fiona landed on my shoulder and bit back a yawn. "Where did you get them?"

"Seize the Clay."

"Really?"

I nodded. "Renee is dying to see a fairy. Do you think you could . . ." I hesitated. "No, I know you can't, but I do think she's receptive."

Fiona blew a raspberry. "Can you imagine her trying to explain a sighting to the detective?"

The potential chat made me chuckle, too. "What have you been up to? Where did you go? On a fly-around?"

Fiona winked. "Mine to know."

Fairies loved protecting secrets. On the other hand, I wanted her to toe the line. "Would the queen fairy approve of your activity?" I asked.

"Yes."

"Good."

As my father would say, quoting Ernest Hemingway, "The best way to find out if you can trust somebody is to trust them."

"By the way, I saw Tish Waterman when I was out," I said. "The detective she hired to find her daughter isn't working out. Have you checked in with Zephyr lately?"

"Funny you should ask. That is exactly where I was." She planted her fists on her hips looking smug. "Did you see me with her?"

"Nope. Just a good guess."

"Well, it turns out Zephyr contacted an intuitive fairy who has a network of fairies in Colorado."

"A network?" I was learning something new every day. I supposed the vast number of fairies in Carmel could be considered a network. "How can a fairy communicate with a network?"

"We have our ways."

"Aha! You do have ESP. I knew it!"

"As if." She snickered.

"What then? Fairy Pony Express? Fairy Western Union?" Curiosity blossomed within me. "Can fairies use a cell phone?"

"*Pfft.*" She did a pirouette midair.

"Fine. Suit yourself. Don't clue me in," I groused. I would find out. Sooner, rather than later.

Hovering in front of me, she said, "Don't you want to know what Zephyr found out?"

"Yes, of course."

"Tish's daughter—"

"Twyla."

"Was in Aspen. She was living with the Children of the Three Divines."

"What is it? A cult?" I'd never heard of it, but that didn't mean anything. There were thousands of cults around the world; some were political, religious, therapy based, or otherwise. "Do you know what the followers believe?"

"Three humans convinced the flock they were divinity in the flesh."

I moaned.

"However, Twyla left the cult about a month ago," Fiona said.

"Don't cults force people to stay?"

Twyla had reached out to her mother via postcard. Had she escaped? Was she on the run and scared out of her mind? Had the cult leaders allowed her defection?

"Where is she now?" I asked.

"That's just it. We don't know."

"Okay, keep on it, and remember to ask Ulani Kamaka to help you."

"She can't see or hear us," Fiona said.

"I forgot." Ulani had instigated her investigation based on my say-so. *Hmm.* "Can you leave her notes? Or tell me what you need her to do, and I'll touch base."

"I like that idea." Fiona paced in the air while stroking her narrow chin. "First and foremost"—she came to a halt, her wings working overtime—"Ulani needs to find out whether other cult members have left the fold."

I fetched my cell phone and tapped in a message to Ulani. She didn't respond instantly. "Anything else?"

"Yes. If they have left, where did they go? To another cult? To any one place in particular? Did they go home?"

"I'll let you know what she says."

Fiona curtsied her thanks.

Joss stepped onto the patio. "Boss, you have a visitor."

I peered through the glass windows into the main show-room and saw Meaghan, dressed in a short-sleeved, embroidered dress. She was inspecting teacups.

"I'll be right back," I said to Fiona, and rushed inside. Just short of Meaghan I paused. Her hair was lackluster, and her eyes were brimming with tears. Cautiously, I approached and rubbed her shoulder. "How are you?"

"As best as I can be. For now."

"And your mom? Is she settled in?"

"She's shuffling around. Trying not to sleep."

"Why doesn't she want to sleep?"

"She's afraid that she'll . . ." Meaghan picked up a Royal Albert Old Country Rose pattern teacup—one of my favorite designs, with red and yellow roses gracing the white porcelain—and turned it left and right.

"She's afraid that she'll *what?*" I asked.

Meaghan's lower lip quivered.

"Kill someone?" I said, finishing the thought. "That's ridiculous."

"Try telling her that." My pal set the teacup down with a *clack*. "Sorry. It's delicate. I didn't mean to—"

"It's okay. They don't break easily. Just like you, me, and your mom." I twisted the handle so it faced right, like all the others on the shelf. "Maybe she should see a therapist."

"I suggested that. I even mentioned Tamara Geoffries, though she's probably too exclusive."

Hearing Tamara's name jolted me. "Has your mom ever consulted Tamara before? Is it possible Tamara knew about your mother's sleepwalking?" I'd wondered whether Tamara might treat her patients with hypnosis. She'd known the effects of somnambulism. Had she staged the crime scene and hypnotized Wanda to say, on cue, *What have I done?*

"No," Meaghan said. "Mom has never seen a therapist. And though she can be a bit of an over-sharer in some ways, I doubt she's told many about the sleepwalking except her doctor and me and a few friends. Why?"

"I was wondering whether she might have confided in Kenny Chu since he was her trainer."

"Nah."

"How about her clients? Or any of the volunteer workers with whom she associates?"

Meaghan's forehead creased. "Wow, when you put it like that, the list of possibilities multiplies." She exhaled softly. "Are you suggesting that someone at the party who knew she'd gone to take a nap set her up to take the fall?"

"It does seem like a stretch, the timing of it all. How would the killer have lured Lana to the bidding room at the exact moment your mother awakened? That's what I can't figure out. Detective Summers didn't see a text message exchange on Lana's cell phone. Did Lana and the killer prearrange a meeting? If that's what had happened, it had to have been someone Lana had trusted."

"Or someone Lana had hated and had wanted to confront. She was on the warpath earlier. Remember how she'd argued with her husband and Kenny? She hadn't pulled any punches." Meaghan fiddled with a lock of her hair. "Plus, everyone in town knew Lana had a set-to with my mother outside Flair Gallery." Meaghan moaned. "All the killer needs is an alibi and my mother will go down for this."

"A verifiable alibi," I reminded her. "Let's talk about this on the patio." I clasped her elbow and drew her through the French doors. Over my shoulder I said to Joss, "Would you mind bringing some chamomile tea to us?"

Joss gave me the *okay* sign. She was ringing up a customer.

I settled Meaghan into a chair by the fountain, hoping the burble of the water might calm her, and then I took a seat. I propped my elbows on the table and reached for my pal's hands, but she drew into herself.

Fiona flew to Meaghan and studied her face. "She needs more than tea."

"Like what?" I asked.

"A potion."

"Who are you talking to?" Meaghan's eyes widened. "Is Fiona here?"

I nodded. "What kind of potion?"

"I have just the thing." Fiona darted into her favorite ficus tree and returned in seconds. She sprinkled something that looked like crushed lavender over Meaghan's head. Meaghan felt it because she reached up to touch it. Then Fiona pulled a teensy jar filled with silvery glitter from the pocket of her dress. She popped the top and whizzed in a circle above Meaghan, but I didn't see anything spill out.

"What is that?" I asked.

"A good wish," Fiona replied. "Meaghan needs to inhale." She drew in a deep breath to demonstrate.

Meaghan inhaled without my coaching.

I squeezed her wrist. "Fiona is blessing you with a good wish."

"Like a genie?" Meaghan asked.

"Like a fairy," Fiona said. "Now she has to close her eyes and count to ten."

"And then what?" I prompted.

Fiona spread her arms. "She makes the wish, but she can't tell anyone what she wishes for."

I relayed the command to my friend. "It's like blowing out birthday candles."

"How soon will it come true?" Meaghan intoned as if in a trance.

"Wishes take time," Fiona said. "But if possible, and they're not for monetary gain, they will come to pass."

Meaghan slumped and muttered, "*If possible*. I heard that."

Joss arrived with a tray set with a teapot, two teacups and saucers, and a plate of biscuits. "These are lemon thyme biscuits. Yvanna brought them in a few minutes ago. I had one. Superflaky." She gestured to a small ramekin filled with clarified butter. "If you add a dab of this, they're perfection. The lemon will be good—"

"For my soul." Meaghan folded her arms on the table, shoulders hunched. "Got it."

Lemon was a natural healer and cleared toxic substances from the body. Would it do the same for toxic energy? Meaghan was all about keeping her chakras clear, but the negativity oozing out of her had to be prohibitive.

Fiona circled Meaghan like a doting nurse. "Have her make a fairy garden. If she does, I think she'll see me. She's on the verge. There's an aura around her."

"Meaghan"—I laid my hand on her arm; she didn't recoil—"let's make a garden. Together. For your mother."

"The tea will get cold."

"I'll make us new cups when we're done. C'mon. Your mom needs it. We'll focus on a theme of lightness and air. Something freeing and positive."

We moved to the learning-the-craft area, and I selected one of Renee's pots, a white one with an ethereal blue fairy painted on it. If I didn't know better, I'd swear Fiona had posed for it—shimmering blue hair, silver tutu and silver shoes, green wings.

"How about this one?" I asked.

"Sure." Meaghan sounded so defeated my heart ached.

"Let's pick out two fairy figurines for the garden. We want them to have a conversation."

"Between the judge and the accused?"

Fiona kicked the back of Meaghan's head.

Meaghan flinched. "What was that?"

Fiona flew closer to me, hand over her mouth, shoulders shaking with delight.

Meaghan squinted. "Fiona, are you laughing?" In a hushed voice she said, "Is that . . . is she . . . blue?" She reached out with a hand.

Fiona whooshed upward and, like an imp, braced her thumbs against her cheeks. She wagged a *nyah-nyah* sign at Meaghan. If only I could have photographed Meaghan's reaction. She was amazed, delighted, and scared all at the same time.

Retaliating, Meaghan mimicked the *nyah-nyah* sign.

Fiona did a happy dance midair. "Yes, yes, yes! She can see me. There's hope." She clapped her hands. "Now chop-chop. Make a garden for your mother, Meaghan. Wanda needs to feel loved and protected. Start with this fairy." Fiona flew to the figurines and hovered above a blond girl fairy in a blue dress who was sleeping peacefully.

"Won't she think we're making fun?" Meaghan asked. "I mean, the girl is *sleeping*."

"We're not done," Fiona said. "Courtney, where's that fairy godmother you purchased?"

I knew exactly which one she meant. I'd bought some specialty Lenox and Lladró items on eBay a few months ago. They weren't designed for typical fairy gardens. They were art pieces, but for this garden, the Lenox one might work. A fairy godmother, given her magical essence, could be larger than everything else.

I went to the office where I kept them under lock and key and returned holding a lithe fairy godmother dressed in a gorgeous pink gown and flowing blue cape. On her head she wore an ornate gold crown. In her hand she carried a gold wand.

"Meaghan, here's the story," I said. "The girl's fairy godmother will wake her from her sleep and break the spell. She will be free."

Meaghan said, "The fairy godmother doesn't have wings."

I chuckled. "Not all artistic representations of fairies have wings. This one is all about the fairy godmother's spirit. Her power."

"Her love," Fiona whispered.

Chapter 19

Fairies love the sound of bells.
—Anonymous

For an hour, Meaghan and I constructed the fairy garden for her mother, adding a reflecting pool of water, solar lamps on shepherd's hooks, and a variety of miniature ferns. By the end, Meaghan's mood was riding high and she was eager to return to her house to bolster her mother's flagging spirit.

With the sun high in the sky—Joss was more than happy to tend the store alone—we headed to Meaghan's house. Fiona didn't accompany us. Believing her duty to Meaghan was complete, she opted to seek out Merryweather. She wanted to give her an update about Zephyr's networking buddies.

Meaghan's charming Craftsman was located four blocks from the beach and decorated in Laguna stacked stone.

As we walked along the slate path toward the front door, I drank in the beauty of the garden, which had been planted with daylilies. Nearing the porch, I noticed a sparkle to my right. A fairy with green hair and wings and dressed in an iridescent green frock was tending to the flowers. If nonbelievers were to encounter her, they might mistake her for a firefly or a cricket.

Realizing I could see her, the fairy waved. I crooked one finger in greeting.

"Do you see her?" I asked Meaghan.

"See who?" Meaghan asked. "Mom is inside. In the kitchen."

"The fairy in your garden."

"Where?" She spun around.

Before Meaghan caught sight of her, the fairy flew away.

So the imp was going to play hide-and-seek.

I giggled. "Sorry. She's already gone."

"You're toying with me."

"Nope. Now that you can see Fiona, you'll see others. Keep your eyes peeled. She's green. I think she's a guardian fairy."

"What's a—" Meaghan flapped a hand. "Never mind. We don't have time for that right now." Balancing the fairy garden we'd created on one hip, she opened the door. "Mom, I'm home."

I followed her inside and drew to a halt. My father and Detective Summers were sitting on the living room sofa and chatting easily. It didn't surprise me that they were talking—they had met after my father left the force and occasionally played golf—but it did surprise me that they were there. At the same time. Why? Summers was dressed in his usual attire—white shirt and chinos. My father was wearing a polo shirt and trousers. Beside him on the sofa lay a summer bouquet of Gerbera daisies, roses, and baby's breath enfolded in green plastic wrap—understated but lovely.

"What are you doing here, Detective?" Meaghan asked, giving voice to my question. Anxiety riddled her tone.

"Visiting," Summers said.

"Oh." What else could she say? She set the fairy garden on the entry table. "Mom!"

"I'm right here, sweetheart." Wanda entered from the hall looking composed and not put out at having been caught in aqua-blue silk pajamas. She carried a tray set with a pitcher of tea, two tall glasses filled with ice, sugar cubes, cocktail napkins, and coasters.

"Courtney and I made this for you, Mom. It's—" Meaghan gestured to the garden but didn't explain the significance of it. I was glad she didn't. Now was not the time.

"How lovely. Thank you." Wanda set the tray on the coffee table. "Kip and Dylan came to keep me company."

"Keep you company?" I said, slightly stunned that she'd referred to the detective by his first name.

"That's right, Courtney." Wanda motioned at one of the Queen Anne side chairs. "Sit, girls."

I did; Meaghan didn't.

The interior of the home boasted old-world charm, with hand-laid walnut floors, intricate handmade Italian tiles, and vaulted ceilings. The blue-and-white décor was calming. Statues and artwork from a few of the Carmel-specific artists Meaghan displayed in her gallery decorated the walls and shelves.

Wanda gestured to the drinks. "Dylan, Kip, help yourselves."

"Thank you, Wanda," my father said.

"Tea, Courtney?" Wanda asked me. "I'll get more glasses."

"No, thanks." Beneath the hem of Wanda's pajamas I caught a glimmer of the ankle monitor, and my heart sank. The detective had not come to remove it.

"I think you realize by now that your father and I are dating, Courtney," Wanda said, taking a seat in the other side chair. She reached to the sofa and took hold of my father's hand. He caressed her thumb with his.

Seeing them together rattled me, but it also made me smile. I couldn't remember the last time I'd witnessed my father fussing over someone. Well, I could. Over my mother. Twenty years ago. He deserved to be loved. Maybe this relationship would help him stop worrying about me all the time. Except Wanda was under house arrest. Would she go to jail for good?

"Detective Summers," I said, "you're not here for a social visit, are you?"

"Actually, I am." He grinned.

"Dylan and I are old friends," Wanda said.

"You're what?" Meaghan screeched, and quickly apologized. "But you're—"

"We went to college together. Small world, isn't it?" Wanda said. "Dylan was into sports. I was into the arts."

Summers nodded. "I always appreciated your sense of style, Wanda. Even back then, you wore the most colorful clothes. And, man, could you paint. I remember attending an art show to benefit the—"

"Wait. What? . . ." Meaghan sputtered, cutting him off. "Mother, you don't paint."

Wanda's cheeks tinged pink. "I did, once upon a time."

Summers crossed his legs and rested an arm on the armrest. "Yeah, about that. I was expecting to see your work in one of our fine art galleries. Why isn't it? Did you hang up your paintbrush?"

Wanda winced. "Yes. Years ago. Before Meaghan was born. I realized there were so many artists who were better than I. Given my personality, I knew I would be a much better advocate for artists as a representative. I had dreams, but I didn't have the talent."

Meaghan said, "Did you keep any of your work?"

Wanda flapped a hand. "I might have a piece or two."

"I want to see it."

"I don't want you to bother."

Meaghan frowned. "It's not a bother getting to know my own mother."

"What did you paint, Wanda?" my father asked.

"Mostly seascapes."

I fingered the locket hanging around my neck. Was my father thinking of my mother right now? Would learning that Wanda had something in common with my mother throw a wrench into their budding relationship? I'd heard that a person, after losing a loved one, often searched for a mate with similar traits, which wasn't always the best thing because then comparisons would be made, whether the person intended to or not. My nana had encouraged my father to find someone different. He'd shunned looking at all.

"I'd like to see your artwork," my father said, and gave Wanda's hand a squeeze.

Wanda blushed. "Meaghan, why don't you fetch some of those mint chocolate brownies I made yesterday? There's also a bowl of fruit in the refrigerator." She was pretending to be the perfect hostess, but I could tell that a sea of worry was roiling beneath her calm exterior. Her eyes were slightly glassy. Her lips were twitching ever so slightly.

Meaghan strode to the kitchen.

A silence fell over the room.

I cleared my throat. Since Summers was here and since he was sort of a captive audience, what better time to pose the few questions that were cycling through my mind?

"Detective," I began. I wouldn't dare call him Dylan, as Wanda had.

"What's up?" He poured a glass of tea, took a sip, and set the glass on a coaster.

"Did you get my message about Kenny Chu not going to the library during the Spectacular, like he said?"

"Are you hoping to discuss the case?" He raised an eye-brow.

"Yes, sir, I am, seeing as it affects my best friend's mother."

"I can hear you," Wanda said, sounding like me the other day.

Why did people think they could talk about others as if the others were on another planet?

"Yes, ma'am," I said. "I know."

Meaghan returned with another tray set with a platter of treats, small plates, forks, and a bowl of diced fruit. "The brownies look good, Mom." She made room on the coffee table for the second tray and sat in one of the royal-blue arm-chairs.

"Well?" I said to Summers, who was biting into a brownie.

"Well, what?" Meaghan eyed me and the detective.

Summers swallowed and set the rest of the brownie on a cocktail napkin. "I did get your message, Miss Kelly . . . Courtney . . . and we're following up."

"We?"

"I've asked Officer Reddick to do the honors."

"So you don't know why Kenny Chu lied?"

"Not yet, but I will. Soon."

I did my best not to grumble. The investigation into Lana Lamar's murder was not Summers's only case. "May I ask you something else?"

"Unless I leave, I doubt I can stop you."

My father stifled a laugh.

Summers cut him a sharp look. "Did you put her up to this, Kip?"

"Me? Heck, no. I wish she'd keep her nose out of things, but she's like her mother, curious to a fault. Plus, she wants to save the world."

"One friend at a time," I said.

"One friend at a time," my father echoed.

Even though Joss's warning about implicating myself resonated in my head, I said, "Detective, about the murder weapon—"

"The letter opener." He folded his muscular arms across his chest. "What about it?"

"I presume it had Wanda's fingerprints on it."

He nodded.

"Did you also find mine?" My fingerprints were on file because we were teaching children in some of our workshops. It was a federal requirement.

"There were no other prints."

"Ha! I knew it. I handled that letter opener multiple times while I made the fairy garden. My fingerprints had to be on it. Can we, therefore, conclude that the killer—the real killer— wiped the letter opener clean, making it possible for only Wanda's prints to be found?"

Summers worked his tongue inside his cheek.

"What about the hilt?" I asked. "I touched it, too, but I don't think Wanda did."

"It's scrolled and too hard to pick up a print."

"How about the bidding gavel, the one Wanda planned to use when announcing the winners for the auction?" I mimed using a gavel. "I saw it lying beneath one of the tables."

"Did your father teach you to study the crime scene?" Summers asked.

My father threw up both hands. "Again, I take no responsibility. She pays attention to detail. It comes from being a talented landscaper and an astute photographer."

Heart, be still. My father was paying me a compliment? Even when I'd worked for him, compliments had been few and far between. He didn't feel it necessary to pat his employees on the back—not even his daughter—for the work that he expected to be done properly.

"What about the gavel?" Summers asked.

"As you know, one of the fairy gardens I created for the event was destroyed. Either the killer and Lana struggled and knocked it over, or the killer demolished it with the gavel, hoping to create a sharp piece of pottery to use as a weapon."

"Good theory," my father said, and whacked Summers on the upper arm.

Summers leveled him with a look. "Or Wanda destroyed it while sleepwalking."

"Did you find dirt on her?" I asked. "No, you did not, but there was dirt on Lana's hands. Oh, and I just remembered"— I snapped my fingers—"there were wadded-up paper towels on the floor, too. Maybe the killer—" I halted. No, the paper towels were a nonissue. Fiona had examined them and said they were spotless.

"What about the paper towels?" Summers asked.

"Nothing."

Summers pulled his notebook from his pocket and jotted down something. "Anything else?"

Wanda was leaning forward in her chair, listening intently to the conversation. So was Meaghan. My father was working hard not to let the corners of his mouth turn up in a smile.

"Yes. I ran into Elton Lamar at Seize the Clay," I said. "He was scheduled for a pottery lesson, but he canceled. Renee, your fiancée—"

"You're engaged, Dylan?" my father said. "Congratulations."

"Thanks," Summers muttered, not taking his gaze off me.

"When are you getting married?" Wanda asked.

"We haven't set the date. Go on, Miss Kelly."

So much for calling me Courtney any longer.

I said, "Renee said that Elton has talent, but Lana didn't praise his work."

Summers frowned. "That's not enough reason to kill your wife. Renee doesn't like my sketches."

I said, "I didn't know you sketched."

"I'm a man of mystery."

My father guffawed. "It seems everyone in this room is."

"My point about Elton," I continued, "is that perhaps he wasn't in love with his wife any longer. She could be so critical. If their marriage was on the outs . . ."

"Miss Kelly."

"Let me finish. Holly Hopewell saw Elton with a beautiful brunette last week. Outside Carmel Bank. Holly didn't think they were an item; she didn't see any public displays of affection. But what if they were involved? What if Elton was seeing the woman on the sly?"

Summers rested his pen and notebook on his thigh. "Your theory is that Lana Lamar taunted her husband, thus forcing him into the arms of another woman, and when Elton asked Lana for a divorce, she refused, so he killed her?"

"Exactly. There is also a money angle."

Summers groaned. "Here we go. Do you have a list of suspects you want me to question? If you'd write down the names, that would help. If you had a badge, that would help even more."

My father chuckled.

Summers sipped his iced tea and set the glass down loudly. "Do you think I can't do my job, Miss Kelly?"

"No. That's not . . ." I sputtered. "I mean, yes, of course you can. You're great at it. All I meant—"

Suddenly, the green fairy I'd seen in the front garden glided into view. She settled onto Summers's right shoulder and began to nuzzle his neck, and then she started to hum the same lullaby Fiona had sung to me the other night. Was she trying to coax the detective into listening to my theories?

"Go on," Summers said, and folded his hands on his lap, oddly appeased. "Your list."

The green fairy sprang off Summers's shoulder, did a spiral in the air like Fiona was wont to do, and sped away.

Inspired by her puckish performance, I leaned forward and said, "Tamara Geoffries held Lana responsible for her husband Jamie's death. Lana was running in the fog at night, and Jamie didn't see her until the last possible moment. He careened off the road—"

"I know about Lana Lamar and Jamie Geoffries's incident." Summers opened his notebook again and started writing. "But didn't Mrs. Geoffrics arrive at the bidding room about the same time as you and Meaghan did?"

I nodded. "However, I don't know where she came from or from which direction. What if she killed Lana, rounded the building, and joined us to establish her alibi? Did you ask her to remove her coat? There was no reason she should have been wearing it."

"It was chilly."

"Not that chilly. Maybe Lana's blood was on her dress. And there was dirt on the hem of the coat. What if it was dirt from the broken fairy garden?"

Summers jotted another note.

"Tamara claims she was in the neighboring yard," I went on, "communing with cats, but that sounds pretty feeble to me. On the other hand, I like Tamara, and I don't want her to be guilty."

Meaghan groaned.

Realizing my last statement didn't help Wanda's cause, I said, "Back to Kenny Chu. I also meant to tell you that he was acting shady at the athletic club. I'd gone to work out Tuesday, and I caught him in the women's locker room."

Summers arched an eyebrow. "He was *in* the locker room?"

I nodded. "He was trying to open Lana Lamar's locker."

My father whistled.

"Are you sure about that?" Summers asked.

"Positive. He offered a lame excuse, alleging he was there to fetch Hattie Hopewell's pickleball paddle for her lesson, except he was in the wrong row."

Summers made a final notation and once again bundled up his pen and notebook. "Okay, thanks for the update."

"Wait, I almost forgot."

He rolled his eyes and snorted like a bull.

Did I dare press harder? Yes, I had to. "I noticed Elton was wearing a bandage on his finger after Lana died. I don't recall it being injured earlier. Did you get DNA from under Lana's fingernails? Is it possible she scratched him? Maybe—"

"That's it." Summers rose to his feet. "We're finished. *Finito. Finis.* You are not an investigator."

"But—"

"No. You're done with this case."

Little green fairy, come back, I wished silently. But she didn't.

Summers said, "Go back to your shop, Miss Kelly, and let me do what I do best. If and when you earn your private investigator's license or, better yet, you become a full-fledged cop, let me know."

"Dylan," Wanda said, her tone admonishing.

"Uh-uh. Look, Wanda, you and I are friends, and I want more than anything for you to be proven innocent, but I will not allow the general public to impede my investigation."

"I'm not impeding, Detective," I said.

Summers gave Wanda's shoulder a squeeze and strode out of the house.

As the door slammed, I huffed. At *myself*. If only I knew how to tread softly. I caught my father staring at me. His mouth was downturned.

Chapter 20

Fairies spark magic. Believe it to be so.
—Daryl Wood Gerber

"Telephone call for you, boss," Joss said from the doorway leading to the main showroom.

I apologized to the customer I was helping on the patio and hurried inside. "Who is it?"

"That reporter."

"I'll take it in the office." I strode down the hall with Pixie trailing me.

As I entered the office and rounded the desk, Fiona appeared, looking eager and excited. "Good things, good things, good things," she chanted.

"Where have you been?" I asked.

"Doing what I was allowed to do. Promise." She held up three fingers like a Girl Scout would and resumed her chant.

I settled into the desk chair. Lifting the telephone receiver, I pressed the flashing intercom button to connect. "Miss Kamaka, how are you?"

Pixie jumped into my lap and mewed. I stroked her head, and she curled into a ball.

"The better question is how are you?" Ulani asked. "I heard Wanda Brownie is still in jail."

"You heard wrong. Wanda is out, although she is wearing a monitor. She and her daughter are quite hopeful for a positive outcome."

Ulani *tsk*ed. "Oh, yeah, run with that. I've read *The Power of Positive Thinking*, too."

Something about the woman irritated me, but I worked against it by inhaling and exhaling rhythmically.

Fiona flitted to the edge of the Zen garden I'd set at the upper right of the desk. "Put her on speakerphone."

I obeyed and said to Ulani, "Why are you calling?"

"I have news about Tish Waterman's daughter."

Fiona pumped a fist.

"I was following an anonymous tip that I found on my notepad, of all places," Ulani went on.

I whispered to Fiona, "What did you do?"

She blew on her fingertips and polished them on the bodice of her dress. "My toes dipped in ink work wonders." She wiggled a foot. "Zephyr heard from an intuitive fairy in Colorado, one who had been living in the forest where the Children of the Three Divines dwelled. She suggested our human detective—Miss Kamaka—look into the finances of the oldest of the three gurus."

I said to Ulani, "Where did the tip take you?"

"One of the cult leaders owns five houses and eight strip malls in the Midwest. The guy really knows how to shelter his investments. Next, I contacted a few colleagues and asked them to check into the properties. A reporter for the *Omaha World-Herald* reached out to me. She, too, had received an anonymous tip, and discovered that one of the houses, which was located in Omaha, had been broken into. Twyla was squatting there."

I couldn't imagine what Twyla was feeling. Terror? Exhilaration? "How did she learn of the properties?" I asked.

"I don't know. Does it matter?"

I looked at Fiona. She grinned. A fairy in the fairy network must have provided the other tip. *Let's hear it for the fairy pipeline*, I mused, however they communicated.

"FYI," Ulani went on, "I have not met Twyla Waterman in person yet. I'm flying to Omaha tomorrow." She took a sip of something. "Thank you for trusting me with this story. It's going to be a great scoop. I haven't told my editor about it. First, I want to make sure that Twyla doesn't bolt."

"Good idea."

"If only I could thank the tipster."

"I'm sure she knows you appreciate the insider information."

After we ended the call, Fiona said, "I told you Miss Kamaka had good detecting skills."

"With a little help from you and your friends."

She twirled and did a curtsy. As she continued to celebrate, an idea occurred to me that might help solve Lana Lamar's murder.

"Speaking of detecting . . ." I murmured.

Fiona drifted midair, waiting for me to finish.

I picked up the telephone receiver and dialed A Peaceful Solution Spa. When a receptionist answered, I said, "Is Tish in? It's Courtney Kelly."

"You can't tell her," Fiona rasped. "She'll be upset. We don't have the complete story."

"Don't worry. I won't."

A minute later, Tish answered. "Hello, Courtney." She sounded cautious, as if she didn't want to get her hopes up. "Have you . . ."

"No. Not yet."

Fiona let out the breath she'd been holding, and Tish wheezed like a balloon losing air.

"Keep positive," I said quickly. Even though I wouldn't tell her about Ulani locating the daughter, in case, as Ulani had pointed out, Twyla bolted, I did want Tish to remain optimistic. "My team is on it. Promise."

Tish sighed. "I'm sorry about earlier. At the pottery shop. I shouldn't have burdened you with my problem."

"You didn't, but that is why I'm calling. The detective you hired. Would you mind sharing his name and telephone number?"

"He's very expensive."

"I don't need him to do any detecting. I want to pick his brain about his former client, Lana Lamar."

"What a good idea. He might know something that could help Wanda. She must be going stir-crazy in jail."

"She's out on bail."

"That's wonderful news. Give her my best. Now let's see." I heard Tish opening and closing drawers. "Ah, here it is. His card." She rattled off the investigator's contact information. Before ending the call, she said, "Please, if your team comes up with anything, even a thread of hope, I want to hear it."

A thread wasn't good enough. I wanted to provide Tish with a clear resolution.

After work, I agreed to meet Ned Needham, Tish's private investigator, at Schuster Wine Tasting, an intimate venue about two blocks from Open Your Imagination. He was on a case and couldn't break from his schedule. I left Pixie snoozing in the office and promised I would return in an hour.

Fiona had flown off yet again. To celebrate with Zephyr, I imagined. How I hoped the queen fairy really did approve of their association. If she didn't, would she whisk to Carmel and exile Fiona to another realm? I would be heartbroken if she did.

The wine-tasting venue was simple in design, with a white oak bar and matching shelving that held wineglasses and un-opened bottles of wine. Silver-framed posters of Carmel Val-ley and Schuster Vineyards adorned the walls. Plenty of sunlight shone through the plate glass windows. A chalkboard held a list of selections for the day, starting with white wines and descending to the reds.

Three guests were huddling at the far end of the bar, sniff-ing and swirling and chatting among themselves. Three more followed me inside and moved to the center of the bar. Need-ham was standing to the right, separate from everyone, a wineglass with a small pour of white wine in his hand. I'd ex-pected him to be a run-down sort of guy. I wasn't sure why. Perhaps I'd read too many noir mysteries. Needham, some-where in his forties, was anything but run-down. In fact, given the particular attention he'd paid to his appearance, I'd bet he dreamed of living in the Gay Nineties. His hair was dyed black; his beard and handlebar mustache were perfectly groomed; he wore a black shirt tucked into black trousers; and his black tie was knotted elegantly.

I introduced myself. He returned the favor in a warm, mellifluous voice.

"Buy you a glass, Courtney?" he asked.

A patron needed to purchase an empty glass in order to taste a flight of six different wines. "Sure. Thanks." I leaned closer. "Who are you observing?"

"The owner. She's not here, but she will be. She doesn't know, so let's keep that between us."

"Will do."

Needham took a sip of his wine and pointed to the de-scription of a sauvignon blanc on the printed tasting menu lying on the bar. "'Full of citrus and pineapple and quite refreshing,'" he recited.

The wine pourer, a slim woman with a ponytail and an easy smile, added a tasting amount of wine to a new glass and nudged it toward me. Like the venue, she was dressed in neutral colors, to blend in, I supposed. "The word *sauvignon* comes from the French word *sauvage,* meaning 'wild,'" she said. "This is un-oaked and high in acidity. The makers like to consider it wild because it also has flavors of gooseberry."

I took a sip and rolled it around on my tongue. It was tart but tasty.

"Do you like it?" she asked. "Only thirty-five dollars a bottle."

"It's nice," I said, not adding that thirty-five sounded steep. I set the glass down, leaned an elbow on the bar, and focused on Ned Needham.

"So why did you need to see me, Courtney? Got a boyfriend you want me to follow?" He nodded to my hand. "I don't see a ring on that finger." When he smiled, the tips of his handlebar mustache lifted.

I felt my cheeks warm. "No, this isn't about me. I heard you were helping Tish Waterman look for her daughter."

"Ah. Tish referred you. Sad case, that one. I thought I'd hit a dead end, but I might have a possible lead that would help revive the search."

For which he expected Tish to pay another five thousand dollars. Was he a con man or legit?

I said, "Lana Lamar referred you to Tish."

Needham polished off the sauvignon blanc and beckoned the wine pourer. "I'll try the pinot grigio," he said to her.

"Sure thing." As she poured, she said, "We make ours like the Italians. It's totally dry with brilliant acidity and a bitter almond note, not fruit forward."

As she moved away, Needham scanned the growing crowd

before returning my gaze. "If you see a squat sixty-year-old with long brown hair, square face, and piercing eyes, let me know. Without drawing attention."

"Will do. About Lana . . ."

"What a tragedy. I heard she was murdered." He tipped his wineglass and studied the legs of the wine. "I also heard the police have a suspect in custody."

"They do. A friend of mine."

"Sorry to hear that."

"She didn't do it."

"They all say that." Needham primped the ends of his mustache with his pinky finger.

"May I ask why Lana hired you?"

The PI raised his left eyebrow. "If I told you, I would be betraying a confidence."

"Even though she's dead?" I tilted my head. "C'mon, I'm sure the police will ask you questions, once they know you were in her employ."

"It was months ago. I doubt they'd think to question me, but if they do, because you'll probably tell them my name, I'll cross that bridge when I come to it."

I reached into my cross-body purse, removed a pre-set fifty-dollar bill, and placed it on the counter.

Needham eyed it and winked. "I'm cheap but not that cheap."

I placed another fifty on top of the first. "It can go to you or to the wine pourer."

He pocketed the money. "Lana wanted to know if a certain man was having affairs."

"Affairs, as in plural?"

"Yep."

"Was the man her husband?"

The corners of Needham's mouth twitched.

I placed another fifty on the bar. This little fishing expedition was getting expensive, but I'd come prepared. After hearing how much the man had charged Tish, I figured he wouldn't tell me anything for free.

"You're not just a pretty face," he said, and added the last fifty to the others in his pocket. "No, not her husband. A man named Kenny Chu."

I recalled the subtle way Lana had brushed Kenny's hand at the Spectacular. Had she been interested in Kenny? They must have seen each other often at Sport Zone. Had their relationship gone further than merely being two people who were avid about sports? According to Lissa Reade, Lana had given Kenny financial advice. Had she hoped to make Kenny a success so she could leave her husband for him, or had she simply been advising a friend? Had Elton believed Lana was in love with Kenny? At the party, after being chastised by Lana, Elton had suggested to Kenny that he, not Elton, go after her and calm her down. Kenny had demurred.

"Did Lana say why she wanted you to investigate him?" I asked Needham.

"She wanted to know if Mr. Chu was having affairs with women who belonged to the club where he worked."

"Where did you start your search?" I asked.

Needham motioned to the wine pourer to move on to the next tasting, a steel-barreled Chardonnay. I dumped the remnants of my sauvignon blanc into a V-shaped container on the counter, said I'd pass on the pinot grigio, and asked for the chardonnay.

As the young woman poured wine into our glasses, she said, "Fermenting in temperature-controlled stainless-steel tanks has the advantage of retaining more of the varietal character, making the fruit aromas of melon and citrus brighter than if this was fermented in an oak barrel. Enjoy."

"Thanks." Needham sniffed the wine in his glass and eyed me over the rim. "Where were we?"

"Lana paid you to follow Kenny Chu. Where did you start? Where did that lead you? To Sport Zone? To individual homes? To a hotel or inn?"

Needham drank the wine in one gulp and pushed the glass aside. "Yes."

"All of them?" I glowered at him. "How about a bit more bang for my buck?"

He waited.

Reluctantly, I pulled another fifty from my purse, but only because I felt this was a strong lead. I would draw the line at two hundred and fifty dollars. I loved Wanda, but I wasn't rolling in dough.

Needham added the bill to the others. "Kenny Chu wasn't having an affair with anyone."

"But you said you followed him to Sport Zone, houses, a hotel or inn."

"I followed him to one house—*his*—and to one hotel where he had a standing appointment for a massage. All on the up-and-up. I questioned the masseur afterward."

I pondered the answer. If Lana had been interested in Kenny and worried that she was one of his many paramours, Needham's investigation had to have calmed her fears. "Do you know if—"

"Gotta go." Needham hopped to his feet. "It's been real."

A squat woman with brown hair plowed from the venue's back room through patrons to the front door, her square face fixed with determination. Needham wasn't stealthy, but he was quick.

Chapter 21

*When I sound the fairy call, gather here in silent meeting,
chin to knee on the orchard wall, cooled with dew and
cherries eating.*
—Robert Graves, "Cherry-Time," *Fairies and Fusiliers*

I returned to the shop frustrated by my conversation with the detective. I was usually good at Q&As, having learned how to coerce a complete profile from a client when working for my father. If only Needham hadn't been on the clock.

Joss had locked up Open Your Imagination and had turned off most of the lights. I let myself in and trudged to the office, where I found Fiona doing a tap dance on the cat's back. Pixie, trying to get the upper hand, kept rolling over, each movement hurling Fiona into the air.

"Hey, you two," I said.

Like children caught in the act, they stopped and sat at attention.

"Where did you go?" Fiona asked.

"You first."

"To celebrate with Zephyr. Merryweather came along. She didn't consider it socializing."

I bit back a smile, glad Fiona was doing her best to obey the rules of her probation.

"And you?" she pressed.

I told her what I had learned from Needham, adding that his answers had provided a slim view into Lana Lamar's life. Had Lana fallen out of love with her husband? Had she fallen *in love* with Kenny? Or was there another reason she'd been looking into Kenny's private life?

"I have an idea," Fiona said. "Why don't we go to Sport Zone and talk to Didi Dubois? She might know what occurred between Lana and Kenny."

"Good idea." I lifted Pixie and peered into her adorable eyes. "I'm taking you to the house. You don't need to go to a sweaty old athletic club."

She purred her agreement.

At home, I ate a couple of slices of cheese and a handful of grapes to curb my appetite and then changed into a pair of blue jeans and an *I Love Carmel* T-shirt. Minutes later, I rode my bicycle to Sport Zone. Fiona, who couldn't fly as fast as I could ride, hitched onto my shoulder. The crisp night air felt wonderful on my face.

Sport Zone's parking lot was packed. I stowed my bicycle in one of the bike racks, attached the combination lock to the tires, and popped inside. The Beach Boys' "Wouldn't It Be Nice" was playing loudly through speakers in the workout room. Nearly all the machines were in use.

Pauline, the perky young woman at the front desk who also served as assistant manager, greeted me by name and scanned my membership card.

"Is Didi in?" I asked.

"She's here somewhere." Pauline glanced over her shoulder. "Over there. In her office."

At the far end of the workout room was a glass-partitioned

room. Didi was inside, pacing back and forth. Her mouth was moving. She held a book in one hand.

"Is she on the phone?" I asked.

"Nah." Pauline chuckled. "She's prepping for tomorrow." She didn't elaborate.

I strode between machines acknowledging a few people I knew.

"Why do they play such loud music?" Fiona asked. "It's hurting my eardrums."

"I think it's to help people drown out the aches and pains of their bodies."

"I prefer our walks on the beach."

"Me too." I tapped on the glass door to Didi's office.

She spun around, set the book she was holding on top of a stack of folders on her walnut desk, and beckoned me inside.

"I hope I'm not bothering you," I said, and closed the door.

"Not at all. I was practicing for my poetry reading tomorrow night at the library." Didi rounded the desk and gave me a hug. "Sit." She motioned to the walnut-and-leather chair.

As I obeyed, I noticed the title on the book she'd set on the folders: *Ledger.* Had she fibbed about the poetry because she was too embarrassed to say she had been reviewing the athletic club's financial accounts? I could commiserate. Running a business was not for the faint of heart.

"I spoke to Wanda." Didi moved the ledger to the brown leather blotter and set a stack of opened envelopes on top, squaring the corners. "We miss her so much. She admitted that the ankle monitor would allow her to come this far, but she's not ready to appear in public. How is she? Really?"

"Hanging in. Listen, I dropped by because I'm hoping you can—"

"Is Wanda eating?" Didi cut in. "The first thing that goes

when you're under stress is maintaining a proper diet. I know. I've lost five pounds since the murder. The strain—"

"She's eating. Her daughter is making sure of it. Plenty of leafy green vegetables," I added. That seemed to appease Didi. "Listen, I was wondering if I could ask you about—"

"There he is," Fiona said.

"Who?" Didi asked.

Had she heard my fairy? No. She was staring straight at me.

"You were wondering if you could ask me about *who*?" Didi asked.

Fiona scowled. "Kenny sure is acting suspicious."

I agreed. He was lingering outside the employees' lounge, eyeing the surveillance cameras. After a long moment, he nudged the door open and slipped inside. What was he up to?

Didi cleared her throat. "Hello-o, Courtney. Who do you want to ask me about?"

I refocused on her. "It's delicate."

"Usually people blurt things out with me. Most everyone knows I don't abide idle chitchat. I've got too much on my plate. So . . ." She waved a hand for me to continue.

"Lana hired a detective to look into Kenny Chu. Apparently, she was worried that he was having affairs with women who belonged to Sport Zone."

"Kenny? Having affairs?" Didi shook her head. "What a ridiculous notion. He's a model employee."

How model was he if he was always sneaking around? What had he wanted from Lana's locker? Why had he made sure the coast was clear before he'd entered the employees' lounge a moment ago?

"Why would she care, anyway?" Didi went on.

"Maybe she was interested in him?"

"Not a chance."

"Or she was concerned that if Kenny were catting around, his actions might hurt the reputation of Sport Zone?"

Didi brandished a hand. "Our reputation is impeccable."

"I didn't mean to imply—"

"Lana didn't own this place. She wasn't even an employee. Why would she—" Didi squared a pencil on the blotter. "Maybe she felt she had a right to snoop because she was
the diva on the pickleball courts and she—" Didi spanked the
table. "Stop, Didi. Do not speak ill of the dead." Tears
brimmed in her eyes. "Oh, how I miss her, Courtney. Warts
and all."

"I'm sure you do."

She pulled a tissue from a box on the desk and dabbed her
eyes. "Go on. Tell me more. Lana hired a private investigator." She wadded the moist tissue and tossed it into a trash
can. "Did Elton tell you about him?"

"No." I opted to be cryptic. I didn't need to share my
sources.

"Did you speak with this PI?"

I nodded. "I think it's fair to say the guy believed Kenny
had nothing to hide. He told me Kenny wasn't having an affair with anyone. Beyond that, he wasn't forthcoming." I
glanced toward the workout room. "Would you mind if I
asked Kenny a few questions?"

"About?"

"His relationship with Lana."

Didi folded her arms across her chest. "Don't you think
the police are doing their job?"

"Yes, of course. Except . . ." I hesitated.

Didi released her arms. "Except they've arrested Wanda
and you believe she's innocent."

"Yes."

"Even though she was found with the knife in her hand."

"Letter opener," I said automatically. "It was part of the
fairy garden."

Didi sighed. "I meant to tell you, by the way, that both of

your gardens were incredible. When I went to bid on *Ocean's View*—did you see that beautiful landscape in the auction?"

"I did." The landscape had been an impressionistic depiction of Carmel, from the angle starting at the ocean's edge and rising to Junipero.

"Anyway"—Didi waved a hand—"when I went to bid on it, I paid particular attention to your lovely gardens. All the details you put into them. What a tragedy to see one destroyed. But back to the matter at hand." Didi clapped. "Let's find Kenny and put this notion of a rift between Lana and him to bed."

"I saw him slip into the employees' lounge." I jutted a finger in that direction.

"Excellent." Didi strode from the office, saying over her shoulder, "Will you come to my poetry reading? It's tomorrow night, and I'd love to have a friendly face in the crowd."

"Sure." I didn't go out much during the week, too tired from work, but for an event showcasing a friend at the library, I would.

Didi entered the employees' lounge first. Fiona and I followed. Like the rest of the athletic club, the lounge was decorated in blue, brown, and white. Furniture included a sofa and a number of armchairs. There was a nook-style kitchen with a sink and modest-sized refrigerator. On the counter stood pitchers or urns of water, coffee, and tea. On the far wall stood a bank of cubbies to receive mail, each cubby marked with an employee's name. Three doors led to other rooms. The one on the left, marked *Security*, was closed. The one to the right leading to the restrooms was also closed. The door in the middle was ajar. No employees occupied the lounge, not even Kenny.

I heard the sound of metal clanging against metal and felt a whoosh of air. "What's through that door?" I asked.

"Lockers."

I peeked into the room. Walnut lockers, like the ones in the regular locker rooms, lined the walls. A covered bench stood in the middle. A door at the far end of the room was closing slowly, its hydraulic arm keeping it from slamming.

"Is that an exit?" I asked.

"Yes."

That would explain the whoosh of air I'd felt. Kenny had left the building.

Fiona whispered, "Why was he in here?"

Maybe I'd misread his stealth earlier. Maybe he was simply clocking out.

"Which locker is Kenny's?" I asked.

Didi roamed the room and stopped in front of one. "This one."

"Would you open it?"

She arched an eyebrow. "That would be an invasion of privacy."

Fiona said, "Tell her what happened in the women's locker room."

"Didi, I came to work out yesterday, and forgot to tell you something that occurred. With Lana's murder being so fresh, I . . ." I hesitated.

"Spit it out."

"I found Kenny in the women's locker room trying to open Lana's locker."

Didi's eyes widened. "He's not allowed in there."

"My thoughts exactly. I suggested that he should have contacted one of the female employees to help him out. He claimed he'd announced that he was entering and that he'd gone there to fetch Hattie Hopewell's pickleball racket for her lesson. He said Hattie liked him to warm it up for her."

Didi's mouth screwed into a frown.

"You don't buy his excuse, either?" I asked.

"Not for a second."

I strode to the rear door, opened it, and peered out. Neither Kenny nor anyone else was lingering in the parking lot behind the building. I turned back to Didi. "Has Elton cleaned out Lana's locker yet?"

"No. The guy is distraught. He said he'd get to it soon. There's so much paperwork that has to be taken care of after a death. I know how he feels. When my sweet Davis died . . ." She battled tears.

I placed a hand on her shoulder.

"Back to Kenny." Fiona whizzed between Didi and me. "Get the facts."

"Back to Kenny," I said, echoing my fairy. "Can we look in his employee locker?"

Didi stood taller. "What are you hoping to . . ." Her mouth formed an O. "You think he might have taken something from Lana's locker, like a memento?"

"It's a possibility."

"That's not a reason to have killed her. Quite the opposite."

"Unless he'd been stealing from her locker on a regular basis and she found out."

"Okay, just this once I'll break the rules, and if Kenny is a thief, I'll confront him, but for the record, I don't think he's a killer." She moved in front of his locker and said, "Look away. I have to do an override."

I swiveled my head, listening to her click the push buttons on the keyless lock. The locker opened with a creak.

Didi gasped. "Oh, my, Courtney, look."

I did. My mouth fell open.

Inside Kenny's locker, tucked at the back so that anyone might not have spied it on a sneak peek, was what could only be described as a shrine to Lana. It included pictures of her playing pickleball, a yellow headband with her initials stitched into it, a black-and-yellow pickleball racket with her name emblazoned on the handle, a slim doll that resembled Lana wearing a silver necklace with a pickleball charm.

"That's Lana's." Didi indicated the necklace. "She told me it went missing weeks ago. She never wore jewelry when she played. It distracted her. So she always stowed it in her locker. She accused the overnight cleaning staff of stealing it. I told her that was impossible. Each of the staff was bonded. I'd never dreamed that Kenny . . ." She eyed me. "What do we do now?"

"We tell the police."

"If you ask me," Didi said, "this looks as though Kenny was obsessed with Lana, which supports my theory. He's not a killer."

"If he was in love with her, maybe he killed her because he couldn't have her."

Didi shook her head. "That doesn't make sense. Why not kill Elton instead?"

"Maybe at the Spectacular, Kenny pleaded his case to Lana, but she told him he would never stand a chance, and incensed, he lashed out."

"But Wanda . . . the weapon . . . the confession."

"She was framed."

We returned to Didi's office, and she dialed the precinct. Dylan Summers was out for the evening. Officer Reddick took the call. He arrived fifteen minutes later, and Didi told me it was okay for me to go home. She would walk him through the tawdry situation. She promised to fill me in on what his inspection revealed. Curious onlookers watched as Reddick and Didi disappeared into the employees' lounge. Kenny was not among them.

As I was bicycling down Ocean Avenue, Fiona on my shoulder, my cell phone rang. I pulled to a stop and answered. Meaghan was desperate for a girls' night out. Her mother was driving her crazy. I agreed to meet her at Hideaway Café.

I pedaled home, threw on a nubby white sweater, whisked

a brush through my windblown hair, and dabbed on lipstick. With Fiona keeping me company, I walked back to the restaurant.

A hostess escorted me to a table on the patio where Meaghan was already enjoying a glass of Chardonnay. The chatter among dinner patrons was muted, the evening temperature divine. I noticed Dylan Summers sitting with Renee two tables over. He was wearing a caramel-colored leather jacket over his day clothes. Renee looked stunning in a green sweater-dress, her hair swooped into a messy bun with tendrils hanging down. She waved at me. Summers swiveled his head and nodded in greeting. I wondered whether I should tell him what Didi and I had discovered at Sport Zone and decided against it. Reddick was on it. Summers deserved his private time.

"It's okay if I left Mom alone, isn't it?" Meaghan asked.

"Don't feel guilty. She'll be fine."

"What if she falls asleep?"

"Then she'll sleep for a while before she might have an incident. You'll be home by then."

Meaghan plucked the sleeves of her V-neck peasant blouse.

I placed a hand on my pal's fidgety fingers to calm her. Fiona flew to Meaghan's hair and caressed it.

"Why is your mom driving you crazy?" I asked.

"She's baking up a storm. We have enough cookies to last through Christmas."

"I like cookies." Fiona waved her arm.

"Tomorrow, she wants to make biscuits," Meaghan said. "If she stays with me much longer, I'll outgrow my wardrobe." She showed me how she could barely wedge a thumb inside the band of her trousers. *"Oof."*

A waitress arrived and asked for our order. We both ordered a garden salad with grilled salmon, and I opted for a glass of the same Chardonnay Meaghan was drinking.

Seconds later, Brady returned with the wine and set it in front of me.

"That was fast," I said.

"I anticipated." His eyes gleamed with warmth. "You look nice."

"Thank you."

"How's your mother?" he asked Meaghan.

"My place has become a test kitchen for the 'Great America Bake-Off.'"

Brady laughed heartily. "If you want to drop her off here, she can help in the kitchen."

"I know she wants to seal some deals," Meaghan continued, "or assuage her clients' creative souls, but she's so distracted and, frankly, negative that she's afraid the wrong words will spill from her mouth and she'll ruin everything, so she's staying home. Out of sight." She sighed. "If only Lana's murderer would be found and my mother exonerated."

"On that note . . ." Brady pulled up a chair, glanced in Summers's direction, and lowered his voice.

Fiona flew to the table and performed a tap dance beside his forearm; he didn't notice her.

"A pair of saleswomen who work for Elton Lamar at his dealership were here for lunch today," Brady said. "One, a redhead, was gossiping with the other, a blonde, about Elton and Lana. I happened to overhear because we were one server short, so it was all hands on deck."

"You're an excellent waiter," I said.

"I paid my dues at Cash Cow."

If I remembered correctly, Brady's father had made him do every job at the diner: waiting tables, bussing dishes, and taking out the trash. *A restaurant didn't run itself,* I'd heard his father say.

"Anyway," Brady continued, "as it turns out, the redhead said Elton blew his top last week because Lana embarrassed him at a sales meeting."

That had to have been the meeting Elton and Lana were arguing about at the Spectacular.

"What did Lana do?" I leaned closer. Brady smelled good, like delectable kitchen aromas.

"It seems that sales were down, so Lana took it upon herself to address the group."

"She certainly was aggressive," Fiona sniped.

Aggressive wasn't quite the word I'd have used. *Formidable* was more apt.

"It seems Lana gave the sales group a pep talk about morale," Brady went on, "and advised them how they could beef up sales."

"But she's not . . . she *wasn't* . . . a salesperson," Meaghan said.

"Exactly." Brady drummed the table. Fiona scooched out of his way. "The two saleswomen were beside themselves with resentment but thrilled that their boss—Elton—steered Lana into his office and gave her a tongue-lashing."

Didi had said that Elton was a different man when not in Lana's presence. She'd said he was fierce at the athletic club. Did he act that way at work? Had Lana threatened to emasculate him by insinuating herself into his business where he held sway? Had that pushed him over the edge?

"What happened next?" Fiona twirled a hand, eager to hear the ending to the story.

I said, "Go on, Brady."

"According to the blonde," he said, "Elton shouted, 'I'm going to kill you.'"

Fiona gasped.

So did I. "Have you told the police?"

Brady shrugged. "It's hearsay."

"The police should talk to these women." I cut a look at Summers.

Brady did, too, and started to rise.

I tapped his arm. "Wait a sec. Mentioning hair color reminds me of what Holly Hopewell said last night, about seeing Elton with a brunette."

Fiona twirled in place, agreeing with me.

Meaghan's eyes crinkled. "What are you talking about?"

"Holly Hopewell saw Elton with a brunette outside the bank." I regarded Brady. "Isn't that right?"

He nodded. "Man, Holly was a hoot the way she popped up from behind the fence between your yards."

"Ahem." Meaghan cleared her throat impishly. "Brady, what were you doing in Courtney's yard?"

"Getting the grand tour," he replied. "She'd been promising for months. I was hoping to spy a fairy, but no luck."

"You almost did!" Fiona exclaimed. "Can you see me now?" She flew in front of his face, taunting him. He didn't blink.

Meaghan snickered. "Yeah, right. You wanted to see a fairy."

"Stop." I whacked my pal with two fingers. "Focus on the present."

"Was the brunette one of his salespeople?" Meaghan asked.

"That's not the point," I said. "If Elton was furious with Lana, and if he was stepping out with the brunette—"

Brady wagged a hand. "Hold on. Holly said she got the feeling that Elton and the woman weren't romantically involved."

"True." I squinted at him. "Could the brunette have been one of Elton's grown daughters from his previous marriage?"

"Enough speculating." Meaghan thumped the table. "The only way we can help my mother is for you, Brady, to tell the police what you heard, and for Holly Hopewell to give the police a description of the woman she saw."

Chapter 22

Never ever step inside a fairy ring. Who knows what lies beyond?
—Anonymous

When I arrived home, I texted Holly asking if she was able to chat, but she didn't reply. The lights were out in her house. Not willing to wake her if she was sleeping, seeing as it was after ten p.m., I headed to bed.

Except I couldn't fall asleep. Again. Drinking a cup of chamomile tea didn't help. Neither did reading a book about soil, usually a guaranteed snooze inducer. Pixie tried, as she had the other night, to comfort me, and Fiona sang a few new lullabies that I hadn't heard before—fairies, she told me, were famous for their lullabies—but nothing worked.

Around two a.m., I drifted into a fitful sleep, racing from one nightmare to another. Each was worse than the previous. In one, Holly sketched Wanda's face and then slashed it to smithereens. In another, Elton Lamar tackled Wanda to the ground and jabbed her with the letter opener. In yet another,

Kenny Chu walloped Wanda with a pickleball paddle. In all, Wanda ended up behind bars, a cell door clanging into place.

At dawn on Thursday, I crawled out of bed, donned jogging clothes, and took a loping run on the beach to clear the cobwebs in my brain. Fiona accompanied me. Throughout the run, she chanted fairy speak. At one point, I was pretty sure she was attempting a fairy spell. She hadn't learned many yet. First, she had to master potions.

When I returned to the house, I luxuriated in an overly hot shower. To bolster my sagging mood, I dressed in a pink blouse and pink-checked capris, after which I ate a hearty breakfast of poached egg, chives, and smashed avocado on sourdough toast—yes, I needed to spoil myself. Soon, I was thinking clearly and even believed I might come up with answers to save Wanda.

At the shop, I set Pixie on the floor, opened the top half of the Dutch door to let in the fresh morning air, and readied the coffee and tea. Fiona whizzed onto the patio and into the ficus trees.

For a half hour, I checked the indoor display tables for issues, none of which needed tweaking, after which I set out a sign for a Thursday Special: *Pick one fairy figurine and get the second, half off.* I liked offering specials, but never on the same day of the week, two weeks in a row. It was sneaky, true, but I didn't want our customers to plan their visits. I had to do whatever I could to drum up repeat business.

The notion made me think of Didi Dubois and the ledger she'd been reviewing when I'd met her at Sport Zone, which led me to wonder what Officer Reddick had decided to do after viewing Kenny Chu's locker. I was about to call Didi to ask when Holly sashayed into the shop.

"Hello-o!" she warbled.

"Good morning. Don't you look youthful." I wasn't

lying. In a bright green smock-style blouse over leggings and multicolored sandals, Holly looked as frisky as ever.

"Not a day over fifty-nine." She chuckled. "I hope our teacup gardens are ready."

"You bet." With the flurry of activity, I'd forgotten that I'd asked the Hopewells to leave their creations for a few days so the glue would settle. Teacup fairy gardens, because they were top-heavy, could be quite perilous if not anchored properly.

"My sisters are on their way, and then we're all going to Hideaway Café for tea and scones. Won't that be fun? We'll make sure to display our gardens on the table while we dine." She winked. "A little PR never hurt anyone."

Joss entered carrying a bag from Sweet Treats. "Morning, Holly. Morning, boss. You beat me today."

"I got an early start," I said.

"How early?" Joss arched an eyebrow.

"Predawn."

"Insomnia stinks." Joss petted my shoulder. "I have some homeopathic sleep aids, if that will help, but in the meantime, I brought muffins. A blueberry lemon one should perk you up."

"I'm *perked* enough." Two cups of strong coffee with my gourmet breakfast had done the trick.

Joss headed down the hall toward the kitchen.

"Hey," I called after her, "are you free tonight? Do you want to go with me to Didi's poetry reading at the library?"

"I'd love to."

I fetched the three teacup gardens for the Hopewells and returned to the sales counter. "By the way, Holly, were your ears burning last night?"

"Oh, that's right," she said. "You sent me a text message. What's up?"

I mentioned my conversation with Meaghan and Brady

about the brunette Holly had seen with Elton. "Perhaps you should go to the police and describe her to a sketch artist."

"You don't think she's the killer, do you?"

"How would I know? Even if she's not, if Elton is having an affair with her—"

"It's no longer an affair if Lana's dead," Holly stated matter-of-factly.

"Yes, of course, but the question is, did Elton kill Lana so he could move on with this woman?"

Holly wagged a finger at me. "As I said before, I didn't pick up a romantic vibe between them. Elton wasn't holding her hand or making eyes at her."

"Even so . . ." I set the teacup fairy gardens side by side.

"All right. You've convinced me." Holly sighed. "I'll go to the police. One must do one's duty, mustn't one?" She lifted her fairy garden and twisted it right and left. "Do the police still use sketch artists, or will I be talking to a computer?"

I smiled. "You'll talk to a person, but that person might put the details you provide into a computer."

Holly placed a hand on her chest. "Phew. I'm not good with computers. I try. Hedda has been giving me one-on-one lessons, but—"

"What have I been doing?" Hedda asked as she entered the shop, her pencil skirt restraining the length of her stride.

"Teaching me the computer."

"You and computers, Holly," Hattie said, trailing her younger sister. "There are classes you can take."

A few customers followed the women inside.

"It's not that hard to learn," Hattie went on. How relaxed she appeared in a Happy Diggers T-shirt over jeans, as if ready for a day in the garden. "You're simply resistant. Just like Dad was when cell phones came out."

Holly made a *pfft* sound. "I can text."

"Not the same thing," Hattie said.

Joss emerged from the hall carrying a plate with the muffins she'd purchased. "Anyone want one?"

The Hopewells declined.

"Oh, how cute are these?" Hedda strolled to the counter and inspected the three petite fairy gardens. "I'm so glad we did this. I want to sign up for another class." She lifted hers and, like her sister, turned it this way and that. "So why were you discussing computers, Holly?"

"Courtney and I were talking about"—Holly lowered her voice—"Elton Lamar. We were wondering if he had a reason to kill his wife. He has such an iffy alibi, claiming he went to Devendorf Park in the middle of the event."

Hedda said, "I was there around nine. I saw a man. It must have been Elton. He was sitting on the bench."

Hattie scoffed. "Why didn't you say so the other day?"

"What other day?" Hedda's forehead wrinkled.

"Sunday, when we were here making the gardens and chatting about . . ." Hattie tapped a finger on her chin. "Oh, I remember now. You didn't arrive until after we'd discussed seeing Elton with an attorney."

I wondered whether Summers had questioned Glinda's attorney boyfriend and whether Glinda had touched base with the detective about what she'd heard Lana say.

"We believe Elton had a financial motive to have wanted his wife dead," Hattie said, "but if you saw him at the park at the time of the murder—"

"I'm not one hundred percent sure it was Elton"—Hedda flapped a hand—"but it could have been him. Whoever it was had blond hair. The glow of the streetlight highlighted it. And I'm pretty sure the man was wearing a tuxedo. The light drew attention to his white shirt, as well."

"Why were you there?" I asked.

Hedda regarded her sisters self-consciously.

"Go on," Hattie said. "Tell her."

"I go to the park on Saturday night to . . ." Tears filled Hedda's eyes.

Holly slung an arm around her. "Her boyfriend died in a bicycle accident at the corner of Junipero and Ocean Avenue two years ago."

"Hedda, I'm sorry," I said. "I had no idea."

"I go there"—Hedda brushed tears off her face—"to talk to him. I know I could do so at home, but there's something about being in the park, beneath the stars, when I know . . ." She lowered her chin. "I know he's watching over me."

Hattie said, "She finds pennies every time she goes there."

"Pennies from heaven." Holly gave her sister a squeeze and released her. "Who'd have thought our sweet Hedda would be anything other than practical, but it turns out she's not all dollars and cents."

"Although she does have a huge stash of pennies," Hattie joked.

"So that settles it," I said. "Elton is innocent. He has an alibi."

"Not so fast, boss." Joss peeled the wrapper off a muffin and broke the muffin in two. "Were your ears on mute? Hedda did not guarantee the guy she saw was Elton."

"True." Hedda bobbed her head.

"Besides, I was talking with Yvanna this morning," Joss went on. "She wanted an update on the murder investigation. You know how fond she is of Wanda. She doesn't think Wanda is capable of murder."

"Like the rest of us," Holly said.

"So we got to talking"—Joss set the half muffin aside and skirted the counter to join us—"and it turns out Elton came into Sweet Treats a week ago with a woman whom Yvanna didn't recognize."

"A brunette?" Holly asked.

"Mm-hm. How'd you guess? Yvanna tried not to eaves-drop on their conversation, but she heard the word 'di-vorce.'"

"Aha!" Holly spanked the counter. "All the more reason for me to go to the precinct and provide a description." She eyed her sisters. "After our tea."

The Dutch door opened letting in a gust of wind. Tamara Geoffries, looking as righteous as a Valkyrie, closed the door with a *clack* and stomped toward me, her hair and the tails of her cloak flying behind her. Pointing, she yelled, "You!"

I swallowed hard. *Me?* What had I done? The Hopewells formed a blockade in front of me. Joss joined them.

Fiona whizzed through the French doors and faced Tamara, her fists at the ready. If I weren't so flustered, I might have laughed at my fairy's bravado.

Tamara drew to a halt and flicked a strand of hair off her face, her gaze hard, her jaw twitching with tension.

I inhaled calmly, stepped around my army of friends. "Tamara. What's—"

"You. Sicced the police. On me." As Tamara cut off each word, her voice skated upward. "How dare you put me in their sights! I did nothing wrong. Nothing."

"Tamara—"

She held up a hand to stop me from talking. "I told you what Lana did to my husband in confidence."

"The police already knew about Lana and Jamie. It was public knowledge."

"Hush!" Tamara raised a second hand, looking for all in-tents and purposes like a crossing guard. "I get that you want Wanda to be innocent, Courtney. So do I. But I did not kill Lana Lamar." Tamara turned on her heel and left as briskly as she'd entered.

Fiona rocketed out of the shop, leaving a trail of shimmer-ing fairy dust behind her. The pair of customers inspecting books on the book stand swiveled. I didn't know if they were watching Tamara or they had caught sight of the fairy dust.

Holly said, "Wow. I didn't have a clue Tamara had that kind of anger in her."

"It's been bottled up," I said. "She misses her husband."

"What a tragedy that was," Hedda said. "Lana. Running. Jamie veering away to avoid hitting her. Did Tamara blame Lana for causing the accident, Courtney?"

I nodded. "I'm pretty sure."

"Which gives her motive," Hattie said. "No wonder she's a bundle of frazzled nerves."

Because of me, I thought glumly. Maybe Tamara hadn't killed Lana, but neither had Wanda.

Silence engulfed us.

After a long moment, I said, "Let's wrap up your gardens, and then, everyone"—I said, addressing the rest of the customers—"come to the register for a free magnet." I'd paid a professional photographer to take pictures of various fairy gardens and had used the photos to create kitchen magnets with our slogan: *Fairy Best Wishes*. Giving away a few magnets for free to promote goodwill would be worth the expense.

The Hopewell sisters paid for their teacup gardens, and Joss helped me wrap them and set them in individual shopping bags. As Holly left with her sisters, she promised once again to visit the police following tea.

Shaken after Tamara's onslaught, I retreated to the patio, grabbed my six-inch stainless-steel shears with micro-tips, and worked on training a bonsai. As I weaved copper wire around the branches and trimmed as necessary, I listened to the burble of the fountain. Doing something normal comforted me. Pixie padded around my ankles mewing her concern.

"I'm fine," I assured her.

I wasn't. I was lying. Even so, I was breathing easier

knowing that the police, despite having Wanda under house arrest, were looking for other suspects.

After lunch, I taught a shy teenager how to build her first fairy garden. She wanted to give her mother something extra special for her fiftieth birthday. She chose an eight-inch fairy pot, a gazebo, a table preset with tea service, a duo of pink fairies—one to represent her mother and the other to represent herself—plus a sign that read: *Fairies love tea.* For a half hour, we planted low-growing plants, taking care with the soil. We were just laying pink-toned gravel groundwork when Fiona returned. The teenager glanced in Fiona's direction and blinked. Her mouth turned up in a shy smile. She didn't say anything, but I knew she could see my fairy.

Realizing she'd been detected, Fiona did a quick pirouette and curtsy. The teenager giggled.

"Courtney," Fiona whispered in my ear, "we need to talk."

I excused myself from my student, urging her to continue tamping down the gravel, and I strode toward Fiona's favorite tree. She winged alongside.

"Where have you been?" I asked.

"I followed Tamara Geoffries."

"Why on earth did you do that?"

"My curiosity was piqued." Fiona inspected beneath her adult wings to see if the second set of wings had grown larger. They seemed about the same as they had the last time she'd checked. She harrumphed and flipped her gossamer hair off her face.

"Don't be in such a rush," I chided. "You'll get there. You're the most curious and righteous fairy I know."

"I'm the *only* righteous fairy you know."

"Yes, why is that?"

"I'm not sure." Fiona shimmied off her bewilderment and continued. "Anyway, back to Tamara. She went home and cried."

"I would imagine she was embarrassed by her public outburst." I righted a string of lights that had slipped off the ficus's branch. "I bet she'd hoped to catch me alone in the shop."

"For a long time, she cuddled her cat."

I nodded. "I'm sure her Angora brings her peace."

"I didn't see the gray one."

"It must have gone back to its home."

Fiona fluttered in front of me. "I think Tamara is innocent of murder."

I regarded her with amusement. "When did you become judge and jury?"

"Let's call it my sixth sense."

"So you're admitting to having ESP?" I poked her tummy.

"A fairy's sixth sense is different than a human's. We are tapped into the universal source."

My mother had often said fairies were connected to nature in ways we humans would never understand.

I poked Fiona again. "You're bragging."

"Bragging is excessive pride or boastfulness. I am not allowed to do so. The queen fairy would not approve." She held up a finger. "Therefore, trust me. I am stating fact."

I laughed. "Okay, for now, based on your sixth sense, we'll cross Tamara off the suspect list."

Fiona kissed my cheek and zoomed out of sight.

Chapter 23

Are those the magic fairy wands glistening on the tree,
or only winter icicles that I see?
—Anonymous

At ten minutes to six, Joss passed through the French doors leading to the main showroom. "Time to close up, boss. Didi's poetry reading begins in fifteen minutes."

"On it." I'd been straightening the patio items for nearly an hour. A group of homeschooled children had visited late in the afternoon. To our good fortune, they had purchased a lot of items, but the remaining figurines were out of place, the environmental habitats were askew, and the two-inch plants had been moved helter-skelter. Preferring an orderly display for the next morning, and choosing not to come in at five a.m. to make it so, I'd set to work the moment the children and adults had departed.

I stood back from my handiwork and smiled. *Done.* "Pixie, time to go."

My cat leaped off the chair she'd been occupying and scurried into the shop.

"Fiona!" I whistled into her favorite tree.

She zipped out.

"Don't you look pretty," I said. She'd dusted her cheeks with gold glitter.

"It's my first time," she said. "We aren't allowed adornment until we have grown our first set of adult wings."

"Like you need any adornment. Fairies are naturally beautiful."

"That's what Merryweather said, but I wanted to try it. It's not too much?"

"You look wonderful."

For Didi's reading, she'd opted to perform in the Barnet Segal Reading Room of the library, an expansive, light-filled space fitted with a fireplace, tables, and easy chairs.

Joss preceded me inside. Pixie squirmed in my arms. I fondled her chin and cooed for her to *hush*. Fiona flew in behind us and immediately disappeared. To search for Merryweather, I supposed.

In addition to the regular furniture, the library employees had set out a lectern and a couple of rows of wooden folding chairs. Didi, who looked striking in a crimson flapper-style dress with matching shawl, was standing to one side of the lectern. Her mouth moved as she leafed through a gilt-edged journal, definitely not the ledger I'd seen yesterday. Sport Zone employees and other locals I recognized were occupying nearly all of the seats. Brady was sitting on one of the folding chairs beside Holly Hopewell.

Seeing him made me smile. I whispered to Joss, "Did you tell Brady about the reading?"

"I'm sure he learned of it via the library newsletter. I would imagine he subscribes, what with his mother being a famous author and all." She elbowed me. "I didn't attempt to matchmake, if that's what you're implying."

Miss Reade, elegant in silver cigarette pants and silver beaded top, stepped behind the lectern. "Welcome, everyone. It is my great pleasure to introduce Didi Dubois, local poet and owner of Sport Zone. Many of you have heard Didi recite poetry in the past. Many of you have read her work, often published in *The Carmel Pine Cone*. But did you realize that Didi has a book of her poems coming out next month?"

"The publisher is small," Didi said, her cheeks flushing.

I joined the audience in a round of applause.

"Small doesn't matter," Miss Reade said, judiciously. "Someone believes in your work and wants to share it with the world. Brava. And, now, without further ado, Didi Dubois." She swept a hand and backed away from her post.

Didi sidled behind the lectern. "Thank you, one and all. I have to admit that I'm sad my sweet friend Wanda Brownie can't be here tonight. I dedicate this reading to her."

Wanda could have come—I'd asked Meaghan to bring her—but Wanda had declined, not wishing anyone to see her with the monitor on her ankle.

Didi closed her eyes momentarily before continuing. "I fell in love with poetry after reading the work of so many talented poets. Edna St. Vincent Millay, Anne Sexton, Emily Dickenson, Ralph Waldo Emerson. Who can forget Sylvia Plath's haunting opening line to 'The Moon and the Yew Tree'? 'This is the light of the mind, cold and planetary.'" Didi took a breath. "But it is Maya Angelou who ignited the fire within me to write my own poetry. Her passion for the truth. Her determination to reveal what others have not said. I dedicate this first reading to her."

She took a sip of water from the glass sitting on the lectern and began.

"'The Day the Light Went Out in My Soul.'" Didi drew in a deep breath. Her eyes glistened. "'How many days must I bear alone? How many tears must these eyes shed? If only I'd seen the beauty of you earlier. The beauty of us. If only I'd known that your soul would expose my own. Would that I could turn back the clock—'"

"Why?" a man shouted from the reception area. The library's front door slammed, adding an exclamation point to his outburst.

He rushed down the stairs into the reading room. Kenny.

People in the audience gasped at the intrusion.

Why *what*? Did Kenny wonder why Didi had started without him? No, his face was flushed with what could only be described as fury. He strode toward Didi. What had prompted not only Tamara but also Kenny to have angry outbursts in public forums on the same day?

I bolted to my feet and bustled to Didi. Brady and Joss did the same.

"Kenny, sit!" Didi ordered. I imagined she'd had to face many combative men in her line of business, including Kenny, seeing as he was her employee. "Sit, I said."

Kenny didn't. "Why did you do it?" he demanded. "Why did you break into my locker? And you, Courtney Kelly!" He aimed a finger at me. "You set this in motion."

How could he possibly know that? A frisson of worry skittered up my neck. Had Kenny seen me? No, he'd rushed out the door. Escaped. Officer Reddick wouldn't have told him. Didi, either. If she had, his wrath would have been spent by now.

"I saw you on the surveillance footage," Kenny went on, clarifying the *how* for me. "Speaking of surveillance, Courtney, you told Detective Summers that I didn't come to the library the night Lana was killed. Now he's hounding me for an explanation. So listen up."

His tone sent a shiver through me, even though I was happy to hear the police were following up on my tip.

"I did not kill Lana Lamar." Kenny flailed an arm at everyone in attendance. "I loved her. Do you hear me? I loved her with all my heart."

Didi rounded the lectern and grabbed hold of Kenny's elbow. "Stop this at once."

Kenny wrenched free and growled, "It's your fault, Didi. You made Lana angry."

"I did no such—"

"All she wanted to do was compete at pickleball, but you were against her from the beginning. She became reckless. Rash. Lashing out at everyone."

Brady said, "Kenny, cool down. Let's take this outside."

Kenny backed up, both hands balled in fists and raised overhead. "Don't come any closer, man. Didi, I want an explanation." He zeroed in on her again. "Why did you do it? Why did you break into my locker?"

"If you must know," Didi sighed, "Lana was investigating you. She believed you were having affairs with women at the club."

"No way. I wasn't."

"That's what I told Courtney, but she caught you breaking into Lana's locker Tuesday, and I had to admit that seemed suspicious, so—"

"She was wrong. I was looking for Hattie's locker."

"Don't lie, Kenny," Didi said. "You took things from Lana's locker. Mementoes. You put them in your own locker. Courtney and I saw them. You had a thing for Lana."

"It wasn't a thing," Kenny hissed. "A *thing* sounds cheap. We were in love."

"*You* were in love," Didi said. "Just you."

"Lana loved me back. She promised to leave her husband and run away with me. We were going to move to Florida."

"Come, come, Kenny," Didi said. "Everyone knows that

Lana wouldn't have done that. She never would have left Carmel and given up the chance to keep winning the pickleball championship title. Not for you. Not for anyone."

I spied Miss Reade standing beyond Kenny, cell phone to her ear. I hoped she was calling 911. Someone needed to rein the guy in.

"Your turn to tell the truth, Kenny," Didi said. "Did you kill Lana because she rejected you?"

"No way." He keened like an injured animal.

"Kenny," I said, my insides revving like a V–8 engine, "do you have a better alibi for the night Lana died?"

He gazed at me, eyes flickering, as if formulating an explanation. "I . . ." He faltered. "I can't say."

"You can't say because you don't?"

"I can't say where I was because I made a promise."

"To whom?" Didi demanded.

"None of your business." Kenny glowered at her. "I quit, Didi. Find another trainer as good as me. You won't be able to." And with that, he headed out of the building.

Fiona and Merryweather flitted to Miss Reade. She gave them an order, and they whooshed out of the library.

At the same time, Didi burst into tears. "I'm sorry, everyone." She gripped the lectern. "I'm too shaken to continue. I—"

Miss Reade slung an arm around her.

I couldn't blame Didi for ending the event. All I wanted to do was go home, putter in the garden, listen to gentle music, and sip wine. Not necessarily in that order. *Chilling is vital for the soul*, my mother had often told me. As a young girl, I'd never truly understood what that had meant.

Miss Reade begged everyone to stay and wait for the police to arrive. An hour later, after we all gave our statements to a fresh-faced female officer, I headed home.

Fiona caught up to me a block from the library.

"Where did you and Merryweather go?" I asked.

"Miss Reade wanted us to keep tabs on Kenny, but we lost him. He was very fast. And sneaky. He cut through a yard and over a fence. The cypress trees obscured his route."

"I'm sure the police will track him down and—"

"Watch out!" Fiona cried.

Out of nowhere, a dark car careened toward me. Headlights off. Clutching Pixie to my chest, I hurdled into a yard, scraping my legs and elbows on the prickly native shrubs. The car zoomed away. It was generic in shape, maybe a Toyota Celica or Honda Civic.

"Did you catch the license plate?" I asked Fiona.

"There wasn't one."

"Dang." I scrambled to my feet and checked Pixie for thorns. When I'd completed the inspection and determined she was fine, I kissed her nose. "Good to go."

Footsteps pounded the pavement.

I hopped to my feet, ready to fight if necessary.

"Courtney!" a man yelled. Brady. Running toward me. Out of breath. "I saw what happened. Are you okay?"

"What are you doing here?" I asked.

"This is my normal route. I got detained at the library. I'd intended to walk you home."

"If you had, you might have ended up in the bushes with me," I joked, though I didn't feel lighthearted.

"Do you know who that was?" Brady asked.

"I don't have a clue. Tamara? Kenny? Both screamed at me today." As I replayed Tamara's outburst, I brushed leaves off my clothes and examined my elbow. The scrape needed Neosporin and a bandage. Nothing more. "She drives a dark blue Toyota. I've seen it in her driveway. For all I know, Kenny could drive one, too, and I won't rule out Elton Lamar. As a car dealer, he has access to lots of cars, most without plates."

"Most of Elton's cars have *Lamar Motors* on the temporary

license plates," Brady said while plucking leaves gently from my hair. "Why would he run you down?"

"I can't fathom a reason other than he might have heard I'd urged Holly Hopewell to talk to a sketch artist about the brunette."

"How would he know you were the instigator?"

"The police could have told him. Summers has been doing his civic duty and following up on all the leads that I or anyone else has given him. On the other hand, Hedda Hopewell established a pretty solid alibi for Elton." I elaborated.

"You should call Summers."

I shrugged. "Maybe this was an accident, pure and simple."

Brady's gaze narrowed. "If you believe that, I have swampland to sell you."

I smiled. "Okay, I'll call him."

"Ask Brady in for wine," Fiona suggested.

"Would you like to stop by my house for a glass of wine?" I said, no longer surprised that my fairy's suggestions influenced me.

"Sure. But let's call the police right now. While we're here."

I let out a sigh. "They are still questioning people at the library."

He matched my exasperated look. "There's more than one cop on duty."

Realizing he wouldn't back down, I telephoned the precinct instead of 911. I asked for Summers. He was following a lead. So I asked for Officer Reddick. When he came on the line, I filled him in on what had happened. He told me to hang tight.

In minutes, Reddick showed up, uniform crisp, eyes alert.

"Hey, Red," Brady said.

"Brady."

As it turned out, Brady and Reddick had known each other for years because they each donated time teaching basketball at the Y in Monterey.

I replayed the incident for Reddick.

Using a large flashlight, he inspected the skid marks made by the speeding car. There were no traffic cams in the neighborhood. He took a few photographs and then said to me, "There's nothing more you can share? Man or woman driving? Passengers? Windows open or closed? Music playing?"

I looked at Fiona. She shook her head.

"Sorry, Officer Reddick, I don't know anything else. It was a sedan, not an SUV. The headlights were off. I dodged left." I did tell him about the various altercations that had occurred throughout the day and added that Tamara Geoffries owned a Toyota. Like Summers, Reddick took notes in a palm-sized notebook. When his inquiry was complete, he slapped the book closed and pocketed it and his pen.

"I'll be in touch if I discover anything," he said. "You get a good night's sleep, Miss Kelly."

As if, I thought.

When Reddick drove away, Brady wrapped an arm around me.

"You'd better not mention a word of this to my father," I warned him. "If he gets wind that—"

"My lips are sealed."

We walked in companionable silence until we reached Dream-by-the-Sea. A breeze had kicked up. The wind chimes in the front yard were tinkling. The merry sound gave me false hope, like all was right with the world. It wasn't.

Chapter 24

*Fairies dance and share secrets
at the bottom of the garden.*
—Anonymous

We drank our wine in the backyard, reflecting on Kenny's outburst at the library and how Didi must have felt after the intrusion. An hour later, Brady asked if I wanted him to stay the night, offering to sleep on the living room couch. I assured him I was fine. I had an edgy cat, a righteous fairy, and squeaky porch steps. Any or all would alert me if someone attempted to break in.

After he left, to err on the side of caution, I propped a shovel by the kitchen door and another by the front door. I was pretty good at basketball, but I was a terror with a garden tool. Years as a landscaper had built up my arm, thigh, and core strength.

Menacing intruder, watch out.

The next morning, having not slept well, yet again— granted, I might have done better had I let Brady stay; sleeping with one eye open was not ideal—I dressed in all white to help me feel spiritually at peace, ate an egg-white omelet with fresh herbs and Boursin cheese to give me daylong energy, and headed to work early. Fiona, who had dined on the juice of honeysuckle, was buzzing with excitement alongside me because, in the wee hours of the morning, she had come up with the brilliant idea that we needed to make a suspect board. When I planned out fairy gardens, she reminded me, I often created a drawing on the marker board in the office to give myself the complete idea—Xs for plants and Ys for fairy figurines. In addition, I sketched out any of the structures I intended to use like a house, gazebo, or fairy door. All of my designs were created with dry-erase pens so I could revise or start over, if necessary. She suggested that I do the same for this investigation.

I agreed.

After pouring myself a cup of mint tea, I retreated with Pixie and Fiona to the office. I queued up the *Secret Garden* playlist on my iPhone and got to work. Whenever I stalled out, I sat at the desk and raked the sand in my Zen garden. Making concentric circles brought me the most comfort.

An hour into the project, as I was staring at the marker board, Joss strode through the doorway.

"Aren't you an early bird!" she exclaimed. "Couldn't you sleep after Kenny's outburst at the library?"

"That was nothing," Fiona said. "Tell her about the car that almost plowed into you."

"What?" Joss had left the library a good twenty minutes before I had.

Quickly, I filled her in.

Joss said, "You must be a wreck."

"I'm managing."

"Why don't you take the day off?"

"Not now. I might be on to something." I motioned with the dry-erase pen.

Joss eyed my handiwork on the marker board.

> *Tamara Geoffries: blamed Lana for death of her husband; outburst at shop claiming her innocence. Drives Toyota. Motive: Vengeance? Alibi: unsubstantiated.*
>
> *Elton Lamar: seen with attorney; also seen with mystery brunette; disparaged by Lana for his creative side; upset that Lana embarrassed him in sales meeting. Drives whatever vehicle he wants to. Motive: Money or divorce? Alibi: corroborated by Hedda Hopewell. Maybe.*
>
> *Mystery brunette: seen with Elton. Who is she? Lover? Daughter? Associate? Did she kill Lana?*

Joss pointed at the next entry. "You don't honestly think Didi is a suspect, do you?"

"I can't rule her out." I studied the marker board.

> *Didi Dubois: feuding with Lana about pickleball and attitude. Motive: didn't want Lana to win the pickleball championship again without jumping through hoops. Alibi: at Sport Zone, resolving security issue and working through her anger.*

"Talk about a weak motive," Joss said.

"It's all I've got."

"My odds are on Kenny."

"Even though he swears he's innocent?"

Joss shrugged. "What murderer hasn't?"

Fiona said, "I agree."

We all stared at the marker board.

Kenny Chu: in love with Lana; made a shrine to her; hot-tempered; sneaky. Motive: rejected by Lana, or did he learn she was having him investigated and lash out? Alibi: The first one was a lie; now he says he was with someone, but he can't say who. Why not?

"Wanda doesn't belong on the board," Joss said.

Fiona threw me a look. "I told Courtney the same thing."

"I agree, but she's the one whom the police suspect," I said.

Wanda Brownie: hated the way Lana critiqued her clients; also wanted Lana's reign as pickleball champion to end; public set-to outside Flair Gallery. Motive: same as Didi's, which was a better reason for Lana to have wanted Wanda or Didi dead. Alibi: sleepwalking; caught in the act. QUESTION: Who knew she sleepwalked?

"Sweetheart, are you here?" my father called from the main showroom.

I skirted my desk. Too late. He strode into the office carrying a bag from Sweet Treats. He came to a halt and gawped at the marker board. "What is this? What are you doing?"

"Why are you here?" I countered. "Do you have a business meeting in town?"

"No."

"Then why are you dressed in a crisp white shirt and trousers?"

"It's a nice look."

"You're going to visit Wanda, aren't you?"

"Don't deflect." Dad sliced the air with a hand. "I'm here because I heard a car ran you into a stand of bushes."

I swallowed hard. Someone had blabbed. Brady had better

not have. Reddick, I decided. Or Reddick told Summers and Summers contacted my dad, which sounded more probable.

"*Almost* is only good in horseshoes," I quipped.

"Why do you do that?" he asked, his tone harsh. "Why do you make everything a joke?"

"I hear customers," Joss mumbled, as she sneaked out and closed the door.

"Chicken," I whispered.

Fiona drifted between my father and me, as if engrossed in a tennis match.

"You could have been seriously hurt," my father continued. "What happened?"

"The more I think about it, the more I suspect it was a drunk driver. The car swerved. I dove. The car tore off. I didn't get a license plate. Don't worry. I'm fine."

Dad scanned the suspect board again. "You don't really believe Wanda—"

The door to my office flew open. Lissa Reade rushed in out of breath. Joss stood over her shoulder.

"Courtney!" Lissa exclaimed. "I'm so glad you're here. Sorry to interrupt. Joss said you were in a meeting. It's urgent. Hello, Kipling." She nodded to my father.

Dad grumbled. He despised his given name, the one Nana had bestowed upon him because she had loved reading the classics. He liked to read them, too, but the formality of his name stuck in his craw.

"You haven't checked out any books lately, Kipling," Lissa said.

"Haven't had time."

"Make time," she ordered, like a schoolmarm. "You don't want your brain to become mush."

Fiona giggled.

Turning to me, Lissa held out a black book with gilt-edged pages, its spine frayed. "Courtney, Didi left her poetry journal on the lectern last night. I can't blame her. She was so upset by Kenny's outburst."

My father raised an eyebrow. "What outburst? What else have I missed?"

"Would you be a dear and deliver the it to Didi?" Lissa asked me. "I'd do so, but I have to see my sister. She's ill."

Joss said, "What about tomorrow's book club, Miss Reade?"

"Don't worry," Lissa answered. "I'll show up for the book club, but my sister really needs some TLC today."

Joss, realizing I was not under attack, waved good-bye and returned to the main showroom.

"Why didn't you leave the journal for Didi at the library's checkout desk, Lissa?" I asked.

"I was afraid Kenny might learn of its whereabouts and, well, he was so angry. Who knows what he might do to something so personal were he to intercept it?"

Lissa's worry seemed misguided, unless there was something in the journal that she believed Kenny might find offensive.

"Maybe Didi wrote a disparaging poem about him," Fiona suggested, giving voice to my concern.

Lissa said, "Merryweather told me . . ." She eyed my father.

He raised a skeptical eyebrow. "Merryweather?"

"A friend," Lissa explained.

"Aha!" Fiona said. "My mentor gave you the warning, didn't she, Miss Reade? She is so clever."

"Anyway," Lissa continued, "I touched base with Didi. I didn't want her to worry. She thanked me and said she won't be at Sport Zone until later today. She's in San Jose at the moment. If you have time, would you mind taking it to her after work?"

"Sure," I said.

"Bless you." Lissa held out the book but lost her grip. It

fell from her hands onto the floor. A page came loose. "Oh, drat. Clumsy me. I knew how fragile it was. Just look at the wear and tear." She clucked her tongue as she tucked the page inside the journal. "Didi has not taken good care of it." She pushed the book into my hands.

"Journals aren't made to last like they used to be," I said.

"How true. Ta-ta." Lissa pecked my cheek and left as quickly as she'd entered.

I set the journal on my desk. "Where were we, Dad?"

His jaw was ticking with tension. "Tell me about Kenny Chu."

I explained about the poetry reading and Kenny's tirade and subsequent flare-up with me. "He left in a huff, and—"

"And someone tried to run you off the road. Courtney—"

"I reported it. Officer Reddick investigated."

"When will you learn—"

"To keep my nose out of things? To not care? Dad, c'mon. Who taught me to be observant?" I aimed a finger at him. "You! Who taught me to be proactive? You. You wanted me to be independent. Strong. A person who thinks outside the box."

"I want to be a fairy that thinks outside the box," Fiona said.

Dad shot out a hand. "But not someone who runs *toward* trouble."

"You did, Dad. As a cop. Plus, I've seen you rush to help people in an accident. It's the right thing to do."

He ran his fingers through his thick hair. "You have a glib tongue, young lady. That's your mother's fault."

"No, sir. I learned that from you. It's the Irish in us."

"Faith and *begorrah*," Fiona trilled.

My father cocked his head. Had he heard her?

"Back to Wanda," I said, changing the subject. "She's on my suspect list because—"

"I know very well why she's on it." He sighed. "I'm going to take her some tarts to cheer her up." He jiggled the bag he was holding. "I thought you might like to accompany me."

"I would love that."

Joss poked her head in. "You can't."

"Why not?" I asked, bristling.

"Because Wanda and Meaghan just strolled in."

I swept past my father and tore into the main showroom. Fiona and my father trailed me.

A slew of customers were milling by the tea sets. Beyond them stood Wanda and Meaghan. They were inspecting a set of wind chimes. Meaghan looked pretty in a navy-blue lacy dress. Wanda had donned a white summer sweater over skinny jeans. Her ankle monitor stood out prominently. I tried not to stare at it.

"Wanda," I said, "it's so wonderful to see you out and about." I threw my arms around her. When I released her, I studied her face. "You look good." I wasn't lying. Her eyes were clear, her skin tone healthy.

Fiona circled Wanda while sprinkling her with silver dust.

"I feel good." Wanda smiled demurely at my father. "Hello, Kip."

"Nice to see you, Wanda."

Meaghan said, "Mom, tell them why you're beaming."

"The tox screen and urine tests came back. They prove that I was dosed with Ambien."

"Dosed?" I glanced between my pal and her mother.

"Mom hasn't taken it. Ever."

"I don't take any prescriptions," Wanda said. "Nothing bad goes into this body except the occasional juicy steak."

"Which means," Meaghan went on, "that someone slipped the drug into something Mom ate or drank at the party."

"That can't be proven, dear," Wanda said.

Meaghan frowned. "She's right. The tests don't show the exact time Mom consumed it, only that it was in her system."

"I don't understand," I said.

"Me, either," my father said. "Why is it a big deal that you ingested it at all?"

"Because"—Meaghan twirled a hand—"Ambien can cause odd dreams. Can you imagine the confusion a sleepwalker might suffer if, say, the sleepwalker stumbled upon a murder scene?"

"Freak-out time." Wanda wiggled her fingers next to her temples.

Fiona hovered beside Wanda and mimicked the gesture. "Freak-out, freak-out."

Meaghan said, "Which would explain why Mom knelt down and grasped the weapon."

I shook my head. "Why would Ambien show up in your system days later, Wanda?"

"Older people hang on to medications longer," Dad stated, as if he'd studied up on the subject.

"Exactly." Meaghan shot a *gotcha* finger at him. "Also, Mom ate a lot at the party, which helped the drug linger."

Wanda nodded. "The drug is probably the reason why I felt sleepy and needed to lie down."

"Does this get you off the hook, Wanda?" my father asked.

"Not exactly."

I said, "Why don't we all have tea on the patio and discuss this further?" I moved to the tea service behind the sales counter, poured four cups, set them on a tray, and added spoons and a container of honey. I carried the items to the patio and set them on a wrought-iron table beyond the fountain. My father brought four small plates and forks and laid out the tarts he'd purchased.

When I sat down, Pixie scampered over to me and rubbed

my ankles with her head. I petted her and gave her a nudge.
Fiona swooped to Pixie and landed like a skateboarder on her
back. The cat whirled around and snarled. Fiona doubled over
laughing.

I chuckled at their antics.

Wanda sat beside me. "What's so amusing? Is your fairy
here?"

"Yes." Meaghan pointed. "She's toying with the cat."

My father coughed his disbelief.

"I can see her now, Kip," Meaghan said. "I couldn't before. It took making a fairy garden for Mom to open my eyes."

Dad grunted.

"She's glimmering," Meaghan said, trying to persuade him.

My father plopped into a chair and folded his arms, having
none of it.

"Wanda, who were you with other than us at the party?"
I asked.

"Everyone." She counted on her fingertips. "Elton, Lana,
the Meeting Hall benefactors."

"Tamara Geoffries?" I asked.

"Of course." Wanda placed a hand on her chest. "She's
such a darling. We have quite a number of deals pending. An
entire estate from San Francisco is due any day. It includes
gorgeous antiques that Tamara has been salivating over. She
has quite the clientele."

Despite the fact that Fiona and I wanted Tamara to be innocent, I couldn't rule out that she could have been the person who had tried to run me over.

"How about Kenny Chu, Wanda?" I asked. "Did you
chat with him?"

"Why, yes. Kenny and Didi wanted to talk about how to
drum up new business at Sport Zone." Wanda lowered her
voice. "Ever since Davis died, the club has struggled financially. Didi has had to cut back on water consumption, and

the electrical bill is through the roof. She even canceled the security system, but I didn't think that was wise. Too much equipment to lose. So I paid for all of it for a month. *Shh.*" She held a finger to her lips. "Didi doesn't know. Next up, repair the roof and the pickleball courts and—"

"You can't cover all of that, Mother," Meaghan protested.

"No. I've done my share, but that's what's next on Didi's to-do list. The club needs more dues-paying members. It's that simple."

"Back to the party time frame," I said. "What did you drink, Wanda?"

"White wine, a sip or two of champagne, a Perrier with lime . . ." Wanda tapped her chin, thinking. "A glass of water, and—"

"Did you hold on to each drink until you finished it?" I asked.

"Of course." Wanda bobbed her head. "I learned my lesson as a teenager about the hazards of drinking a beverage after it had been out of sight."

Meaghan shot her mother a worrisome glance.

"Sweetheart, don't go to the dark side." Wanda petted Meaghan's shoulder. "I learned to be cautious because a tricky sixteen-year-old thought it would be funny to put cough syrup in my cherry Coke at a party. I got so sick that I was in the bathroom until sunrise. That's why I taught you to be watchful."

Meaghan rolled her eyes at me. "She's not kidding. I can't tell you how many half glasses of soda I had to abandon during college."

"Were you watchful at the Spectacular, Wanda?" I asked.

"Absolutely."

My dad said, "What does it matter how the Ambien got into Wanda's system? Obviously, the killer gave her something on purpose to make her sleepy."

"Unless"—I squeezed the liquid from my tea bag into my cup and set the tea bag on the saucer—"the authorities think Wanda dosed herself."

"Dosed myself?" Wanda scoffed. "Why on earth—"

"So you could claim sleepwalking as a defense."

Meaghan scowled at me. "They wouldn't. They couldn't. Why are you being such a Debbie Downer? Besides, how could my mother be sure she'd wake up exactly when Lana entered the bidding room? The timing would be ridiculously hard."

Fiona flew to the table and alit on the rim of my tea. "Good point. How did the killer plan that?"

I wasn't sure. Did he or she lure Lana there, stage the scene, and then wait for Wanda to wake up and take the fall?

"Wanda, how many people know you are a sleepwalker?" I asked.

"A few of my friends. Plus, a few people at Sport Zone. I had an episode at the club once. I fell asleep in the office. Life had simply caught up to me. Kenny was locking up. He'd just finished a lesson with Elton Lamar. I frightened the two of them when I emerged from the employees' lounge and didn't respond to their questions. Later, Kenny teased that I was acting like a zombie, arms jutting in front of me like this." Wanda demonstrated. "My eyes were open the whole time, he said—that's typical for a sleepwalker—but I couldn't remember having seen anything. I must have been groping for a door or something."

Meaghan drummed the table. "Victoria Judge took the evidence to the police. She's at the precinct right now. We're waiting—" Her cell phone rang with a "Don't Worry, Be Happy" ringtone. She fished it out of her purse. "It's her. Miss Judge." She pressed Send. "Hello, Victoria." She listened. "Yes. Uh-huh. Okay." My pal's mouth turned up on both ends. "Thank you." She ended the call, set her cell phone on the table, and took hold of her mother's hands. "Mom, you're exonerated. One hundred percent. We can go to the precinct and they'll remove the ankle bracelet."

Wanda let out a delighted squeal. "Wonderful. Absolutely incredible. Kip—" She pivoted to face him.

"I'm coming with you." He was beaming.

Meaghan threw her arms around her mother. So did I.

"Group hug!" I yelled.

My father held back. Fiona didn't. She whizzed to Wanda, knelt on her shoulder, and caressed Wanda's hair. Reflexively, Wanda smoothed her hair. In the nick of time, Fiona sailed off and escaped being squished. She giggled.

"What was that tinkling sound?" Wanda asked.

"Mom. That's Fiona."

Wanda peered overhead.

"By the way"—Meaghan clutched my arm—"I saw the fairy in my garden."

My father grunted. "Oh, c'mon. Now you're seeing others? Hogwash."

Meaghan nodded. "It's true. She's got green wings and a green dress and—"

My father exhaled forcefully.

"Courtney!" Joss appeared in the doorway leading to the main showroom. Her face was pinched with worry. "Detective Summers is here. Are you expecting him? Is something wrong?"

"Relax. Breathe. It's all good." I moved inside to greet him. "Detective, you've come to the right place."

"I happen to know that." Summers grinned and hooked his thumb. "I was around the corner when I heard the news. As luck would have it, the Brownies were seen by one of our patrol cars entering your establishment, so I decided to come over and do the honors myself. Where is—" He peered toward the patio. "Ah, there she is."

He made a beeline to Wanda. I followed.

"Mrs. Brownie," Summers said, maintaining the formality he preferred when in a public setting, "I am sorry for any inconvenience you may have experienced. You no longer need to wear that contraption. May I?" He motioned for Wanda to sit in a chair. She did. He bent down and, using a tool he took from his pocket, removed the monitor. "You are free to roam."

Wanda hooted with glee.

"But?" I asked. I'd noticed something hesitant in the detective's tone.

Summers threw me a look. "But don't leave town."

"What?" Wanda chewed her lower lip. "I thought—"

"We might need you as a character witness when we do find the killer."

Liar, liar. Summers hadn't completely ruled Wanda out as a suspect, probably for the same reason I'd surmised. If the police concluded that Wanda had given herself the Ambien, all bets were off.

Chapter 25

❧⚜❧

*May you touch dragonflies and stars, dance with fairies,
and talk to the moon.*
—a fairy blessing

My father and Wanda left together to celebrate. Meaghan, elated and at peace, headed to Flair Gallery. With her mother cleared, she could get back to business. Joss and I stayed at the store and kept on task, although I continued to think about the other suspects I'd written on the marker board in my office. True, with Wanda cleared I no longer needed to figure out who had killed Lana Lamar, but the question remained. Equally important was the other nagging question: Why had the killer implicated Wanda?

Close to noon, a gaggle of forty-something do-it-yourselfers arrived en masse with lunch bags in hand. Their leader, a buoyant woman, had arranged for them to occupy four of the tables on the patio so they could conduct their own fairy garden workshop. She planned to videotape the event and share it on her social media page. Who was I to argue? I wouldn't shake a finger at free publicity.

Minutes after I'd shown the women to the learning-the-craft corner, I heard a stir in the main showroom. I peered through the window and spied Kenny Chu facing Joss, his arms thrown wide. In his skintight orange workout outfit, Kenny reminded me of an Oscar Mayer whistle. He wasn't aiming a weapon at Joss and he wasn't as red-faced as he had been last night at the library, but even so my stomach knotted. What did he want? I was certain he hadn't come to build a fairy garden.

Drawing in a deep breath, I hurried into the shop. "Kenny, how can I help you?"

Joss's face was ashen. Her lower lip was trembling. Had he threatened her? I gently nudged her aside, and though I wasn't much bigger than she was, it was my shop, my home turf.

"Speak," I said to Kenny.

"I . . ." He checked his watch and glanced over his shoulder.

Fiona zipped into view. "Maybe he's waiting for someone."

"Kenny," I repeated, "talk to me."

Pixie romped into the shop and brushed against him. Kenny peered at her and back at me.

"Are you okay?" I asked. "Do you need some water?"

"There you are." Tamara Geoffries scuttled into the shop, out of breath, and drew alongside Kenny. She pushed off the hood of her cloak and flipped her hair over her shoulders. Her face was taut and her eyes strained. "I thought we'd agreed to meet in front," she said to Kenny.

Why had they agreed to meet at all?

"What's going on?" Fiona asked.

I shook my head, as confused as she was. Had Tamara hoped to have a clandestine meeting with Kenny? If so, she was out of luck. Everyone in the shop was staring at them.

Kenny sputtered again and wrapped an arm around Tamara's shoulders.

When she didn't shrug him off, I recalled wondering at

the Spectacular whether they were dating. I'd sidelined the idea. Had I been wrong? Were they star-crossed lovers planning to elope? *Get real, Courtney.* They were of age and neither was married.

"Tamara, please explain," I said.

She met my gaze calmly, her anger of yesterday no longer evident.

"May we talk in private, Courtney?" she asked.

"You and me? Or you and Kenny?"

"The three of us."

"I'm coming along." Joss squared her shoulders, doing her best to look formidable. She would need another six inches and fifty pounds to pull it off.

"How about we chat by the fountain?" I suggested. In plain view, for all to see. "The water will drown out our conversation from others."

"Uh, okay." Kenny frowned, not convinced.

I squeezed Joss's arm. "I'll be fine."

Fiona followed Tamara, Kenny, and me to the patio and hovered by my shoulder.

"I'm sorry about last night," Kenny began. "At the library. I don't know what came over me."

"A guilty conscience," Fiona quipped.

Tamara placed a hand on his arm. "Tell Courtney everything," she said in her dulcet, soothing tone.

Kenny nodded. "I'm here to confess."

"To murdering Lana?" I gasped.

"What? No!" His face drained of color. "To my alibi on the night of the murder. I know I said I couldn't at the library, but now I can—"

"From the beginning," Tamara coached.

"I wasn't in love with Lana Lamar." Kenny licked his lips. "I mean, I was. Once. When we first met. I adored her. I worshiped her. I obeyed everything she said. I fell in line. I . . ." He faltered and licked his lips.

"Keep going," Tamara cooed.

"Lana was smart and savvy and well invested."

Had Kenny and Tamara rehearsed riffing off each other? Had they plotted to kill Lana together and pulled it off? Was this scenario a trial run before they told the police their story?

"Your alibi," I said, steering the conversation back to Kenny's confession.

"That will come," Tamara assured me.

"I could tell Lana wasn't in love with Elton," Kenny continued, "so I thought I stood a chance"—he sucked back a sob—"if I became the man she wanted me to be."

"Kenny was her pawn," Tamara said. "She duped him."

"I knew Lana would only fall for a rich man, so when she told me how I could increase my income, I jumped at the bait."

"Lana scammed him," Tamara said, "and Kenny lost every cent he had. She suggested he invest in this, that, and the other thing, as if she were educated in the market. She wasn't. She had no business doing what she did. Lana blindsided Kenny."

"I took out loans," Kenny said. "I refinanced my house. Hedda Hopewell—"

"Arranged these loans for you," I cut in.

He nodded. That would explain why Lissa Reade had seen him entering the bank daily.

Fiona sailed around Kenny's head. She wasn't spritzing him with anything, but I heard her utter, "*By dee prood mahaw*," the same incantation she'd said the other day to help lighten Didi's spirit.

"Kenny was addicted," Tamara said. "He was Lana's slave."

"I hated her. Despised her."

"But you didn't kill her?" I asked.

"No."

Fiona landed on my shoulder. "I get it now. Don't you see? Tamara Geoffries is Kenny's doctor."

"Tamara," I said, "is it true that you're a therapist as well as an antiques dealer?"

"Yes. I'm an LMHC, licensed mental health counselor. I was a full-time therapist in San Francisco until I met my husband, Jamie. When he asked me to marry him, I moved here to be with him and turned to my second love, selling antiques. My mother had sold them. I'd learned everything about them as a girl." She lifted her chin and met my gaze. "Why?"

"Is Kenny your patient?" I asked.

"Yes."

"The rumor is that you only consult the rich and famous, but, by his admission, Kenny is broke."

"Kenny is . . ." Tamara paused. "Kenny *was* my trainer at Sport Zone. When I saw what Lana was doing to him, I took pity on him, ended our trainer-student relationship, and offered to advise him for free." She petted his shoulder. "Go on, Kenny. Tell the rest of your story. Share your alibi."

"That night . . ." Kenny looked past me at the do-it-yourselfers. "Are you sure they can't hear us?"

"Positive," I said. Neither the leader nor any of the participants were looking in our direction. "Go on."

"I was in session with Tamara—Dr. Geoffries—last week, and we got to talking about what I should do about Lana, and . . ." Kenny pressed his lips together. "That night, at the party"—he hung his head—"I told Tamara I wanted to do something that would hurt Lana and she said, 'Let's go somewhere and talk.'"

Tamara said to me, "What I told you, Courtney, wasn't a complete lie. We went next door."

"Midway through our talk," Kenny said, "Tamara suggested—"

"This is where it gets dicey," Tamara cut in.

"She suggested I sabotage Lana's fortune."

"I told him Lana loved money and suggested he hit her where it hurt."

"How would he do that?" I asked.

"I wasn't sure," Tamara said. "We were batting around ideas."

"But see"—Kenny opened his hands—"I worried that if I told the police what we talked about, it might compromise Tamara's reputation."

"What I did wasn't ethical," she admitted.

"So we didn't tell anyone that we'd met." Kenny dropped his hands to his sides, shoulders slumped. "Tamara told you she went to visit the cats, which was true, and I lied about going to the library."

"The cats!" Fiona piped up. "They could prove Tamara isn't lying."

"Cats can't talk," I blurted.

"Don't be ridiculous," Tamara replied. "Of course they can't."

I eyed Fiona, blaming her for my misstep.

"But there was cat hair everywhere," Tamara went on. "Maybe—"

"Maybe it would still be on my jacket." Kenny's eyes lit up.

At the party, I'd noticed Kenny had removed his jacket. Later on, I'd wondered, like Detective Summers had, whether Kenny had taken it off because Lana's blood had splattered onto it.

"What did you do with your jacket?" I asked.

"I took it off and stowed it in the trunk of my car because it was covered with cat hair. I thought it would give us away."

"Maybe now it could prove your alibi," Tamara said.

"Is your jacket still in the trunk?" I asked.

"Yes." Kenny bobbed his head. "I've been meaning to take it to the dry cleaner."

I screwed up my mouth as another notion took hold. "You could acquire cat hair anywhere."

"Not the gray cat's hair," Fiona said. "That cat is unique."

"Tamara, you said the ghostly gray cat with the white muzzle lives on that property."

"Yes."

"Did you see it that night?" I asked.

"It sat in my lap."

"And mine," Kenny said.

Were they lying? Why concoct such a far-out story?

"Why did you put on a coat that night, Tamara?" I asked.

"Because it was cold. I get cold easily."

"The hem of your coat had dirt on it," I said.

"From sitting on the ground by the crypt."

Fiona said, "Maybe Kenny's jacket has dirt on it, too, and the dirt will match the soil of the neighbor's property."

I eyed her with awe. She was getting good at this detecting thing.

I touched Tamara's arm. "You and Kenny need to tell the police your story. Kenny, give them your jacket, and Tamara, provide your coat." I mentioned what Fiona had said about testing the soil and the cat hair. "If the evidence proves out, both of you will be off the hook."

Leaving Elton as the main suspect. If only he didn't have a verifiable alibi.

As Kenny and Tamara left the shop, Ulani Kamaka entered, her A-line skirt fluting around her toned thighs. Over her shoulder, a fairy flew into view. Zephyr, I presumed. What a beautiful fairy she was, with lavender eyes, lavender wings, and silver hair. She wore a two-toned dress that matched her features and toted a flute in a bow-and-arrow-style pouch.

Fiona darted to Zephyr. The two chatted animatedly in fairy speak. I sensed that something was, as Fiona loved to say, *afoot*.

"Miss Kamaka," I said, "nice to see you. Were you able to—"

She pinched my elbow. "Come with me."

Unable to resist her fervor, I said to Joss over my shoulder, "Back in a few." To Ulani, I said, "Where are we going?"

"Sweet Treats."

We headed out of the shop and through the courtyard, taking the steps two at a time. Fiona and Zephyr trailed us. At Sweet Treats, Ulani whipped open the door. Customers stood in line, many peering into the glass display case filled with pastries, cakes, and cookies. The three retro pink stools were occupied at the counter. Yvanna was behind the counter packing an order into a Sweet Treats bag. Her boss was weaving through the four café tables serving up coffee.

"Follow me," Ulani said.

Tish Waterman was at one of the tables. Opposite her sat a younger woman, late thirties, who was the spitting image of a younger Tish. Short dark hair. Whip thin. She had to be Tish's daughter, Twyla. Her shoulders were hunched and her gaze cautious, as if her experience with the cult had drained all confidence from her. On the other hand, Twyla had had the wherewithal to escape and hide. She was a survivor. Both women were wearing all-white ensembles, as if they'd exchanged wardrobe notes before meeting. I imagined Tish had worn white to express her hopefulness. White wasn't typically her color.

On the table between them sat a plate of sugar cookies. Tish had bought some the other day under the advisement of

Zephyr, who had suggested that the aroma might lure Twyla home.

I strolled to the table and said to Tish, "This must be your daughter."

Tish's eyes glistened with tears. "Yes. Twyla, meet my friend Courtney."

I choked up. *Friend.* How one's fate could change in the blink of an eye.

"Nice to meet you," Twyla said, her voice thin.

Fiona and Zephyr, each shimmering with good vibrations, circled Twyla's head.

Tish grabbed my hand and said, "Bless you."

"Bless the fairies," I said. "And Ulani Kamaka."

Tish beamed at Ulani. "Thank you so much."

Ulani said, "Think nothing of it," but I could tell she was hoping to get the exclusive on the story. In my humble opinion, she had every reason to expect Tish to grant her wish.

"I'll leave you to it," I said.

Tish gripped my hand harder. "Wait. Don't go. Twyla, sweetheart, I have to share something with Courtney."

"Do you want me to leave?" Twyla asked.

"No!" Tish nearly screamed the word. "No, sweetheart, I just don't want you to think I'm ignoring you."

"Mo-om," Twyla said as if she were still a teenager. "We've got lots of time. Go on. Talk."

Tish released my hand. "Courtney, I was thinking about what I'd seen at the Spectacular."

"Are you referring to the gray cat?"

"No. I saw Elton and Lana Lamar exchanging words. I told the police as much. But then, yesterday, when I was in Percolate getting a latte to go, I recalled seeing Elton at the café a week ago sitting at a table for two with . . ." She hesitated. "With an attractive brunette. I don't think they were in love. In fact, I think they were involved in a business deal. He gave her cash"—Tish mimed the gesture—"so it couldn't have been about him selling her a car. At least, it didn't seem so."

"Oho!" Fiona trilled from over my shoulder.

She must have jumped to the same conclusion I had. Elton had sought the services of a professional. Why? Had Lana denied him sex?

"I took a picture," Tish went on. "I know it was rude of me, but something about their negotiation stuck in my craw. I live a life born of caution nowadays."

Twyla shifted in her chair.

Tish opened the photo app on her cell phone and swiped to the picture. "See?" She had captured the brunette's image in profile. Even from that angle, I could see she had sharp cheekbones and penetrating eyes. Aloofness bordering on contempt oozed from every fiber of her being.

Something about her seemed familiar. Where had I seen her before? And then I remembered. On a flyer at the precinct. When Meaghan and I had gone to see Detective Summers. The brunette was a wanted criminal.

"Tish, you have to show this photograph to the police."

Chapter 26

Do not think the fairies are always little. Everything is capricious about them, even their size.
—W. B. Yeats, *Fairy and Folk Tales of the Irish Peasantry*

At noon, as I waited for Tish to touch base and tell me how the police had reacted to her revelation, Fiona flew to me and asked whether I'd heard from Kenny and Tamara. I hadn't. Fiona was concerned that they'd put one over on us. Her unease made me reconsider my conversation with Lissa Reade about Kenny and how often he would visit the library to day-trade using the computers and how she would see him enter Carmel Bank daily. Lana's bad advice had caused Kenny to lose everything. Was Fiona right to be worried? Had Kenny killed Lana? Had he convinced Tamara to lie for him?

Unwilling to sit and wait for news to come to me, I asked Joss to watch the shop and contacted Hedda Hopewell. I invited her to join me for lunch at Devendorf Park, stating that I needed to pick her brain about a financial issue. She was more than happy to oblige.

Fiona went with me to buy a couple of sandwiches and iced teas at Deli Delicious.

At a quarter to one, we arrived at the park. Considering the near-perfect weather, the site was chock-full of people. Walkers. Joggers. History buffs studying the statuary. A family of six were picnicking on a blanket. A handsome bleached-blond man in swim trunks and tight T-shirt was playing Frisbee with his Dalmatian. A silver-haired woman was training her Goldendoodle to heel.

I sat on a bench beneath the gigantic oak and waited. And waited. Fifteen minutes later, I checked my iPhone. No messages.

"Yoo-hoo, Courtney, here I am." Hedda, wearing a long-sleeved dress and a sun hat as large as mine to protect her fair skin, arrived out of breath. "Sorry I'm late. A customer came in at the last minute." She planted herself on the other side of the deli bag and crooked an arm over the back of the bench. "It's always something, isn't it?"

I unpacked the lunch and handed her a sandwich. "Hope you like tuna."

"Adore it." Hedda peeked beneath the bread. "Pickles. Perfect." Before taking a bite, she said, "Okay, what's up?"

"I want to speak to you about Kenny Chu. He said he did a few transactions with you. I'm sure you can't reveal anything about them, but can you at least confirm that he did?"

"Kenny is a regular. A tad wild with his investments, and that's not talking out of school. Everyone at the bank knows it. For a fit guy, Kenny often comes in sweating bullets." She sipped her tea. "These young people think they can hit it big if they simply guess how the market will react day by day. Me? I believe in spreading the risk between stocks and bonds. I'm conservative, and I advise every customer of mine to do the same, but do they listen?" She wagged her head. "Kenny, sad to say, has made some very bad investments."

So Kenny wasn't lying about losing his shirt. Score one for truthfulness.

"Watch out!" a man yelled.

A Frisbee landed at our feet. The blond and his Dalmatian jogged over to retrieve it. Fiona whisked to the Dalmatian and gave the dog's ears a pat. She adored canines.

As the man rose, he locked eyes with Hedda. The wrinkles around his intense eyes crinkled, revealing his age—around sixty. "Hey there, ma'am," he said to Hedda. "Remember me?"

Hedda shook her head.

"Last Saturday night. You were by the statue of the monk. I was here, on the bench. No dog."

The dog took that as a cue and head-bumped Hedda's hand. Fiona spiraled into the air.

Hedda stroked the Dalmatian as she regarded the man. "That was you?"

"Yep. All dressed up with no place to go." He hooked a thumb. "After any business dinner, I enjoy sitting in the park and going over the conversation." He smiled easily. "I've seen you before. In the bank and around. I'm Jeremy." He blinked, as if seeing me for the first time. "Sorry. Jeremy Batcheller." He thumbed his chest.

"Batcheller Galleries?" I asked.

"The same." He regarded Hedda again and offered a winning smile. "I see you're busy. I didn't mean to intrude. How about I stop by the bank soon? Say hello. Maybe we could grab a coffee."

"Sure," Hedda said, breathless.

"Let's go, Polka Dot." Jeremy tossed the Frisbee and the Dalmatian ran off. He tore after the dog, his calf muscles something to behold.

I tapped Hedda's arm. "Well, well. I think someone likes you."

"It was him." Her tone was breathy, as if shocked.

"What do you mean? Him *who*?"

"He was the man who was in the park the other night.

Not Elton Lamar. I mistook Jeremy's dark suit for a tuxedo. His hair"—she wiggled her fingers beside her temples—"is similar to Elton's."

Fiona kicked my shoulder. "So Elton doesn't have a verifiable alibi after all."

After a long silence, Hedda said, "I haven't dated since . . ."

I nodded.

"I probably should."

"If you want to."

"Jeremy seemed nice." She smiled demurely.

"And he was very much into you. A potent combination."

As Fiona and I returned to the shop, Fiona whispered, "*Psst.* Look."

Across the street, Elton Lamar was entering Hideaway Café.

I didn't know what I hoped to learn by following him into the restaurant, but I did.

Brady met me at the hostess desk. "Table for one?"

And a fairy, I mused, but kept that tidbit to myself. "Perfect. I could use a cup of tea and a moment to collect my thoughts." The hostess was leading Elton to the rear patio. "Outside, if there's room."

"For you, I'll make room." The way Brady's eyes twinkled made me smile. Was he ever depressed or sullen? "This way."

Brady set a menu on a table for two and pulled out a chair for me. "Chamomile?" he asked.

"Earl Grey. Thanks. And honey."

"Talk about a potent combination," Fiona teased as Brady left.

"Cut it out," I snapped.

Toward the rear of the patio, I spied Elton sitting by himself, viewing his cell phone. A lithe woman in a white linen suit joined him. I recognized her. She was one of the premier travel agents in town. *Do you need a getaway?* her local TV ads asked. She could pull strings. *A safari for two?* She was your gal. I passed her offices often on my strolls around town. Images of the far-off places she posted in the windows made me salivate.

Elton was doing all the talking. The travel agent was nodding. Was Elton planning to leave town?

Brady returned with a pot of tea and a white china teacup and saucer, plus a plate of miniature lemon cookies. "Thought you might be hungry." He perched on the chair opposite me and took a cookie for himself. "If you aren't, I am." He chuckled low. "Any fairies about?" He searched overhead.

"Mine and the café's," I said.

His eyes widened. "We have one?"

I nodded. "I haven't met her yet. She's quite shy."

Fiona wasn't allowed to make friends with her. We didn't know her name.

"Well, well. Does everyone in Carmel-by-the-Sea have a fairy?"

"Don't be silly. Of course not. Fairies like to live where the energy is positive."

Brady raised an eyebrow. "Who are you kidding? I heard Tish Waterman has one, and she is as bitter—"

"Not anymore. Her daughter has returned, safe and sound. Tish's negativity is receding as we speak."

"So there!" Fiona cried.

Brady folded his forearms on the table and leaned in. "How did that come about?"

"Magic."

He took another cookie. "Speaking of fairies, are there any gremlins and such in Carmel? Are they referred to as gremlins in this day and age?"

"I'm sure if there are, they're called gremlins. I haven't had the pleasure of meeting one, thank you very much."

"What about trolls and pixies?"

I laughed. "Yep. And warlocks and witches, and don't forget the unicorns and fairy horses."

"You're pulling my leg."

The queen fairy had told Fiona stories about all sorts of other spirits roaming the earth. Was it true? I didn't relish meeting a witch.

Fiona said, "What do you think Elton and that woman are talking about?"

I looked over my shoulder. Elton was gazing at the multiple brochures the agent was handing him.

"Why do you keep looking at Elton?" Brady asked.

Caught in the act, I felt my cheeks flame with heat. "Don't you think it's odd that he's seeking the advice of a travel agent so soon after his wife's demise?"

"Maybe he intends to have a memorial for Lana in her hometown. Wasn't she born in Texas?"

I blanched, having not thought of something so reasonable. Why were my thoughts constantly running to the nefarious? "You're right. Bad me." I sipped my tea and ate a cookie. "Delicious."

"The trick is to double the zest."

For a few minutes Brady and I talked about his business— it was thriving. He was toying with new recipes to expand the menu. Shop talk apparently bored my fairy. Fiona yawned and flew off. I, on the other hand, was entranced. When Brady ran out of things to say about food, he asked me about my business, which surprised me. I couldn't remember the last man who'd been interested. Certainly not Christopher, who had thought my career as a landscaper had been perhaps the most boring profession I could have undertaken. I wondered if my ex-fiancé knew I'd opened my own shop. And then I wondered why I cared.

"Psst." Fiona returned, wings fluttering at high speed. "You've got to see this."

"See what?" I asked.

Brady peeked overhead. "Who are you talking to?"

"Guess."

He narrowed his eyes as if that would help him see her. After a long moment, he rose to his feet and shook a leg dramatically. "I'm getting a spasm from all the leg-pulling."

"I'm not lying." I really wanted him to be a believer. "You'll see one someday. Promise."

"I'll hold you to that." Brady petted my arm, sending a shiver down my spine, and headed into the restaurant. "Tea is on me," he said.

Fiona tugged a lock of my hair. "Come with me. Now."

"Okay, okay." I grabbed my purse and trailed after her. "What's the urgency?"

"Elton Lamar left. He went outside."

I took a quick look over my shoulder. Too absorbed in my conversation with Brady, I hadn't seen Elton or the travel agent leave. So much for being an ace sleuth. "Where is he?" I asked.

"Getting into a car."

I hurried out of the restaurant and paused on the sidewalk. I glanced to the right and saw why Fiona had been insistent. Elton was climbing into a dark-colored Honda, very similar in shape to the car that had tried to run me down, no *Lamar Motors* stamped on a temporary license plate.

In fact, no license plate at all.

Chapter 27

Every time a new story is told, a fairy is born.
—Anonymous

I rushed after the car but realized it was fruitless. I wouldn't be able to stop Elton on foot. Outside Seize the Clay, I drew to a halt and bent over to catch my breath. My morning jogs had not prepared me for a mad dash.

"Are you okay?" Renee Rodriguez asked, stepping from her store.

"Not. A. Sprinter."

She gripped my elbow. "Why were you running so fast?"

"It's a long story." I stood upright and finger-combed my hair.

"Come in for a cup of tea and tell us about it."

"Us?"

"Dylan is visiting." Renee guided me into the store.

Fiona followed. "It's so calm in here," she whispered, entranced. "I'll be back." She flew off, inspecting each of the areas.

Drinking in the white décor and Zen-like atmosphere made my shoulders relax. Detective Summers was standing near the register. Was he off duty? Dressed in blue shorts and white polo, he looked ready for a day at the beach. A few customers roamed the shop. Renee's capable assistants weren't shadowing them, but they were remaining close, if needed.

"What brings you in?" Summers asked me as we moved away from the register, an easy smile gracing his face.

"Courtney was chasing someone or something," Renee said. "She said it's a long story. Care to share?" She gazed at me, truly concerned.

"Elton Lamar was at Hideaway Café meeting with a travel agent, and my—" I stopped short of saying *my fairy*. "Someone mentioned that he was getting into his car outside, and it turned out it was the same kind of car—"

"That tried to run you down," Summers said. "Nondescript. Dark-colored car. No license plate." So Reddick had read him in on the incident.

Renee looked incredulous. "Someone tried to run you down? When?"

"Last night," Summers said. "After a poetry reading at the library."

"Were you hurt?" Renee seemed genuinely concerned.

"A few scrapes. No major injuries."

"Who would have done such a thing?" she asked.

I said, "My first guess was that it was Kenny Chu. He disrupted the poetry reading. He was quite upset with Didi Dubois and me because I'd coaxed Didi into peeking in his employee locker." Before Summers could ask why, I said, "There were legitimate reasons. We found a shrine to Lana inside."

"Pardon me," a female customer said to Renee. "I'd like to purchase a set of cerulean dishes."

Renee excused herself from us and followed the customer to the display.

Summers said, "By the way, Miss Kelly, investigating without a license can rub people the wrong way."

"I wasn't—"

Summers offered a wry smile.

I responded by scowling.

"Do you suspect anyone other than Kenny of charging at you?" Summers asked.

"Tamara Geoffries owns a dark blue Celica," I replied. "However, I don't believe Kenny or Tamara is the culprit. Haven't they stopped in at the precinct to talk to you yet?"

"Not that I know of."

I filled Summers in on their visit to the shop and their corroborating alibis.

"You think they're telling the truth?" he asked.

"Perhaps, but Elton Lamar has access to a whole host of cars, many without license plates."

Summers's gaze narrowed. "Why would Elton Lamar try to run you over?"

"Honestly, I can't fathom a reason other than that I'd encouraged Holly Hopewell to go to the precinct and talk to your sketch artist about the brunette she saw with Elton. If Holly didn't come in—"

"She did."

"And you saw the sketch?"

"I did."

"Good, because if Holly hadn't shown up, I was going to say you need to talk to Tish Waterman. She saw Elton with the brunette at Percolate a week ago, and she thought it was odd the way Elton and the woman were negotiating, so she took a photograph of the two of them. She showed it to me earlier. By the way, I've seen the brunette before. At the precinct. Among the wanted criminal flyers."

"I know." Summers grinned. "I'm actually an astute guy."

"I'm sorry. I didn't mean to imply—" I opened my palms. "So who is she? What did she do? Rob a bank?"

Summers worked his tongue inside his cheek.

"C'mon, spill, Detective," I begged.

"She's a professional killer."

I gawped. "Are you kidding me? A hit woman?"

Fiona flitted to my shoulder. "What's going on? Your voice shot up an octave."

"That's it, Detective," I went on. "Mystery solved. Elton hired the brunette to kill his wife. Tish will corroborate that Elton gave her money."

Summers raised a hand. "Hold on, speed demon."

"A trained professional"—I chopped one hand against the other—"could have set up Wanda to enter the crime scene at just the right time."

"Stop!" Summers barked. Automatically, he glanced over his shoulder. Renee was handing the customer her purchase while glowering at her fiancé. Lowering his voice, Summers said, "You're wrong. The brunette did not kill Lana."

"How can you be sure?"

"Because she was with Elton."

"That's another thing," I said. "Elton didn't leave the party, as he'd claimed, and go to Devendorf Park. Hedda Hopewell was there at that time. At first, she thought she'd seen him and corroborated his whereabouts, but today she realized she had seen the owner of the Batcheller Galleries that night, not Elton." I drew in a deep breath. "Elton lied."

"Yes, he lied about going to the park, but he did leave the party." Summers spread his hands. "To meet with the brunette. I know, because she is an undercover cop. Elton had been planning Lana's murder for nearly a month."

"Honestly? Why did he want her dead? To inherit her wealth?"

"Lana didn't have any money. She was broke."

"Really? Lana told Kenny Chu she was an expert investor."

"She wasn't. She was running through her personal funds like water. Elton was putting up all sorts of financial roadblocks to stop her from bleeding him dry, but they weren't working; hence, wanting her dead."

"So Elton's business is not struggling?"

"Nope. It's thriving. We've been waiting for him to pay the UC so we could haul him to jail for intent to kill."

"Did he pay her that night?"

"No. He waffled."

"Elton paid her when Tish saw him," I countered.

Summers wagged a hand. "No, actually, he didn't. We know about that incident because the UC and Elton saw Tish take the photo and, seconds later, Elton asked for the money back. Now that Lana Lamar is dead, no crime, no foul."

"Will Elton do time for intent?" I asked.

Summers shrugged. "It'll be up to the court to decide."

Fiona said, "A change of heart is a good thing. Maybe Elton realized he loved Lana after all."

Renee rejoined us. "I couldn't help but overhear you guys." She bussed Summers's cheek. "Ain't love grand? You think you know someone, and then, oops, it turns out you don't."

"You know me," Summers teased.

"I do."

They gazed at each other lovingly.

Fiona spiraled into the air and landed on Summers's shoulder. "Ask him if he has other suspects."

I did as bidden.

"Lana Lamar had a lot of enemies," Summers admitted. "Due to her rising debt, she owed a couple of people money. Not only that, but Lana rubbed a number of people at her husband's car dealership the wrong way, two in particular who happened to have attended the Spectacular."

I doubted any of them would have run me off the road. Perhaps that had been an accident, after all.

"If only the Meeting Hall had installed enough surveillance cameras," I said, "including one to cover the murder site."

"If only." Summers pecked Renee on the cheek and walked me out of the shop. On the sidewalk, he gripped my arm gently but firmly. "Listen, Miss Kelly, I've got this. Wanda is free. I want you to back off."

I promised I would.

The afternoon sped by because one hundred people from a tourist bus flooded in. For hours, they browsed Open Your Imagination and other shops in our courtyard. Fiona had toyed and teased a number of them. Two elderly women had asked if they could adopt Pixie. *No way*, I'd told them politely. For a few who begged for a class, I provided an impromptu one on making fairy gardens in eight-inch pots.

By the end of the day, I said to Joss, "I don't know about you, but I'm dog tired. What a day!"

"Me too." Joss swept the floor and emptied the contents of the dustbin into the trash can behind the counter. "But you don't get the luxury of going home to a glass of wine quite yet, boss."

"Why not?" I orbited the main showroom twisting teacup handles and righting wind chimes that were slightly askew. "I've earned it."

"Because you have to take the poetry book back to Didi at Sport Zone."

"Yikes." I'd forgotten my promise to Lissa Reade. "Maybe I'll work out while I'm there to revive myself."

"Instead, I'd opt for a steam."

A steam. That sounded nice.

Joss closed out the register and took the till to the office.

When she returned, I said, "Maybe you and I should have a spa day on one of our days off. We'll get Meaghan and a few others to join us."

"Great idea. *Ooh.*" She pointed at me. "I'll bet a grateful Tish Waterman will give you a discount."

I chuckled. "Don't count on it. She may have her daughter back, but she hasn't lost her business sense." I retreated to the office to fetch Didi's book of poetry and retrieved Pixie. "I'm taking you home, girl, and then I'm going out for an hour or so."

She purred her disapproval.

"Don't worry." I tapped her nose. "After that, it's dinner, a good book, and bed."

At home I threw on a sweater and inserted the journal into one of the oversized pockets, and then I rode my bicycle to Sport Zone with Fiona on my shoulder. She was up for adventure.

Pedaling hard, I said, "Get behind my neck, Fiona. It'll block you from the cool air."

Minutes later, we arrived at the athletic club. As I set the bicycle in the rack in the parking lot, attached the combination lock, and removed the journal from my pocket, I heard the unmistakable sound of a pickleball game on an outdoor court. Because the game was played with a hard paddle and a polymer ball, much like a Wiffle ball, the noise was akin to table tennis on steroids. I peeked through the mesh fabric covering the court's fencing and, beneath the halo of outdoor lighting, spied Hattie Hopewell playing a game with Cliff.

"Psst." Fiona tugged my hair. "Isn't that Didi?"

I pivoted and spotted Didi pulling up in her Mercedes, which was sputtering and spasming. Seconds later, two other cars, a muddy Dodge Dart and equally muddy Prius, drove in. Didi remained in her two-door coupe, mouth moving; she appeared to be talking on speakerphone.

The driver of the Dodge Dart, Pauline, and the driver of the Prius, her twin sister, clambered out of their cars at the same time. Both were laughing heartily. Both were dressed in jeans and long T-shirts, which were splattered with grime.

"We're not making this an everyday event, Sis," Pauline said. "My hair can't take daily washing."

"Mine, either," her sister replied.

As I neared Didi in her Mercedes, Pauline spun around from the trunk of her car, a gym bag in hand. The bag arced upward and connected with my arm, making me drop the poetry journal. Pages, many more than the one that had escaped at the shop, went flying.

"Oh, no," Pauline said. "I'm sorry."

We scrambled to collect the loose pages before any hit the muck that was dripping off Pauline and her sister.

Red-faced, Pauline said, "I'm such a klutz."

"It wasn't your fault. The book's spine is broken." I took the pages from her, relieved that Didi hadn't seen what had happened. "Why are you so dirty?"

"My sister and I went mud sliding. We've been three times this week, but I'm drawing the line. So much fun, but so sloppy!" She sputtered out a laugh. "We've got to run and clean up before our shifts."

"Go," I said.

As I waited for Didi to get out of her car, I read one of the single sheets Pauline had handed me.

The memory of you comes in the night
And swallows me whole.
The wind blows its mournful tune
And I catch my breath.
You are gone and naught will return you to my arms.
Yet she, and she alone, brings disgrace to your name.
She ruins the legacy that once was yours.
Did she, with vileness, prey upon you like a wraith,
Forcing you into submission until you died?
Demanding, taking, reviling
What you had created?
Her selfishness. Her ego.
Dominance over all is what she craves.
Giving nothing, ceding nothing.
How dare she do this to you, even still,
When you have no fight, no will.

"How sad," Fiona whispered, obviously picking up on the bitterness I was sensing from the poem.

It was no secret that Didi missed her husband something awful. She'd taken on the burden of Sport Zone to keep his memory alive. Was the *woman* a metaphor for his business? Had he given all he'd had to it, thus alienating Didi? I didn't understand poetry. English literature hadn't been my strong suit in college.

Didi opened her car door, which creaked in need of oil, and climbed out. She closed the door and locked the car using a remote key. "Hi, Courtney," she said, seeing me for the first time.

Swiftly, I slipped the poem into the journal. I didn't want her to think I was prying. "I brought this for you," I said, offering the book, noticing it looked ragtag after the spill. "Sorry, but the spine gave way, and—"

"No worries." Didi tucked the book into her purse and smoothed the lapel of her Balmain jacket. "My fault. I've been rough on it."

"How are you doing after last night's—"

"Fiasco?" She fanned the air. "I'm fine. But Kenny? Quitting in front of everyone? How embarrassing."

"I'm sorry."

"Don't be sorry for me. Be sorry for *him*. There are better ways to conduct oneself. He's gone off the rails." Didi leaned closer and lowered her voice. "If you ask me, after what we discovered in his locker, I'm convinced he killed Lana."

"Except he has a solid alibi."

"He does?" She arched an eyebrow. "I thought Lissa and you proved he didn't go to the library as he'd claimed."

"Correct, but as it turns out, he was with Tamara Geoffries." I didn't elaborate.

Didi frowned. "I was so certain he'd killed Lana, given his outburst. Thank heavens the police have come to their senses and exonerated Wanda."

"You heard."

"On the drive home, I called her while I was stuck in bumper-to-bumper traffic. We're having dinner tomorrow night to celebrate." She waggled the journal. "Did you read any of the poems?"

"I—"

"Many are personal ramblings. Not meant for publication. Have you ever written poetry?"

"I kept a diary. When I was a girl. I stopped when I was ten." After my mother's death, I hadn't wanted to record any more thoughts or feelings. They'd been too painful.

"I find writing poetry cathartic."

"I find exercise cathartic."

Didi smiled and turned to go inside. Over her shoulder, she said, "Coming to work out?"

"I was considering it, but on second thought, I've got to catch up on my blog and such." So much for my promise to my cat to cool my heels. "I'm going to head home."

"I hear you. PR for one's business is never done." Didi waved. "See you, and thanks again."

"By the way," I said, before she walked away, "I've heard of a bookbinder in San Francisco who might be able to fix that for you."

"I'd love the name."

Chapter 28

The Realm of Fairy is a strange shadow land,
lying just beyond the fields we know.
—Anonymous

After dining on a simple tossed salad and a turkey burger made with thyme and rosemary, I moved to the computer on the desk in the living room and reviewed the archived posts on the website's blog. Pixie mewed her dissent. I caressed her ears and told her to snooze.

Since starting the blog, I'd written twelve of them, including "How to Become a Fairy Whisperer," "How to Enter the Realm of the Fairies," and "Knock Three Times"—a symbolic way to invite fairies into one's life. For tonight's post, I recalled the bitterness I'd sensed in Didi's poetry and decided upon the theme: Open Your Heart to Possibility. My mother used to say, *Positive is as positive does.* My father had teased her about her attitude, calling her a Pollyanna. How I wished I could be more like her.

Fiona floated to the top of the computer display and planted her fists on her hips. "Just do it," she ordered.

"What?"

"Just do it. Like that commercial. Be like your mother."

I gawked at her. "Did you hear my thoughts?"

"You said it out loud."

"No, I didn't." I was certain I hadn't uttered a word. Or had I? Living alone, one could talk to oneself without even realizing it, especially one with a cat and a fairy.

Fiona was giggling.

I cocked my head. "You *can* hear my thoughts, you imp. Have you always been able to?"

She blew a raspberry. "For me to know. By the way, your cell phone is ringing."

I looked toward the kitchen where I'd left it. I didn't hear a ring. Maybe I'd set it on *vibrate*, except I didn't hear a buzz. "You're off your rocker," I said.

And then the phone jangled. Loudly.

Again I ogled my fairy. "Did you intuit that?"

Fiona did a pirouette.

"Can a righteous fairy learn to intuit?" I asked, as I hurried to the kitchen. "Is Merryweather teaching you this skill? You'd better not be doing something that will irk the queen fairy."

"As if."

I scanned the cell phone readout: *Brady.*

"Hurry or he'll hang up," Fiona warned.

I answered and gave her a long sideways look. How had she known it was him? My mind was doing a two-step trying to catch up with what this new revelation might mean.

"Hello," I answered. "Aren't you at work?"

"Yep. Friday nights can be a bear." Brady sounded almost as tired as I felt. "I needed a moment to regenerate."

Running a restaurant couldn't be easy. So much staff to manage. Very little time off. Demanding customers.

"I had a moment free between seatings," he went on, "and I was thinking about you."

A flutter of joy whooshed through me, but I tamped it down. We were friends. That was all. Besides, he was probably wondering why I'd run out of the café earlier.

"Everything okay?" Brady asked, confirming my suspicion.

"Yes." I gave him a quick recap about Elton Lamar, per Detective Summers.

"I can't believe Elton was going to hire a hit man . . . *woman*. Do you think it will be front-page news tomorrow?"

"I think the police will keep it under wraps until they find the killer."

"Sure. That makes sense."

I didn't think what Summers had shared was confidential, but to be on the safe side, I begged Brady to keep mum.

He promised he would. "So . . ." He took a sip of something. "Sorry. I needed water. Got to keep hydrated. What are you up to tonight?"

I moved to the sink and poured myself a glass of water. "I'm blogging."

"I've read a few of your pieces."

"Have you now?" I smiled, realizing I'd spoken with an Irish brogue. My father spoke with a brogue occasionally, to make me laugh.

"Yep. I combed your entire website. Nice photos of Carmel and the Bay Area and beyond. I love your use of light and dark."

"Thanks."

"However"—Brady cleared his throat—"I believe that you've been holding out on me."

"What do you mean?"

"When are you going to take me hunting for fairies in the woods?"

In my blog "How to Enter the Realm of the Fairies," I'd written about searching for fairy doors in the forest and in areas near water. Fairy doors weren't physical doors; they could be elements of nature that visually drew the eye and let the observer view the realm beyond. Last spring, I'd spent many of my days off taking photographs of the most beautiful places in Northern California to support my blog.

"Let's plan a trip," I said. "By the way, there are fairy doors on the beach. We passed one the other night."

"And you didn't point it out?"

"Ah." I hummed. "That's the trick. You have to be able to see them for yourself."

Brady harrumphed. "You'll teach me."

"Maybe." I chuckled.

So did he. "I've got to get back to work. Sleep well."

I wished him the same, ended the call, and returned to the desk in the living room.

Fiona, who was lounging on the keyboard, sat up and grinned like the Cheshire Cat. "Well?"

"Well, what?"

"How's Brady?" she asked in a singsong voice, reminding me of how Meaghan used to tease me about Christopher back in college.

"Fine."

"Just fine?" she asked.

"Very fine."

"Courtney li-ikes Brady," she chanted. "Courtney li-ikes Brady."

Gently, I flicked her off the keyboard. She soared into the air, laughing her wings off.

Saturday morning, I awoke feeling slightly groggy. Had Fiona dosed me with a potion? No, she wouldn't do that without warning me. She knew I liked to keep a clear head.

But the notion made me think of Wanda. Who had altered her reality at the party? Was Summers following that facet of the investigation? Without hard evidence from a drinking glass or piece of food, I would imagine it was a moot point, unless the police found a bottle of Ambien in the killer's medicine cabinet. I made a mental note to ask Summers if he'd inquired at pharmacies about any of his suspects' prescriptions. Who else did he have on his radar?

Abandoning my exercise routine, promising myself a long walk following the afternoon book club tea, I fed Pixie, downed a blueberry-chia protein shake, served pomegranate seeds to Fiona, dressed in a yellow smock dress embroidered with flowers, and headed to work.

The weather outside was phenomenal, a mere dusting of clouds in the sky and a temperature of seventy-five degrees. Perfect short-sleeve weather. People were out in droves. The silver-haired pastor of the nearby Congregational church was walking her aging Shar Pei. Tish Waterman was walking with her daughter, Twyla. Each held a mug of something. They appeared lost in conversation.

A block later, Fiona shouted, "Stop!" We were nearing Tamara Geoffries's house. "Look!"

The gray cat with the white muzzle was perched on the wicker chair by the front door. Alerted by Fiona's yell, the cat swiveled its head. Pixie wriggled in my arms, eager to give chase. I held her firmly.

Without warning, Fiona zoomed toward the gray cat, but before she could reach it, it bolted to the right and out of sight.

She whizzed back to me, her forehead pinched. "That darned cat is so elusive."

"Almost as elusive as a ghost."

"It's not a ghost."

When we arrived at Open Your Imagination, I was bubbling with energy, ready to tackle the day ahead. We had a big crowd coming in for the book club. Nearly thirty. Lissa Reade had selected *Death Overdue*, an autumn-themed book set in a library, featuring a librarian and resident ghost. Thinking of the framework of the series made me wonder what relationship Tamara might have with the gray cat. Why was it always roaming around her property and not remaining where it belonged, on the property next to the Meeting Hall? Tamara had said the cat was born the night her husband died. Was Fiona wrong? Was the cat a spirit and possibly the reincarnation of Tamara's dear Jamie?

I set Pixie on the floor and gave her a nudge. "Go. Have fun." She scampered to the patio. Fiona followed her. "Morning, Joss."

"Morning." My petite assistant was setting out a display in the front window that included autumn leaves, Vintage Hall's Jewel Tea autumn-themed china cups and saucers, copies of today's book, and gauzy wraiths.

"Looking good," I said. "Were you inspired by your outfit or vice versa?"

"Ha!" Joss had donned an orange shirt and orange-checked capris. "We have a delivery coming soon; four boxes of environmental figurines plus two boxes of fairy doors. The stacked-stone door is my favorite."

"I like the green one etched with ivy."

"Good morning!" Meaghan called as she and her mother breezed into the shop. Meaghan was wheeling her harp encased in its bag. Both of them were clad in white—Meaghan in a lacy top over a flowing skirt and Wanda in a slimming V-neck jumpsuit. "Shall I take my harp to the patio?" Meaghan asked.

"Yes, thanks."

Meaghan would play at today's event until Miss Reade opened the discussion, if Miss Reade showed up. I hoped her sister was feeling better and she wouldn't cancel. On the walk to work, I'd sent her a text. She had yet to respond.

I followed Meaghan and her mother as they strolled to the far end of the patio by the learning-the-craft corner. "Were your ears burning?"

"Do tell." Meaghan removed her Celtic lever harp from its case.

I said, "Last night, I was thinking about the way you used to tease me in college."

"Well deserved," she joked.

"And, Wanda, this morning"—I switched on the miniature lights that weaved through the ficus trees—"I was wondering whether the police knew more about the Ambien found in your system."

"Not to my knowledge."

Wanda perched on a chair at a wrought-iron table. Pixie bounded into her lap. Fiona flew to Wanda and hovered in front of her face, but Wanda didn't react. Giving up, Fiona settled on Pixie's head. The cat reared and bounded to the floor.

Laughing at their antics, I opened a closet beyond the learning-the-craft station, wheeled out the lectern for the book club, and locked it in place.

Wanda said, "I spoke with Didi yesterday. She thinks the police botched the collection of evidence big-time."

"When did you call her, Mother?" Meaghan strummed her harp and tuned it softly.

"I didn't. Didi rang me. She was driving home from San Jose. She sounded quite forlorn. A business meeting she'd had in San Jose didn't go well. I think she's looking for a loan. Anyway, we got to chatting, and Didi said she thought the police should have kept the Meeting Hall roped off longer than they did."

I said, "They do their best."

As I fetched six terra-cotta broken-pot fairy gardens from around the patio to set as decoration on each table, I reflected on the various evidence I'd seen the police gather: fibers, fingerprints, the mallet, the shards of the fairy garden pot, and its figurines and plants. I doubted a bottle of Ambien had been anywhere among the—

I gasped.

Fiona flew to me. "What's wrong?"

"The Ambien used on Wanda; it was planned. A person doesn't typically walk around with sleep aids. It proves premeditation. Why didn't I realize that before?"

"Because you're not a trained professional," Fiona teased.

"Why hasn't Didi reached out to Carmel Bank?" Meaghan asked her mother as she zipped up her carry case and stowed it in the closet with the soil, oblivious to my tête-à-tête with Fiona.

"She did," Wanda said. "They turned her down. As I said the other day, Sport Zone has been quite a drain on her accounts. She blamed Lana."

"Why blame her?" I asked.

"Because Lana and her narcissistic attitude were driving away customers. Pickleball players were leaving in droves to join a club in Monterey. A club needs members and monthly dues to survive."

"Was that the only reason Didi disliked Lana?" I asked.

"I don't know." Wanda fiddled with the belt of her jumpsuit. "Why do you ask?"

Meaghan and I joined her mother at the table. Fiona perched on the rim of the broken-pot garden centerpiece.

I said, "I met up with Didi last night outside Sport Zone. I was returning her poetry journal. She'd left it at the library."

Wanda moaned. "Heavens. I heard about that fiasco."

Meaghan asked for a recap. Quickly, I filled her in.

"Anyway, last night as I was attempting to return the

book," I continued, "I ran into Pauline—literally. She accidentally whacked me with her gym bag, and the book went flying. Loose pages spilled out. As I waited for Didi to exit her car, I perused one of the poems. It was quite bitter in tone, about Didi's husband and a woman. At the time, I'd thought the woman in the poem was a metaphor for Sport Zone, but, now, I'm wondering. . . ." I tapped the table. "Is it possible that Lana—"

"Had an affair with Didi's husband?" Meaghan cut in.

"No," Wanda said. "Never. Davis was devoted to Didi. When he died, Didi was bereft. Almost as broken as this pot. When Lana . . ." Wanda hesitated and rotated the fairy garden so that the front would face the center of the patio.

"When Lana what?" I prompted.

"When Lana started grandstanding and browbeating Didi and the board, she made me so angry."

"Mom," Meaghan warned. "*Shh*. If the police hear you—"

Wanda waved her off. "I'm innocent. The police know it. Let's talk about lighter subjects. Courtney, the other day, Didi said she attended a class and made one of these." She gestured to the broken-pot garden. "How did she do? Given her current state of pique, I can imagine her wielding a mallet. Bam, bam!" She mimed the action and cackled. "Oh, my, can you imagine her chasing after Lana with it?"

A couple of customers moseyed onto the patio.

Fiona spiraled into the air. "*Shh*," she warned. "They'll hear."

Meaghan grasped her mother's arm. "Mom, stop. Didi didn't kill Lana."

Wanda blanched. "Of course she didn't. I didn't mean to imply—"

"Didi couldn't have," I said. "She was nowhere near the Spectacular at the time."

Wanda tilted her head. "Where had she gone?"

I told them how Didi had received an alert about a break-in at Sport Zone and had gone to check it out. "It turned out to be nothing, no break-in, but she was so frustrated by an argument with Lana that she stayed at Sport Zone to work out the tension."

Wanda frowned. "Didi couldn't have gotten an alert about an alarm. I mean she *could* have, but I would have, as well. As head of the women's association and occasionally Didi's backup, I have the same Ring alert system." She fetched her cell phone from her purse, swiped through messages, and displayed it to us. "As you can see on the night of the party, I didn't."

Fiona hovered above the display. "Is she saying Didi lied?"

I gaped at the display. "Wanda."

"Yes, dear?"

"Did Didi know you were a sleepwalker prior to the other night?"

"Yes, but . . ." Wanda winced, as if the weight of the world had landed on her shoulders. "No, no, no. You have to be wrong. Didi didn't drug me and kill Lana. No, it can't be true."

"Courtney"—Fiona settled on the pot's rim again and kicked her heels against the terra-cotta—"do you remember how Didi acted at the pottery-breaking class? How she hit the pot with such force?"

I nodded. The pot had shattered. Had she been reliving the moment when she'd struck Lana?

I said, "Wanda, if Didi lied about being at Sport Zone, is there a way to prove it?"

"We have surveillance cameras."

I sighed. "Too bad the security system is broken."

"No, it's not. I told you yesterday morning that I paid for the repair."

I nodded, recalling that Wanda hadn't let Didi in on the

secret because she'd feared Didi would be embarrassed to receive help.

"Would there be a tape of last Saturday night's goings-on at the club, Mom?" Meaghan asked.

"We reset the videos every two weeks," Wanda said.

"If the system is up and running," I said, "that would explain how Kenny knew I was the one who'd encouraged Didi to break into his locker."

Fiona whistled and whooshed to my shoulder. "Didi must have realized the same thing. Knowing you would figure that out sooner or later, she tried to run you down after the poetry reading."

"But she drives a—" I flashed on my meetup with Didi last night. What if she, given the iffy condition of her aging Mercedes, had borrowed Pauline's car on the night of the poetry reading? Pauline drove an unimposing Dodge Dart, similar in shape to a Honda Civic or Toyota Celica, and thanks to the three mud-sliding forays with her sister, the license plate had been impossible to read.

Did Didi kill Lana? She had shown up at the crime scene with a shawl over her dress. If she'd stabbed Lana, perhaps Lana's blood had splattered onto the dress. Didi's poem had suggested that a woman had preyed upon and destroyed her husband. Had that woman been Lana? Early in the evening at the Spectacular, Didi had given Wanda a celebratory glass of champagne. Had she dosed the drink with Ambien? She must have.

One thing niggled at me: Why would Didi have framed her good friend to take the fall?

Chapter 29

The longing of my heart is a fairy portrait of myself.
—Mark Twain

"Hello-o, I'm here," Lissa Reade said as she strode through the door connecting the main showroom to the patio.

Thankful she had arrived and hearing that her sister was on the mend, I guided Lissa to the lectern.

During the book club event, while Yvanna and her sister served tea and Lissa Reade put the group through its paces, asking typical mystery book club questions like *who*, *what*, and *why*, I stewed over the likelihood of Didi being the killer. Fiona orbited my head. She didn't pepper me with questions or douse me with a potion; she was merely showing support. As I pondered the possibility, I studied Wanda. She was sitting stone-faced at one of the tables. Clearly, she was as distraught as I was that her good friend might be a murderess.

When the tea disbanded and patrons began to browse the figurine shelves or study the premade gardens, I approached Wanda. "I need you to do me a favor."

"Like what?"

"What time are you supposed to meet Didi for dinner?"

"Six thirty."

"Call her and tell her you're going to be late. Offer to pick her up at her house."

"Why?"

"So after she leaves Sport Zone, you and I can steal inside, and you can show me the security footage."

Wanda moaned. "If she hasn't erased it."

Meaghan grabbed my arm. "Uh-uh. We're calling the police."

"What if I'm wrong?" I asked.

"The police follow bad leads all the time."

"Summers asked me to butt out," I said. "If I call him, he'll realize I've been theorizing. If we're wrong, no harm no foul."

Fiona winged between us. "Sherlock Holmes would gather all the evidence first."

"You're no Sherlock Holmes, Courtney," Meaghan grumbled.

"And you're no Watson." I stared her down.

"Oh, yes, I am. I'm coming with you."

The four of us—Wanda, Meaghan, Fiona, and I—headed to Sport Zone. On the way, Wanda phoned Didi, who was thrilled that Wanda would pick her up at home. At present, she was leaving her Mercedes with a mechanic—it was giving her trouble—confirming my guess that she might have borrowed Pauline's Dodge Dart on the night of the library event.

When we arrived at Sport Zone, we paused at the entrance to the parking lot and double-checked to make sure Didi's priority spot was, indeed, empty. It was.

At the front door, Fiona said, "I'll remain outside and stand guard."

"So will I," Meaghan said.

Wanda and I gave them a thumbs-up gesture and strode inside. Pauline, wearing a blue jacket emblazoned with the club's logo, was on duty as the assistant manager.

Wanda said, "Hello," as she waltzed past her.

"Great to see you're out of jail," Pauline said.

"Thanks. I'm going to check for women's association mail."

The gym was extremely busy. Nearly every machine was in use. Beyoncé's "Crazy in Love" reverberated through the speakers.

Wanda led me to the employees' lounge. None of the staff were present. All of the adjoining doors were closed. A stale coffee smell permeated the room. To follow through on her promise, Wanda moved to the cubbies and withdrew two envelopes from the women's association slot, after which she moved toward the door marked *Security*.

"Hold it," I said. "Isn't there a guard stationed inside?"

"No. Didi worried that she would mistakenly hire a pervert and the guy would spy on women in the locker rooms. Whoever is on duty roams the property. The tapes are for backup."

Wanda slipped into the room. I followed. Unlike the setup at the library, where the images appeared on split screen via Miss Reade's laptop, the athletic club's system could be viewed on an adjoining bank of televisions that hung above a large rectangular desk.

Wanda sat in the ergonomic chair and deftly scrolled backward through the closed-circuit videos until she landed on images for the date of the murder. "Nothing has been erased, as far as I can tell."

Methodically, we reviewed the tape for last Saturday night. Partial lights were on in the athletic club, but there was no activity. No one was working out on the machines. No one was playing on the pickleball courts or the racquetball courts.

"Didi closed Sport Zone that night," Wanda explained. "She knew it would be a ghost town because so many members were attending the Spectacular."

Wanda zoomed forward to the approximate time the murder had occurred. All of the footage was the same, partially lit but lifeless. Didi never put in an appearance to tend to a security alert.

Wanda gazed at me. "She lied to you."

I pulled my cell phone from my purse and dialed the precinct. I reached the clerk and asked for Detective Summers. He was investigating a burglary at an art gallery. Reddick was with him. I asked her to put me through to Summers's voice mail and left a message, outlining what we'd found.

"What do we do now?" Wanda asked.

"We wait. He'll respond. Is there any way to copy the video?"

"I don't know." Wanda hit a button. The images on the screen froze. "Didi will get suspicious if I don't show up at her house."

"Good point. You need to leave. Do you think you can keep the secret while having dinner with her?"

"No. I'll blab everything. I—"

The door to the security room opened. Didi peeked in. She eyed the bank of televisions and frowned. "What are you two up to?"

I glanced past her. Why hadn't Meaghan or Fiona alerted us? Hadn't they seen her enter Sport Zone?

"Hi, Didi," Wanda said, acting as if she weren't surprised by Didi's arrival. "You look nice. Did you forget that I said I'd pick you up at home?"

Didi had donned a bohemian-style blue dress, cross-body purse, and matching heels. "I forgot my purse in my locker. I needed my credit cards." She patted the purse. "I repeat, what are you two up to?"

Wanda forced a smile. "I was showing Courtney the security system we have. She's considering getting something for her shop. Burglaries are on the rise in Carmel. It's a wise business decision, don't you think?"

I had to commend her for how calm she was. My heart was pounding a mile a second.

"If only our surveillance system worked," Didi said, "so you could show her all the bells and whistles."

"But it does," Wanda said. "I paid to repair it."

"But you knew that already, didn't you, Didi?" I stated. "Kenny drove the point home at the poetry reading."

"Cut the crap." Didi reached into her purse and pulled out a snub-nosed revolver.

I wasn't a weapons expert—I wouldn't know the difference between a Ruger and a Smith & Wesson—but I was certain the gun could kill at close range. My insides snagged.

First Didi aimed the gun at Wanda and then waggled it at me. "Let's go, ladies."

"Where?" I asked.

"I'm not sure yet." Didi stepped to the side to let us pass. "There must be a good cliff for both of you to jump off of. Wanda, on your feet. Now!"

Wanda started to stand but faltered. I helped steady her. So much for her courageous spirit. She was shivering like an aspen.

"You're not going to kill us," I said.

"Why not?" Didi asked.

"Because you like us."

"Not anymore." Didi stepped to one side. "After you."

Where were Meaghan or Fiona? I wondered until it dawned on me. "Did you enter through the employees' locker-room entrance, Didi?" I asked.

"Yep. No one saw me."

Not Pauline or any of the club's members, and not Meaghan or my intrepid fairy.

As Wanda and I moved into the employees' lounge, Didi slid the security door closed. Softly.

I cleared my throat. Loudly.

"Uh-uh, Courtney." Didi tapped my shoulder with the gun. "Don't try to alert anyone."

"I can't help it," I said, clearing my throat again. "I'm allergic to cleaning fluid."

"Cut it out. You didn't cough the other day when I showed you around. Move. You too, Wanda."

Wanda whimpered.

"Why did you kill Lana?" I asked, looking for something I could use to disarm Didi but seeing nothing within reach. The coffeepot and kitchen utensils were clear across the room.

"You know why, Courtney. I saw you reading my poem. By the way, that made my blood boil. My poems are personal. I choose who gets to read them." Didi tapped my back with the gun, urging me forward. "Move."

"Lana and your husband." I edged forward reluctantly, not eager to leave the club, hopeful that Summers, or anyone, might appear. "Were they having an affair?"

"No, but he was in lust with her, which is why he gave in to her whims and nearly ruined us. Lana is the reason this place is falling to pieces. She's the reason we're in arrears. She browbeat Davis into resurfacing the pickleball courts and into buying new pickleball tutors. Everything needed to be top-notch, or she wouldn't stay. Davis thought having a champion like her representing our club mattered to sales, so he buckled every time."

Someone knocked on the door leading to the gym. The doorknob jiggled. We hadn't locked it. Didi must have done so before revealing her presence to us. Shoot. Even Fiona couldn't pass through locked doors. There were no windows, although there was a vent. Maybe—

"Wanda, open that." Didi gestured to the door leading to the employees' locker room.

Wanda obeyed and passed through it. I followed. The locker room looked like I remembered, walnut lockers on each wall and a bench down the center. The exit at the far end was closed. No employees were around. One of the lockers on the left, beyond the bench, was slightly ajar. Probably Didi's. She must have heard us in the security room and, in her haste to confront us, left it open.

"Keep moving," Didi ordered.

Stalling for time, I drew to a halt and said, "How did you entice Lana to meet you in the bidding room?"

"I texted her."

"There wasn't a message on her phone."

"I'm not stupid. I erased it," Didi said. "I wrote that I needed to talk about the women's association. I told her I was going to demote Wanda and put Lana in charge."

"No," Wanda mewled.

"I wouldn't have, Wanda. You're my friend. But I was not above appealing to that woman's ego."

An idea came to me. I nudged Wanda to move left of the bench, toward the open locker. "Speaking of friends," I said, "why did you give Wanda the Ambien?"

Didi raised an eyebrow.

"We know about it," I said. "Her attorney ordered a tox screen. You framed her. On purpose."

Wanda looked over her shoulder. Her face was streaked with tears.

"I'm sorry, Wanda," Didi said, "but I needed someone to take the heat, and I knew you'd get off. I was sure of it. Because of the sleepwalking."

Wanda continued past the open locker.

"When Lana showed up," I said, "you didn't waste a second, did you? You sneaked behind her and attacked her with the bidding mallet."

Didi grinned. "If she'd figured out what I was up to, she would have attacked me first. She was nothing if not fierce. I couldn't take the chance."

"You hit her and stabbed her with the letter opener from the fairy garden," I said, edging past the open locker.

"Actually, I didn't know about the letter opener yet. I smashed the pot, thinking it would be poetic justice to pierce her with a shard right through her cold heart. But the shard wasn't sharp enough," Didi went on. "That's when I spotted the—"

I flung the locker door backward. Into Didi. She stumbled. A shot rang out. A bullet slammed into the ceiling. I turned to attack while she was off balance, but she hadn't lost control of the gun. Dang.

"That was foolish," Didi snarled, re-aiming it at me. "Don't do it again."

I peeked in the locker. Definitely Didi's. Pictures of her husband were taped to the door. Her blue pickleball paddle hung on a hook. On the floor lay the dress she'd worn to the Spectacular, wadded into a ball. A prescription bottle lay on top of it. Ambien, no doubt. She hadn't come to Sport Zone during the party, but she had come here directly afterward to get rid of the evidence. Wanda and I hadn't proceeded that far with the surveillance footage. If only I'd thought to question Didi's alibi earlier.

Before I could second-guess myself, I did *do it again*. I smacked the locker door a second time. Didi lurched backward so it wouldn't hit her. This time she lost hold of the gun; it clattered to the floor.

While she scrambled to retrieve it, I reached into the locker and grabbed the pickleball paddle. As Didi started to rise, I swung the paddle using a cross-court dink stroke and clipped her on the side of the head. She staggered to her right.

Fueled by rage, I whacked her again. She tripped over the bench and landed with a thud. I straddled her, prepared to strike again if she moved.

At the same time, a siren whooped and the exterior door to the locker room flew open. Summers and Reddick strode in, guns drawn. Meaghan hovered behind them.

Fiona swooped into the room and landed on my shoulder. A smattering of golden dust trailed her. "Are you all right?" she asked.

I looked at Didi, quivering on the floor, and whispered, "Never better."

Chapter 30

❦

*"Deep within the winter forest among the snowdrift wide,
you can find a magic place where all the fairies hide.*
—Anonymous

After Summers cuffed Didi and led her to a patrol car, I said
to Fiona, "How did you do it? How did you get the detective
to pause his investigation for the art theft and check his messages?"

Hovering midair, she planted a fist on one hip and smiled.
"You were my inspiration."

"Me?"

"You always worry that I might do something to upset the
queen fairy, so I thought, *What would Courtney do?* Be more
responsible, of course. So I contacted Merryweather and suggested we invite Zephyr and her intuitive fairy friend to create
a fairy ring. As it turned out, the intuitive fairy lives here in
Carmel."

"Where?"

"In Meaghan's garden." She raised her hand for a high five.

"That's fate, right? I told Merryweather about her, knowing that Wanda and Meaghan, by virtue of her familial connection, were at the root of the problem. Merryweather was as pleased as punch that I'd paid attention. She reached out to Callie—that's the intuitive's name. Together, the four of us were able to create a ring of energy and telepath a message to Detective Summers."

"Telepath?"

Fiona fanned her fingers on either side of her head. "Woo-woo stuff, but it worked." She held a finger to her lips. "*Shh. Don't let on. The detective won't like it.*"

No kidding.

Wanda joined me and gazed into the air. "Is she here?" She must have seen me conversing with Fiona.

I nodded.

"Hello, little fairy," Wanda whispered, and then said to me, "Courtney, dear, you were heroic."

"You were the hero." I slipped my arm around her and squeezed. "I was amazed by how quick thinking you were when Didi arrived. It was your banter that gave the police time to get here."

"Do you really think so?"

"I know so."

"Well, I felt inspired."

Fiona caressed Wanda's hair. "Maybe she's closer to the fairy world than she knows."

The next day, Fiona, Joss, and I went to Pilgrim's Way bookshop to listen to Eudora Cash talk about her latest novel, *The Pirate's Affair.* Over sixty women and men were in attendance. We found standing room at the rear of the shop.

Joss, who was a big fan, said, "She's pretty."

I nodded. Brady's mother hadn't changed much since I'd

seen her last. She still wore her strawberry-blond hair in a twist with tendrils. Like Brady, she had a dimple in her right cheek that appeared every time she cracked a joke.

After her spiel, in which she talked about how she'd researched the pirates off the coast of California—she shared some rollicking tales—Joss and I each purchased a book and we waited in line to have Eudora autograph it.

When I made it to the front—Joss nudged me to go before her—Eudora looked up at me and grinned.

"Courtney. It's lovely to see you. Brady said you'd be coming in." She rose from her chair and rounded the table to give me a hug. "I'm glad you and he have reconnected. He sings your praises. You must come to dinner soon. Promise?"

I did.

Then I introduced Eudora to Joss. Eudora didn't hesitate. She gave Joss a warm hug, too. After we left with our autographed books, Joss couldn't stop gushing about how nice and normal Eudora was.

Fiona flitted to me and crooned, "Brady's mother said he sings your praises."

"I heard her."

"I bet she doesn't say that to everyone."

My cheeks warmed.

Monday afternoon, Meaghan threw a party on the rear patio at Hideaway Café to celebrate her mother's total exoneration. Wanda's artists, her clients, and some of her Sport Zone friends were in attendance. My father remained by her side as she greeted each guest.

I was surprised but not surprised to see Dylan Summers show up with Renee Rodriguez. As a longtime friend, he had to be pleased that Wanda had been proven innocent.

Meaghan, like the consummate hostess, was chatting with everyone she met. Dressed in a white crocheted dress, she looked ready for a wedding. I scanned the crowd for her boyfriend but didn't see him. What was his excuse this time? Maybe Fiona was right; he wasn't good enough for Meaghan. She and I would need to have a frank discussion soon.

I scanned the patio for my fairy and glimpsed her with Merryweather and Zephyr in a tree. Her wings were billowed. She was turning in a circle. She caught me staring at her and whizzed to me.

"Guess what?" she rasped as she hovered midair.

"I couldn't possibly." I held out a finger.

She alit on it. "Do I look different?"

"As in older? By a day maybe," I teased.

"Very funny. Look. Beneath my wings."

With a fingertip, I lifted one wing. "Oh, wow. Your second set of wings have bloomed."

She nodded emphatically. "Because I helped you help Wanda."

"Does the queen fairy know of your progress?"

"Merryweather said she will provide a full report." Fiona whooped with glee and spiraled into the air. "Isn't it wonderful? Maybe soon, the queen fairy will let me socialize."

"I hope so. For your sake."

"You and I need to talk," a man said from behind me.

I spun around.

"Detective," I said. "Nice to see you."

Dylan Summers didn't smile. In fact, his mouth was tight and his jaw ticking. Renee was with him. In a cherry-red sheath, she radiated strength.

"What do we need to talk about?" I asked, doing my best to appear as confident as Renee.

"How can I entice you to keep your nose out of my investigations?" he asked.

Fiona plopped onto my shoulder. "Do you need backup?"

I tapped her foot with a fingertip to keep quiet.

"This time, you really crossed boundaries," Summers went on.

"Wanda is my friend."

"She was exonerated."

"Not completely, not until you found another suspect. Was Didi Dubois ever on your list?" I asked, instantly regretting my accusatory tone. "I'm sorry. What I meant was—"

"Cut her some slack, Dylan," my father said, appearing on Summers's right. "Obviously she has some talent."

Renee elbowed Summers. "Exactly what I said to you."

Heart, be still. Renee and Dad were taking my side?

"Of course, my daughter has some questionable beliefs about life in general," my father quipped.

I threw him a sharp look, warning him not to bring up the fairy thing. He bit back a smile, and I realized he was goading me.

"By the way, that was some news about Elton," my father went on.

Renee nodded. "Who'd have thought he'd been that desperate?"

"Money problems can create all sorts of wedges." Summers slipped his hands into his pockets. "He's selling his car dealership to focus on his defense."

"Speaking of selling, Sport Zone is on the market already," my father said. "Apparently, Didi needs to divest of all her assets to afford a defense attorney. She's hired some big shot from San Francisco."

"She'll lose," Summers said.

"I hear they're going for temporary insanity," Dad went on.

Fiona tapped my shoulder. "That won't work. Not since Didi dosed Wanda with Ambien. That's premeditation. You know what Sherlock Holmes would say."

"'No way, José,'" Renee chimed.

I laughed, knowing that wasn't what Holmes would say.

"The drugs were premeditated," Renee added.

Fiona high-fived me for making the right assumption, which made me laugh even harder.

My father frowned. "What's so funny, Courtney?"

"Nothing, sir. Gallows humor." I swept Fiona off my shoulder. She soared into the air. "I'm sorry Didi felt the need to end Lana's life instead of fighting her in court. I'm sorry she will go bankrupt defending herself. For all her faults, she was a nice woman and a talented poet."

"I agree," Renee said. "Hey, I'm thirsty." She signaled toward the open bar.

Before leaving, Summers aimed two fingers at his eyes and then pointed the same fingers at my eyes. I got the message: he was watching me. *Fine.* I was watching him, too. If the law decided to investigate someone I cared about, beware. I would always come to his or her aid. I would not yield. And if the past few moments had taught me anything, I'd say my father had my back on this.

Dad kissed my cheek and headed to Wanda.

"Courtney." Joss moseyed to me. She was with the three Hopewell sisters. "You'll never believe what we heard."

"What?"

"Sport Zone is up for sale."

"I just learned about it myself."

Hedda leaned forward. "Well, what you didn't hear is that Tamara Geoffries is going to loan Kenny the money so he can buy it."

"Honestly?"

I'd seen Tamara and Kenny join the party. They were at a table for two in the far corner. To my surprise, both of them were holding cats—Tamara, her Angora; and Kenny, the illusive gray cat.

Fiona whisked to me and said, "Do you see Kenny and the cat?"

I gawked at her. Was she once again tapping into my mental musings? If so, I needed to talk to her about boundaries. "I do."

"I think the gray cat has warmed up to him to let Tamara know it's okay to move on. She can fall in love again."

Meaning Fiona believed the gray cat was, indeed, the reincarnated spirit of Tamara's husband, Jamie. *Hmm.*

"Who are you staring at?" a man asked from behind.

I whirled around and nearly smacked into the tray of appetizers Brady was holding. "I wasn't—"

"Yes, you were. I know staring when I see it." He grinned. "You're checking out Tamara and Kenny."

"Are they a couple?"

"Seems like they might be. Tell me about your dad and Wanda."

My father was holding Wanda's hand, his thumb gently caressing her knuckle. Sweet.

"Yep, they are a couple, too," I said.

"Is there something in the café's water?" Brady asked.

"I don't know. You should ask the owner. Maybe even report the problem to Health Services."

Brady set the appetizer tray on a table and moved closer to me. The dimple that graced his cheek nearly made me swoon. Softly, he said, "Maybe we should drink the water."

My cheeks blazed hot. "Wh-what?"

"Told you," Fiona sang as she zipped between us. "Told you, told you, told you. Brady sings your praises." In a flash, she whizzed from view.

Somewhat dumbfounded, I said, "What do you mean, we should drink the water?"

Brady smiled. "I think we should go on a formal date. Get to know one another better. Who knows?" He gazed deeply into my eyes. "Maybe if I fall in love with you, I'll see that fairy you promised."

RECIPES

From Joss:

This is my mother's lemonade recipe. She has been making it for years. She once told me the salt was key to giving it its flavor. If you're really daring, add a half teaspoon of Tabasco sauce. Your mouth will thank you.

Adult Lemonade

(Serves 8–12)

4 cups water, divided
1 cup sugar
1 cup fresh lemon juice, about 4–6 lemons
juice of 1 orange
juice of 1 lime
pinch of salt

To make the simple syrup:
In a saucepan, pour 2 cups water and 1 cup sugar. Bring to a simmer and stir until sugar dissolves, about 5–7 minutes. Cool.

To make the lemonade:
Make sure your citrus fruits are at room temperature before you squeeze them. Remove all pulp and seeds.

In a pitcher, mix lemon juice, orange juice, lime juice, salt, 2 cups of water, and the simple syrup.

Add more sugar, if desired. Serve with ice and slices of lemon.

From Brady:

I find that my diners love home-cooked meals. One of my father's favorite entrées that he serves at the Cash Cow and has allowed me to serve at Hideaway Café is baked fried chicken. It's simple to make with very little mess, and it turns out tasty and moist every time.

Baked Fried Chicken

(Serves 12)

1 cup flour
1 teaspoon salt
1 teaspoon white pepper
1 tablespoon chopped dried parsley
1 cup seasoned bread crumbs
3 eggs
12 chicken thighs
1 teaspoon paprika
½ cup canola oil

Preheat oven to 350 degrees F.

Pour the flour, salt, white pepper, and parsley onto a shallow plate. Onto another shallow plate, pour the bread crumbs. In a separate bowl, beat the eggs.

Dredge each piece of chicken in egg, roll in the flour-spice mixture, and then roll in the bread crumbs.

Pour oil into a 9 x 13 pan and set the chicken pieces in the oil, skin side down. Bake for 30 minutes. Remove from oven, turn the chicken over, sprinkle with paprika, and bake for another 30 minutes. Remove from oven and set chicken on paper towels to drain. Serve hot or at room temperature.

To make this even a little less messy, line the 9 x 13 pan with aluminum foil before adding the oil.

From Courtney:

I'm sharing two versions of these muffins, gluten-free and regular. Yvanna gave me the recipe, but I've tweaked it by adding more zest, as Brady suggested. Who doesn't love more zest? These are perfect for a tea or for any day of the week when you need a pick-me-up. The berries pop and the lemon muffin is deliciously lemony. Enjoy.

Blueberry Lemon Muffins (regular version)

(Makes 12)

Blueberry Filling Ingredients:
2 cups blueberries, rinsed
1½ tablespoons sugar
½ tablespoon flour
¼ teaspoon salt
¼ teaspoon cinnamon

Lemon Muffin Ingredients:
1⅓ cups flour
4 tablespoons brown sugar
1½ teaspoons baking powder
¼ teaspoon cinnamon
¼ teaspoon salt
6 tablespoons unsalted butter, cold and cut into pieces
8 tablespoons cream cheese
¾ cup milk
2 eggs
2–4 tablespoons lemon juice (from fresh lemon)
1–2 teaspoons lemon zest
1 tablespoon granulated sugar + ⅛ teaspoon cinnamon to
    sprinkle on top
whipped topping, if desired

Preheat oven to 350 degrees F.

Line 12 cupcake tins with cupcake liners. Spray with non-stick spray.

In a bowl, toss the blueberries with the sugar, flour, salt, and cinnamon. Set aside.

In a pastry blender or food processor, whisk together the flour, brown sugar, baking powder, cinnamon, and salt. Add in the butter and pulse until the mixture looks crumbly.

Add in the cream cheese and pulse, then add milk, eggs, lemon juice, and lemon zest, and mix until the dough has come together but is just combined. It will resemble cooked corn meal. It could be thinner if you added more lemon juice or used jumbo eggs instead of large eggs.

Using an ice cream scoop or large spoon, put about 2–3 tablespoons of dough into the prepared cupcake liners. Pat with wet fingers if necessary, to make it even. Set some of the berry mixture on top of the dough. Top with the rest of the dough and pat to make it even. Sprinkle with granulated sugar mixed with extra cinnamon.

Bake for 18–22 minutes until the muffins are a warm brown and a toothpick comes out clean. Remove from oven and let cool for 20 minutes.

Blueberry Lemon Muffins (gluten-free)

(Makes 12)

Blueberry Filling Ingredients:
2 cups blueberries, rinsed
1½ tablespoons sugar
½ tablespoon gluten-free flour
¼ teaspoon salt
¼ teaspoon cinnamon

Lemon Muffin Ingredients:
1⅓ cups gluten-free flour (I prefer sweet rice flour)
¼ teaspoon xanthan gum
1 tablespoon whey powder
4 tablespoons brown sugar
1½ teaspoons baking powder
¼ teaspoon cinnamon
¼ teaspoon salt
6 tablespoons unsalted butter, cold and cut into pieces
8 tablespoons cream cheese
¾ cup milk
2 eggs
2–4 tablespoons lemon juice (from fresh lemon)
1–2 teaspoons lemon zest
1 tablespoon granulated sugar + ⅛ teaspoon cinnamon to
    sprinkle on top
whipped topping, if desired

Preheat oven to 350 degrees F.
Line 12 cupcake tins with cupcake liners. Spray with non-stick spray.

In a bowl, toss the blueberries with the sugar, gluten-free flour, salt, and cinnamon. Set aside.

In a pastry blender or food processor, whisk together the gluten-free flour, xanthan gum, whey powder, brown sugar, baking powder, cinnamon, and salt. Add in the butter and pulse until the mixture looks crumbly.

Add in the cream cheese and pulse, then add milk, eggs, lemon juice, and lemon zest, and mix until the dough has come together but is just combined. It will resemble cooked corn meal. It could be thinner if you added more lemon juice or used jumbo eggs instead of large eggs.

Using an ice cream scoop or large spoon, put about 2–3 tablespoons of dough into the prepared cupcake liners. Pat with wet fingers if necessary, to make it even. Set some of the berry mixture on top of the dough. Top with the rest of the dough and pat to make it even. Sprinkle with granulated sugar mixed with extra cinnamon.

Bake for 18–22 minutes until the muffins are a warm brown and a toothpick comes out clean. Remove from oven and let cool for 20 minutes.

From Courtney:

I love having easy appetizers at the ready in my freezer. Because I don't like huge dinners—I sleep better if I eat half of what I think I need—a light dinner of appetizers satisfies me. These morsels are so easy to make and reheat nicely in the microwave. Enjoy.

Cheddar Artichoke Appetizer

(serves 6–8 as side dish; serves 12 as appetizer)

4 green onions, diced
1 14-ounce can artichoke hearts, in water, drained and diced
1 tablespoon oil
4 eggs slightly beaten
6 soda crackers (for a gluten-free option, use gluten-free
    crackers)
1½ cups cheddar cheese, shredded
1 teaspoon pepper
1 teaspoon Tabasco sauce

Preheat oven to 325 degrees F. Oil an 8-inch square pan.

Sauté green onions and artichoke hearts in oil for about 3 minutes on medium, until green onions are tender. Cool and set side.

In a medium bowl, mix eggs, crackers, cheese, pepper, and Tabasco sauce. Add cooled green onions and artichokes.

Pour mixture into the prepared 8-inch square pan. Bake for 35–40 minutes.

Serve hot or cold.

For side dish, cut into 2-to-3-inch square portions.

For appetizer, cut into 1-inch bite-sized pieces.

From Yvanna:

    I adore cinnamon. My grandmother used it in everything. Soups. Casseroles. Cookies and cakes. Whenever I make these scones, I think of her. Make sure you use heavy cream. It adds a lush quality to the scone. By the way, my sister must eat gluten-free, so I often make a separate batch for her. You will see that recipe below. Buen provecho *or, as the French say,* bon appétit.

Cinnamon Swirl Scones (regular version)

(Makes 16 scones)

⅔ cup brown sugar
2 tablespoons softened butter
1½ teaspoons cinnamon, divided
3 cups flour
⅓ cup granulated sugar
1 tablespoon baking powder
½ teaspoon salt
½ cup cold butter
1 cup heavy cream
1 whole egg, slightly beaten
1 teaspoon vanilla

    Preheat oven to 425 degrees F.

    In a small bowl, combine brown sugar, butter, and 1 teaspoon cinnamon to form soft crumbs; set aside.

    In a large bowl, combine flour, ½ teaspoon cinnamon, granulated sugar, baking powder, and salt. Cut in the cold butter until the mixture resembles pea-sized crumbs. Make a well in the center.

In a small bowl, combine the cream, egg, and vanilla. Pour the cream mixture into the well of the flour mixture and mix. The dough will become firm. Pour half of the brown sugar mixture into the dough and knead. There should be streaks of the brown sugar visible.

Lightly dust a cutting board with flour and turn the dough onto it. Knead and fold the dough a few more times. Sprinkle brown sugar crumbs into each fold.

Divide the dough in half and form each into a ½-inch-thick round. With a moist knife, cut each round into 8 wedges. Place wedges onto a cookie sheet lined with parchment paper and refrigerate about 10 minutes.

Bake for 11–15 minutes in preheated oven. The scones should be golden brown when you remove them from the oven. Cool on wire racks for 20 minutes.

If desired, you may also wrap the unbaked scones and freeze for up to three months. Remove from freezer and bake a few at a time. They may require more baking time.

Cinnamon Swirl Scones (gluten-free version)

(Makes 16 scones)

⅔ cup brown sugar
2 tablespoons softened butter
1½ teaspoons cinnamon, divided
3 cups gluten-free flour (I like using sweet rice flour mixed
    with tapioca starch)
½ teaspoon xanthan gum
1 tablespoon whey powder
⅓ cup granulated sugar
1 tablespoon baking powder
½ teaspoon salt
½ cup cold butter
1 cup heavy cream
1 whole egg, slightly beaten
1 teaspoon vanilla

Preheat oven to 425 degrees F.

In a small bowl, combine brown sugar, butter, and 1 teaspoon cinnamon to form soft crumbs; set aside.

In a large bowl, combine gluten-free flour, ½ teaspoon cinnamon, xanthan gum, whey powder, granulated sugar, baking powder, and salt. Cut in the cold butter until the mixture resembles pea-sized crumbs. Make a well in the center.

In a small bowl, combine the cream, egg, and vanilla. Pour the cream mixture into the well of the gluten-free flour mixture and mix. The dough will become firm. Pour half of the brown sugar mixture into the dough and knead. There should be streaks of the brown sugar visible.

Lightly dust a cutting board with gluten-free flour and turn the dough onto it. Knead and fold the dough a few more times. It will not be as supple as regular flour. That's okay. Add water sparingly, if necessary, for elasticity. Sprinkle brown sugar crumbs into each fold.

Divide the dough in half and form each into a ½-inch-thick round. With a moist knife, cut each round into 8 wedges. Place wedges onto a cookie sheet lined with parchment paper and refrigerate about 10 minutes.

Bake for 11–15 minutes in preheated oven. The scones should be golden brown when you remove them from the oven. Cool on wire racks for 20 minutes.

If desired, you may wrap the unbaked scones and freeze for up to three months. Remove from freezer and bake a few at a time. They may require more baking time.

From Courtney:

This recipe might look complicated, but it is not. My mother taught me that you can always look at a recipe in three parts—the wet ingredients, the dry ingredients, and any additions. That way it is less intimidating. Warning: the aroma of delicious chocolate will make you salivate while you wait for warm cookies to come out of the oven.

Double Chocolate Cookies

(Makes 24–36 cookies)

½ cup unsalted butter, room temperature
½ cup granulated sugar
½ cup dark brown sugar, packed
1 large egg, room temperature
1 teaspoon vanilla extract
1 cup flour
½ cup + 2 tablespoons dark cocoa powder
1 teaspoon baking soda
1/4 teaspoon salt
2 tablespoons milk
1½ cups semisweet chocolate chips

In a large bowl, combine the butter and sugars. Beat together on medium-high speed until light and fluffy, 2–3 minutes. Blend in the egg and vanilla; scrape down the bowl if needed.

In a separate bowl, whisk together the flour, cocoa powder—remember the extra 2 tablespoons—baking soda, and salt.

Add the dry ingredients to the wet ingredients and mix until incorporated.

Add in the 2 tablespoons of milk and fold in the chocolate chips.

Refrigerate the mixture for 2 hours.

When ready, preheat oven to 350 degrees F. Line 2 baking sheets with parchment paper. For each cookie, roll about 2 tablespoons of dough into a ball and place on the baking sheet. Flatten slightly. They should be far apart. They will spread.

Bake at 350° F for 10–11 minutes. Remove from oven. Let cookies cool on the baking sheets for about 5 minutes, then transfer to a wire rack to cool completely.

Keep in a tightly sealed container. Individual cookies may be frozen if wrapped in saran and sealed well.

From Yvanna:

These biscuits are very flaky and delicious. If you didn't know, lemon is very good for the soul. It is a natural healer and helps clear toxins from the body. When I was growing up, my mother would always squeeze lemon juice into our water. It is a flavor that brings me comfort.

Lemon Thyme Biscuits

(Makes 8–10 biscuits)

2 cups all-purpose flour
2 teaspoons baking powder
¼ teaspoon baking soda
2 tablespoons whey powder
1 teaspoon salt, plus more for sprinkling
1 tablespoon finely grated lemon zest
1 teaspoon chopped thyme, plus more for sprinkling
4 tablespoons cold unsalted butter, cut into chunks
1 cup buttermilk

Preheat oven to 425 degrees F.

In a medium bowl, whisk the flour, baking powder, baking soda, whey powder, salt, lemon zest, and thyme. Using a pastry blender or fingers, cut the butter into the flour mixture until it forms pea-sized pieces. (You may also do this in a food processor.) Stir in buttermilk until mixture is just moistened. It will be a loose dough.

Turn the dough onto a lightly floured surface and knead a few times until it comes together. Don't over-knead. On a cutting board, roll out the dough to ½-inch thickness, and then cut biscuits using a 2-inch round cutter (or the top of a drinking glass). Arrange the biscuits on an ungreased cookie sheet. If desired, reroll the scraps and make more biscuits.

Note: If you want natural-looking biscuits, don't roll out the dough at all. Set large spoonfuls of biscuit mixture on the cookie sheet and pat down so they aren't too thick.

Brush the tops of the biscuits with water and lightly sprinkle with salt and extra thyme. Bake for 12–15 minutes or until golden brown. Serve warm with butter.

From Meaghan:

This is the best darned brownie recipe I've ever concocted, and I can make them gluten-free, too! So moist. I'm sharing both recipes. And mint? It's one of my favorite additions for brownies. Goes beautifully with a strong cup of coffee.

Mint Chocolate Brownies (regular version)

(Makes 12–16 brownies)

½ cup unsalted butter, plus 1 tablespoon, divided
1½ cups sugar
½ teaspoon salt
1 teaspoon vanilla extract
¾ cup Dutch-process cocoa
3 large eggs
¾ cup flour
1 teaspoon baking powder
1 cup mint chocolate chips

Preheat oven to 350 degrees F. Line a 9-inch-square pan with parchment paper and rub with 1 tablespoon butter.

In a medium saucepan, melt the ½ cup butter over medium-high heat. Add sugar and salt and stir until the mixture turns a pale yellow.

Transfer the mixture to a large mixing bowl. Blend in the vanilla and cocoa, and then add the eggs. Mix until shiny, about 1 minute.

Add in the flour and baking powder. Stir in the mint chocolate chips.

Pour the batter into the prepared pan. Make sure you spread it to the edges.

Bake for 32–36 minutes until the top of the brownie is set. Insert a toothpick in the center to make sure it's cooked through. A tad of chocolate at the tip is fine.

Remove from oven and cool 15–20 minutes before cutting. For the prettiest brownies, wait until they are completely cool. No crumbs!

Once cool, cover any brownies that you're not eating tightly with plastic or store in sealed glass containers.

Mint Chocolate Brownies (gluten-free version)

(Makes 12–16 brownies)

½ cup unsalted butter plus 1 tablespoon, divided
1½ cups sugar
½ teaspoon salt
1 teaspoon gluten-free vanilla extract
¾ cup Dutch-process cocoa
3 large eggs
¾ cup gluten-free flour (I like a combo of sweet rice flour
    and tapioca flour)
1 teaspoon baking powder
1 teaspoon whey powder
1 cup mint chocolate chips

Preheat oven to 350 degrees F. Line a 9-inch-square pan with parchment paper and rub with 1 tablespoon butter.

In a medium saucepan, melt the ½ cup butter over medium-high heat. Add sugar and salt and stir until the mixture turns a pale yellow.

Transfer the mixture to a large mixing bowl. Blend in the vanilla and cocoa, and then add the eggs. Mix until shiny, about 1 minute.

Add in the gluten-free flour, baking powder, and whey powder. Stir in the mint chocolate chips.

Pour the batter into the prepared pan. Make sure you spread it to the edges.

Bake for 32–36 minutes until the top of the brownie is set. Insert a toothpick in the center to make sure it's cooked through. A tad of chocolate at the tip is fine.

Remove from oven and cool 15–20 minutes before cutting. For the prettiest brownies, wait until they are completely cool. No crumbs!

Once cool, cover any brownies that you're not eating tightly with plastic or store in sealed glass containers.

From Brady:

The clientele at Hideaway Café crave comfort food. In addition to standards like meat loaf and burgers and fried chicken, I like to provide flavorful appetizers. Cheese, a natural comfort food, is what makes these puffs so tasty. Don't scrimp on your cheese selection. If you don't like cheddar, try Gruyère or Monterey Jack. Both melt well and combine nicely with mushrooms.

Mushroom Cheese Puffs

(Makes 18 appetizers)

2 sheets of puff pastry
2 tablespoons oil
1 sweet Hawaiian onion, diced fine
6 garlic cloves, minced
16 ounces fresh mushrooms, cleaned and diced
salt to taste
12 ounces sharp white cheddar cheese, grated

Thaw pastry sheets and lay them on a cutting board.

Preheat the oven to 400 degrees F and grease 18 muffin cups.

Preheat a large skillet over medium heat. Add the oil. Cook the onion and garlic until the onion is transparent, about 5–7 minutes.

Add the mushrooms to the pan and season with ½ to 1 teaspoon salt. Sauté the mushrooms over medium heat until tender. Drain off any liquid and transfer the mushrooms to a large mixing bowl. Let them cool slightly.

Mix in the grated cheese.

Roll the puff pastry out and cut the sheets into 9 squares each. You should have 18 small squares.

Place 18 squares in the muffin cups. Fill each square with about 1½ tablespoons of the mushroom mixture. Fold the square over the top of the mixture. Pinch the tops.

Bake for 15–17 minutes, until the pastry is golden brown. Serve warm but not hot!

From Courtney:

Nana always made sugar cookies at the holidays. She nicknamed them freezer cookies because they kept so well for months in the freezer. When I asked her what the secret to them was, she said the cream of tartar. It adds a lovely flavor that no spice can achieve. Make sure you bake them until they brown slightly around the edges. Bet you can't eat one.

Nana's Sugar Cookies

(Makes 24–36 cookies)

1 stick butter
½ cup sugar plus 1½ tablespoons sugar
1 egg
1 cup flour
1 teaspoon cream of tartar
24–36 pecan halves or colored sprinkles, if desired

Preheat oven to 375 degrees F.

In a mixing bowl, cream butter, sugar, and egg. Add flour and cream of tartar. Whip.

Drop by spoonfuls onto ungreased cookie sheet. Press each with the back of a spoon to a dollar-sized pancake shape. Add a pecan half or colored sprinkles to each cookie, if desired.

Bake at 375 degrees F for 10–12 minutes. Cookies should be lightly brown around the edges when removed from oven. Let cool 1 minute, then remove from cookie sheet and set on wire racks to cool. These get very crisp.

Store in an airtight box or freeze.

Read on for an exciting preview of Daryl Wood Gerber's
next Fairy Garden mystery . . .

A HINT OF MISCHIEF

Forthcoming from Kensington Publishing Corp. in Summer 2022

Chapter 1

❧❧❦

"Thief!" a woman cried outside of Open Your Imagination, my fairy garden and tea shop. I recognized the voice as Yvanna Acebo, who was a baker at Sweet Treats, a neighboring shop in the courtyard.

I hurried from the covered patio through our main shop, grabbed an umbrella from the stand by the Dutch door, and headed outside, quickly opening the umbrella so it protected me from the rain. "Yvanna, what's going on?"

Yvanna, dressed in her pink uniform, was standing at the top of the stairs that led through the courtyard, her back to me, hands on her hips. No umbrella. She was getting drenched.

"Yvanna," I called again. "Were you robbed? Are you okay?"

She turned. Rain streamed down her pretty face. She swiped a hair that had come loose from her scrunchie off her cheek. "I'm fine," she said with a sigh. "A customer set her bag down on one of the tables so she could fish in her purse for loose change. Before we knew it, someone in a hoodie slipped in, grabbed the bag, and darted out."

"Man, woman, teen?"

"I'm not sure about any of it." Her chest heaved. "That's the second theft in this area in the past twenty-four hours, Courtney."

"Second?" I gasped. Carmel-by-the-Sea was not known as a high-crime town. Well, that wasn't really true. We had seen two murders in the past year. Flukes, the police had called them. "Where did the other theft occur?"

"Across the way." She pointed to the Village Shops. "At Say Cheese."

"The thief must be hungry," I said. Say Cheese had a vast array of cheeses, crackers, and condiments. "Were you scared?"

"No. I'm miffed." A striking Latina, Yvanna was one of the most resilient women I knew and tough as nails. She rarely took a day off. She had a family of six to feed—two cousins, her grandparents, her younger sister, and herself.

"Call the police," I suggested.

"You can bet on it."

We didn't have CCTV in Cypress and Ivy's courtyard yet. Maybe our landlord should consider it, I mused. I returned to Open Your Imagination, stopped outside and flicked the water off the umbrella, slotted it back into the stand, and then weaved through the shop's display tables while saying hello to the handful of customers. Before heading to the patio, I signaled my stalwart assistant, Joss Timberlake, that all was under control.

"Do not argue with me," Misty Waters exclaimed. "Do you hear me? I want tea. Not coffee. Tea!" Misty, a customer, was standing by the verdigris bakers' racks on the patio, wiggling two female fairy figurines. When she spotted me, she laughed a full-throated laugh. "Oh, you're back, Courtney. Everything okay outside? Did I hear the word thief?"

"You did."

"Hopefully nothing too dear was stolen."

In addition to my business, the courtyard boasted a high-end jewelry store, a collectibles shop, an art gallery, and a pet grooming enterprise.

"Bakery goods," I said.

"And no one got hurt?"

"No one."

"Phew." Misty gazed at the figurines she was holding. "I swear, I can't get over how young I feel whenever I visit your shop. It takes me back to my childhood, when I used to play with dolls. I'd make up stories and put on plays. At one point, maybe seventh grade, I thought I was so clever and gifted with dialogue that I'd become a playwright, but that didn't come to pass."

Misty, a trust fund baby who had never worked a day in her life even though she had graduated Phi Beta Kappa and had whizzed through business school, had blazed into the shop twenty minutes ago, hoping to hire me to throw a fairy garden birthday party for her sorority sister. In the less than two years that the shop had been open, I'd only thrown three such parties, each for children.

"Let's get serious." Misty returned the figurines to the verdigris bakers' rack, strode across the slate patio to the wrought-iron table closest to the gnome-adorned fountain, and patted the tabletop. "Sit with me. Let's chat. I have lists upon lists of ideas." She opened her Prada tote and removed a floral note-pad and pen.

Fiona, a fairy-in-training who, when not staying at my house, resided in the ficus trees fitted with twinkling lights that surrounded the patio, flew to my shoulder and whispered in my ear. "She sure is bossy."

I bit back a smile and said, "The customer's always right."

"How true," Misty said, oblivious to Fiona's presence.

To be fair, Misty was a force. Tall and buxom, with dark auburn hair, sturdy shoulders, a broad face, and bold features,

I doubted she had ever been a wallflower. Every time I'd seen her at this or that event, always dressed in stunning jewel tones as she was now, her red silk blouse looking tailor-made, I'd been drawn to her like a moth to a flame. She was a great story-teller.

Pixie, my adorable Ragdoll cat, abandoned the mother and child customers she'd been following for the past three minutes, and leaped into Misty's lap. Misty instantly started stroking the cat's luscious fur. Pixie didn't hold back with her contented purring.

"Sweet kitty," Misty crooned.

"Pixie doesn't like just anyone," I said.

"Of course not. She knows a cat lover when she sees one, don't you, Pixie?" Misty tipped up the cat's chin. "Yes, you do. You know you do. I have three handsome friends for you to play with, Pixie. A calico, a tuxedo, and a domestic short-hair that I rescued. I love them all." She returned her gaze to me. "Now, Courtney, where were we?"

"You want to throw a party."

"For darling Odine." She stressed the O in her friend's name. I'd met Odine a few times and was pretty sure she pro-nounced her name with the accent on the second syllable. "She's the first of us to turn forty," Misty continued. "I'm the last." That fact seemed to tickle her. "She has always loved fairies. She displays fairy art everywhere in her house. And have you visited Fantasy Awaits? That's Odine's shop."

"I have."

Odine Oates owned a jewelry shop located in a nearby courtyard. Carmel-by-the-Sea was known for its unique courtyards. All of the jewelry at the shop featured fairies, sor-cerers, or mythical creatures. She burned incense, played lighthearted orchestral music, and offered exotic sucker can-dies to all of her customers. For her décor, Odine had commissioned a local artist to recreate well-known fantasy art-work, including the famous Cicely Mary Barker fairies, on four-feet by six-feet canvases. The art made quite an impact.

"I remember that place," Fiona whispered. "It was scary."

To a fairy Fiona's size, I imagined seeing giant-sized fairies, gnomes, and dragons would be frightening. She wasn't more than a few inches tall with two sets of beautiful green adult wings, one set of smaller junior wings, and shimmering blue hair. Her silver tutu and silver shoes sparkled in any light. By now, she should have grown three full sets of adult wings and lost her junior wings, but she'd messed up in fairy school, so the queen fairy had booted her from the fairy realm and had subjected her to probation.

"I want to have the party in my backyard," Misty went on.

Although at one time Misty's family had owned a gran-diose Spanish estate on the iconic 17-Mile Drive, the road popular because it led to Pebble Beach Golf Course, beaches, viewpoints, and more, she had downsized last year, wishing to live in Carmel proper so she could walk to restaurants and art galleries in a moment's notice. She had purchased a gray and white home on 4th Avenue with the charming name of Gar-dener's Delight—many homes in Carmel had names—and had hired my father's landscaping company to revamp both the front yard and backyard. Her gardens were the envy of all her neighbors.

"Here we go." Joss placed a tray set with the fixings for chamomile tea, two Lenox Butterfly Meadow pattern teacups, and a plate of lemon cookies on the table. "May I pour?"

"Please," I said.

"Boss, we have a ton of things to do," she said, filling Misty's cup first. "A shipment is coming in and a busload of tourists is about to disembark. They'll be swarming the court-yard in less than an hour."

"She won't be long," Misty said on my behalf. "I'm very

organized. This will only take a few minutes." She held up her notepad.

Joss raised an eyebrow, which made her look even more elfin than normal.

"I like your shirt, by the way," Misty said to Joss.

"This old thing?" Joss plucked at the buttons of the parrot-themed shirt she'd bought in Tijuana. "It's fun. I like color."

"So do I." Misty opened her notepad, silently dismissing Joss.

Over fifty and seasoned in the picking-up-clues department, Joss winked at me and returned to the main shop. Through the windows, I watched as she moved from display to display, straightening teacup handles, garden knickknacks, strings of bells—fairies loved the sound of bells.

Misty took a cookie, bit into it, set it on her saucer, and started reading the bullet-pointed list she'd created. "I want to have fairy doors and windchimes everywhere."

Something breakable inside the shop went *clack . . . shatter.* Joss *eek*ed and then Fiona chanted, "Oh no, oh no," and my stomach snagged. Joss waved to me that she was all right and held up a multicolored windchime. Was the accident a freak moment of timing or fate? Fairies hated breakage of any kind.

Fiona zipped off to check on Joss. She couldn't help pick up the broken pieces, of course, but she could offer Joss a whisper of encouragement. Joss, like me, could also see Fiona.

Misty hadn't seemed to notice the fracas, too intent on her list. "I want the guests to make fairy gardens. You'll instruct them, of course."

In addition to selling fairy gardens and items for fairy gardens, I taught a weekly class and gave private lessons about how to construct them. I experienced a childlike joy whenever I completed a project.

"I want party games and favors," Misty went on, "like you would for a child's party, but more adult."

That would take a bit of thinking on my part. Children relished games like the lily pad relay and a fairy tale obstacle course. What would adults enjoy?

"And I'll want you to paint a mural on my back wall."

"Me? Paint?" I snorted. My talent was purely in the gardening department. My mother had been the painter. A painting that she'd titled *Starry Night*, like the Van Gogh painting, hung on the bedroom wall in my cottage. My father hadn't been able to part with any of the others.

"Hire someone." Misty flourished the pen. "I want the mural to feature lots of flowers and vines with fairies and pixies frolicking throughout. I saw one on the *DIY Garden Channel* and it was stunning. I'll download some pictures and email them to you."

Fiona hovered above Misty's head, waving an imaginary wand, I thought, until I realized she was mimicking Misty's gestures with the pen. I couldn't very well say *Cut it out,* so I frowned. Fiona stopped and soared to a ficus branch so she could hold her belly while laughing.

Later, my sassy fairy and I would have to have a chat. Because she was classified as a righteous fairy, which meant she needed to bring resolution to embattled souls, she could earn her way back into the queen fairy's good graces by helping humans, such as myself. But she had to toe the line. She couldn't act like an imp all the time.

Only last year did I learn that there were classifications of fairies. Four, to be exact. Intuitive, guardian, nurturer, and righteous. Up until then, I'd always thought fairies were merely a type, like air fairies, water fairies, and woodland fairies, Fiona being the latter. Also, up until then, I'd forgotten about fairies. As a girl, I'd seen one, but I'd lost the ability when my mother passed away. That is, until Fiona popped into my life.

"All righty then," Misty said, standing. "Come up with a plan."

"Would you mind leaving me your list?" I asked.

"I'll text you a copy. Oh, and I'd like to have the party Saturday."

"In three days?" I gulped.

"No, silly, next Saturday. Ten days. Ample time."

Ten! Ha! The last birthday party I'd thrown had taken me a month to prepare. On the other hand, because it had taken a month, the birthday girl's mother had thought she could make numerous changes to the menu, favors, and events. A tighter timeline might make this party, for adults, easier to manage.

"Can do?" Misty asked in shorthand.

"Can do," I chimed.

As Misty left the store, Fiona followed me to the modest kitchen behind my office. I set the tray fitted with tea goodies on the counter, filled the sink with soapy water, and started by washing the teacups.

"Something feels off to me," Fiona said, perching atop the teapot. "That's the right word, isn't it, *off?*"

"Yes, that's the correct word. What feels off?"

"She's in too much of a hurry."

"Or she's not as organized as she claims," I countered. "I'm sure everything will go as steady as—"

A teacup slipped from my hand and plunged into the water. When I lifted it, I realized it had cracked in two.

"Oh my." Fiona clasped her head with her hands. "This is not good. Not good at all."

Suddenly my insides felt jittery, probably because I'd recently learned that I should trust my fairy's instincts. According to her fairy mentor, Merryweather Rose of Song, the more mature Fiona became, the more her instincts would become fine-tuned. "What isn't good?"

"Misty. Her excitement for this party. She's too eager." Fiona fluttered her wings.

"She seemed fine to me."

"What about the way she said her friend's name?"

"I'm not following."

"She said, 'O-dine.' " Fiona stressed the O as Misty had. "But that's not how you say her name. Remember? I went with you to her shop. You bought that necklace for Joss."

A dragon pendant with an emerald eye. Joss adored dragon paraphernalia.

"Odine made sure we knew how to pronounce her name," Fiona went on. "She chanted, 'Odine. Odine. Odine.' "

My fairy was right. Odine had intoned her name sounding much like a sorceress preparing for an incantation.

Fiona swatted my hair. "I'm telling you. Something's off."

And then lightning lit the sky, thunder rumbled overhead, and Fiona nearly swooned.